PENGUIN BOOKS

THE PERFECT AGE

Heather Skyler was born and raised in Las Vegas, Nevada. She is Editor-in-Chief of the *Beloit Fiction Journal* and lives in Madison, Wisconsin with her husband and their son, Malcolm, and daughter, Lux. This is her first book.

The
Perfect
Age

● ● ● ● ● ● ● ●

Heather Skyler

PENGUIN BOOKS

PENGUIN BOOKS

Published by the Penguin Group
Penguin Books Ltd, 80 Strand, London WC2R 0RL, England
Penguin Group (USA), Inc., 375 Hudson Street, New York, New York 10014, USA
Penguin Group (Canada), 10 Alcorn Avenue, Toronto, Ontario, Canada M4V 3B2
(a division of Pearson Penguin Canada Inc.)
Penguin Ireland, 25 St Stephen's Green, Dublin 2, Ireland
(a division of Penguin Books Ltd)
Penguin Group (Australia), 250 Camberwell Road,
Camberwell, Victoria 3124, Australia (a division of Pearson Australia Group Pty Ltd)
Penguin Books India Pvt Ltd, 11 Community Centre,
Panchsheel Park, New Delhi – 110 017, India
Penguin Group (NZ), cnr Airborne and Rosedale Roads, Albany,
Auckland 1310, New Zealand (a division of Pearson New Zealand Ltd)
Penguin Books (South Africa) (Pty) Ltd, 24 Sturdee Avenue,
Rosebank 2196, South Africa

Penguin Books Ltd, Registered Offices: 80 Strand, London WC2R 0RL, England

www.penguin.com

First published in the United States of America by W. W. Norton & co. 2004
First published in Great Britain by Hamish Hamilton 2004
Published in Penguin Books 2005
1

Printed in England by Clays Ltd, St Ives plc

For John and Malcolm

Acknowledgments

I'd like to thank Elizabeth Sheinkman, Jill Bialosky, Simon Prosser, and Carla Riccio for believing in this book.

Exuberant, loving thanks to my sister, Jennifer, for her endless support and radiant praise. Many grateful thanks as well to my parents, Juliet Roberts and Paul Burns.

I want to thank Kay Sloan for being an exquisitely kind and wise writing teacher.

Also, I have great amounts of gratitude to heap on the following friends for their advice, support, and camaraderie: Tenaya Darlington, Jennifer Wong, Heather Lee Schroeder, David Ebenbach, Guy Thorvaldsen, Ron Kuka, Dean Bakopoulos, and Andrew McCuaig.

Finally, thank you to Baby Lux.

Your whole life you are two, with one taken away.
—Stanley Plumly

Book One

The
First
Summer

. . . .

The Daughter

EVERYONE WANTS TO put oil on Helen's shoulders, on the raised line of bones running down her neck to the low-dipped back of her black swimsuit. First, the pool manager, Gerard, squeezes a clear puddle of Panama Jack #4 into his palm, rubs his hands together, and motions with a quick upward nod that she should turn around. His palms are rough, she notices, as he kneads the oil into her shoulders, moving each strap aside as he works. When he's finished, he claps his hands together and says, "You wouldn't want to burn your first day on the job."

"But I put on sunscreen before I left this morning," she tells him. "SPF fifteen. Waterproof."

"Well, you need to wear the products that we sell here."

She nods silent agreement and thinks of her boyfriend, Leo. If he were to see her here like this, being touched by another, even this over-forty walnut-colored man (the result of too much oil?), there would be no end to the shouting and sorrow, the jealous accusations and her subsequent pleading for forgiveness.

LATER, as she sits in her designated lifeguard chair, raised high over the vast blue hourglass of the pool, watching only an old woman on a raft and two couples standing with pink drinks in the shallow end, she feels yet another pair of hands placed on her shoulders. It is Miles this time, the twenty-something head guard she met when hired. "Time for some more oil, don't you think?" he asks.

"I think the oil is making me burn," she tells him, glancing over her shoulder at his tanned handsome face, then back into the pool below.

"A week of sunburn, and then you'll be used to it," he says, as if this were a solemn truth. She doesn't mind the feel of his hands on her back as much as she had Gerard's, is even a little flattered, but still there is a level of embarrassment to this treatment high up in her chair, being caressed in front of everyone. Though no one even seems to notice. Is she some sort of prude? Beyond the walls of the courtyard she can see only the tops of giant neon signs, floating in the desert air like alien ships.

"Um," she begins, trying to drum up conversation. How does one talk to someone over twenty? "So what do you do during the winter?"

"Premed at Reno," he tells her, running his hand one last time from the top of her neck, beneath damp hair, all the way down her spine. "You sure are bony," he says, then adds, "How'd you ever pass the lifeguard test?"

"I'm a good swimmer," she tells him. "It wasn't a big deal."

THERE ARE TWO pools in the inner courtyard of the Dunes Hotel. An expanse of deck between them like a creamy sweep of beach. Yellow deck chairs sit in perfect rows, beginning at the side of each pool and disappearing back into the outer ring of palm trees. A bar adorned in palm fronds in order to give the impression, Helen thinks, of a more primitive time, rises amid the chairs, but the waitresses, milling around its front, ruin this with their gold lamé bikini tops and skirts, their heavily lined eyes, and teased-up, hair-sprayed bangs. But this is Las Vegas, after all, and if Helen has learned anything about the city in which she's lived her entire fifteen years, it's that subtlety is not a valued trait.

Her time in the lifeguard chair grows dull. She watches Miles for a moment, presiding over the teardrop-shaped pool, then Gerard, sitting between the pools beneath a red umbrella at a sort of raised lectern, where she stored her bag this morning. She has to remain alert, she reminds herself, scanning the water below for trouble, but there are only three adults in the pool now, so she allows her mind to roam over the memory of the evening just behind her. Television and pizza at Leo's house, though she cannot recall a single show they saw—only hands, the long fingers scarred in spots from playing drums, playing up and down her back, beneath her bra strap, which was easily undone, and then around to her small breasts, untouched, as yet, by anyone. Such pleasure! She has never known such pleasure—and such fear. Would his mother wake and see her there, top twisted up around her neck, half naked really, on this woman's pewter-colored carpet? And the other fear of course is this: Is she now expected to have sex?

AT LUNCH SHE wanders into the hotel and finds a sandwich shop, where she buys a roast beef and cheddar on wheat, chips, and a Coke. The air conditioning makes it overcold inside, and she wishes she had brought a book as she sits and watches the tourists pass by her table, walking from the pool outside deep into the casino's interior.

It occurs to Helen that she's never eaten lunch in a casino, and it strikes her, suddenly, as bizarre. Through the glass walls of the sandwich shop she watches the slow progress of people playing slot machines, pulling down handles with no sense of hope or elation at all as far as she can tell. In fact, the place reeks of sadness at this time of day. There is none of the nighttime whooping at wins, only the steady plugging in of quarters by people who don't yet seem awake, despite the fact that it's after noon.

A cocktail waitress walks by, carrying a tray of drinks, and Helen, along with a few men at nearby tables, watches her disappear between a row of slots, her legs and half-revealed ass flashing at them from the shiny confines of tan pantyhose. Helen wonders what a fifteen-year-old girl on her lunch break in Ohio might be seeing right now. Surely not slot machines and ass cheeks. What is life like in other cities? she muses. Is it just like it is here, only with different scenery? Or is this life—*her life*—something unusual?

A man approaches her table and clears his throat, cracking a hole in Helen's reverie so that she is forced to look up. He is older, maybe thirty-five, and wears black swim trunks and a T-shirt that reads "Mustache Rides: 5 Cents." He does not have a mustache, and even if he did have one, Helen knows she still would not understand the meaning of his shirt. This man has the clean-cut look of a talk show host, a row of snowcapped teeth, gestures when he speaks that seem aimed to sell her something.

"Eating all alone?" He opens his arms, palms up, as if to show her the people swarming all around who surely would love to join her.

She nods and takes a sip of Coke.

"I saw you out there in the lifeguard chair. Maybe you'd like to have a drink or something, after work?"

She stares at him a moment, then says, "I'm fifteen years old."

"Oh, Jesus," he says, and laughs, hand cupped over his mouth. "That can't be true."

"It is." She smiles at the man, almost, it seems, against her will. Her lips rise, exposing teeth, without a prior thought of doing so.

"Well, I suppose I'll have to come back in three years or so."

She watches him walk away, feeling, for the first time since that morning, light and strong with confidence. Helen finishes her Coke and chips, then returns to the sun and pool.

ON THE RIDE home that evening her mother quizzes her. "Did you reapply your sunscreen after lunch?"

"Yes."

"What's your boss like? Does he seem like a nice person?"

She shrugs. "He's all right."

The sun sits like a blister above the pale shelf of mountains to her left as artificial air purrs against her knees. At a stoplight, Helen sees a cluster of half-naked women emerge from the side door of the Stardust Hotel. They are all in rhinestone g-strings and tiny triangle bikini tops. Many hold feathered headpieces in their hands. They all light cigarettes.

"Amazing," her mother says, shaking her head at the sight. "What some women will do for money."

They're just showgirls, Helen wants to say. What's so wrong with dancing for a living? But she says nothing, just averts her gaze and stares at her mother's hands on the steering wheel, which are thin and delicately veined as leaves. Her mother is a third-grade teacher and has the summer off, so she will drive Helen to work each morning, pick her up each evening after five.

"What did you do at Leo's last night?"

"Watched TV."

"Which show?"

Helen shrugs. "Some movie, I think."

"You *think*?"

"I don't remember the name."

"Did his mother watch it with you?"

Helen turns to her mother, who is beautiful, dark hair curved perfectly around her oval face, green eyes, which she always lines in colors—deep lavender or black—that make them even more green, two gemstones, jade perhaps, or tourmaline, set into her softly aging skin. "No." Helen shakes her head. "But she was reading on the chair beside us."

"So, HOW DO you like it?" Leo asks the next evening, after her second day. He traces the bare skin of her shoulders, and she flinches away.

"They're burned," she explains, then shrugs and says, "It's fine, I guess. I don't think anyone is bound to drown. Everyone just drinks and lounges on rafts. I've only seen one little kid anywhere near the pool. I got to yell at two boys today, older than me probably, to get on the diving board one at a time. I felt sort of stupid."

They are lying on his bed. Leo pulls up her tank top and kisses the white skin of her stomach. His mother is out on a date, and his older brother is in the kitchen making something that smells like burned beef. Leo undoes the top snap of her shorts then begins on the zipper.

"I don't know about this," she says, sitting up.

"I thought you had a good time the other night."

Helen sits on the edge of the bed, bare feet touching the carpet below. Her shirt is twisted around, and she straightens it with a quick downward tug. "I did."

"Don't you know how much I love you?"

"Yes."

"Then what's the matter?" He puts his arm around her and scoots close so that their legs are touching.

"If I got pregnant right now, it would be the worst thing in the world."

"We'll use a condom."

"It could break."

"And we could die tomorrow too. Lots of things *could* happen."

She sighs and runs both hands through her hair, rubs her eyes with her knuckles. Leo swoops in to kiss her mouth, a long, urgent kiss that causes her to waver. Maybe it is time? "Let's just wait. At least till I'm sixteen. It seems better, somehow, if I'm at least sixteen."

"That's two months away!" He crosses his arms over his chest and turns slightly to the side. A thick shank of sandy brown hair hangs across his face, shielding his expression. After a long, silent moment, he moves his hair behind his ear and turns to her. "Look, we can't just go back to holding hands. It doesn't work that way."

She hopes he is not about to tell her again that since he has already had sex in the past, it is more difficult for him to wait. Besides, he is seventeen and likes to remind her that there are other older girls all too willing to go out with him. But he says nothing more, just waits for her answer, his dark, sullen eyes round and finely lashed as a child's. "Just give me some time to think about it," she says, finally.

"Okay." He stands and walks to the closed door of his bedroom. "Come on, I'll take you home."

"DID YOU AND Leo have a fight last night?" her mother asks the next morning, weaving through their neighborhood toward the main road, which will take them to the Strip. "You seem upset."

"No."

A quick, inward breath, and then: "You're not having sex, are you?"

"*No*," she says quickly, perhaps with too much force. "Of course not."

"I couldn't handle that," her mother says. "The idea of some guy manhandling my daughter. You're just a child."

"*Mom*," she says, fighting the urge to roll her eyes toward the roof of the car. "Come on. I said I wasn't."

When they park at the Dunes, her mother says, "I think I'll walk you in today. I should meet your boss, and there's a shop I want to look at in the hotel."

Gerard is waiting at the lectern, his beige shirt, a lighter brown than his walnut skin, open to the waist, a pen in his mouth as he ponders the schedule. "Hey, it's my favorite lifeguard," he says, looking up at her approach.

"Hi." Helen smiles, then yanks off her tank top and shorts and shoves them into her bag. She wears a whistle now, and its heavy silver curve rests in the inward dip just beneath her ribs.

Her mother holds out her hand to Gerard and says, "Kathy Larkin. The mother."

Gerard takes her mother's proffered hand and smiles broadly. For the first time since Helen's met him, he lifts his mirrored sunglasses to reveal two wrinkle-shrouded eyes. "It's so good to meet you," he tells her. "Helen is doing great."

Helen can't think of a single thing she's really done, other than sit up in the chair and sweep the deck, but she doesn't mind the praise.

Her mother kisses her good-bye on the cheek, then begins

walking toward the casino. Gerard gets out the Panama Jack oil in preparation for the daily ritual.

Helen turns her back to him, her tender shoulders stinging with anticipation. Her mother is almost to the casino door when she turns, again, toward Helen, hand raised for one last wave. Gerard's hands are moving up and down her arms so that she can't lift one to return the wave, can only smile back at her across the shimmering surface of the pool. Helen waits for her mother to come running, to bat this man's hands away and tell him to keep them to himself. She holds her breath, preparing for the coming battle. Whose side will she take?

But her mother turns away again, without a step of hesitation, and disappears inside the dark doors of the hotel.

"Okay," he says when he is finished. "All set. Go get in the chair."

A MAN IS at the pool that day who was there the day before. He is nondescript: brown hair, brown eyes, a heavy brow and softly fading jaw. Yet he stands out because he wears a jacket. A light jacket, to be sure, a puffy sort of Windbreaker, black with silver letters on the back that read "The Big Apple: Take a Bite." Beneath that he wears a black T-shirt, black swim trunks, a pair of black suede thongs, nothing that would cause him to stand out, except the jacket. And the fact that he's been watching her, from the comfort of a lounge chair across the pool, for two days straight.

Today, when she takes her first break, leaving her chair to stand beneath a palm tree and eat a pear, this man approaches her, says hello, and hands her a card. "Charles Link," it reads, "Big Apple Models."

"I think you're very beautiful," he says.

She looks around to see if anyone has heard. Gerard is watching them from the shade of his umbrella, too far away to hear, and the yellow deck chairs on either side of them are empty. "You do?"

"Yes, your features are very uniquely arranged."

"Eyes, nose, then mouth?" She laughs and takes a bite of pear.

"You laugh"—he smiles—"but I'm serious. I'd like to take you to New York. Let me see your eyes."

She removes her sunglasses and looks at him, blinking against the light.

"Perfect," he says, leaning close and taking her chin in his hand, tilting her face to the sun.

She worries he might try to kiss her, and she wonders if she ought to yank herself away, but in a second he releases his hold.

"You have a lot of potential," he says, then crosses his arms over his chest, jacket squeaking, and asks, "So, what do you think?"

She shrugs and looks toward the water. "I don't know. I'm in high school."

"You're at the perfect age right now. You wouldn't want to wait another month, another *day*."

But I can't leave, she thinks, I'm in love. Instead, she says, "I don't know. I don't think my parents would like it if I left."

"How 'bout if I call them?" He pulls a pen and another card from his inner jacket pocket, then readies his hand for writing.

"Okay, I guess," she says, and gives him her home telephone number.

BACK UP IN the chair, the sun boils against her bare legs; the surface of the pool beneath her feet is littered with leaves from a windstorm the night before. She'll have to scoop them out after lunch. How did she miss them this morning? Charles Link stands beneath the umbrella now, chatting with Gerard, and she watches the two men from behind her sunglasses when no one is in the pool. Is this man in the jacket really who he claims to be? The idea of leaving with him for New York City does not seem real enough to even consider. She cannot imagine leaving school, her family, Leo. How could she leave Leo? But the notion that this man thinks her beautiful enough to be a model is a sort of drug, lulling her, on this long, hot afternoon, into a certain tree-shaded peace.

Helen is quite tall; she knows this all too well from bending one knee when she stands next to Leo in an attempt to match his height. And very thin—too thin, she's often been told, meanly, by people passing by her in the halls at school. She likes her hair, which is a thick sandstone brown and shimmers with health in the sun, and the color of her eyes because they match her mother's green—but beautiful? Her knees turn in, and her skin always sports at least one blemish, and without waterproof mascara she thinks her eyes look sleepy and naked. Often she looks in the mirror with worry, with the desire to be different. Once in a while, however, she feels her beauty and, inside these moments, a sort of fragile power.

LEO COMES OVER to her house after work, a relief to Helen because at her house they are not even allowed to shut her bedroom door behind them. They are forced back into holding hands. Not that she doesn't enjoy their deeper intimacies. His hands on her bare skin are a narcotic. That of course is the problem. She might be careless if she lost herself too deeply in the pleasure of his touch. She does not want to marry Leo. Helen wants to go away to college, become a lawyer or a writer, maybe teach history classes at the university, like her father. Or should she be a model? Even swimming in the deep pool of this new and excruciating love, she can see the surface of her life, shimmering above. And the surface, the future, does not include Leo.

But tonight he is here, waiting on the couch as she brings out a plate of sugar cookies, and tonight she is completely immersed in his presence. Helen sets the cookies on the coffee table, then settles in beside Leo and kisses his cheek.

"Have you been thinking about what we discussed?" he asks.

She nods.

"Well?"

"Let's not talk about it tonight." She takes his hand to soften this.

"It's all I think about. Being with you. Absolutely with you."

She looks away from his gaze and leans forward for a cookie.

"My mom's going away for the weekend," he continues. "You can come over for the whole day Saturday. You can tell your parents you're going for a bike ride or something."

Before she can reply, her father walks into the room. He still wears his blue dress shirt from work over jeans, his bare, pale-toed feet lost in thick carpet. "Who's this Charles Link person, Helen?" There is an edge of irritation in his voice as he reaches up to adjust his glasses. "He claims you gave him our number. I hope that's not true."

"A man I met at the pool today." Leo's grip on her hand tightens, and she squeezes back a pulse of reassurance. "He wanted to talk to you."

"So you just give out our number to strange men now?"

"He thinks I should be a model." She shrugs, embarrassed, and takes a bite of cookie. She knows what her father thinks about such nonsense and wonders why on earth she gave that man this number. She obeyed his request without a thought of saying no.

"I know what he thinks. He told me what he thinks, but what do you think? I thought you wanted to go to college. Isn't that still true?"

"Yes, of course," she tells him, wanting to erase his frown of disappointment.

"And I don't want you talking to strange men. Who knows if this guy is even who he says he is?"

"Okay," she says. "Sorry."

"Don't be sorry, just be careful." His brows remain drawn together as he looks now at the plate of cookies on the table. "Don't spoil your dinner. We're going to eat soon," he tells her, then retreats into the study.

Alone with Leo again, she tells him about the incident at the pool. He is already unhappy with her job, with the idea of her wearing a bathing suit all day in front of strangers, and this only deepens his resentment. "You'd go to New York and just leave me?" he asks, those eyes again, those child's eyes, serious with worry.

"No. I'm not going anywhere."

"Then why did you give him your number?"

She finishes the cookie in her hand, thinking, then says finally, "I don't know."

THE NEXT DAY the man is at the pool again. Same jacket and black shorts. Same chaise lounge and same stare.

"I'm leaving tomorrow," he tells her during lunch. They sit together in the cold casino. He has bought her a salad and a sandwich. He drinks only a Diet Coke, and she begins to feel self-conscious as she chews. "Your father didn't sound amenable to my plan to make you famous."

She shrugs and swallows. Takes a sip of water. "I could have told you that."

"You have a boyfriend?" he asks.

"Yes."

"Does he know what a lucky man he is?"

She shrugs again and takes another bite of salad.

"You keep my card," he tells her. "You never know."

"Okay," she says, searching all the crevices of memory to recall where she might have put it. Maybe in the garbage can beside the lectern.

He takes her chin between his fingers, while she chews her salad, and she looks up at him, thinking once again he wants to see her eyes. But then he leans across the table and he kisses her. A quick, dry kiss that tells her this: He is not really an agent from

New York. He stands and leaves before she has time to say a word, and she wipes off her mouth with a napkin, then looks around to see who might be watching. No one.

Walking back out to the pool, she feels so stupid. Will she ever learn all she needs to know to live? Gerard is waiting under his umbrella, and when she reaches him, he says, his face more serious than she's seen it yet, "You know, that guy's for real. Another girl who used to work here, she's in *Vogue* and all sorts of other mags all the time now. He's for real."

She nods, removes her outer clothing, then goes to sit back in the chair. She thinks about the kiss. She thinks of Leo. Of her father standing barefoot on the carpet. Her mother's face turned toward her in the car: "Are you having sex?"

Last night in bed she read some poems out of a new book from her father. The book was a gift for starting her first job, and the author is Rilke (Ril-kah, her father corrected when she asked, "Who's Rilk?") The poem she'd especially liked was called "Evening."

Sitting here now, she can recall only something about your life's being changed, alternately, into stone and stars. The line had been much cleaner, and of course poetic, and brought to mind the dark silhouette of a girl cut through with bright shapes. Beneath the cumbersome afternoon sun, Helen feels hard and bright at once, both stone and star. It's this heat, she thinks, the way it makes you feel as if you were just fired in a kiln.

ON SATURDAY she rides her bike to Leo's, so early he is still asleep. She goes around the back to knock on his bedroom window, and he pulls aside the curtain, his face creased from lying on the sheets, then smiles.

Inside, the house is cool, and his bedroom smells of musty sleep. She yanks off her tank top, then her shorts, and sits in her black bra and purple underwear upon his unmade bed.

He kisses her and kisses her, then gets a condom from his top dresser drawer.

AT WORK the next morning she sits in the chair watching the pool. Up here, in this quiet heat, she unravels in her mind the way Leo felt, moving over her, into her, out of her again so quickly. Finished before she even got used to the idea of their connection. Tonight, again, she'll visit him, and anticipating this, her body heats up. "You are so beautiful," he told her after they were finished, his naked boyish body beside her on the bed. "I've never seen anyone as beautiful as you."

THERE IS A child in the pool today. A girl of eight or nine, whose pink and silver two-piece seems out of place against her uncurved frame. She splashes in the shallow end all morning; then her mother rents a raft for her and she floats around beneath Helen's feet, splashing water up at her and laughing.

On Helen's break at three, the girl follows her to her spot beneath the palm tree and, looking up at her, says, "When I grow up, I want to be a lifeguard, just like you."

Helen laughs and thinks she might explain that she is not grown up. This is not her career, just a summer or two during high school, just a job to make a little money. Instead, she asks, "Can you swim?"

The girl shakes her head no, smiles, then runs away and jumps into the deep end of the pool. She splashes crazily the moment she hits water, and Helen gasps and drops her pear, then runs across the deck, between the chairs, and dives into the deep end. The girl is flailing, screaming with the realization of what she has just done, and Helen approaches slowly, aware from her training that this little girl, made strong by fear, could pull her under, drown them both.

"I'm going to help you," Helen tells her, treading water only a foot or so away. "Just be calm." Then she is beside the girl, her arm looped across the child's flat pink chest, pulling this fierce screaming little body to the side. The pool is vast, and seems larger still today, sun hammering her neck and shoulders as she scissors-kicks and keeps the girl's head abovewater.

And then there is another set of arms, taking Helen's hand away from this girl's body, taking both her shoulders and moving her aside. It is Miles, and he takes the girl into his arms and swims the short, remaining distance to the side, pulls her out, and sets her, safe and frightened, on the deck.

Helen is beside them both in seconds, treading water in the deep end, looking up at Miles, at the girl. "Why?" she asks him as the mother runs toward her daughter, then wraps herself around the child with a wail.

"Are you all right?" the mother murmurs. "Are you okay?" Then: "Thank you," this to Miles. "Thank you thank you thank you." She takes the child over to a lawn chair and wraps her in a towel.

"Why did you do that?" Helen asks again. "I had her. Her head was above the water. I was fine. Why?"

He shrugs, the muscles in his shoulders puckering with movement, then smoothing out again as he gives her a smile meant to charm away her anger, her dismay. "I thought you might need help. That's all. You've never saved a life before."

Helen frowns, embarrassingly close to crying now, stops the movement of her legs, and submerges herself beneath the water, looking up to the distorted pool deck far above. Miles's face, wavy and misshapen, a haze of yellow hair around it, gazes down at her. Behind him stretches mottled sky, blue and endless as a desert. Helen presses all the water from her lungs so that she starts to sink. Down she travels, bubbles rising from her mouth like unearthly, vivid stones, and when her toes touch bottom, Helen holds her breath for as long as possible. Then, when she can no longer bear it, she kicks off against the concrete with both feet and hurtles toward the surface.

The Boyfriend

HE LOVES HER AND HE DOESN'T LOVE HER. There is her beauty, cool and languid as a falling leaf upon his skin. When she rises from his body and goes home—to her parents, her sister, dinner together at that long teak table—he places his hands on his chest to feel the imprint she has left. Surely she has left a mark upon his body.

His own dinner is soup from a can, cream of chicken or tomato. Maybe a sandwich. If his mother is home, there is something hot, spaghetti and meatballs or beef Stroganoff, set down for him on the kitchen table. She stands as she eats. Always hurried and hunched over the sink, a few questions politely tossed to him about his day.

"How was school?"

"Mom," he says, "it's summer."

She laughs. "Oh, right. How's Helen? I haven't seen her for a while."

"She's fine."

"A sweet girl," she says. "Treat her nice." She likes to tell him this at least once a week. Probably, he thinks, to ease her conscience. Surely she must know what they've been doing in his bedroom. Once, a month or so ago, Helen met his mother in the hall on her way out of his bedroom to the bathroom. She was dressed, of course; they weren't that careless, but still, he thought, the mangled hair and sleepy, still-flushed face—perhaps a scent? He wasn't sure. But surely, his mother had to know.

"A date tonight?" he asks her.

She nods, then leans to swallow water from the tap.

"Ron again?"

"Of course." She fluffs the frosted tips of her hair with her fingers. "Who else?"

"I thought maybe you'd dumped him." He smiles and puts spaghetti in his mouth.

"Honey," she says, moving to stand near him. Her small frame casts a shadow on his plate. "No one dumps an orthodontist."

"Why not?" he asks. "None of us need braces."

"Leo, Leo." She sighs and runs her hand through his hair, touches his forehead with the back of her hand as if to check for fever. "You're too young, my dear, for us to even have this conversation."

HE LOVES HER and he doesn't love her. At her house the next evening, after he has eaten dinner with her family—lemon chicken on a bed of pristine rice, salad, and a loaf of hard-crusted bread—he sits beside her on the couch. In this house she is different. Bright and quick and nervous. Her long, tanned legs crossing and uncrossing until it makes him crazy. Naked, in his bedroom, she is completely his. The white imprint where her swimsuit rests all day, the portion of her body that she keeps from view, has been saved, he likes to think, for him alone.

"Has anyone else," he asked her once, last week, "ever seen you naked?"

She shrugged and laughed a little. 'I don't know. Girls in gym, I guess. My sister."

"But no men?"

"No," she said. "At least none that I'm aware of."

"What's that supposed to mean?"

"Nothing," she said, and kissed his shoulder.

And he let his breath out, closed his eyes, then pulled her body onto his and pressed it as firmly to his own as Helen would allow.

He rises now and says, "Let's take a walk."

Helen stands, then slips her bare feet into sandals; her toes, he notices for the first time, are painted a pale pink, and for a minute he is angry, so angry, that her feet are pretty, that she's painted them for someone. Who?

Outside, walking past the lit-up houses, he holds her hand but doesn't speak.

"What's wrong?" she wants to know.

"Nothing." He wills himself not to say a word, not to look

down at her toes, aglow like pearls, no doubt, beneath these giant streetlamps.

"Come on." She tries again. "Tell me what's the matter."

"Nothing." Said with too much force this time, so he stops her and puts his mouth on top of hers, tongue searching around inside that darkness until he has forgiven her.

HE WANTS HER and he doesn't want her. Leo doesn't have a job this summer. He has received a scholarship to music camp, a chance to live in Lee's Canyon for two weeks—an hour's drive into the surrounding mountains—and play the drums his every waking hour. But the camp is three weeks away, and with Helen at work all day, he has begun to feel lonely, at loose ends. In the morning he practices for two hours on his own patched-together drum set, the bass drum and two cymbals he bought with money saved last summer from his job at the Mirage. The snare drum was a gift this year from his band teacher, but the rest—a few toms, one more cymbal, a cowbell, and a set of wind chimes—is stolen, from grade schools where he's gone with the other drummers to do demonstrations, from high schools late in the afternoon, when the doors are still unlocked and no one seems to be watching. Helen knows only about the stolen wind chimes. That is the only crime to which he has confessed, leading to an argument that almost broke them up. He justified the theft to her as he always justifies these forays to himself. "Look, I don't have any money; they have tons. If I don't have the means to practice, I'll never be good enough to get into an orchestra." He used that last word for her. *Band* sounded too low a dream to justify his crime.

"Who do you think you are?" she asked him, arms crossed over her chest, tears beginning to roil in her eyes. "Raskolnikov?"

"Who?"

"Never mind," she said, then turned and left, riding away on her bike, hair waving out behind her like a flag of burnished gold.

AFTER PRACTICING each morning, he makes himself a sandwich, does the dishes from the night before, then walks to Odyssey Records, where he browses for at least an hour, listening to every kind of music he can find. Lately he has been sitting inside the sample headphones in the corner, listening to a band from Africa that uses only steel drums. Now he wants to own one of these as well, a drum that can sound like a xylophone, like a cool rain of color, but he promised Helen that he will no longer steal, so he has to sit inside this wanting and do nothing, just listen to the layered sound, the clean beauty of the music, without owning the instrument that he could use to create these sounds himself. It seems to him that the world will always be filled with wanting, never enough with actually having.

After this trip to the record store, it is usually one o'clock, five hours left until Helen will arrive on her ten-speed, hair still wet from the swimming pool, her skin an even creamy brown from that day's sun. Five hours of empty time until the moment when his day begins.

Sometimes he practices for a few more hours. Sometimes he washes his car, then drives across town to see his father. But this past week he has been going to the Dunes Hotel and watching Helen.

HE WANTS HER and he doesn't want her. She sits in that chair above the pool like some sort of visiting royal, though she is almost oversexy, he thinks now from his distant lounge chair, to be a princess. Did she look this way last month, he wonders, before they made love in his bedroom for the first time? He remembers her shoulders as neat and precise, a perfect geometry of skin and bone, but now there is a sultry shimmer in the movement of her collarbone, a slippery quality of light in the curve from neck to black swimsuit strap. He sits in a distant yellow chair, across the pool from Helen and seven or eight rows deep, beneath a palm tree. He wears a new pair of mirrored sunglasses and a blue baseball cap. His other shield is a magazine, *Vogue* or *Mademoiselle*—whatever he has lifted from his mother's bedroom end table that morning—which he holds before his face so he can peer at her in secrecy. This is his third day at the pool, and on all three days she has not so much as looked his way. Her gaze remains focused on the water, roaming across from shallow end to deep in search of danger. Once a waitress approached his chair, tray balanced on one supple hand, and asked if he would like a drink. He said a quick "No, thank you," certain she would call him out, tell the manager he was an impostor, not a hotel resident at all, and send him home. But she just frowned a bit, then turned on heels so high he thought she'd topple and walked across the deck to approach yet another lonely man.

He watches as Helen crosses and uncrosses her legs, adjusts her sunglasses, fans herself with a piece of paper she has folded and brought up into the chair. Miles, the other guard, relieves her every hour and a half. This time he climbs the stairs behind her before she notices his presence, and Leo watches as this man lays his hands, those foreign, evil hands, on his girlfriend's shoulders!

Leo drops his magazine and stands with a small cry: "Hey!" The waitress glances at him, then turns back to her customer. Helen looks up, across the pool and deck, right at him. She must see him, standing here in his swim trunks, white chest blazing like an admission of guilt. Even though her eyes are hidden by black sunglasses, it seems obvious she is staring directly at him. Trying to think what to do, he decides to raise his hand in greeting. He is here to surprise her, to take her out to lunch, but as he lifts his hand, she turns and looks behind her up at Miles, then stands and exchanges places with him before climbing down and retreating to a distant palm tree, where she sits on a lawn chair and begins to eat a pear.

Blood pumps through Leo with such force he cannot sit back down, so he pulls on his T-shirt, grabs his car keys and the magazine, and leaves. The parking lot is even hotter than his lounge chair, the car like a pit of fire, vinyl burning his legs as he sits, shuts the door, then rolls a window down for air. He closes his eyes and leans his head against the seat, his throat burning with the obscenities he wants to yell but doesn't. Are the pink toenails, he wonders now, for this guy, Miles?

"Excuse me." A soft female voice speaks at his window.

Leo opens his eyes to a plump girl who wears some sort of uniform. A short-sleeved, polyester shirt, maroon, with "The Dunes" in white above her left breast, and beneath that "Hi, I'm Traci." Her hair is permed and obviously dyed a sharp banana yellow.

Eyes dark brown and lips lined in a maroon to match her shirt, then colored in a pale bubble-gummy pink.

"You got a light?" she asks.

"No," he says, then. "Oh, wait a minute, there's one built in the car."

She takes this as an invitation, walks around the front, opens the passenger door, then climbs in beside him. "You wanna split this?" She holds up a joint, white and tightly rolled as a cocoon. "My break is almost over anyway."

"Okay," he says, looking at the dashboard clock. He has an hour until Helen's mother will pick her up, in this very parking lot. "What the hell."

The lighter pops out, and the gentlemanly way he offers it to her, hand cupped around the silver cap as if it were a flame, makes him feel he is cheating on Helen. So when he kisses this girl, half an hour later, his mind pleasantly adrift in heat and heightened feeling, it seems a natural progression of the offered lighter and not a further step in his transgression.

They talk a little, and he sees her teeth are pretty, the two front ones crossed a bit in modesty. Her legs, emerging at mid-thigh from white, polyester shorts, are up on his bench seat, crossed Indian style as if she were in someone's living room, and he likes the way her skin is so pale he can see the fine violet veins in her eyelids when she closes them to inhale.

After she goes back to work, he sits awhile in his car, feeling that the kiss with Traci somehow justifies Miles's hands on Helen's shoulders, cleans the slate so that he can love her once again.

"PLAY THE CHOPIN," Helen tells him. "That one piano tape you played before."

He is naked, hunched beside his bedroom stereo, searching for the music that will somehow seal this girl to him, attach her to his body in such a way that she cannot easily detach herself and drift past him. He finds the tape and puts it in the player, then rises to return to the bed, but the first notes of music—those cold deep blue piano keys—spread melancholy through his limbs, and he thinks of his betrayal, today in the car with Traci, and knows he is not worthy of this girl before him, her body long and patterned brown and white upon his dark blue sheets.

"I love this so much," she says, and throws her propped head back upon the pillow as he lies beside her. "Can you do Chopin on the drums?" She laughs, muscles in her stomach emerging in her skin like stones, and he wonders if she's making fun of him.

"Maybe on the timpani," he says.

"So, what'd you do today?" She looks across the sheets at him, those green eyes with gold splayed out around each iris as if sunflowers grow inside her.

"Um, nothing much. Went to see my dad."

"How are the clocks?"

Is she mocking him again? He cannot tell. "Same as always."

"I'm thinking about buying one for my dad for his birthday. What do you think?"

"I think you're crazy. Do you want him to disown you?" He attempts to inject scorn into his voice, instead of the worry that he feels. She'll leave him soon. Of course she will. Her father teaches people about the art and history of Russia. His father makes clocks with dice in place of numbers!

"Maybe you're right." She rolls onto him, hair falling around his face so that all he can see is her. She kisses him, quick and light, then says, "I have to go."

HE NEEDS HER and he doesn't need her. The next day he is at the pool, watching her from the same chair, *Vogue* in front of his face like a ridiculous shield. She wears a hat today, a black ball cap with "The Dunes" scrawled in cursive maroon across it, so it is even more difficult to see her face. She blows her whistle at some teenage boys, then stands to shout at them: "Don't run on the deck!" Her voice carries to him, sweet and slightly hoarse across the pool, so uncertain of the order it is yelling that he wishes he could go to her, climb the lifeguard chair, and take her in his arms. But everyone would see him, would know that he does not belong here.

When she takes her break at three and goes to stand beneath her palm tree, he leaves, retreating once again to the blazing parking lot. Traci stands against the wall of the building, eating a sandwich and shading her eyes against the sun, and he walks over to her. "How's it going?" he asks.

She smiles. "Great. Even better now."

"Want to take a ride?" He nods toward his blue Nova, hands shoved deep into the pockets of his shorts.

She shrugs and checks her watch. "All right."

He drives away from the Strip, toward Industrial Road, the bleak street lined with bars and strip clubs that separates them from the highway and the mountains beyond, but he assumes she needs to be back to work soon, so he doesn't go too far away from the hotel. For a while they say nothing, simply let the scalding wind blow over them. Traci lights a cigarette with a lighter from her pocket, blows smoke out the window, then says, "I get off work at eight tonight."

He nods, eyes concentrated on the road ahead. The Crazy Horse Saloon moves by them on the left, the silhouette of a well-curved woman imprinted on its sign, and he feels both at home—he has lived in this city, after all, for almost eighteen years—and as lost as he has ever been. What compelled him to drive down this awful road?

"Maybe you'd like to ask me over? We could watch TV or something? I have a car."

"Um," he says, hesitating. Helen will be gone by then, ensconced at home, in that living room of hers, those dark brocaded sofas and end tables made of a wood so beautiful Leo thinks they cannot be created from real trees, not the knobby, rotting things that grow in his backyard. He looks across the seat at Traci. Her face is turned away, rounded cheeks, ripe with too much blush, blowing smoke out his window. "Okay. Why don't you come over?"

TRACI ARRIVES at half past eight, wearing a tight turquoise T-shirt and white shorts. A thin gold chain hangs from her neck, her name written in cursive as its pendant, and Leo has a sudden premonition that this girl will want, at some point, for him to wear this necklace. He decides right then, as he ushers her inside, that no matter what happens, he will not wear it.

"You look nice," he tells her. And she does. Out of that maroon uniform and in this more forgiving light, she is almost pretty. The colors of her hair and makeup do not cry out so harshly, and her plump, short-limbed body reminds him of rising bread: fresh and white and soft.

She moves past him to the living room and sits on the couch, kicking off her sandals and drawing up her legs into a crossed position, as she did the other afternoon inside his Nova.

"Do you want something to drink?" he asks her. "We've got water, milk, Pepsi. Oh, and Tang."

"No, thanks," she says.

He flips on the TV, then sits beside her on the couch. His mother is out with Ron, and his brother is just out, who knows where. He puts his hand on Traci's leg, and she leans her face up to be kissed, so he puts his mouth on hers and tries to think of nothing but their tongues. But of course Helen slides into his mind, those sunflower eyes gazing at him just this afternoon from across the blue stillness of his sheets, the fan above them drawing airy patterns on their skin. "I wish I didn't have to go," she told him. "I'm sick of setting the freaking table. Plus, I love you." He stood in the driveway as she pedaled away on her ten-speed, turning to blow him a kiss and ramming her front tire into a lamppost in the process. Not enough to cause her harm—she hadn't even toppled—but still he ran across the concrete to her side. "Are you all right?"

"Of course," she said, then smiled. "I'm a lifeguard."

The moment he allows his hands to wander under Traci's turquoise shirt, he hears the front door open, and he yanks his hands and mouth away with an overwhelming feeling of relief. It is his mother, home earlier than usual, and her face looks streaked a bit around the eyes, as if she had been crying.

"Hi, honey," she says wearily, tossing her purse on the carpet, and then, seeing Traci. "Well, hello. Leo, maybe you should introduce me to your friend."

Shame spreads through his limbs at her tone of mild accusation, and he jumps up from the couch, moving his body as far away from Traci's as he can, then introduces her as "a friend of mine." Both women nod a wary, soft hello; then Leo moves to hug his mother. "Welcome home," he tells her.

She laughs a little. "Such treatment! What's gotten into you?" Then a tear leaks out and slides halfway down her cheek. "I'm sorry," she says, turning to Traci, who is still curled up on the couch, looking much too comfortable, Leo decides. "It's Ron," she explains to Leo with a shrug. "He says he doesn't want to see me anymore."

Traci rises from the couch. "Maybe I should go."

Leo nods and says, "I'll call you." Though they both know he doesn't have her number, or even know her last name, for that matter.

"See you at the Dunes?"

"Okay."

She lets herself out the front door, and Leo and his mother sit down side by side upon the couch. "What's she talking about? The Dunes?"

"Oh, nothing. She's just a friend of Helen's at the Dunes. You know, where she's a lifeguard?"

His mother looks at him, the beginning of a frown tugging down her features. "Some friend."

"What's the matter with Ron?" he asks. "Has he lost his mind or something?"

"Leo. Are you going out on Helen? Please tell me that is not the case."

"No, of course not."

"You don't understand what you have in that girl."

"What?" He is suddenly annoyed. "What exactly do I have?"

"If you don't know already, I can't tell you." Her face begins to fold in upon itself, black mascara puddling beneath her eyes as she starts to cry.

"What is it?" Leo wants to know. "What reason did Ron give you?"

She shrugs and covers up her face. "Who knows? Do men ever give a reason?"

"I don't know. What was Dad's?"

"Oh, honey. Let's not get into *that*."

He puts an arm around her and pulls her small, frosted head onto his shoulder, rocking her a little as she cries and trying to decide what he's going to do about the mess he has created.

THE NEXT DAY he drives again to the Dunes, but this time he doesn't go anywhere near the pool, only waits in the parking lot until Traci emerges, sipping from a can of Pepsi and squinting against the sun. He honks once, and she raises a hand in greeting, then walks over to his car and gets inside.

"Hi," she says, and smiles. "Didn't think I'd see you here today."

"I came to tell you something."

She waits, sipping at her Pepsi, and he wonders, suddenly, if maybe he could love her. It wouldn't be so hard to do, would it? He could pull that plump white body over his like a blanket, like a soft quilt of nothingness. He thinks of Helen and her sharp edges, the way her hipbones sometimes leave indentations in his skin. When she imprints these marks—one time there was even a small bruise—he tries to lie in bed and keep watch until they fade, tries to calculate the exact second when every trace of Helen has evaporated from the room. "I have a girlfriend," he tells Traci.   She nods, solemn. "I figured." Then she pulls a pack of cigarettes from the back pocket of her shorts and offers him one.

They sit smoking for a while in silence, sharing her lukewarm Pepsi and looking out the windows at nothing, at the hot car-crowded blacktop, at the white, concrete back of the hotel. Finally, he asks, "Do you like Chopin?"

"Who's that?" she asks. Then her face becomes as animated as he's ever seen it. "Is that the new guy at the Mirage who does that dance with the pots and pans as music? I've heard that's a really cool show."

"No," he says, and throws his cigarette stub out the window. "That's not who I mean."

She frowns and looks down at her hands. "I guess I'd better get back to work."

He watches her walk across the parking lot, then disappear into the building, but still he doesn't leave. As he sits there in his smoky Nova, music opens from some wound inside of him, cool blue-green notes, a sea of yearning played out in piano keys, different from the way he yearns for sex, though this music, this feeling, as he sits here, sweating in his car, are still somehow connected to Helen.

Soon he sees a familiar car enter the parking lot and pull into a space a row ahead of his. The back of Helen's father's blond head is visible in the driver's seat, staring straight ahead and waiting for his daughter. If her father turned to look behind him, he would probably see Leo, though there is a row of cars between them, and light does glare off his windshield.

Leo stays right where he is, the music of him flooding the entire car, the parking lot, and when he sees Helen's long-limbed form emerge from the door where Traci disappeared only twenty minutes ago, it takes every ounce of strength he owns not to honk his horn, to cry her name out the window so she'll notice him. Will she look across the lot and see him sitting here? Will she recognize this familiar car, in which she's ridden with him for nine months now?

She walks across the lot to her father's car, smiling at something—some song in her head, maybe something Miles said to her? She swings a canvas bag beside her and steps lightly, with a rolling lift onto her toes. Without looking to her left or right, she opens the passenger door of her father's car and gets inside.

They drive past Leo, slowly, cocooned in their air-conditioned haven as waves of heat break over him. If he called out to her now, she would not even hear him through the glass. They are only two cars away from Leo's as they leave the lot, but neither of them turns their head, and he is left, once again, alone with the concrete back of this white hotel and the sounds of a composer who died more than a century ago.

The Father

THE FIRST NOTE SLID BENEATH his office door says this: "A May/December romance in July, sounds mighty nice to me." Edward reads the torn-off piece of paper in his hand, then sits down at his desk. A May/December romance. He isn't sure, but he thinks this is the term used for a liaison between a younger person and an old. Is he the old one in this equation? He must be; after all, he is almost fifty, and there are few women past his age wandering the halls of this university. The note is handwritten, neither masculine nor feminine in form. A neat, slightly slanted cursive with none of the quirky loops that most girls use. Though the words are almost too evenly arranged to be a boy's.

Or is he stereotyping once again, as his wife, Kathy, has accused him of doing on more than one occasion? "Well, men and women *are* different," he always tells her in response, "are they not?"

A knock on the door makes him jump, and he slips the note into his top desk drawer, then leans back in his chair. "Come in."

A student from his Russian film class enters, a densely muscled twenty-something who usually sleeps in back once a movie starts. All the boys seem so thick these days, Edward thinks as this young man enters, then walks to stand before his desk, so bulked up in the arms and chest. Whatever happened to the fashionably lithe grace of a Jimmy Stewart? The suave thinness of a Fred Astaire? Now everyone aspires to have muscle, to have muscle on top of muscle and to walk as if he were carrying a body made of lead.

"Um," the boy begins. His name is Carl, Edward thinks, or maybe Carter. "I need to turn in my second paper late. Is that okay?"

"What seems to be the problem?"

"Well, I guess I didn't really understand the symbolism in the last flick. But Melanie said she'd help me."

"If it's late, you'll get a lower grade."

"I know." The boy glances at a photo of Edward's daughters on his desk, in which they stand back to back in band uniforms, Helen holding out her flute, Jenny cradling an oboe. "Hey, I know that girl," he says, picking up the picture and pointing at Helen. "Isn't she a lifeguard at the Dunes?"

Edward nods. "That's right."

"Is she your daughter?"

He nods again.

"Wow," he says, and sets the photo down.

Edward ponders briefly the meaning of his "Wow." Is it meant to say, *How could this girl, this young beauty be* your *daughter?* He decides to ignore the comment and get this boy out of his office. "I'll expect the paper no later than a week. Otherwise you'll get no credit. Now, if you'll excuse me"—Edward stands—"I have to go pick up said daughter at the pool."

When Carl (he's almost sure it's Carl now) leaves, Edward picks up the photo, taken just last year when Helen was a sophomore, Jenny a freshman (or freshgirl, as she likes to say; he's raised her well). Helen looks more like him in this picture than she does at present. Lately she has begun to curve away from the awkwardness he sees here as she stands in red and white polyester, "LVHS" in a black diagonal across her chest. Those charming pointed elbows, akimbo as she holds her flute. Braces gleaming in her mouth like something precious. But those are removed now too, and today, when she ran past him to the door on her way to work, that lifeguard whistle swinging crazily against her tank top, all liquid limbs and bright teeth, he was struck by this thought: She is becoming her mother.

In the hot car on his way to pick up Helen, he thinks about the note. Is it a proposition of some sort? Will the sender soon make herself known?

He arrives at the Dunes ten minutes early, so he decides to go inside, into the hotel courtyard where the pool resides, and see exactly what this place is like where Helen works. He rarely ventures anymore into this section of Las Vegas, this part of town where tourists outnumber residents and lights fill every space of sky they can. Down a cool corridor, then back out into heat, Edward steps past the outer rim of palm trees, then begins to make his way through the crowded maze of yellow chaise lounges, toward the water, where he can see Helen's distant figure, perched like a bird—a cardinal in her red one-piece—up in the lifeguard chair. Drawing closer, he notices a man standing beside the chair who has the pale, hairless body of a rodent; he is gazing up at Helen with a smile, dark glasses shrouding half his face, and Edward feels something in his chest constrict, expand, collapse, then crackle into fine sprays of anger.

He navigates the remaining lawn chairs fast and loops around the right curve of the pool until he is standing on the other side of Helen's chair, sweating now in his tie and cotton shirt, his lightweight linen jacket.

". . . the test wasn't all that hard," he hears her saying to this man. "I've been swimming since I was like two, so I'm used to it."

"So," the man says. He is twenty, maybe twenty-five. "Can I call you then?"

"No, you can't call her," Edward says, in the tone he uses to reprimand a talking student. "She's still in high school."

"Dad." She turns to look down at him, dark glasses shielding her expression. Is she grateful that he's saved her?

The man looks up at Helen. "Are you a senior?"

She shakes her head. "Almost a junior."

"So I think you'd better leave her be," Edward says.

"It's cool, dude." The man exudes his words, like butter

through a fist. "Don't freak out." He looks again at Helen. "Nice to meet you anyway," he says, then turns and walks away.

"Dad," she says, "can you please just wait for me inside the car?" Then she looks across the pool at an approaching guard, a man in red swimming trunks coming toward them, presumably to take her place. Is this a look of pleading that she gives the guard? Or one of irritation? Edward can no longer read her.

IN THE CAR, on their way home, he says, "I'm sorry, Helen."

She shrugs. "It doesn't matter. But I am expected to be nice to the patrons of the pool. It is part of my job."

"I thought he was bothering you."

The shrug again. "He was."

A couple of blocks of silence as they turn off the Strip toward home. They pass a gas station with a flashing sign. An Elvis look-alike stands in jeans and a T-shirt beside a pump, washing the front window of a white Lincoln. When they drive by Luv-it, Helen's favorite place for frozen custard, Edward sees a dead ringer for Marilyn Monroe licking a scoop of vanilla ice cream. He wonders if he's imagined the likenesses, then remembers there's an impersonator's conference in town this week, being held just down the street at Vegas World. Past this they dip into neighborhoods scarred by yellow lawns, each one leading to a house so cheap and thin it would never withstand a winter in Ohio. The home of Helen's boyfriend rolls by them on the left, and Helen turns to look at it, presumably to see if Leo might be visible. When they get home, she'll ride back here on her bike immediately.

"Can Leo come for dinner tonight?"

"No, not tonight."

"*Dad.*" The whine almost makes him crumble. How like a child she still sounds! "That's what you always say."

"Helen, he has a mother who feeds him."

"But he's leaving in a week for music camp!"

"I realize it's a tragedy, but no." He utters this with stern confidence, but can't help but feel he is only impersonating a father.

IN BED THAT NIGHT, his wife already sleeping, the white curve of her shoulder and half a back dimly visible beside him, Edward thinks about the man from the pool. *It's cool, dude. Don't freak out.* A vernacular so crass it makes his face burn merely recalling it now. He is a father! It seems to Edward that at some point, unbeknownst to him, there began to be a loosening of all standards. The English language is marred so often now by words he doesn't care to recognize, as if a pristine painting, a Rembrandt or a Caravaggio, had been slashed across its center and thrown onto the ground, left to weather through the elements alone. *May/December romance*, on the other hand, is a term he likes, if only because it has a quaintness to its cadence, an old-fashioned tint, a pink tinge of humanity.

His wife's shoulder moves slightly as she breathes, and Edward watches it, thinks to touch it, wake her up, but does nothing to disturb her. At dinner tonight Helen sulked while Jenny chatted on about her day of swimming at a friend's house. Later, in the kitchen, his wife wanted to know why he had banned Leo from the table for a week now. "Invite the poor boy over," she said, handing him a dish to dry. "Helen's driving me crazy. Besides, better to have him here where we can watch them."

"I just don't want to have to entertain after a day of teaching ridiculously inept students."

"*Entertain.*" She rolled her eyes and blew out a poof of breath as if to show him the absurdity of this line of reasoning.

"Is it so much to ask that I just want to eat dinner with my family?"

"I suppose not. But you can't always have your way, you know." She smiled, then handed him another dish, and they finished cleaning up in a not unpleasant silence.

The truth is that he likes Leo. More than Kathy does; he's sure of that. But this boy's presence in their home, sitting at their table next to Helen, has begun to unsettle him. When Leo's here, Edward thinks too much of his own first love, Janie Langtree. Tree, he used to call her or, when they lay alone together on a dark summer lawn near campus, Willow, fireflies aglow on either side, their bright bodies one of the few things he misses about Ohio. But why is this a problem? he wonders now, glancing at the clock beside the bed: one-thirty. It's not as if he wished he had married Tree, but watching Leo and his daughter, those liquid looks they send across the table, or their small, inadvertent touches when they sit side by side, fiddles with his insides, stirs up some old longing so that he cannot concentrate on his book after dinner or sleep the dreamless sleep he likes.

THE SECOND NOTE says this: "Don't worry, I'm older than your daughter." It is waiting on the pale gray carpet of his office, and when he picks it up and reads it, Edward feels a chill move through his limbs, then quickly looks around the room as if to find the writer waiting somewhere between the bookshelves and the dying rubber plant, perhaps behind the Russian flag he has hung across his window. But of course he is alone.

He sits down at his desk and moves his mind's eye across the women in his class. Could one of them have written this? There are the two sorority types who sit in back, near Carl, but he can't imagine it is one of them; they've hardly looked his way the entire class; rather, they sit chatting in the corner, passing notes as if still in high school.

There is the dark-haired girl with glasses who sits up front and answers every question with a thoroughness that makes his heart sing. But he can't picture this girl, either, sending secret letters, wasting precious study time to pen these notes to him. There is a stunning black woman who wears halter tops inappropriate for school and an Asian girl here for the summer from Hong Kong who paints her nails during the break. Then there are a few nondescript types who neither speak nor show up late. They turn in B papers and seem, for some reason, to be asexual, maybe just because they are not particularly attractive to Edward. But he can't see any of these women wanting him. He is not unattractive. No potbelly, but no real muscle definition either. A full head of reddish-blond hair and tortoise glasses, which he tries to keep in fashion. He wears a suit every day, and his aging face is always cleanly shaven, but these are not traits that appeal to women in their twenties, are they?

Maybe this is just a joke. The idea makes him slightly sick.

And who would know the ages of his daughters? Everyone. He's mentioned them in class a couple of times at least. Many students have been in his office, seen the photo on his desk. The sender could be anyone.

AT THE DUNES today, waiting in the parking lot for Helen, he sees Leo's car in his rearview mirror, Helen's boyfriend's handsome head and crown of lank brown hair visible through his front windshield. Edward gets out and walks over to the Nova, an unsightly peacock blue with missing chrome by the front headlight. Leo's window is rolled down, and when Edward approaches, he sits up straighter and tucks his hair behind his ears.

"Hello, Leo," Edward says. "Were you picking Helen up today? Did I get something wrong?"

The boy shakes his head. "No, I was just . . ." He hesitates and scratches at a scab on his left arm. "In the neighborhood."

"How's the drum practice coming along?"

"Good." Leo nods with firm conviction. "I've really got to stick with it. It's my only ticket out, you know, of this hellhole."

"The Nova?" Edward asks.

"*No*." He looks offended. "Las Vegas."

"Oh," he says, and straightens up to gaze over Leo's car at the distant row of mountains, serrated and brown, at the scorched blue sky above. "I've always said Las Vegas has a harsh beauty to it. It's not an easy place to love."

Before Leo can respond, Helen appears at Edward's elbow. "Hi, Dad. Hi, Leo." This last "hi" in a sweeter voice, one that she will never give to him, her father. "Can I ride home with him, Dad?"

"Um. I guess so. I'd ask you to dinner, Leo," Edward adds, "but I'm afraid that doesn't leave Kathy with enough notice."

Helen rolls her eyes, but Leo nods. "That's all right, Mr. Larkin. I understand."

In bed that night he awakes from a dream about Tree and turns to Kathy. He touches her shoulder and says her name; then her nicknames begin to pile up inside the darkness. "Katherine," he whispers first, then: "Katerina, Kat, Catherine the Great. CTG. Come on, CTG, wake up."

She rolls toward him, eyes half open. "What?"

"I'm feeling amorous."

"Go back to sleep."

"I can't."

He leans across the sheet to kiss her shoulder, neck, her mouth, wrinkled from its press upon the pillow. "It's been so long."

She kisses back this time when he tries her mouth, so he gently eases up her nightgown and moves on top of her.

It is not unsatisfying, this lovemaking. It is not unsweet in its familiar touches, in the cry she leaves between them, imprinting on his closed eyelids a field of lightning bugs, which slow him for a moment until he can recapture a more lustful image. Her hair is slightly damp with sweat, recalling summer lawns beneath his back, and his hands find waist and spine so that he feels connected to her bones. Still, there is no birdsong, no brilliant swimming from his brain down to his abdomen and back. No bright skies opening so wide he thinks he'll weep before they crash down then encircle him in blue.

Afterward they lie side by side, knuckles touching, breathing deepening in tempo with the air conditioning's hum. He wonders, as he always wonders, what pleasure she has taken from this union. He is not young enough, he knows, to learn how to ask this of his wife, so he lies in silence, then decides to ask a different question. "Kath," he ventures, "do you think I'm handsome?"

"Um," she murmurs, half asleep already. "Yeah, of course."

"But not like Leo."

"Like Leo? He's seventeen years old!"

"I know, but still. I never looked like him."

"And I never looked like Helen."

"Yes, you did," he tells her. "You know you did. You still do." Then he leans across the sheet and kisses her good-night.

THE THIRD NOTE says: "I too miss the lightning bugs." Edward drops the piece of paper, as if the words have burned him, then kicks it a few times until it is beside the wastebasket. He bends to pick it up with the intention of throwing it away, then changes his mind and shoves it into the front pocket of his khaki pants. Who is this person? Has he made mention of the lightning bugs in class before? It is not out of the question, he decides. It is one of the things he likes to toss into a conversation, the way he misses the fireflies of Ohio. But still, who would take notice of such an offhand comment and then write it in a note?

In class that day he watches them all as they take a quiz in silence. No one even glances up at him. Maybe he is looking in the wrong arena. He searches memory for other women in his life. There is Carmella, the department secretary, though he thinks she may be older than he is, canceling out the May/December note. Jane Dempsey teaches "The Victorian Era," but he can't imagine this broad-bottomed redhead who laughs at anything and everything wanting *him*, and besides, there is a rumor she is lesbian. May Petrocelli, professor of the most popular class on campus, "The Holocaust," is pretty in her flowing hippie skirts, he'll give her that, but she has a husband, the provost of the university, no less, and Edward crosses her off the list without a second thought.

Then the smart girl in the front row finishes her essay and looks up. Edward thinks she is about to look at him, to give her-self away, but she looks above him at the clock, then stands and turns in her paper, setting it on his desk and walking out without a backward glance.

THAT EVENING, after dinner, he sits beside Kathy on the couch, each of them paging through a magazine; the sound of Jenny practicing her oboe croons out into the living room like an off-key love song, one he can't quite catch the words to. Kathy's legs, white and long in shorts, are tucked up under her, and Edward notices pale blue veins that show beneath her skin and thinks: Those veins are there because she bore my children. Still, he is a bit repelled by these blue branches climbing quietly beneath her thighs, by such white white limbs, and he wonders why she doesn't get a little sun. After all, she is a teacher and has the summer off. He looks down at his own pale legs and sees that veins are visible beneath his skin as well. They are growing old together as they sit here on the couch! Who could possibly be writing him these notes?

WHEN HE STEPS inside his office the next day after lunch, the fourth note waits patiently, lying white and thin upon his carpet. "Please meet me in the campus cactus garden, after class tomorrow." He sits down behind his desk, then swivels toward the window.

This is not the first time he has been presented with the possibility of an affair. The last time was two years ago, and he took the opportunity then, slept with the curator of the local history museum for two months before she called it off in tears beside the fountain in the museum's courtyard just after dusk, Venus in the sky behind her like an omen, like an egg, like a brilliant prick of nothing in the sky.

He remembers driving home that night, to dinner, to his wife and daughters, and how vivid everything had been. The chicken crisply floating on the plate beside the painted green of broccoli. Red wine a brilliant shimmered dark inside its glass. Helen spilled a cup of cranberry juice on their pale carpet, and the stain, instead of making him a little crazy as it usually would have, blazed before him on the floor like a heart, his own heart, the shadow of a heart, and then once again it was a stain, this was his family, and the colors settled once more into dullness.

His Russian flag, covering half the drapery rod, shimmers in the air conditioning's wind, and Edward recalls the scene in last week's movie—the one half his class had slept through—when

Lev, the movie's hero, clasps one fist around the handle of a sickle, the other round the handle of a hammer. The man holds both these tools before him, as if in awe, then looks toward the red Russian flag waving up above his porch and sees the symbols of these instruments printed there as well. The movie was shameless, a transparent vehicle of propaganda, but Edward was affected by that scene. In his hands, Lev holds the thing itself, not merely the picture—yellow printed on a cloth of red—which he was raised to honor.

Is it because Edward is an only child, a victory after many miscarriages, that he wants now to meet this woman, this strange girl who slides notes beneath his door? Was he raised beneath the love saved up for two or more? Had he been taught to want too much, to ask for more than should be offered?

There is a knock on his door, and he turns and says, "Come in."

It's Carl once again, holding a paper in his hand. "I finished early. Well, earlier than the late-paper deadline."

"Fine," Edward says. "Just put it on my desk."

The boy sets the paper down, then stands a minute with his hands behind his back. "So, how's your daughter?"

"She's fine," he answers, then asks, "When were you at the Dunes pool anyway? It's just for hotel guests."

"Oh, me and my buddies sneak in now and then to swim. No biggie."

Edward nods.

"So," Carl asks, "does she have a boyfriend?"

"Yes, she has a boyfriend," Edward says. "And he's in high school, just like her."

"Hmm." Carl nods. "You must be proud of her."

"For what?"

He shrugs and begins to back out of the office, the muscles in his bulky forearms jumping. He must be wringing his hands, Edward thinks, behind his back. "She's a very pretty girl."

WHEN HE DRIVES today to pick up Helen, he waits until ten past five, then goes inside to find her. Gerard, the manager, tells him she went home early, that she wasn't feeling good. At a pay phone, inside the Dunes, he dials home. He thinks he sees Liza Minnelli playing blackjack at a nearby table, but when he squints for a better look she changes into an ordinary middle-aged woman with spiky black hair. When Kathy answers the phone, she tells him that Helen isn't there, that she never came home early. "Don't worry," he reassures her. "I'll check at Leo's. I'm sure that's where she is."

Leo's car is in the driveway at his house, but when Edward rings the doorbell, no one answers. He rings again and stands there, lightly sweating in his linen suit, angry with a mist of worry hurrying to overtake him. He walks around the side of the house, stepping between two fat palm trees, and tries to find a window through which he might look, but all the blinds are drawn. Then he notices that the last window in this row is half open, though the shades are still shut tight, and he moves to stand beside it, where he waits, for what, he does not know.

Edward thinks he can hear breathing through the window. Maybe a quiet moan, or was that the far cry of a car horn? And then a low, clear voice, a girl's, says, "I think you'd better check and see who's at the door."

"Are you crazy?" This is Leo's voice. "It might be Helen."

Edward's face grows hot, and sweat beads quickly on his upper lip. He raises a fist and knocks hard on the window without thinking, the sound loud and brittle above the pulse of nearby traffic. Then, before he can think what to say, what to shout at Leo through the window, he runs, gets inside his car, and guns it out into the now-empty street.

WHEN HE ARRIVES home, Helen is there, waiting on the porch, still in her swimsuit, covered only by a loose tank top, which says "The Dunes." She rises when he reaches her. "I'm sorry, Dad. I got a ride home early with a friend. I forgot to call you until it was too late."

"What friend?" His voice sounds shaky to his own ears, and he worries Helen will detect his frazzled state.

"Zoe."

"But your mother said that you weren't home."

"We went to get frozen custard on the way. My throat hurt, and we thought that it might help."

"I went all the way to Leo's to try to find you."

"I'm sorry, Dad," she says, then glances up at him. "Was he there?"

Edward gazes out at the lawn, listens to the pulsing hum of the cicadas, then looks back down at his daughter. "No, he wasn't there."

THE NEXT DAY there are no notes, only the distant glow of a meeting, in the cactus garden after class. Edward has decided he must go, how can he not? But what he decides to do once he gets there is another matter.

In class he looks at every face with hesitation. Is it she? Or she? Or she? They are going to watch the movie adaptation of *Anna Karenina* tomorrow, and as he prepares them for this film, with excerpts from the book, he feels ridiculous. Could any novel make more explicit why he should not stray from Kathy? Does he want to end up like Anna, beneath a speeding train?

He stops at his office after class to set down his briefcase and eat a mint. When he steps out into the hall to leave, Carl is waiting beside his door.

"Professor Larkin, did you grade my paper yet?"

"You just gave it to me yesterday."

"Oh, right. I guess I'm pretty anxious about my grade. Sorry, I realize that you have a life." He laughs and rolls his eyes.

"I'll look at it tonight," Edward says, then begins to turn away.

"I saw your daughter yesterday."

"Yesterday?" The day she left early. "Where?"

"Um. At Luv-it. You know, that frozen custard place."

"I know it."

"We talked for a while. She's really cool."

"That's great, Carl. Now, if you'll excuse me."

"Where are you headed? I'll walk out with you."

"I'm just taking a stroll," Edward murmurs. "To clear my mind. I'd like to be alone."

"Okay. Until tomorrow, then, Dr. L." The boy holds out his hand. Edward takes it with hesitation, then completes the handshake with a firmness meant to show a confidence he doesn't— at the moment—feel.

THE CACTUS GARDEN is behind the Science Building. It is an intimate, secluded plot of land woven through with pathways. In the center sits a gazebo, surrounded by a purple spray of sagebrush. He hesitates at the edge of the garden—no one is in sight—then takes a breath and steps between two Joshua trees onto a path, sun pressing on his neck like a weight, like a burden of light.

He approaches the gazebo, and as he draws closer, he detects a pair of legs inside; they are crossed, one sandaled foot swinging back and forth, and then, when he steps beneath the archway, an entire body is made visible. It's the girl who sits in front with all the answers, and he smiles at the sight of her—of course she is the writer—sitting with a book and sipping from a straw that is stuck into a box of juice. He softly says her name. "Jessica."

She looks up. "Oh, hi, Professor Larkin."

He is caught off guard by this greeting, so formal for a secret meeting, and decides to take it slow, to play it nonchalant. "How can you stand this heat?" he asks, then moves to sit beside her on the bench.

She shrugs. "I like it."

Her eyes are green, almost the color of his daughter Helen's, and as he sits here thinking what to do, drumming up what words to say, he thinks of Leo, of his betrayal yesterday. Who was that girl inside his house? Why would this boy deceive someone like his daughter? "What are you reading?" he asks.

"*Anna Karenina*. For class." She shrugs again, then laughs. "I love it."

And her words and actions remind him once again of Helen, the looseness of her shrug, the nervous laugh she has not yet learned to curb, the simple, clear-toned way she declares her love for something as complex and finely layered as a book. *You don't love books*, he had once told Helen. *You learn from them. You dissect them. You read them to see what knowledge they will bring you.*

"My daughter Helen loves that book as well," he tells Jessica. "We couldn't get her to sleep at night when she was reading it."

"You must be very close to her."

He thinks about this for a minute. "Not really. You know, I love my family very much, but sometimes that alone is not enough."

Enough for what? is the question he expects, and he does not have an answer. Enough to spray the world clean each day, enough to split apart the heavens on a nightly basis so he can taste each piece of food, each word he speaks, as if it were something new.

"My parents both died when I was five," she says instead. "My aunt and uncle raised me, and they're great, but you know, it's not the same. At least I don't think it is."

"I'm so sorry," he tells her, and lays a hand on top of hers. He feels no passion in this touch; there is not the blaze of light between them he had hoped for. He removes his hand and says, "I can't do this."

"Do what?" He notices fine stars of sweat along her hairline.

"Just thinking out loud," he says quickly. "About something

at home I have to do." He waves a hand through the air. "I apologize."

They are quiet for a minute, and she pulls her bare legs, white and long as his wife's, away from his, so there is not even the possibility of contact.

He thinks he should leave, then says instead, "Can I ask you a question?"

"Okay."

"I think my daughter's boyfriend is deceiving her, seeing another girl behind her back. They're just kids, but still, I know she loves him very much. Do you think I should tell her? You're closer to her age. I thought perhaps you'd have some insight."

She looks away, out toward the blazing garden, and says, "You probably shouldn't get involved. She'll work it out alone."

"I think you're right; thank you very much for the advice," he says, then stands. "Enjoy your book."

Stepping out of the gazebo, he doesn't see a single soul, but walking through the garden, he thinks he hears the distant ring of laughter—the shrill giggles of a girl or maybe two—and he decides the notes have been a joke. Most likely they were written by the two sorority girls, he thinks, looking around at the buildings, at the empty, dying grass; after all, they both failed the last exam.

LEO COMES TO dinner at their house that night. They eat late in the summer, after the air has cooled a bit, though not by much at all this time in July. Lamb chops and feta cheese, green salad with a tahini dressing, and a chilled cucumber soup, which Leo seems to like though he was hesitant about tasting it.

"Great dinner, Mrs. Larkin," he says now, from his space next to Edward, across from Helen.

"Thank you," Kathy says, and smiles, and Helen looks at Leo with such love that Edward can't believe she's just fifteen. Where has she learned to love this way?

"Yes, it's delicious," Edward adds, but can't help feeling that his praise has come too late, that his words are just an echo of this boy's beside him, and he feels a silent, crazy anger burning in the base of his stomach.

"So, Leo, are you excited about music camp?" Jenny, his second daughter, asks in a grown-up voice Edward barely recognizes.

"Very excited," he says, and winks at her.

Edward can tell Jenny is pleased by this response, and he sees that in a couple of years she will have a boyfriend too. How will he survive this span of time?

"How's your film class going, Mr. Larkin?" Leo asks him.

"So-so," he says, and takes a sip of wine. "I'm showing the movie adaptation of *Anna Karenina* tomorrow, so things will hopefully liven up."

"I never liked that book," Kathy says, and frowns. "Imagine, leaving your child for your lover."

"But she didn't *want* to leave her child," Helen interjects. "Was she supposed to ignore her heart? She didn't realize what she was going to lose when she fell in love."

"She should've known," Kathy says. "She should've thought ahead."

Edward sits there listening as if to a lecture on his own behavior, trying to draw meaning from their words, to glean some sideways information from this discussion. But this novel is about a woman from another century, he thinks, another life, and he eats the remainder of his soup in silence.

After dinner Helen and Leo announce that they're going to take a walk. Kathy reads in the yellow chair, and Jenny finishes up the dishes. Edward pages through a magazine for a minute or two in the den, then reads a bit of his book before he realizes that he is absorbing nothing, that he doesn't care a whit for the people in its pages.

He wanders through the living room, past Kathy, then opens the front door and steps onto the porch. He hoped to find a full moon, something beautiful to look at, but it is waning, dented on its eastern edge and covered by a stripe of murky cloud. He lowers his gaze to the lawn, then sees, with the help of a streetlight, Helen and Leo, kissing in the back of Leo's car, oblivious to his nearby presence on the porch. He watches for a minute; Leo's back is to him, his shaggy head half covering the creamy, lifted half-moon of his daughter's face, his wide drummer's hand wrapped in passion around the side of her neck. Her hands aren't visible. Where are Helen's hands? Then one appears, moving up and down on the back of Leo's white T-shirt, a motion Edward used to use to soothe her when she cried. Perhaps she has learned to love, in part, from him?

The door behind him opens, and he quickly turns. "Kathy?"

But his second daughter steps onto the porch and walks to stand beside him. "No, it's me."

"Don't look now," he says, and nods toward the scene in Leo's car.

Jenny moves her gaze toward Helen and Leo, and for a moment, Edward detects such longing in her face, that slight widening of her eyes, the quiet crease between her brows. How young she is, he thinks, yet her reaction is so much like his own. There are so many years of this life, he decides now, lost to yearning, lost to wanting what we don't yet have, or to what has been left behind with time. "It'll happen for you someday too," he tells her.

She looks up at him, this little, gawky beauty he has made, then frowns. "Gross, Dad."

He laughs, an immediate release of pleasure. Then Jenny begins to laugh with him, her braces sparking in the moonlight as she tosses back her head. Helen and Leo must hear them because they separate, then quickly exit the backseat of his car and walk, keeping space between them, toward Edward and Jenny, who are still laughing on the porch.

"What's so funny?" Helen asks with a tentative smile; she tosses an embarrassed glance across the grass to Leo.

"Oh," Edward says, catching his breath. "It's too hard to explain."

THAT NIGHT he cannot sleep, so he takes his briefcase into the kitchen and begins reading Carl's paper. It's poorly organized with lots of typos and shoddy use of detail from the film, but there is a bit of insight to the thing, a glimmer here and there of a mind that might one day be interesting.

At the paper's end there is a handwritten note, and the writing looks familiar. But no, it's not as slanted, less neat and even. Still, he never saved one of the notes, so he can't compare them now, except in memory. "I apologize for the tardy nature of this paper," Carl has written, and then, beside an asterisk: "Please give my regards to your lovely daughter!"

Edward writes a red "78%" on the front page of the paper, then rises and wanders through the house in his blue seersucker bathrobe, his mind ablaze with questions. Was the secret writer Carl? Or was it the two girls in the back of the class? Or was it none of them? Either way, it doesn't really matter. In any case, it was some sort of joke on him. But for what purpose? Maybe just a game to pass the time of summer school. Perhaps there was no intent of malice, and truly, he does not feel pain from this deception, only confusion and a mild murmur of embarrassment along his bones.

He returns to the bedroom, sheds his robe, then crawls between the sheets beside his wife. Edward folds himself around Kathy's back, curves his free arm across her body and matches bent knee to knee, like a mother cocooned around her child, like lover spooned to lover, like a second skin that will protect her— surely his skin must be good for this at least—from the elements outside.

The Mother

SHE HAS A NEW ROUTINE that she cannot explain, even to herself. Each morning upon rising, Kathy dons her violet robe, then shuts herself inside the bathroom, where she peers into the mirror above the sink. When she is satisfied she has studied herself well, she pulls a small blue notebook from the pocket of her robe and writes down any changes that she sees, any mark of age the passing days have wrought upon her face.

She began doing this last week, on the first of August, and so far every entry has been the reassuring "nothing different." But today there is a change. "August 8, 1990," she writes, "the beginning of a cold sore on the right bow of my lip." It is just a haze of redness now and a slight tingling beneath the skin, but she knows the signs. Whenever she is under stress, these sores emerge.

Last week, in the pocket of her husband's khaki pants, the slacks he wears to teach his class, she found a tiny slip of paper that said this: "I too miss the lightning bugs." The writing was not his, and the *g*'s had a carefree girlish swoop, the type her daughters might employ, but the writing does not belong to either one of them.

IN THE CAR, driving her daughter Helen to the Dunes Hotel, Kathy asks, "Have you ever seen a lightning bug?"

Helen glances up from the letter in her lap, then shakes her head. "Not in real life. I read a book about them once. Their butts light up when they want to mate." She laughs.

Kathy wants to ask *what* exactly Helen knows about mating but doesn't want to begin a fight, so instead, she murmurs, "They're beautiful."

Helen is back into her letter, received yesterday from Leo, who is at music camp this week.

"Can't you read that later? Have a conversation with your mother?"

"I'm just *re*-reading it, so I can talk at the same time."

"What's Leo got to say for himself anyway?"

"Um." She glances up again. "He really likes his private drum teacher but says orchestra sort of sucks."

"*Helen*."

"What's wrong with *sucks*? It's not a swearword."

She thinks about it for a minute, then says, "It just sounds ugly."

"Anyway. The food isn't good, but the other drummers are cool, and there's a dance tomorrow night, but he promised me he wouldn't dance with anyone. Just hang out. Isn't that sweet?"

The Dunes looms up ahead, and Kathy turns right, then left into the parking lot. "For God's sake, it's just a dance."

"You wouldn't care if Dad danced with someone else?"

If you only knew, Kathy thinks, what your father has done already with someone else. "Your dad doesn't even like to dance," she says. "So I wouldn't have to worry, would I?" She smiles at her daughter and brushes Helen's hair out of her eyes. "C'mon, I'll walk you in."

HELEN'S BOSS, Gerard, is in his usual place between the two pools, standing at a lectern beneath a wide red umbrella. Helen drops her bag beside him and says hello, then turns and says good-bye to Kathy before walking to the pool's edge, where she sheds her clothes down to that second skin of hers, a black one-piece, and dives in.

Kathy stands beside Gerard, and they both watch as Helen begins swimming laps, the crisp scissors of her rising elbows, the turning flower of her face. They could be two pleased parents, Kathy thinks, admiring their daughter.

"Her stroke's really improved," Kathy comments.

"Yes, she's a beautiful swimmer. Do you swim too?" He turns his brown face toward her, eyes shielded by mirrored glasses, black hair crushed beneath a ball cap, which reads "The Dunes." He is most likely forty or forty-two, five years or so younger than she is herself.

"I used to, but don't much anymore."

"In my country they say the daughter can do nothing better than the mother." He raises his shades and winks at her, then drops them back onto his nose.

"Really." She laughs. "What country is that? I'll have to visit."

"A very old one."

IN THE CAR, on the way home, Kathy plays the radio. Mellow rock, which her husband, Edward, never tolerates when they drive together. Classical and baseball are the only two to which he'll listen. But she likes these love songs, despite the fact that they are sung by men and women not yet old enough to know, she thinks, what love is really all about. The way it dips and fades, then buzzes back to life when you find a note from another woman to your husband. Though this rejuvenated love is edged in hatred and distaste, a small amount of fear, which alters the original, transforms it into something different altogether. Can you still call this altered feeling love? she wonders, turning off the Strip into the beige network of neighborhoods. Or does it require the invention of an entirely new word?

"AUGUST 9: Cold sore in full bloom. Dark circles under eyes from lack of sleep." She pauses, pen in hand, eyes focused on her face, then begins to write down everything that's wrong, unsure of what is new and what's been there for years. "Three faint (very faint) horizontal lines across my forehead; crow's-feet, deeper when I smile, two lines from the edges of my nose curving down around my mouth; a small broken vein beneath my left nostril;

chicken pox scar on chin." She leans back and sets the notebook on the sink, exhausted. She should just stop looking in the mirror; she knows this, but it beckons to her, calls her with its shiny surface, which once provided such reassuring pleasure. She shoves the notebook back into her robe, dots base on the dark beneath her eyes, puts a dab of medicine on her sore, then goes downstairs for breakfast.

Edward sits in his usual place at the kitchen table, crunching buttered toast and reading the *Review Journal*. "Good morning," he tells her, without looking up. And then, a glance at her face elicits "Ooh, a cold sore. What's the matter?"

She shrugs. "Nothing."

"*Kathy*." He sets down the paper. "I know you."

"Oh, it's just"—she waves her hand dismissively—"you know, the change of season or something."

"It's still summer."

"Yeah, but August always feels different. Don't you think? More of a separate entity."

"I have no idea what you're talking about."

He crunches once again into his toast, and the sound brings to mind the shallow break of sparrow bones.

"I thought you said you knew me."

He looks up, as if waiting for her face to tell him how to read this comment. She smiles, so he chuckles in response, then dips back into the paper.

KATHY KNEW about the first affair. (She numbers it now as the first since she found the note.) Edward thought she was unaware of his betrayal, but of course she knew about it. How could she have failed to see the changes in him? That callow tone of voice he took on, as if he were a high school boy once more. That lightness in his walk, his extra-ardent professions of his love for her. *Come on*—she thought once when he told her how much he'd missed her that day at work—*give me a break.* But there was no real proof, nothing to confront him with, and she sees now, thinking of that thin slip of paper, that strangely knowing line about the lightning bugs, how lucky that was.

WHEN THE MAILMAN arrives that day, she happens to be on the porch, leaving to get some frozen custard. He hands her one letter, a fat envelope from Leo to Helen, thicker than usual, the blue ink address smeared a bit as if by tears.

"Is that it?" she asks him.

He shrugs and says, "Yep. Looks like someone wrote you quite a letter."

"It's not for me," she explains. "It's for my daughter."

"Oh." He nods knowingly. He is young and very handsome, with a crooked nose and dark red hair. Pale freckles on his forearms like a haze of cinnamon. She imagines, for a moment, kissing him, then taking him inside the house, but the fantasy seems so cliché she is ashamed. The mailman. She can do better, can't she? She's a schoolteacher, after all, not just some lonely housewife.

But as he turns and walks away, the jumping muscles in his calves make her blood leap a bit, and she wonders what it might be like to separate the act of love from love itself. To divorce mind and heart from body and simply listen to your skin. She has never known such pureness of desire; her couplings have always been weighted by the complicated mix of history and heart, the space between her face and Edward's a dense network of memory. Perhaps a simple sweaty contact might be nice, and maybe, she thinks, getting into her car and leaving the house and driveway behind, this is all that Edward wants.

In the car she chastises herself. The note from Edward's pocket is most likely nothing. What kind of love note would that be? He probably found it on the ground and picked it up. That is something he would do, attempt to neaten a room, pick up a scrap of paper in the cactus garden on campus with a huff of irritation.

She is spending too much time alone this summer. Her notion to pass on teaching summer school this year was a mistake. Her friends all are away on their annual vacations, and with her younger daughter, Jenny, off visiting a friend in California, there is no one to absorb her loneliness, to distract her active mind from silly things. She needs some sort of plan. After eating custard, she'll go buy a book, not one of those thin modern novels she's been reading, but something heavy and old, weighted with the wisdom of time.

AT LUV-IT, she sees Helen's boss, Gerard. Kathy gets into line behind him and asks, "Why aren't you at the pool?"

He turns and lifts his glasses. "I'm sorry. Do I know you?"

"Helen's mother. Kathy." She raises her dark glasses too, and the meeting of their unclothed eyes, both squinted up against the sun, seems intimate.

"Oh, right. I'm sorry. I didn't recognize you without Helen

attached. I'm not at the pool because it's lunchtime, and it was too hot to eat real food."

"My thought exactly."

They sit together on a bench, surrounded by a lake of asphalt, casinos rising a block or two away like some ancient, rotting city. Cars river past on Oakey, thrumming out their own familiar rhythm. Kathy takes a bite or two of her sundae, wondering what to say to this man. What might they possibly have in common other than her daughter?

After a few minutes Gerard turns to her and says, "You have a cold sore on your lip."

"I'm aware of that, Gerard, but thank you."

"I've offended."

She laughs. "No. It's okay."

"In my country they say a cold sore is a sign that you're in love."

"You don't even have an accent. I bet you were born right here in Las Vegas."

He smiles and shrugs. "But are you?"

"Am I what?"

"In love."

"No, Gerard." She rolls her eyes. "I'm not in love."

"Hmm." He sits back and takes a bite of ice cream. "Not even with your husband?"

"Oh. Well, yes. Of course. I thought you meant it in a different way."

They are quiet again, but Kathy feels off-balance now, exposed, as if her skin has suddenly become see-through. A small ember of anger burns softly in her throat, threatening to ignite; but then their forearms brush as they both take a bite of ice cream, and Kathy can only describe the feeling of Gerard's skin meeting hers as electric, every fine hair on her arm rising in immediate response.

Kathy reaches down and smooths her skirt, wishing she were able to wear lipstick, but her cold sore will heal more slowly if she does. A teenage girl, who seems half naked in her denim shorts and half shirt, pedals past them on a ten-speed, and Kathy thinks of Helen sitting even more nakedly in a chair right this second, raised high above a swimming pool surrounded by strangers. Every inch of that young body, her *daughter's* body, is no longer known to her. Now Leo is its keeper. Something in the second forearm brush she shares with Gerard, a near stranger whom she finds only partially attractive, tells her this: Helen is having sex with Leo. Kathy had forgotten the current a new touch of skin can carry, the way it seems more potent in its moment than any rules passed down by parents.

When they stand to leave, Gerard says, "I'm having a thing at my house a week from Saturday. You should stop by." He presses a card into her hand that says, "Gerard Rasmussen, Entrepreneur." Beneath this are an address and a phone number.

"Maybe," she says, and smiles across at him. They are exactly the same height.

"You know, I see Helen's face inside you when you smile."

She feels the rising heat of a blush, so murmurs a quick, "Thank you," then walks across the asphalt to her car and quickly gets inside.

AT WALDENBOOKS on Maryland Parkway, Kathy meanders down every aisle, smoothing the sparse hair on her forearm and thinking of Gerard. She cannot imagine him in bed. What is his body like beneath those loose printed shirts? Too tan, most likely, and hairy as a desert fox. But not, she admits, without any appeal. His shoulders have a strength and breadth that Edward's lack, and his hands are wide and ringless, *masculine*. Kathy never could abide a dainty-handed man.

But more to the point, she cannot imagine herself in bed with a man other than her husband. When they first coupled, she was twenty-five, lithe and coppery with sun, no stretch marks or sagging skin, not a wrinkle to be found on any part of her. Sex was easy then; she could please simply by being naked. The first time now, she thinks, must be different, less linked to the beauty of the body. Or maybe she was wrong *ever* to think of sex this way.

She stops in her present aisle and looks down at a row of books. She has ended up in front of Virginia Woolf. Once, over dinner early in their marriage, when Kathy was reading *Mrs. Dalloway*, Edward said, "You know, Virginia Woolf didn't like sex. No one knows if she ever even did it with her husband."

Kathy laughed and said something like "Really? At least I'm not that bad." But the joking tone felt sour on her tongue, and she was unable to shake the feeling that Edward was commenting on her, that he sensed she didn't much enjoy their lovemaking. Another time, late at night after quiet sex beneath the ceiling fan, he mused, not unkindly, into the darkness, "I wonder if your father's being killed when you were just a teenager affected you in some deep way we can't even understand."

Kathy feigned sleep at this, uncertain if she was being insulted or finally understood.

She picks up *To the Lighthouse* now and pages through it. Too short, she decides, and sets it back. The only book of girth in this section is a biography by James King set beside the novels, so she buys it, then leaves the store and plunks the book onto her passenger seat with a thud of satisfaction. This should keep her busy for a while.

It's almost time to pick up Helen, so she drives to the Dunes and reads in her air-conditioned Honda for half an hour. A young bride walks in front of Kathy's car, her long white dress and veil limp and rumpled from the heat. The groom is nowhere in sight. Kathy watches as the woman disappears behind the door leading to the casino.

The door to the pool's courtyard opens next, and a woman in a hot pink g-string bikini wanders out, talking softly to a parrot on her shoulder. Her muscles flash and ripple in her bronzed skin as she passes, and Kathy wonders if she's in some sort of show involving the parrot.

She spends ten more minutes reading about Virginia Woolf, then looks up again, waiting for her daughter to emerge. When Helen steps out from behind the white door into the parking lot, she seems smaller than Kathy recalls, and not as radiant. Her hair is lank with water, and the zinc on her nose, half rubbed off, creates an imbalance in her features. Her knees are sunburned and turn in more than usual, most likely because she's tired. She gets into the car without a word, then sees Leo's giant letter on the dashboard and smiles.

"How was work?" Kathy asks.

"Hot."

Helen tears open the envelope, and Kathy pulls out of the lot, back into the traffic of the Strip, thinking this will be yet another conversationless car ride with her daughter. She turns on the radio, and synthesized piano music pours over them, a girl with a scrunched-up baby voice wailing about lost love. Kathy reaches to change the station, then realizes Helen is crying. "Sweetheart," she says, turning the radio completely off. "What's the matter?"

Helen shakes her head as if to say, "It's nothing," then releases a fierce, birdlike sob, causing Kathy to turn down a side street and pull over.

"Helen, tell me. What is it?"

Her daughter turns, leans across the gearshift, and puts her face into the curve of Kathy's neck, then loops an arm across her chest and shoulder. The embrace shocks her skin—it's been so long since Helen's clung to her—and Kathy attempts to turn her body and complete the circle; but this is awkward in the car, so she holds on to her daughter as best she can, trying to decide what tack to take. Should she wait it out or prod Helen further? Is Leo injured? Dead? In love with someone else?

She has parked beside a run-down Laundromat, and Kathy watches as two girls walk toward its doors carrying giant gray-green duffel bags. Beside the Laundromat is a 7-Eleven, and beside this sits an empty lot of sand, strewn with the array of tumbleweed and debris that these spaces always contain. The ugliness of Kathy's surroundings quietly invigorates her: At least

I don't have to do my laundry here, she thinks: At least our yard has grass and flowers; at least our house is filled with good food and soft chairs, with vibrant rugs and perfect wineglasses. At least my daughter is healthy and intelligent and loved.

After a few long minutes Helen's sobbing begins to soften, and she says, into Kathy's shoulder, "Leo kissed another girl. He wants me to forgive him, but I don't think I can."

Kathy nods but can think of no adequate response. It occurs to her that she has been waiting for Leo to fumble, to fall and push off-balance the delicate structure he has built with Helen. How long has she been expecting news like this? she wonders. The entire ten months they've been together? Or even before that, before Helen met Leo in the marching band and brought him home to meet them, possibly before she was even old enough to want a boyfriend.

"Will you drive me up there Saturday? I need to see him face-to-face." Helen lifts her head now and wipes her eyes with the heels of her hands, then leans back into her own seat. "Please?"

"Oh, honey, I don't know. Maybe you should wait it out. He'll be home in another week."

"I can't wait," she says, her face small and plaintive, freckles emerging on her nose beneath the cried-off zinc.

Kathy does not say what she wants to say, that it's time now for Helen to leave this boy behind. Why muddle through this mess if she doesn't have to? Why should she learn to compromise so early? Instead, she pats her daughter's shoulder and says, "Okay, I'll take you up."

THE NEXT MORNING—Friday—Kathy's notebook is missing. Her hand clenches and unfurls inside the empty pocket of her robe before she hurriedly goes to search the path from bed to closet to bathroom. The notebook is nowhere in sight.

In the shower she tries to calm herself. Why does she care so much about the silly record of her face? Why should it embarrass her? It's not, after all, a real diary. There are no secrets revealed, no mooning passages about Gerard. She laughs at this idea and feels slightly better. Gerard, she decides, is not the type one moons over. He is strictly meant for sex, or maybe just a dangerous, thrilling kiss behind the palm trees of the pool. He doesn't linger in the mind the way a man you might marry would. He is present, or he is not. There is no dreamy in between.

Edward is already gone by the time she makes it down to breakfast. Helen arrives at the table with swollen eyes and eats her cereal in pained silence, so Kathy pulls out her new biography and reads it while she eats her Grape-Nuts, reads about Virginia's beautiful, aloof mother, her moody father, and wonders when she'll get to the part about Virginia's not liking sex.

WHEN SHE DROPS Helen at the pool, Gerard gives Kathy a smile across the deck and waves her over to him. She follows Helen to the lectern and gives her daughter a quick kiss on the cheek before she approaches the pool for morning laps.

"Your sore is looking better," Gerard tells her.

"Does that mean I'm falling out of love?"

He laughs and pats her shoulder. "You are too beautiful for that."

The comment makes no sense, but she is flattered just the same. "So, Rasmussen. Is that Hungarian?"

"You're getting close."

"Croatian?"

"No. Of course not."

They hear a splash behind them and turn to watch Helen begin her laps. Her stroke still has the same lanky ease it always has, and Kathy feels a certain glimmer of relief. She will get over Leo.

"So, have you thought about next Saturday?" Gerard asks her.

"I'm not sure I can make it. What time again?"

"The party will be going on all night, I'm sure." He takes his glasses off, and she tries to decide if he's attractive. His eyes are slightly bloodshot, perhaps from sun, but their broken beach-glass color and dense lashes are appealing, and he almost has a dimple in his left cheek when he smiles. She wants, right now, to touch this almost dimple, to press her thumbnail into that minor crease and deepen it.

"I'll see what my schedule looks like," she says by way of explanation, then glances once more at her daughter and leaves the pool.

At lunchtime Kathy decides to surprise Edward at his office. He doesn't answer when she knocks on his door, but it's unlocked, so she lets herself inside and sits behind his desk to wait. She thinks his morning classes last until twelve; then he returns to his office to set down his things before leaving to eat lunch. She swivels his chair toward the bookshelf beside her and sees a row of translated Russian poetry books. An idea occurs to her, and she rises and pulls one off the shelf, then pages through it, heart beating much too fast as she searches for the line that's a recurrent picture in her mind, a lawn lit as if by stars.

There are no poems about insects at all as far as she can tell. She pulls another book quickly from the shelf and pages through. One poem about a sacred beetle. One with the word *lightning* by itself. (The sight makes her heart increase its pace.) The next book has only poems of love, no bugs included, and the last one has a revolutionary bent.

She swivels back to Edward's desk. His clock reads fifteen minutes after twelve, and she listens for footsteps in the hall, then, satisfied he's not approaching, begins looking through the papers on his desk. He is very neat, so there are only two. A student's paper titled "Anna and the Train," and a letter with the envelope made out to Mary Ward at Miami University of Ohio, his alma mater. She picks this up and looks at the envelope more closely, a sturdy business white which does not allow her to see any of the contents inside. It is not heavy or thick. The address is not smeared by tears. It tells her nothing.

His file drawers, connected to his desk, are neatly organized with topics like Russian Film before Perestroika and After the Wall, a New Aesthetic. There is nothing suspicious in the drawer at all and she leans back, exhausted, in his chair, then turns it all the way around to face the window and wait.

When she hears him open the door a few minutes later, she

does not turn around, does not want to see whether his face reveals joy or disappointment at her visit.

"Kathy," he says immediately, "what a pleasant surprise."

She turns toward him and tries to smile but feels weak from her search and a little bit ashamed. Still, she asks, "Who's Mary Ward?"

"Mary Ward," he repeats, setting his briefcase on the desk. "I don't know."

She holds up the envelope.

He smiles, then says, "If confessions are being made here, I think it's your turn." He takes her blue notebook from his inner jacket pocket and tosses it neatly onto the desk, where it seems to sizzle, to undulate with the heat rising through her throat.

"Where'd you get this?" She snatches it up, then throws it back onto the desk, unwilling to claim it completely.

"Under the bed. I found it when I was straightening the dust ruffle. So"—he perches on the desk's edge across from her and smiles—"what is it? Some type of skin cancer notebook? A preventative measure of sorts?"

"Don't tease me," she tells him, searching her mind for an explanation; none is forthcoming. "I don't know. It's private."

He picks it up and hands it to her. "You know, Kath, you don't need to worry. You're still beautiful."

Still is the word she's attracted to, the one that continues to beat its wings before her as the rest of the sentence falls away. Decline, it suggests, will inevitably follow.

"Thanks," she says, then waves the letter from Mary at him once again.

"That letter is for the woman to whom I send my alumni dues. Why?"

She shrugs, breathes out, and says, "Just curious. By the way, I came to take you to lunch and to tell you that I have to take Helen to Lee's Canyon tomorrow to see Leo. Apparently he cheated on her."

"*What?*"

"Kissed another girl."

"Oh, he *kissed* another girl." Edward shrugs and says, "Not as bad as it could be, I suppose. And, I have to admit, it doesn't surprise me. He's only seventeen years old after all." He opens his briefcase, as if they were finished with this discussion, then begins removing the papers inside.

"What's his age have to do with it?" Kathy wants to know.

"When you're seventeen, a week away feels like a year. He probably forgot about Helen after the third day." He looks up at her now and adds, "Not that I condone that type of behavior or think that our daughter is in any way forgettable." Frowning, he asks, "Do you think he and Helen are, you know, having sex?"

"Possibly." She shrugs and wrinkles up her brow. "Probably."

"What do you think we should do about it?"

"I have no idea." Kathy feels the heat of tears begin to build, and then it is too late; they are running down her face. She takes a tissue from the box on Edward's desk and wipes at her cheeks.

In seconds he is around the desk, crouching awkwardly beside her chair so that they are at eye level. "What? Sweetheart, what is it?"

She shakes her head. "It just makes me so upset, the idea of that boy touching our daughter, and then, on top of that, going off with some other girl."

"I know," he says, then leans across the space between them and kisses her forehead. "I know." They don't speak again until she is finished with her tears and they stand to leave for lunch.

SATURDAY DAWNS hot and heavy with the strident cry of cicadas. The notebook is back in her robe, and she takes it out and pens the date—"August 11"—but can't bring herself to write another word. She peers into the mirror, closely, scanning every inch of her face. The cold sore is almost gone. No dark circles today. Same green eyes and thin dark brows. Same subtle, upward slope of cheekbones and smallish, fragile mouth. Is she *still* pretty? Was she ever? It's as if she is too close to her own face to truly see it. She knows the bones too well to appreciate it as a stranger might. What, for instance, might Gerard think about her face?

When she goes downstairs for breakfast, Helen is already waiting, sitting at the kitchen table with a glass of orange juice, dressed in a sky-blue halter top and cutoff shorts. Too sexy, Kathy wants to protest, but says nothing.

In the car, they play the radio—Helen's choice of station; something annoying she calls alternative rock—and take turns sipping from a water bottle. The sky is an unrelenting blue, hard and artificial as a solid piece of plastic, and the edges of the city— minimarts and low-end casinos—are bleak in their newness, their bright, sterile facades blinding in the sun.

As they leave Las Vegas behind them and begin their climb into the mountains, Kathy turns off the AC and rolls down her window. Helen does the same, and they share a smile at the altered air, the hint of coolness to the breeze. Joshua trees and pale green shrubs dot the hills that are rising around them. Higher up, the Joshua trees transform into piñon pines, the hills become mountains and the air is even cooler, though it is still at least eighty-five degrees, Kathy thinks, testing it with a hand out the window.

"So, what are you going to say?" Kathy asks.

"That I hate him and it's over."

"Are you sure?"

Helen turns her eyes on Kathy, still red-rimmed and puffy from another bout of crying the night before. "I think so."

THE CAMP IS down a long dirt road shaded by pine trees and aspen. At the end of this road the sky widens, and they are in a large clearing, rimmed at the edges with wooden cabins. Kathy parks the car, and they both step outside, then begin to look around at all the kids walking by carrying instruments or leaning against cabin walls and trees, to see if Leo is among them. He is not, so Helen and Kathy begin to walk, looking for the name of Leo's cabin, Timpani.

A boy with a bass drum strapped to his stomach walks by and smiles at Helen. Two girls play a flute duet beside a drinking fountain. An older man with a conductor's wand strides past without a glance, rubbing his temples. And then there is Leo, leaned against a tree, one leg bent and propped up on the other in such a way that provides a flat surface where he is beating rhythms with his drumsticks. His hair is lighter and longer than

Kathy remembers its being, and when he looks across the space between them and sees Helen, he smiles, drops his leg, and waits.

"I just need a few minutes," Helen tells her.

Kathy nods, then watches Helen walk across to Leo, the space of back between her halter and her shorts glowing golden brown. Hair brushing pointed shoulder blades. Left leg winging in a bit with each step as it has since she was five. This is her daughter, *her daughter*, and she both wants to watch this exchange and can hardly bear to see it unfold.

Helen keeps some space between herself and Leo, arms crossed over her chest in defense, it seems, against his brilliant drummer's smile, his glossy crown of hair. Kathy watches for a minute as they talk, then turns and wanders off, between two cabins into a meadow.

She sits down on the grass and leans back on her hands, bending her knees and tilting her face to catch the sun in such a way that reminds her of being a teenager, sitting in exactly this position beside Lake Mead with her own first boyfriend, Joey Ingersoll. The position suggests pleasure, she thinks, even abandon, but she always felt a little uneasy around Joey, uncertain how to talk to him, nervous about the sunburst of yearning that expanded in her stomach when he kissed her. What was she supposed to do with such a feeling? Better not to experience it at all, then, she decided, better to feel *less*.

Fifty feet or so away, a boy stands with a tuba, practicing his chords in the quiet air. She watches him and listens, the fat, deep tones an unromantic sound she's never really liked, but the sight of him, a teenage boy wrapped in this huge gold creature of an instrument, pleases her. He begins a song, and to her surprise, she recognizes it. A favorite pop song from ten years ago that she hasn't heard in ages. She closes her eyes and tries to dredge the words from memory, as the melody swells out around her. "When time was all that ever rested between us, I'd say I loved you before I even thought it; you caught the words with your hand raised high . . . the sky behind you lit with fireflies." No, that last line is not right. The words were something else, maybe "the sky behind you rising into bright." The other lyrics swim around her now, almost disguised by the thick sound of this boy's tuba. "You knew where to rest your fingertips on my eyelids before I ever closed my eyes, and I was so beautiful, you didn't even have to tell me." She cannot recall the chorus, or the song's name or singer; only that stanza has remained. When the boy is finished, Kathy claps, and he turns toward her, appearing startled to see another human being in this meadow, then gives her a gracious little bow.

"Mom," she hears behind her, and turns to see Helen and Leo, holding hands at the edge of the meadow. Kathy gets up and walks over to them.

"Hi, Mrs. Larkin," Leo says. "How are you?"

"I'm fine," she answers.

"Leo has to go to orchestra practice, and he wanted to say good-bye. We can have our picnic in this meadow, don't you think, Mom?"

"Sure."

Leo reaches out a hand toward Kathy, and she looks at it a moment, then takes it and shakes. "Thanks for bringing Helen up to see me."

He turns and kisses Helen, lightly on the lips, both their eyes closed against Kathy, against the sky and yellow aspen trees, against the tuba player, who is exiting the meadow a few feet away. It is a kiss so innocent it causes Kathy to rethink her idea that they are having sex. Maybe she is wrong. Leo whispers something in Helen's ear, squeezes her shoulder, then says, "I'll write you a letter tonight."

KATHY AND HELEN retrieve their lunch from the car, then spread a yellow blanket out on the meadow's soft pearl-green ground and sit down together to eat. They have tuna fish sandwiches and chips, a pickle, and two plums. They refilled the water bottle at an outside fountain and share it as they did in the car.

"You think I'm pretty stupid, don't you?" Helen says.

"Of course I don't."

"It's just . . . I know he loves me. That doesn't happen every day, you know? Love."

"Many more boys and men will love you in this lifetime, Helen." She is aware of how trite this sounds, how like a fortune cookie, but this doesn't lessen the truth behind the words. Her daughter is beautiful, will grow more beautiful still, and it is apparent from her first attempt that love will come easily, will float over her bones like a garment she has always been meant to wear.

When they finish eating, they both lie back and look at the sky, softened now by a layer of cirrus clouds. The sun is warm on Kathy's face, and she closes her eyes and listens to the sound of Helen's breathing, which is deepening toward sleep. She thinks about the note in Edward's pocket, about the blue notebook in her robe, about Virginia mourning her dead mother as she lay in bed at night, breeze in the trees like the strains of a harp. She thinks of her own long-dead parents and how empty the world can sometimes feel when she remembers they are gone. She thinks about Gerard and his party and decides that maybe she will go. Why not? She and Edward have no plans, and she can make up some excuse. Maybe she will even kiss Gerard, very lightly on the lips, the way her daughter just kissed Leo. Nothing serious, just some small contact to remind her that she is, after all, a human being.

She props herself up on her elbows and looks at Helen, who is sleeping beside her. Her daughter's face is fifteen years old. There is a small patch of red on her chin, but otherwise all the planes are smooth. Strange, Kathy thinks, how we can pass down something like a face, the color of skin and the shape of bones beneath, the green of eyes and the curve of lips. But there it is, the replica, almost, of herself at age fifteen, and she touches Helen's cheek, carefully so as not to wake her, and knows she loves this likeness of her face, this person resting beneath, more than she has ever loved herself.

The Party

SUMMER IS ENDING. Helen sits in the lifeguard chair and watches an empty pool, music looping down from some hotel room like a memory, distant and languid, note caving in upon note so quietly she can't make out the words. Gerard sips a diet soda beneath his umbrella. Miles sweeps leaves around the edges of the deck, though where these ordinary leaves have come from, Helen can't quite figure, since the only vegetation in sight is a ring of palm trees. Two hotel guests, both middle-aged women, well oiled and talking to each other with their eyes closed, heads leaned back to catch the sun, sit in yellow lounge chairs at the pool's edge.

Helen spritzes her face and neck with a water bottle she keeps on the chair and wonders what time it is. Leo will be here at noon to take her to lunch, and she doesn't know how she'll survive another second in this chair, sun cutting into her shoulders and back with such force she feels like quitting this job right now or, at the least, diving into the pool. In Las Vegas, August is the hottest month, the hardest month to survive, and she spritzes her face again, then leans back.

Miles is close to her now, sweeping beside her chair, and he looks up and says, "Going to Gerard's party tonight?"

"My mom said I couldn't."

"So? Are you a prisoner or something?"

"Are you going?"

"Haven't missed one yet."

"What are they like?"

He shakes his head and smiles. "Weird."

Helen laughs, and of course Leo manages to arrive on the pool deck at this exact moment, so that ten minutes later in his Nova on the way to Wendy's he asks her, "What did Miles say that was so funny?"

"When? What do you mean?"

"You know what I mean. You were laughing like a hyena when I walked in."

"I don't remember."

"Yes, you do."

"How do you know what I remember and what I don't?"

"Look, Helen, you know I don't like that guy. I wouldn't do something if I knew it was hurting you."

A thick silence descends, the untruth of his statement wavering between them like a force field. Rather than press forward and electrocute herself, Helen decides to change the subject. "Want to go to a party tonight?"

Leo shrugs and turns into the Wendy's parking lot. "Okay."

INSIDE, she orders a Frosty and large fries, then chooses a seat by the window and waits while Leo gets them ketchup and napkins. From her table she watches him. A recent haircut has made him less attractive, and he's taken to wearing this salmon-colored polo shirt she can't stand.

He sits down across from her and bites into his cheeseburger, a dollop of mayonnaise dropping onto his shirt in the process. "Shit," he mutters, wiping at the stain with a napkin, then looking across at Helen with a frown. "What's with you today? Why didn't you get a burger?"

"I'm thinking of going vegetarian."

"Great." He smirks. "Just what we need, another vegetarian. I feel better about the world already."

"It's not about that. It's personal. I'm trying to think more about what I do, on every level, that's all."

Leo nods, pressing his lips together, and says, "Hmm," as if he can respect this reason.

They eat for a while in silence, and Helen thinks that perhaps the rest of her lunch break will be all right, that they have somehow found a balance. Leo has been home from music camp for less than a week, yet every day has been a struggle. Despite their reconciliation on the mountain last Saturday, the equilibrium of their relationship has been disturbed, and Helen wonders if the damage is permanent.

When they are almost done with their food, Leo speaks. "You didn't mention my haircut."

"It's cute."

"*Cute.*" He sneers.

"Handsome." She tries again.

"You don't like it."

"Yes, I do."

"Look, you're the one who wanted me to be a preppy geek."

"What?" She leans back against her chair, away from him. "I never said that."

"You didn't have to." He wipes his mouth with a napkin and looks out the window. Helen does the same, wishing they didn't have to speak at all. Then everything would be just fine between them, wouldn't it? Cars at a stoplight curdle in the heat while the restaurant's air conditioning sends goose bumps up her legs and arms. Everywhere, she thinks, the temperature is wrong. Across and down the street she can see the white buildings and green lawns of UNLV where her father teaches. Helen wonders if he's ever had a terrible, awkward meal like this with her mother.

"I'm sorry," Leo says. "I guess I'm just freaked out about these honor band tryouts tomorrow. I really want to make first chair."

"You will," she tells him, then reaches across the table for his hand; their cold, French fry–salted fingers meet in the middle and remain interlocked until they rise to leave.

THAT EVENING Helen dresses for the party carefully. She can't make it look as if she were going anywhere out of the ordinary; still, she's never seen Miles or Gerard out of her pool uniform, wet hair and a bathing suit, zinc on her nose like a tribal print, and she wants, for some reason, to impress them. So she blow-dries her hair in the bathroom, curving the long ends under. Puts on eyeliner and mascara, two pats of powder, and a pale pink lipstick called seashell, which matches the paint on her toes. Helen is slipping into her denim miniskirt and black tank top in her bedroom when her mother knocks, then enters. "What are you doing tonight?"

"Going to the movies with Leo."

"Which one?"

"Um, I don't know. Whatever's at the Huntridge. I forget."

"Your hair looks pretty." Her mother crosses the room and touches the crown of her head. "It looks nice when you do it this way."

"Thanks." She bends to put on her black sandals, flat so she doesn't tower over Leo. "What are you and Dad doing tonight?" Helen rises from buckling her sandals, and notices that her mother is dressed nicely too, her lips painted perfectly with red, dark hair loose around her face in a new style.

"Oh, nothing. I might meet a friend for coffee, or I might just stay home."

Helen notices a bracelet on her mother's wrist that she hasn't seen before, a thick silver band with strange markings. "That's pretty," she tells her. "What are those prints on it?"

"Oh, I think they're Egyptian hieroglyphics. Supposedly they spell my name."

"Cool."

There is a honk outside, sharp and insistent, so Helen kisses her mother on the cheek, grabs her purse, and runs outside to Leo.

IN THE CAR, Helen gives him directions from a slip of paper in her purse. A wind has begun that only seems to make it hotter outside, but Leo doesn't have air conditioning, so she keeps her window down. At a stoplight on Maryland Parkway, Leo kisses her, then leans back and inspects her face. "Who's the lipstick for?"

"You."

He reaches over and rubs it off with his thumb. "You taste better without it."

The light turns green, and they roar through the intersection, Leo giving the car just enough gas to show her he is a little angry, she thinks, looking out the window at fast-food restaurants, a church, a junior high school, air moving over her face so quickly now she closes her eyes.

Since Leo's return from music camp, Helen has tried to forget that while he was there, he kissed another girl, but when he acts this way, the image returns: some nondescript blond girl leaned against a tree, Leo covering her like a shroud, his hands in her hair, on her waist and below, the sounds of a trumpet or maybe a flute crooning to them, a song somber and dark, the sky crowded with hot clouds as she sits alone, a mere hour away in her lifeguard chair, missing him.

At the next stoplight, Helen pulls down the sun visor and opens her purse, then reapplies lipstick in the small, cracked mirror before her, willing Leo to say something, to begin a fight over this. To her surprise he says nothing, just turns on the radio and adjusts the dial until he finds something he likes, Iron Maiden she thinks it is, then continues on toward the party.

When they reach Gerard's address, Leo pulls into an empty stretch of curb across the street and cuts the engine. There is music seeping out of the house, a small beige stucco building with a dying lawn, and through the front window she can see two girls in red dresses dancing in a strobe light. A man she doesn't recognize walks out of the front door and sits down on the stoop, where he lights a cigarette; he's wearing a hat with a beer can on top and a tube coming down to his mouth that he drinks from after blowing out his first lungful of smoke.

"Helen, I don't want to go to this."

"I do."

"Wouldn't you rather go to my place and make love?"

"We can later. This looks fun."

"You go then. I'm going home."

"*Leo.*" She touches his arm.

He says nothing, just leans on the steering wheel and looks past her at the man on the porch. "That's not a cigarette he's smoking, you know. This party's gonna get busted."

She opens the door and climbs out into the night, heat beating against her as she shuts the car door, then turns and leans down to look through the window. "Please come with me."

He shakes his head, so she leaves his car behind and crosses the street, steps past the man on the porch, then goes inside without a glance back. When she turns to look out the peephole, Leo's car is already gone.

GERARD'S HOUSE IS a catacomb of dark, tiny rooms. The room to her left contains the dancing girls, and Helen sees that a man sits in the corner sketching them on a notepad. He has short hair and a mustache, and when Helen looks into the room, he looks up. Wordless music, filled with beats and synthesizers, courses over her, and when the man speaks, she doesn't quite hear him. "What?" she calls across the room, hoping her words carry through these two girls in red dresses. One is young, perhaps her own age, and the other much older. She thinks they may be a mother and daughter from the similarity of their pale, scrunched-up faces.

"I said," the man shouts, "do you want to be in the picture? I have another dress in the back."

She shakes her head. "No, thanks."

He flashes her a peace sign with his fingers, then looks back to his notepad.

She continues down a hallway toward what appears from its bright light and yellow and white interior to be the kitchen. There are two shut doors on her right, and from inside one she thinks she hears, beneath the music, the deep burble of voices. On her left there is an open bedroom, where she sees three adults, two men and a woman, jumping on a queen-size bed.

The heart of the party is in the kitchen. Women of varying ages sit all along the countertops, drinking from beer bottles or wineglasses, and men mill about on the floor. One man leans between the legs of a woman and kisses her neck. One leans backward against a woman, her arms laced across his chest, head leaned down to his. Plastic red chili pepper lights are looped around the edges of the room and another music source, a boom box in the corner, plays heavy metal. Everyone is talking, or shouting over the music, and Helen feels momentarily lost in the din. Then there is a tap on her elbow, and she turns to find Miles, holding out a wine cooler and smiling. "Hey. Didn't think you'd make it."

She accepts the drink and takes a sip, surprised by its sweetness. "I wanted to see what was so weird about these parties." She nods toward the long countertop. "What's with the segregation? Aren't men allowed to sit down?"

"One of Gerard's rules." Miles laughs. "No male butts on his countertops."

She laughs too and takes another sip of cooler. Down the hallway she can see more people enter through the front door, and for a moment she thinks Leo is among them. Her blood heats up at the sight of sandy hair, blinking off and on in the strobe light; but then the owner of the hair turns, and it's another guy, so she turns back to Miles. He looks different away from the Dunes. His hair is lightly spiked up with gel, and in place of his trademark red swim trunks and bare chest, he has on khaki shorts and an orange T-shirt that reads "Princeton University," although she remembers he goes to the University of Nevada, Reno. Helen searches for something to say that will sound knowing and adult, but all she can come up with is to ask about his major. "So, how's premed going?"

"Great. It rocks."

"Cool," she says, and takes another sip of wine cooler, trying to wash away thoughts of Leo, then smiles up at Miles. He is much taller than she is, and she likes the way she has to lift her head to meet his eyes.

"You look great tonight." He touches her bare shoulder. "Though I prefer you in a swimsuit."

"Thank you," she says, feeling a blush begin to build beneath her skin.

Just then Gerard appears, stepping in through the kitchen door, the backyard a dark sea behind him. Out of his pool manager swim trunks and Hawaiian shirt he looks even more different than Miles does. Tonight he is wearing crisp linen pants the cool color of sand and a black polo shirt. His Dunes ball cap has been discarded, and his dark hair is combed sleekly back against his skull. In this bright kitchen light, his tan is muted, and Helen can see the gold gleam of an earring in his left ear. His dark eyes scan the room, and when they catch on her, Helen can see his surprise. He waves, then crosses over to her and Miles. "I didn't think you were allowed to come to this gathering," he says into her ear.

"I'm not."

He smiles, but worry slides across his features as his eyes light on the wine cooler. He takes it from her and says, "I'd better get you some juice instead."

He walks over to the refrigerator, and Helen asks Miles, "What's with him?"

"Who knows?"

Gerard returns with a tumbler of dark red liquid. "Cranberry juice," he says, and hands it to her. "Sorry, but I'm out of ice."

"I've drunk alcohol before you know," she tells him. "I'm not that young."

"Oh, yes, you are," he says, and pats her shoulder. "You're my little innocent lifeguard. And I wouldn't corrupt you for the world."

Miles laughs at this, and Helen frowns. The cranberry juice is warm, and her lipstick comes off on the rim of the glass, leaving her imprint behind. She thinks of Leo and wonders if he's gone home or is circling the neighborhood in his Nova. Also, for the first time, the idea that she has no way home without him enters her consciousness with the fierce throb of a nightmare. If she misses her curfew *and* she is discovered at this party, she will be in very big trouble.

Gerard turns toward the crowd, lifts his arms, and shouts above the din of music and chatter. "Why isn't anybody dancing? Come on!"

At least half the people follow him down the hall to the strobe light, and Helen excuses herself to find the bathroom, which is off the other end of the kitchen. A candle burns on the back of the toilet; beside it are two ceramic figurines, a purple horse raised up on its back legs and a girl in a full white dress holding the number fifteen before her. It's one of those dolls you buy a daughter to celebrate her current age, and Helen picks it up and studies it, thinking how disappointed she would be if someone gave her such a gift.

She flicks on the light, and as her eyes adjust to the new harshness, she is surprised by what she sees. Photographs cover every space of wall, overlapping, flapping off in the breeze from the bathroom fan, black-and-whites and color Polaroids. Everyone in the pictures looks sort of like Gerard, especially a girl with waist-length black hair, who Helen guesses is his daughter, though Gerard has never spoken of her. In one picture, she holds the figurine from the toilet and smiles what Helen interprets as a fake, half-grateful smile. Behind her, a cake ablaze with candles sits on a picnic table.

On the other wall there are only girls in bathing suits, with the occasional guy lying on a raft or looking sternly down from a lifeguard chair. Miles is in one of the photos, and Helen smiles at how young he looks, his legs skinny in wide red shorts as he waves to the camera from his sitting position on the diving board. All of them, she guesses from the whistles looped around their necks, are ex-lifeguards. There is a girl with red hair and braces. Another with a birthmark on her cheek. One with cleavage spilling out of a purple bikini top beneath a face so round and pimpled it doesn't seem to match the chest. There is another picture of Miles, older by a few years, and then, heart rattling against her rib cage, she sees a picture of herself. She is on the pool's edge, poised to dive in for her morning laps. Her legs look skinny, knees turned slightly in, and her face is faraway, focused so intently on some inward picture that she doesn't even notice she is being photographed. What day was that? Helen wonders, stepping closer. And why does the act of being photographed without her knowledge strike her as a violation?

She has little time to ponder this, because beneath the picture of herself is one that jars her even more. It is a photo of her mother, smiling beneath Gerard's red umbrella, cocktail waitresses in the background like dragonflies floating in their gold lamé. *Her mother*. Well, she often drops Helen at the pool and stays to chat with Gerard for a minute or two; still, this picture strikes her as very wrong, and she untapes it from the wall and puts it in her purse.

Helen places toilet paper on the seat before she sits on it, and when she is finished, she washes her hands and splashes water on her face, then goes back into the kitchen. A man in the corner is mixing something magenta in a blender, a girl beside him saying over and over, "Speed it up. Speed it up." The buzzer on the stove goes off, and a woman in an orange dress leaps off the counter, puts on an oven mitt, and pulls a chocolate cake out of the oven. Helen goes in search of Miles but finds him dancing with the younger red-dressed woman, so she sits in a chair by the window and watches the cars pass by outside, hoping to see Leo's Nova.

Gerard walks past her and pats her on the head, then retreats down the hallway and into one of the closed rooms. The song ends, and a slower one begins, a sentimental ballad, the type her mother likes. Miles taps her shoulder, so Helen rises and takes his outstretched hand, then puts her arms around his neck and begins to dance. His hands are at her waist, and he pulls her closer as the song progresses, drawing a circle at the small of her back. "I didn't know Gerard had a daughter," Helen says into Miles's ear.

"I don't think he does."

"There were all these pictures in the bathroom."

He shrugs and tugs her even closer. "Well, there are a lot of things I don't know about Gerard."

Over Miles's shoulder, Helen can see down the hallway into the kitchen. Gerard is leaning against a counter now, talking to a woman who has her back to Helen. From this distance, it appears to be a familiar back: slender shoulders and a thin, exposed neck, the swing of airy black hair as the woman shakes her head. And then the woman turns to lean on the counter, and Helen's breath catches in her chest, causing it to painfully constrict, leaving her bereft and airless. The woman is her mother.

Helen watches for a moment, mesmerized, as the song continues to spiral out around her, Miles's hands dipping lower on her hips. Despite her proximity to the kitchen, Helen feels she can safely watch her mother and Gerard from her position on the dance floor, shielded as she is by very dim lighting and an array of couples. Her mother, *her mother*, takes a proffered cigarette from Gerard and leans in for a light. She inhales, then coughs into her hand and laughs before she takes one more puff, then gives it back to Gerard with a frown and shrug. He takes the cigarette and throws it into the sink beside them, then walks out of view for a second, returning to hand her a piece of chocolate cake.

For a second Helen is worried about what's in the cake, if it will harm her mother in some way; but then the greater fear of being caught at this party overwhelms her, and she leans into Miles, trying to fit herself against him as closely as she can, as if his body were a place to hide. Her mother bites into the cake, leaving a large crumb on her upper lip in the process, and when Gerard leans across to remove the crumb, plucking it off with two pinced fingers as if he were tidying a flower bed, Helen wonders how well they know each other, if they've met privately before, and if so, what any of it may mean.

"Why is your heart beating so fast?" Miles wants to know, leaning back to look at her.

"I think I need some air," she tells him. "Let's go outside."

She leads him in the opposite direction from the kitchen, out the front door, then down the steps and over to the side lawn by the driveway, where Helen leans against the stuccoed wall and pulls him in front of her to act as a shield. Should she leave now, she wonders, escape while her mother is otherwise occupied? Or wait it out here in the half dark with Miles, who has taken her chin into his hand and is raising her face to his.

She kisses him, with caution at first, thinking of both Leo and her mother and hoping she is sufficiently hidden here against the rough wall. Then she thinks of that girl in the mountains, probably leaned against a tree beneath Leo much as she is leaned against this wall beneath Miles right now, so she releases herself to the kiss, pulling Miles closer and opening her mouth, feeling as if she wants to take something from him, to pull out some knowledge he has kept from her, wanting even to become him for a moment, then return him back to himself, broken and changed.

Although his is only the second mouth she's ever really kissed, Helen knows already how to please him—this part is easy—where to rest her hands behind his neck, how to wander through his hair with one set of fingers while the others find the buried notches of his spine or stroke behind his earlobe. He pulls her down onto the dry strip of grass so they are sitting, still kissing, still hidden by the shadows. His mouth has a different shape to it from Leo's, smaller at the edges, more compact with smoother teeth, and she experiences a sudden pulse of excitement at the mere thought that she is doing something wrong.

But then the back door slams, and her insides collapse as she moves away, all pleasure draining down into the dry ground beneath her as she separates from Miles and pulls him back, deeper into the shadow cast by the stucco wall. The clack of sandals sounds on pavement; then a figure appears from around the back of the house. Helen knows the walk, though there is a different lilt to it tonight, and watches as her mother walks past them, only three feet or so away on the driveway, then crosses the street and gets into her Honda.

After she drives away, Miles whispers, "Wasn't that your Mom?"

"No," Helen says too quickly, so that it comes out false and high. "What would she be doing here?"

"It just sort of looked like her for some reason." He shrugs, then tugs Helen against him once again.

"You know," she says, pulling back and trying hard to smile. "I have to go. I really do. I'm sorry." She stands up and brushes dead grass off her skirt, then walks down the driveway, sandals clacking just as her mother's did. "I'll see you Monday," she says, turning, and watches as he frowns at her from his spot on the lawn.

SHE WALKS FIVE BLOCKS before she realizes she needs a plan. Her house is much too far away to walk, and her curfew is in a mere hour and a half. Besides, she has to admit that the neighborhood is a little creepy: A rusted-out muscle car, parked in the middle of a lawn, eyes her with its black, broken windows, and a flickering streetlight seems a reminder of the strange man from the party, sitting with his pad and pencil in the strobe light's glow. *Do you want to be in the picture too?*

She crosses over to the main street, Maryland Parkway, and spots a 7-Eleven down the block with a pay phone. Leo's phone rings twice before he picks it up.

"Please come get me," she says, glancing at two men watching her from inside a Trans Am parked in front of the convenience store. Across the street she sees a gigantic church with two jutting wings. Its dark cross seems cut out of the sky.

"I knew it was you." And then a few beats of silence before he asks, "Where are you?"

Helen goes inside the 7-Eleven, where she buys a cola Slurpee, then thumbs through a magazine while she waits. The clerk is an elderly woman with fake pearls at her neck who keeps looking at Helen and sadly shaking her head, as if she were doing something wrong just by being here alone.

Leo arrives by eleven and when she gets into his familiar car, Helen leans back with a sigh of exhaustion and relief.

"What happened?" he asks her. "Why'd you leave your *great* party?"

His eyes look red, and she wonders if he's been crying or getting stoned, then decides she doesn't want to know. "You were right. It wasn't so great. And"—she pauses to breathe in—"my mom was there."

"What? Did she see you? Now she'll never let you go out with me again!" He slams his fist on the steering wheel, and Helen moves farther away from him.

"Relax, she didn't see me. I don't think she was there because of me. I think she was just hanging out with Gerard. It was weird."

"Well"—he shrugs—"maybe she's starting to loosen up. Maybe she'll quit worrying so much about what *you're* doing all the time and get her own life."

The idea should please her, but it doesn't. For a moment she closes her eyes and imagines her mother poolside in a black bikini, deeply tanned and holding a dark brown drink. Gerard is rubbing oil into her calves. Helen attempts to place her father there instead, his pale professor's hands fumbling with the snap top of the oil, his half frown of distaste at the slippery mix of skin and lotion in his palms.

"Let's go back to my place," Leo says. "You still have an hour."

"I don't really feel like it," she tells him. "I'm tired."

"Oh, so you basically just called me for a ride home. Now I'm your personal chauffeur."

"We could go get ice cream or something," she suggests.

His face is dark. Only his hands are visible in the steady beat of shadows between streetlights. "No," he says. "Just forget it."

She turns back to the window, watching the houses roll by, low to the ground, their pastel faces cloaked in darkness. Beyond these homes is the faint, toxic glow of the casinos. A line she read yesterday in an Anne Sexton poem suddenly becomes clear. *Everyone in me is a bird.* Helen feels the line's meaning now, the beating wings of her mother, the light quality of Leo and Miles, all flying through her ribs, circling her stomach, passing airily over her heart on the way up and out her mouth. Though what she is left with is a rattled chest, as if an entire flock of crows has carved out a flying space behind her ribs.

They are only about ten blocks from her house now, so she turns to Leo and says, "Why don't you let me out here? I feel like walking."

"It's not safe."

"I'll be fine."

"You really don't understand the world, Helen. Do you?"

She shrugs and looks out her window at the quiet sidewalks. She hasn't seen a person for at least five blocks, but now they pass an illuminated living room where she can see a shirtless man flipping through channels, his bare skin a ghostly flash of rippled green in the television's light, and thinks that maybe Leo is right: It's not safe out there.

THE LIVING ROOM windows of her home are lit but curtained. Her mother's Honda is in the driveway, but her father's car is still gone. She wishes, suddenly, that her sister, Jenny, were not away in California, that she didn't have to enter a house containing only herself and her mother.

"Well, aren't you going to wish me luck?" Leo asks, sliding across the bench seat so that he is beside her.

"Of course," she says, turning to kiss him and trying to recall what exactly he needs luck for. They separate after an awkward fitting together of lips and hands, and she remembers just in time: honor band. "I'm sure you'll do great."

HER MOTHER IS reading on the couch when Helen walks through the door. She wears her red summer robe and sips from a glass of water. The bracelet has been removed. "How was the movie?" she asks.

"We didn't end up going. The line was too long, so we just drove around instead. Got some ice cream."

She nods, then looks back into her book.

"What did you end up doing?" Helen ventures.

"Me?" She looks up again. "I just read. Your father's over at Andy's, watching the game."

Helen moves toward her and kisses her good-night, trying to decide if she can detect the smell of smoke or a spiral of Gerard's cologne, but there is nothing, only the fresh green scent of her herbal shampoo. "Good night," Helen tells her, watching her face for a waver, a flicker of someone different, but her mother just smiles calmly and says, "Good night, sweetheart," so Helen retreats to her bedroom and shuts the door. She takes the photograph out of her purse and looks at it more closely. It tells her nothing except that in it her mother looks happy and a little shy at being the object of the camera's eye. Helen puts it in a drawer, beneath a stack of tank tops, then undresses, washes her face, and gets into bed.

ON MONDAY her mother drives her to work. Helen sits quietly in the passenger seat, her canvas bag pressed close to her leg, the photo of her mother tucked inside like a concealed weapon. Why has she brought it along? It's only making her stomach begin to ache.

Helen glances at her mother and tries to decide what's different about her today, because something is. She is always nicely dressed, but today she seems even more perfectly turned out, wearing a long, loose blue skirt and white blouse. Her face is animated by a small smile as she turns onto the Strip, and her silver hieroglyphic bracelet bangs against the steering wheel, then slides farther down her forearm. "It's a gorgeous day," she says.

"Mom, it's a hundred and three degrees already."

"But look at how clear the sky is, so blue I can almost taste it. There's not an ounce of smog in the valley after that windstorm last night."

"I guess so," Helen says.

Casinos float by on either side of the car, insubstantial as a movie set. The mountains to her right are so clear and crisply scissored out of the sky they seem unreal as well.

"How were Leo's tryouts yesterday?"

"I don't know. I never called him back."

"Is the world ending or did I miss something?" Her mother smiles widely now, emphasizing what Helen reads as a flirtatious tone. Is she gearing up to see Gerard?

"I just didn't feel like talking. That's all."

Her mother walks her into the courtyard. Gerard waves immediately and stands, as if wanting to appear more gentlemanly. After they have walked past the first row of chaise lounges, Helen hesitates, then stops and says, "I forgot something in the car." She leaves the courtyard, walks down the cool corridor past the bank of elevators and out into the boiling parking lot. When she reaches her mother's car, Helen takes the photograph out of her beach bag and tucks it beneath the windshield wiper on the driver's side, the picture facing in so her mother will see the image of her own face the minute she sits down to leave.

Back inside the courtyard, Helen approaches her mother and Gerard with caution. He is speaking; she is laughing, both close enough for conversation, but too close? Closer than they usually are? Helen can't be sure. They are almost the same age, Helen realizes for the first time. Maybe Gerard is younger by a year or two, but really, they are peers. "There's my best lifeguard," Gerard says when Helen finally reaches them. "It's gonna be a hot one. Better get in the pool."

She swims her morning laps faster than she usually does. It's as if she wants to exhaust the image from her body, swim until her breath has expelled that moment when she saw her mother leaned against Gerard's silver counter, laughing and eating cake. Her arms lift and fall in rhythm with her breathing, legs beating the water, then tucking under her to turn and kick off from the wall. When she finishes, her mother is no longer there and Miles is waiting at the pool's edge with her towel; as she hoists herself out of the water in the deep end, he bends toward her as if to wrap her in it, but she shrugs him off and says, "It's too hot. I'll just dry up in the chair."

She almost expects her mother to run back onto the pool deck, waving the photo above her head in rage, but the deck remains quiet, so Helen leans back and stretches out her legs with a sigh, scanning the water below in her daily attempt to prevent disaster.

At noon she half hopes to see Leo, but he doesn't show for her lunch break, and she decides it is probably for the best because they would inevitably argue and the rest of the day would be even more soured than it already is. She has not spoken to Leo since he took her home Saturday night, and she knows that by the time she does call him back, he will be angry. And who can blame him? His big tryouts were yesterday, and she doesn't even know how things went for him. She's supposed to be supportive, she reminds herself. Loving. Almost like a wife, she thinks, despite the fact that she is not yet sixteen.

HER FATHER PICKS her up from work at five. "Where's Mom?" she asks, getting into his car, which is cool and soothing, a strand of violin music weaving through the interior, a water bottle and a peeled orange waiting for her on a paper towel beside him.

"She has a headache," he tells her, then pulls out of the parking lot. "Aren't you glad to see *me*?"

"Sure." She puts on her seat belt, then adds, "Thanks for the orange."

"How was work?"

"Okay."

She eats three wedges of fruit, then takes a long swallow of water. The view seems different from her father's car, she notices, as the casinos and tourists scroll by, more distant and contained, like pieces inside a glass dome rather than actual people who can speak, go to parties, have sex in a dark back bedroom.

"My work was okay too," her father says, nudging her with an elbow. "In case you were wondering."

"Oh, sorry," she says, looking over at him. His reddish blond hair is sparked with late-afternoon sun, and she tries to decide if he is handsome, but she can't see him this way. He is her father and he is old and she can't tell what other people might see when they look at him. Other women. Like her mother, for instance.

"Is something bothering you?" he asks.

Should she tell him, she wonders, unveil her mother's secrets? But what does she really have to tell? *I saw Mom eating cake and smoking at a party I wasn't supposed to be at. And, there was a picture of her on the bathroom wall.* "No," she says, and shakes her head. "I'm fine. Just tired, that's all. And hot."

HER MOTHER is lying on the queen-size bed in her room—blinds closed against the sun, air conditioning humming, a wet washcloth laid across her eyes—and Helen is stricken with worry that she's injured her, that the picture strapped beneath the windshield wiper made her physically ill.

"Mom," she whispers, moving to sit on the edge of the bed. "Are you all right?"

Her mother removes the washcloth and opens her eyes, anger roiling briefly through her features, then settling into something softer, closer to contempt. "Where'd you get that picture?"

"What picture?"

"The one you put on my car this morning."

"Um." She hesitates, hearing a quiver in her voice. " I just found it around the pool."

"You were at Gerard's party Saturday, weren't you?"

"No," she says immediately. The lie floats between them, and Helen hopes it will descend and be accepted. When the silence lasts too long for her to bear, Helen asks, "Why would Gerard take a picture of you?"

"I don't know." She sits up and rubs her eyes, mascara trailing down her cheeks. Helen worries she might begin to cry, so she moves to sit closer to her on the bed, though she stops just short of touching her. "I guess," her mother says, and shrugs, "we're friends."

Helen nods and looks down at her hands. "He's nice."

They both sit for a minute, not moving, their breathing muted by the air conditioner. Her mother sighs, then asks Helen for the second time this summer, "Are you having sex with Leo?"

Helen shakes her head no but doesn't dare look her mother's way, aware that if she does, the truth may fly out of her mouth or eyes, some small opening she can't control. *Everyone in me is a bird.*

She feels her mother's arm loop around her shoulder, and Helen leans into it. "I just worry about you," her mother says. "That's all. Sometimes—no, who am I kidding?— *all the time*— I worry."

AFTER DINNER, Helen rides her bike to Leo's, but when she reaches his house, she passes it and decides to ride the extra blocks to Luv-it first and have a cone of frozen custard. The sun is lowering. It's the time of day when the light changes, deepens to a dense, brilliant marigold, so that the small white ice-cream stand, lost in its sea of asphalt, looks almost like a shrine.

She parks her bike at the bike rack, then gets in line behind a couple, two teenagers who kiss, then separate, then kiss again, while they wait for their vanilla shakes to be made. The boy is tall and wears a ball cap backward, acne climbing up beneath his cheekbone like a cluster of army ants. She is small with long black hair and dark eyes made even blacker by makeup; her mouth is thin and sullen until she smiles and accepts her shake. This girl is familiar, in her features, in her gestures as she reaches up to rub her boyfriend's shoulder, and Helen is almost certain that this is the girl from Gerard's bathroom, that standing before her now is Gerard's daughter.

Helen buys a chocolate cone, then sits on an outside bench across from the couple and tries to watch them without being obvious. It seems to her that in some other life, some strange parallel world, she could've been this girl, who looks a little trashy in her tight red T-shirt and short shorts, cellulite creasing into view at the top of her thigh as she slides closer to her boyfriend and whispers in his ear. Her father would be a pool manager, and her mother, well, would be her mother, but different if she were with Gerard. Maybe a bit more careless with her clothes and hair. More likely to go to parties and smoke cigarettes. Darker skinned from lying by the pool and harder in some way. She wouldn't teach school and she would wear perfume.

In what ways has she herself changed since she's been with Leo? Helen wonders now. At the most basic level, she thinks different thoughts. The pictures that ferry through her mind almost always carry him. She worries more. About getting caught having sex, getting pregnant, about wearing, doing, or saying something that will make him angry. Her mind is awash with worry.

Yet the tradeoff is that she is loved. That is how her *self* has changed. It now knows love from someone other than her family.

"Do you have a problem or something?" It's Gerard's daughter. Helen has been staring at her without thinking.

"No. Sorry." And then: "Are you Gerard Rasmussen's daughter?"

"*Who?*"

"No one. Never mind. I thought I knew you."

"Well, you don't."

There is such anger emanating from this girl, an anger so alien to Helen she can say nothing back, so she stands and leaves, throwing her napkin in the garbage can and releasing her bike from the rack. In another life, she thinks, she could have been the owner of this anger, a type she sees in Leo too, from time to time.

Helen gets on her bike and rides toward Leo's house beneath a sky striped with color. A wind moves through her hair, a whisper of coolness to it she hasn't felt in months, and she realizes, as she moves along the sidewalk, that she is grateful, maybe for the first time in her life, for the parents she's been given.

Book Two

The
Second
Summer

· · · · · · · ·

Locust Shells

THERE IS A NEW GIRL WORKING at the pool this summer, Ernestine, and even before Gerard lets out a low whistle at the sight of her swan dive, even before Miles has fetched this girl's first Diet Pepsi, Helen knows that she has been dethroned. Or rather, she realizes, for the first time, that last summer she reigned.

Ernestine. The name belies her beauty, or not beauty exactly but something even more alluring. Sex appeal is the term, Helen guesses, that most men would use. She is straight-hipped as a boy, but voluptuous on top, and has a flat-footed slap to her walk that she manages to make charming.

"Please, just call me Ernie," she tells Helen when they are

introduced this first day of June. "You know, as in Bert and Ernie of *Sesame Street*."

Helen nods and says to call her Helen, " You know, as in of Troy."

Ernie looks perplexed, then smiles widely, dimples denting evenly into both her cheeks. "Well, I hope you don't start any wars this summer."

Helen blushes, embarrassed that Ernie's gotten her vain joke, and begins to fidget with the whistle hung around her neck. "Gerard wants me to train you," she tells her.

"Great!" this girl exclaims, and Helen wonders how she'll make it through the day.

THERE IS LITTLE to show her. Helen goes over the different kinds of lotion that they sell. "Try not to let new people buy the SPF two oil," she advises. "They come back to blame you when they burn."

"What do you use?" Ernie asks.

"Sunblock. Fifteen or thirty. It depends. How about you?"

"Just baby oil."

So that's how she's managed to be this perfect, creamy nutmeg, Helen thinks, when she herself is still pinkish white with winter, a faint shorts tan striped across her legs from the last month of Phys Ed. She wishes, for a moment, that she didn't worry about burns and cancer and future wrinkles, that she didn't have a father who insisted she protect herself against this enemy, the sun. Simply to exist in the present moment, that's the ability this new girl exudes, and it creates a jealousy in Helen, a momentary wish to be someone different.

Ernie and Miles take the first shifts up in the chair. Helen waits her turn beneath the red umbrella, sitting on a long-legged stool on the opposite side of the lectern from Gerard.

"So, how's your mother?" he asks. His face, as usual, is unreadable behind mirrored glasses.

"She's all right, I guess," Helen says, though in fact, just this morning she found her mother alone in the backyard, staring at the oleander trees as if they were speaking, as if meaning were written on their leaves. "I'm ready to go," Helen told her.

"Your father's going to take you."

"Okay," she said, then asked, "Are you sick?"

"No, just thinking, that's all."

"Well," Gerard says now, after a thoughtful sip of his soda, "please give her my regards."

HER OWN STINT in the chair is oppressive. She has forgotten how boring this can be, especially when only two people are in the pool. Every hour and a half they rotate, so that Helen now sits in Miles's former chair, Miles sits where Ernie sat, and Ernie lounges cozily beside Gerard, laughing now at something he's just said. Is he preying on her mother too?

It's only 10:00 A.M., but already the day feels fragile, about to crumble at the edges. Helen is acutely aware that she is too tall, composed of too many angles folded awkwardly into this white fiberglass chair; she feels prudish in her black one-piece next to Ernie's yellow string bikini, and even her hair feels too long, scratching wetly at her shoulder blades, compared with Ernie's short dark layers, dipping over her Ray-Bans in a sexy peekaboo.

It doesn't help that Leo is out of town visiting his sister in Denver for the month. He provides a daily dose of praise that she didn't realize until now is somewhat necessary to her confidence.

Helen reminds herself that she is here to do a job, to save people who are drowning, not for some unspoken beauty contest, some battle of the teenage girls. Besides, Ernie seems nice and fairly smart. Maybe she should try to become her friend. But at day's end, when Miles walks Ernie to her car, tossing only a brotherly wave in Helen's direction, she realizes that she hates this girl and that she hates herself for hating her.

HELEN'S MOTHER takes her to the Dunes on her second day of work and walks inside the courtyard with her to "see how it looks this year." Gerard waves from his lectern—it's as if he never leaves that spot—and they cross the pool deck into the shade of his umbrella, where Helen begins to strip down to her swimsuit, trying both to listen and not to listen, watching them for a moment and then turning to the pool.

She does a back dive off the side of the deep end, then swivels around and begins to swim. After five laps she stops in the shallow end and stands to stretch her arms, interlocking them in front and pulling forward, crooking first one elbow behind her head and tugging down, then the other. Her mother is still here, sitting in the chair beside Gerard, one white linen–panted leg crossed and swinging, her black sunglasses giving her the glamour of an aging star, silver necklace sparking in the sun as she throws back her head and laughs. Why is it that Gerard never manages an amusing line when Helen's in his presence?

There is a gentle splash behind her, and she turns to find Ernie, waist high in the pool, doing stretches similar to her own. "Who's that lady?" Ernie whispers. "Gerard's girlfriend?"

"No." Helen frowns at her. "It's my mother."

"Oh, sorry." She shrugs an apology, then dives under and swims away.

Gerard's girlfriend! What an awful thought. Though as she continues to stretch and watch them, she can see why Ernie made this mistake. They both look so happy sitting there together. She has not seen her mother laugh like this in months. And Gerard, Gerard is practically transformed. His mirrored shades are raised, and his face is animated—almost intelligent—as he listens to her mother talk.

Last summer her mother told Helen that her voice changes when she talks to Leo, becomes softer and airy, happier, and Helen began to think of this voice as her true one, the one she uses in her mind to talk to herself. Somehow, Leo has drawn it out into open air. She wonders now if another person could alter more than just your voice, could change your entire being, make your better self, your most *you* you rise to the surface.

But the idea that her mother and Gerard might be able to do this for each other is repellent and irritates Helen so much that when her mother waves good-bye to her, Helen pretends not to notice and ducks back underwater.

HELEN AND ERNIE take the first shifts in the chair today. Miles sweeps the deck for a while, then grabs a bottle of oil from the lectern and climbs Ernie's chair to rub some into her shoulders.

Helen recalls his doing that to her last summer and how awkward she felt, whereas Ernie strikes her as completely at ease with his attention, laughing and leaning into his hands, while still managing to keep her eyes on the pool. Helen can't figure out why Miles seems so much more appealing to her this year, why she now wishes he'd cross the deck and climb the chair to talk to her. His hair's a little shaggier, giving him a slight rock star quality, and there's an extra dose of confidence to his walk, garnered, she supposes, from completing yet another year of college. Or maybe, she decides, it's simply that he's no longer interested in her. The idea depresses her—how can she be so predictable?—and she looks away from Miles and Ernie back to the pool, where one lone woman floats beneath her on a raft. It's too early in the summer for the pool to fill up, too early in the summer for disaster to occur.

Later, under Gerard's umbrella, drinking from a water bottle, she tries to decide if she misses Leo. She thought this month of separation would be difficult. Last summer his time away at music camp had been excruciating, but now she feels none of last year's dark yearning for his presence. In fact, she hardly misses him at all. He calls her every two nights from Denver, but his voice is small and far away, distant in her ear as an echo. What she does miss, she decides, is being touched every day. Funny how a person can grow so used to that, she thinks, how a person can miss the contact, though not necessarily the conversation, of another human being so acutely after only a week has passed.

She turns to watch Gerard pore over the schedule, brow crumpled up in thought.

"Here," Helen says, reaching out her hand to him. "Let me do it."

He looks up and smiles. A very nice smile, Helen begrudgingly admits. "Okay, little miss bossy. Give it a shot." He slides the schedule across to her, and she fills it in for the next two weeks, trying to make sure that Miles and Ernie never have the same days off.

"So," Gerard asks her as she writes, "what's your mother like? I can't quite get a read on her character."

Her stomach flutters at this question, and she tries to determine how exactly to answer. Should she make up something distasteful, so he'll lose interest? "She's weird," Helen says, without looking up.

He laughs at this. "Weird, huh? I don't see that side of her, but that's good to know. I like weird."

She slides back the completed schedule, takes a breath, and asks, "Why are you so interested anyway?"

He shrugs, palms up. "Just trying to get to know my employees a little better." He reaches across to pinch her cheek, and she flinches at his touch.

"Helen!" she hears Miles shout from the chair. "Get up here, please. I'm sweating to death."

She takes a final sip of water, then goes to relieve him from the heat.

HER MOTHER PICKS her up at five but doesn't come inside. Helen finds her sitting in the parking lot, gazing through the windshield of her Honda at the wall of the hotel. Inside the car, pop music floats around, innocuous and drab, but when Helen reaches to change the station as she often does, her mother grabs her hand. "Wait. This is my favorite song."

"It is?" Helen listens to the synthesizers, a man's voice coating the notes with words she can't decipher, something, as usual, about love.

Her mother taps long fingers absently against the steering wheel, still looking at the wall.

"Can we go now or what?" Helen wants to know.

Her mother shifts into reverse, then turns to her and says, "Quit being such a snot."

Helen begins to protest, then decides against it and says, "Sorry."

"Everything, Helen, is not about you."

"I never said it was."

Her mother pulls out into the traffic of the Strip, just missing the tail end of a group of big, blond, German-looking tourists. "It's your whole attitude."

"What did I do?"

"Just think a little before you act. All right? That's all I'm asking you to do. Just to think a little bit."

AT HOME, Helen finds Jenny and her boyfriend, Ricky, kissing on the back patio. They separate when Helen lets the screen door of the kitchen slam, and Ricky stands to go. "Hey, Helen." He nods, somehow managing to evoke an aura of being both cocky and shy. "Gotta go, Jen." He bends to kiss her, his head of moussed curls barely moving in a sudden breeze. "I'll call you later." Jenny follows him inside to walk him to the door, and Helen sits down to wait for her return.

Ricky is sixteen, the same age as Helen, yet he seems much younger to her, much lighter and at ease. Lately Helen has begun to feel both young and old at once. The world is still composed mostly of questions, yet there is a new weight to things. She can feel certain daily lies beginning to pile up inside, growing incrementally heavier each time she tells her mother *no, of course I'm not having sex*, or is compelled by Leo to pledge *yes, I do love you more than anything or anyone in the entire world*. At day's end she is so tired from this heaviness, so obviously altered, that her unchanged image in the bathroom mirror is a surprise.

Jenny arrives back on the patio, smiling and humming, and sits down across from Helen. "Let me ask you something," Helen says. "Do you think Mom would ever cheat on Dad?"

Jenny laughs. "Are you crazy? No way. Never."

"What makes you so sure?"

"I don't know. She seems too old."

"She's only forty-five."

"*Only.*" Jenny laughs again. "That word doesn't belong in that sentence."

They sit for a bit, watching the oleander bushes buckle and sway in the hot breeze. Then Jenny turns to Helen and says, "Can I ask *you* something?"

Helen nods, and her sister continues. "How did you know when you were ready to have sex with Leo?"

Helen frowns and looks up to think. She remembers a vague yearning to learn more about the world, wanting to speed up her rate of adult knowledge intake and leap into the second realm of living. But of course those things hadn't happened. Other than a different sort of closeness to Leo and a few mechanical facts, she was none the wiser about life. "I can't really explain it," she tells her sister. "A big part was that I knew we were in love."

"I think I might be in love with Ricky, and he's been wanting to, so . . ."

"Why not wait until you're sure?" Helen blurts. "There's no need to rush."

Jenny sighs. "If I don't soon, he'll probably break up."

Helen understands she means Ricky will end the relationship, but she is given an image of him splitting into pieces, like a puzzle undone. Helen wants to provide wise counsel, the perfect advice she herself never asked for or received, but she doesn't know how to guide her sister, what these words of advice should be, so she asks, "You really think that you might love him?"

Jenny shrugs, her thin shoulders smooth and round as eggshells. "What the hell do I know?"

SUNDAY IS the day that Helen gets to practice driving. She's had her license since December, but because her family owns only two cars, she usually has to ride with either her mother or her father or with Leo, who by no means will let her get behind the wheel of his precious Nova.

Sometimes Jenny or one of her parents joins her on these practice rides, but today Jenny is off with Ricky, and her mother dropped her father off at his office, then went to grocery shop, so Helen finds herself alone behind the wheel. Usually she takes a route away from the city, through town toward Sunrise Mountain, or follows Charleston out to Red Rock Canyon, but today she makes a change. Today she heads straight down Maryland Parkway past the strip malls and office buildings, past the Boulevard Mall and Sunrise Hospital, toward Gerard's house.

She remembers his address from the party he threw last year at the end of summer, but today the house looks different. In bright sun, its stucco walls are more pockmarked than she recalls, and the rectangle of mustard-colored grass beside the driveway, where she made out with Miles in the dark, is bald in spots and appears even more scratchy than she remembers it against her legs. She parks across the street, against the curb, and steps out into the heat, looking up and down the block for a sign, something to tell her why she's traveled here.

She finds it in seconds: the blue top of her mother's Honda glowering at her from its parking space, partway down the block behind a convertible Volkswagen. To be certain that it's her mother's car, Helen walks over and looks into its windows. She hasn't wanted it to be true, but as she cups hands around her eyes and looks inside at the familiar interior—a book in the backseat, a bottle of Evian wedged beside the parking brake, black sunglasses tucked beneath the driver's visor—she realizes she already knew that she would find her mother here.

Gerard's house appears deserted. Maybe, she tells herself, they're just out somewhere for coffee. Still, she approaches the squat structure, trying to figure out what the hell to do. Should she ring the doorbell? Sit waiting on the stoop? Peer through windows? The last option strikes her as the only reasonable choice, but she pauses in the driveway, worried she'll be seen or heard and worried, most of all, that what she's going to do right now may change her life for good. She steps closer to the wall, into a thin alley of shade; pale cicada carcasses cling at eye level to the stucco wall, and when she pulls one off, it crumbles in her hand.

Before she can decide what to do, a laugh ascends from somewhere inside the house. Helen thinks it is her mother's laugh, though it sounds different from the way it usually does, more loose and varied, maybe younger too, though Helen can't decide if a laugh contains an age. She edges slowly down the wall toward the windows of the kitchen but can't yet bring herself to glance inside, so she walks past the windows into the backyard, though it doesn't seem large enough or even alive enough to be called a yard.

A dilapidated motorcycle sits on a slab of concrete beneath a clothesline, tools set neatly on a red cloth beside the bike. Dead grass stretches out to a high wooden fence. Helen sees movement in the weeds of the yard's far corner, and then a turtle wanders out, making its way toward her across the lawn. Gerard has mentioned this turtle at work; he purchased the turtle to keep him company, claiming he didn't want anything as high maintenance as a dog or cat. After hearing this story, Helen imagined Gerard asleep in a large bed with the turtle tucked in beside him. The picture makes her smile and calms her enough so that she can walk back to the side of the house and look through the windows.

The kitchen is empty, its gray counters vacant except for an open gallon of ice cream, fifteen feet or so away from the window. She thinks the label reads "Chocolate Chip," her mother's favorite flavor.

In the next second, her mother wanders into view; she is barefoot but fully clothed, wearing the same long white skirt and sleeveless top she left the house in. She crosses the kitchen to the ice cream, which she begins eating from the carton with a spoon. Helen holds her breath and moves away from the glass, leaning against the wall with her eyes closed, debating whether she should run or risk another look.

When she chances a second glance, she sees Gerard appear on the edge of the kitchen. He is completely naked and moves to put his arms around her mother's middle from behind, laying his cheek on her shoulder, face turning toward Helen; she pulls back from the window but then sees that his eyes are closed. His bliss is palpable even from across the kitchen and through this dusty glass; the certain shape of his happiness floats toward Helen and secures her to this spot. She cannot move, cannot turn away from them. He is dark from the sun except for the space his swim trunks usually cover, the half-moon of his ass as pale as any skin Helen's ever seen.

Her mother's lips move, saying something quiet to Gerard, and in that same moment he opens his eyes and looks directly at Helen. Before she can decipher if he's really seen her, before she can wait and learn what happens next, she runs, down the driveway, across the street into her father's car, and turns it on; it dies; then she tries again, sweat flushing across her chest and back before she's able to release herself from the curb and out into the street.

Did he see her? She can't be sure. There was, she hopes, enough space between them, enough glare across the windows, enough sleep left in his eyes to make her presence shadowy and vague. In her rearview mirror the street is empty. No one is running after her. She continues on her way toward home, car growling beneath her, cicadas shrilling through the heat like a distant scream, the one she can feel building in her throat.

To settle her nerves, she decides to lengthen her drive, so she turns left on Tropicana and heads for the Strip. Once she reaches it and turns right, traffic slows, so she relaxes her foot on the gas pedal and tries to empty her mind by focusing on everything going on around her. There, up on her left, is the Dunes. Ernie and Miles are working today, and she wishes she were too, that she hadn't had the time to drive all the way out to Gerard's and spy.

A billboard that she sees every day on the way home from work fills her window. It shows a row of women, lined up in black high heels and G-strings, asses to the camera. Floating in silver script above their heads, the caption reads: "The Crazy Showgirls of Rock and Roll: No ifs, ands, or . . ." A cab pulls up beside Helen, sporting a large display poster on its top of bikini-clad women splayed out provocatively on sand, advertising some new show called *A Day at the Beach*. At a stoplight in front of Caesars Palace, she sees men passing out pamphlets to tourists. Helen has seen enough of these booklets littering the gutters to know they advertise women you can order up to your room, like a tray of food.

Usually all this strikes her as amusing, completely unrelated to her actual life. But today it seems to stain her, to invade her skin to the point of leaving a sticky film on her limbs. Has the city infected her mother as well? Have all the years spent surrounded by sex sent her falling toward Gerard?

She is relieved finally to reach Oakey, where she turns right and heads toward home through the familiar neighborhoods, the ranch houses that look as if they could fit into any western U.S. town. When she passes Leo's house, the sight of his Nova sitting vacant beneath the carport, waiting for his return from Denver, pains her. She hasn't received his usual call for the last two nights, and she tells herself that he has probably fallen in love with another girl.

HELEN HOPES to find her own home empty, but when she steps inside the front door, her sister is sitting in the living room, crying on the couch. After moving to sit beside her, she puts an arm around Jenny's shoulders, waiting to hear what's wrong. What else could possibly be wrong?

"Ricky dumped me," Jenny murmurs into her hands, rubbing her reddened face with her palms.

Helen nods and pulls her closer. "Oh, honey," she says, feeling suddenly like a mother, like her own mother's replacement, "I'm so sorry."

"I couldn't do it." Jenny shrugs and looks up at her. "I guess I got scared."

Helen can feel a deep relief moving through her, cooling her overheated limbs like a salve. "You did the right thing," she tells her.

"I don't know what stopped me. People used to get married when they were twelve, you know. They had kids by the time they were my age."

"Who told you that?"

"Ricky."

"Well, that's because they *had* to." Helen laughs. "This is supposedly considered progress."

"Right." Jenny grimaces and leans closer to her sister. "Progress."

They sit for a while in silence, the clock on the mantel clicking at them. Outside the front window Helen can see a giant blue and white sky racing over the neighborhood; below this, their ant-red driveway seems to emit a rising pinkish heat. Inside the living room it is cool and quiet, the muted colors providing calm, as they are meant to do.

"Where did you drive today?" Jenny finally asks.

Helen shrugs. "Oh, nowhere really. Just around."

FOR DINNER that evening they eat the grilled halibut and salad her mother made when she got home, an hour or two after Helen. Talk across the table consists of the Russian films her father found today in the university archives, Jenny's breakup with Ricky, Helen's day of driving. "It went fine," is all she offers when her mother asks about her progress. "I've got it down."

It seems to Helen that her mother is eating more than usual and maybe drinking a bit more wine, the flushed planes of her face rising and falling with conversation. She is vibrant with color and chatter, waving her fork through the air as she offers words of consolation to Jenny. "There'll be other boys," she tells her. "It may not seem like it right now, but trust me."

"Don't tell her that," Helen says, her angry tone creating a sudden silence. "Don't make it sound like Ricky didn't mean a thing to her."

"Helen, I certainly didn't mean to imply that Ricky was unimportant."

"But on the other hand," her father interjects with a laugh, "maybe he was."

"He was a jerk," Jenny says, and shrugs. "Who needs him?"

"That's my girl." Her father chuckles and puts an arm around Jenny.

Helen pushes back from the table and stands up. "Can I please be excused?"

Before anyone can answer, she has left the table behind, escaped to the kitchen, where she scrapes and rinses her plate, then runs the faucet over her hands and rubs them across the hot skin of her face. Laughter reaches her from the other room, first her mother's, then Jenny's and her father's, and Helen leans against the sink and stares out at the darkening backyard, thinking for the first time all week that maybe she does miss Leo, just a little bit.

AT THE POOL on Monday, Gerard acts as if nothing were different. There is no variation in his gaze or manner to suggest he saw her through the kitchen window. Ernie and Miles arrive at the same time, kissing lightly beneath the lifeguard chair before Ernie climbs the ladder and settles in for her first shift. Helen ascends the other chair, where she leans back into the seat as deeply as she can and splays her legs out over the platform, feet resting only on the blazing air.

She watches Gerard, sitting beneath the red umbrella, sipping a Diet Coke, and tries to decide if she hates him. He seems so innocuous right now, so different from the man glimpsed in the kitchen, that yesterday's vision feels unreal. Is this really the person who huddled lovingly at her mother's back?

At lunch Ernie joins her, without asking, in the casino. Helen tries to talk to her, to distract her mind from other matters and simply listen to this girl. "I think I'm really falling for Miles," she tells Helen. "Isn't he adorable?"

Helen shrugs, then nods.

"We've only been dating for a couple of weeks, but I don't know. He might be it."

"Have you ever been in love?" Helen asks her, for no real reason, just to make conversation.

Ernie looks at the ceiling then takes a bite of her ham sandwich. "No, not really. How 'bout you?"

Helen thinks of Leo, but he seems so far away right now, as if he were already someone from her past, a boy she used to *think* she loved. "I don't know," she says at last.

THAT EVENING her mother is late to pick her up. Helen waits in the parking lot; the sun is at its deepest heat, burning past the high white walls of the Dunes directly into her bare legs and arms. Down the street she can see the clear, cool fountains of Caesars Palace, rising and falling, and she briefly considers running over and jumping in. Miles appears through the exit door and sees her standing there alone. "You need a ride?" he calls, crossing the lot to his minitruck.

She debates a moment, then yells "Okay," leaps off the curb, and sprints across the asphalt into the waiting cab of his Toyota.

"Where's Ernie?" Helen asks as they pull out onto the Strip.

"Oh." He waves a hand. "Some family thing tonight. Her sister's dance recital or something. I don't know." He turns on the radio, then says, "Hey, why don't we go to the lake?"

"Right now?"

"Yeah. We're both dressed for it." He smiles. "Why the hell not?"

Helen thinks about her mother, possibly pulling into the Dunes parking lot right this second and wondering where her daughter is. "Okay," Helen says. "Let's go."

THEY STOP at a 7-Eleven on the way out of town. Miles goes inside to "get some refreshments," and Helen waits in the cab of his truck, eyeing the pay phone by the door. Should she call her house and let them know what she's doing? She will only be yelled at for leaving without asking first; she will only be questioned about the safety of Miles's driving, about the safety of Miles himself, and she decides to leave the trouble she is already in for later. Helen rolls down the window, props her feet up on the dashboard, and decides that for the first time in a while she is happy.

As THEY DRIVE, the desert grows empty around them, convenience stores transforming into tumbleweed, corrugated sand replacing taverns. The desolation of this stretch of road is absolute, and Miles and Helen are silent until they top a ridge and see the lake below them, filling in the giant emptiness with cobalt blue. Helen smiles at the sight. "I can't wait to jump in," she tells Miles.

"Me neither."

He takes her to the cliffs, a more secluded spot than Boulder Beach, a cove tucked away from the larger expanse of lake, and a place where the stoners from her school supposedly hang out. She's been here once or twice with Leo, and there have always been a few people around at least, but today the sand below the bluff on which they park is completely vacant.

They climb down the hillside to the small strip of beach, where Miles lays down a blanket and a bag from the 7-Eleven. To their left, across the water, sandstone-colored cliffs rise like ancient structures, though Helen's not sure they're tall enough to be called cliffs. She herself has jumped off one into the water, and it wasn't all that long a drop.

They both strip down to their swimsuits, then make their careful way across the rocky shore into the water. It is lukewarm from the heat, but a better alternative than the sun-baked beach, and they swim out to a jutting rock and climb it. They sit for a minute before jumping in and making their way back toward the sand.

As Helen steps onto land, the sun is beginning to descend, moving to meet the red rocks that surround the farther reaches of the lake, and as Miles gets out of the water, he is backlit by a thick burnished gold, his face and body so shadowed by the glare he could be anyone at all.

He settles down beside her, then opens the 7-Eleven bag, pulling out a six-pack of berry wine coolers and a bag of powdered doughnuts. "Dinner?" he asks, ripping open the dough-nuts, then twisting the tops off two wine coolers.

Helen takes everything he offers, drinking quickly from the sweet cooler and eating three doughnuts before Miles has had one. He laughs at her and leans to brush powdered sugar from the edges of her mouth with his thumb. Is this how it began with her mother and Gerard? Helen wonders. With a touch that seemed both necessary and invasive, both innocuous and intimate? She remembers the party at his house last year and the moment when Gerard leaned to remove a crumb of chocolate cake from her mother's upper lip. Did everything begin in that minute, the tra-jectory that would carry them separately through the school year, then back into each other's presence beneath the red umbrella? Helen wants to travel the same path, to understand what's hap-pening between her mother and this man, so before she can think about it too much, she leans across the blanket and kisses Miles, close-lipped at first, then opening herself to him completely, searching the dark corners of his mouth for some sort of answer, an explanation for the way the world works.

After a few minutes she pulls away. "I'm sorry," she tells him. "I know you're seeing Ernie."

He shrugs. "I like her, but she's 'saving herself,' whatever that's supposed to mean."

Saving herself. Helen turns the phrase over in her mind. Is the alternative drowning? There *is* a sense of being underwater as she leans her body toward Miles and kisses him again, but it is not an unpleasant sensation, not at all.

They separate, and Miles takes a long swallow from his cooler, then smiles at her. The sun has disappeared behind the mountains, and the sky behind him streams out blue and purple as a bruise. "I thought you were all serious with Leo."

Now it's her turn to shrug. "I sort of am."

Before she can feel guilty about this half-true answer, she reaches across for Miles, grasps on to his bare arm, and pulls him toward her, against her, on top of her. They kiss for a while before separating once again to crawl out of their still-wet swimsuits, and Helen thinks of the locust shells that will be everywhere soon, and wonders at the beauty of being able to shed your outer body every summer and start again.

Their coupling is quick and fumbling and polite. An embarrassed "thank you" from Miles when she helps him get the condom open; a mumbled "sorry" in her ear when his watch catches in her hair. Helen does not love Miles. She knows this, knows it especially well now that they are physically connected. Yet she wants to tell him that she does. When he extracts himself and lies down beside her, she wants to say *I love you, Miles*, so she struggles quietly to keep these words inside her chest, since they aren't even partway true.

He softly hums beside her now, half asleep already it seems, though he reaches now and then to rub her stomach. Neither of them speaks, and she guesses that they won't, hopes they won't, until they get inside his truck and reach the city. Helen rises from the blanket and returns to the water, where she wades in until she is waist-deep, then dives under and swims out into the darkness. Far out from the beach she stops, then flips onto her back to float. A gibbous moon swims above her in the sky, though whether it is waxing or waning, she can't recall. The symbolism strikes her as important, and she wishes she could remember. Is this a beginning or an ending?

Maybe, she tells herself, it's neither one. Just a middle. Just a new episode of her life linked to all the others from her past, waiting to be joined to more. The idea that life might be just that, a straight line without cycles, without predictable periods of growth and diminishment, without time laid out for rising and resting, without any coherent *meaning* really, frightens her. So she closes her eyes against the moon and tries to summon a thought that will ground her. Being punished for this excursion with Miles is what she should be worrying about, but she is not as nervous as she thinks she ought to be.

Helen thinks about Ernie and Leo, the way she's just betrayed them both. Though if neither of them finds out what she's done with Miles, is this still a betrayal? If no one is hurt, is it actually wrong? Helen knows, somewhere inside her water-cooled limbs, that it is, but she floats on the other possibility for a while, immersed in this soupy, too-warm water, in this giant man-made lake, wondering where she's going to find the desire to return herself to shore.

Love Song for a Snare Drum

SHE IS DIFFERENT NOW when they make love. More like Leo thought he wanted her to be—looser and fluid, moving in almost perfect rhythm with his hips—but he already misses the way she used to do it—a little awkward, too shy to make a sound—and after the act today, when they lie side by side beneath his ceiling fan, he knows that something is wrong between them.

He rolls onto his side to watch her. A blemish burns red on her chin, and a streak of black mascara is drawn from the corner of her eye across her cheek. Still, he thinks, her beauty remains intact. She has not diminished at all in the year and a half they've been together, only expanded in size so that now she fills his entire orbit.

There is not a second of his day when she is not circling through him, and sometimes, like right now, it seems difficult to breathe.

"What are you looking at?" she asks, turning toward him with a smile.

"That zit on your chin."

"Oh." She covers the lower half of her face with a quick hand. "I forgot it was there."

"You never told me what you did while I was gone." He's been back from Denver for a week and it seems to him they've barely spoken, only met at his place every afternoon, after Helen has finished at the Dunes, and fallen into the deep blue-sheeted pool of his bed.

"Um, just sat around missing you, I guess." She laughs and rolls on top of him. He can never tell when she is mocking him and when she's serious. "What more can I say?"

"Well, your sister broke up with Ricky. That's pretty big news. You could give me the story or something."

"Oh"—she frowns—"there'll be other guys."

Other guys, he wants to scream! Where has she learned to be so cold, so nonchalant? "Yeah, but Jenny really liked him."

"Not enough, apparently." She kisses him as if to still his voice, her hair descending on his neck and shoulders like a light and sudden rain. He has the instant wish to grow his own hair long so he can keep this cool sensation with him. In seconds she pulls her mouth away, extricates her limbs from his, and climbs off his bed to stand beside the stereo and dress. "I have to go," she explains, pulling on her black underwear and cutoff shorts, her bra and V-neck T-shirt.

Leo lies there, watching her, trying to devise words that will keep her with him. "Stay here for dinner," he says.

"Actually, I can't. I've been assigned to make the meal tonight, my first attempt."

"Really?" He sits up. "What are you making?"

"Lemon chicken, I think."

"Why aren't I invited to this big event?"

"Oh, I don't want to poison you. Just my family." She laughs, then says good-bye, and before he can dress to walk her out, she is gone, the sound of the front door shutting so faintly and delicately it makes him angry. The sound was one of shame, he thinks, of sneaking out.

HE IS WORKING, for the remaining two months of summer, at his father's clock shop. It's a claustrophobic store located on Las Vegas Boulevard between a pawnshop and a wedding chapel. Lots of brides and grooms come in to buy last-minute gifts, reminders of their brief time in this city, and their presence has made Leo begin to think more and more of marriage.

He is an adult now, after all. In June he turned eighteen and graduated from Las Vegas High School. He didn't get the music scholarship he'd hoped for, but he did qualify for a Pell grant that will pay almost all his tuition for UNLV, so in September he'll escape the faces of these clocks, their dice neatly stacked and glued onto colored plastic squares, hands moving through time in slow motion, it seems to him, as he listens to his father, clearing his throat over and over in the back room, where he makes these sad creations. There is only a swamp cooler to defuse the heat, and Leo stands behind the glass display case that doubles as a counter and sweats, listening to the AM talk radio to which his father is addicted.

The door swings open, brass bell ringing, and a young woman steps inside. Perhaps, Leo thinks, she is a bride, because she is dressed in a lacy white blouse tucked into a white miniskirt, and there is something frail and frilly crumpled in her hand, which Leo decides has to be a veil. Her white pumps click across the floor until she stands across from him, looking down into the display case at the clocks. "Hey," is all she says.

"Hey," he says back to her, hoping his father can't hear that he's not trotting out the prerequisite, "Hi, I'm Leo. How can I assist you today in Buying Time?" That's the name of the store, Buying Time, and he's tried for years to convince his father that it sounds depressing, but his father only laughs and says, "It's clever. Don't you get it?"

The woman before him is young, he decides, maybe twenty-one or twenty-two, but her mouth is hardened like a smoker's, and her hair appears to have been bleached so many times it looks stiff and brittle as the yellow grass in his backyard. She wears it short and spiked up from her face like Billy Idol's.

"I need something different," she tells him, looking up at last. "Something really unique."

"Okay," he says, stepping around from behind the counter and leading her over to the newlywed section. He picks up a clock with a white background. The dice are black with white dots, and painted in between each stack of numbers is a red top hat or a dove.

"Mmm." She frowns. "I don't think he'll like it."

He holds up some other clocks with wedding themes. Blue bells against a silver background. A painted rainbow lifting from a field.

She shakes her head again, and he notices that her hair doesn't move at all. "Too cutesy," she complains, then turns to him and asks, "What's *your* favorite one?"

If he were to tell the truth right now, he'd admit he hates them all, admit that they remind him too acutely of the man in the back room. His father is always telling people that Leo is a musician, "an artist just like me." Once when Leo tried to tell him that he couldn't really call making these clocks art, his father grew silent, his old mouth becoming soft and wrinkled as it dropped more deeply into the creases of his face. "Maybe you're right," he said quietly, then cleared his throat and disappeared into the back room.

That day, in an effort to apologize, Leo made a clock of his own, working beside his father for the entire afternoon. When it was finished, his father had bet him twenty dollars that it would never sell.

He takes this woman now over to his clock. It's practically hidden in the back corner of a shelf, and he can feel the soft skin of dust that has gathered on its face as he takes it in his hands. It has a swirly psychedelic background adorned by clear dice with dark blue dots. Black music notes float behind the hands as small as insects, expanding to the size of butterflies the farther out they go. It doesn't look as professional as his father's clocks. The music notes are unevenly spaced and blurred a bit around the edges, and he notices for the first time that he put two dice adding up to nine where eight o'clock should be.

"Cool," she says, taking it from him. "Yeah, I want this one."

He points out his mistake, and she frowns for a second, then says, "Who gives a crap? We all know when it's eight o'clock and when it's nine."

As Leo is ringing up the purchase, the woman unclamps her fist and flounces out the veil she has been holding. "Wish me luck," she tells him as she attaches it to her spiky hair. "I barely know this guy."

"Then why get married?" Leo asks, shrugging so she won't think he is being mean.

"I'm pregnant," she whispers.

Leo can't hide his distress at this statement, can feel his forehead drawing inward, his mouth turning downward in concern.

"Just joking," she tells him, slapping his arm. "I guess I love him. Isn't that enough?"

The veil is cockeyed on her head, and instead of answering her question, Leo leans across the counter and adjusts the combs until it's centered.

"Thanks," she tells him, then takes her package and leaves, veil flapping out and skewing crooked once again in the wind from the open door.

"Leo," his father shouts from the back room, "which one'd you sell?"

"Um." He hesitates. "Just one of those wedding clocks," he shouts back, then sits on his stool and waits for the next customer.

He picks Helen up at the Dunes at five-thirty. Inside the court-yard he finds her beneath the red umbrella talking quietly to Miles. Gerard and this new girl, Ernie, Helen's mentioned are nowhere to be seen. Leo approaches with caution, stepping through the maze of yellow lawn chairs, the late-evening sun a weight upon his neck and shoulders. The two pools are starkly empty, their usual blue clarity blurred by leaves and palm fronds from today's heavy wind. Helen's head is close to Miles's, con-spiratorial and intimate, and Leo can feel anger begin to ricochet against his insides.

"Hey," he says coolly when he reaches them, trying to mimic the insouciant demeanor of the bride he'd met today. Who could be so calm before a wedding?

"Leo." Helen smiles when she sees him and leans away from Miles. "You're early. I still have to clean the pool."

"Actually," he says, "I'm late."

"Don't worry about it, Hell. I can finish up," Miles says, Leo's insides catching fire at the use of this new nickname for *his* girlfriend.

"Well, that's sweet of you," Helen says, leaping off the chair. She turns to Leo. "Let's go."

In his Nova, he is silent, waiting for her to ask him what the matter is, as she usually does, but Helen says nothing, simply looks out her window at the passing casinos, humming a song he doesn't recognize.

He turns on the radio to drown her out, then, when a minute's passed, turns it down and asks her, "Why did Miles call you Hell?"

"Oh, I don't know. I suppose he thinks it's clever."

"You two seem to have grown pretty close while I was gone."

She shrugs. "I wouldn't say that."

"Helen, I want to know what's going on."

She turns completely toward him now, arms crossed over her narrow chest. "Nothing is going on."

HIS MOTHER IS home when they arrive, making a peanut butter sandwich at the kitchen counter. The blinds over the sink are closed, and the room seems thin and dingy, the overhead light already on despite the barrage of sun outside. His mother wears her reading glasses and looks above their fake gold frames to ask, "Hey, you two, want a sandwich?"

"No, thanks," Leo says, turning toward his bedroom.

Helen surprises him by saying, "I'd love a sandwich," before she sits down at the narrow kitchen table. "I'm starving," she tells him, by way of explanation.

"I'll be in my room," he announces, then steps into the darkened hallway.

FROM BEHIND HIS closed door he can hear his mother's voice, low and graveled by years of smoke, weaving in and out of Helen's higher tones. The words are unclear; but he can tell they're having a good time, and when Helen laughs, he can no longer stand it, so he turns on his stereo and lies down on his bed, listening to his favorite new tape, Berlioz, which he slipped into his pocket on his last visit to Odyssey Records, where he did buy an Iron Maiden record, he reasons, at full price. The *Symphonie Fantastique* moves throughout the small confines of his room, pushing at the walls until he feels almost peaceful. He read on the tape's cover that Berlioz wrote this song to win a woman, and Leo tries to decide if he could write something for Helen to play for her on his drum set. But the idea seems feeble—no love songs are written for the timpani or snare drum—and when he hears Helen laugh again, the bright sound lifting through his music, he squeezes his eyes tightly to keep himself from crying.

Later she enters his bedroom, smelling of peanut butter and cigarettes, a splash of milk against her black tank top. She undresses, then lies down beside him, pulling up his T-shirt so the cool skin over her ribs is touching his stomach. He turns to look at her, his face so close to hers she is difficult to see. "I don't think you understand," he tells her, "how much I love you."

She sighs and flops away from him. "Maybe I don't."

They lie there for a while in silence, the ceiling fan humming above their bodies as if nothing were the matter. Music hovers over them, and its dark, soothing beauty is the only thing holding Leo back from placing his face into the curve of Helen's collarbone and crying, salting her shoulder with another impermanent fluid.

"What's this we're listening to?" Helen asks at last.

He tells her, "Berlioz," then asks, "What do you think?"

Peripherally, he can see her close her eyes. Her breathing deepens as if she were trying to absorb the sound. After a few seconds she says, "It's pretty depressing."

THE NEXT DAY at his father's shop a man comes in carrying a package pressed tightly to his chest. He is short and thin-shouldered with the alert, handsome face of a beagle. After stepping carefully across the scarred linoleum, he reaches Leo and sets his package on the counter. "I need to return this."

Inside the plastic bag is Leo's clock, the one he sold just yesterday to the Billy Idol bride. Leo extricates it from the tissue paper and holds it in his hands. The weight of it feels dangerous, as if he had created a bad omen, something so tainted by his anger it can't withstand a marriage. "Why?" is all he can manage to ask this man, who is standing there waiting, arms akimbo, sunglasses perched in his brown hair like a nervous bird.

"Well, you can see right here," the man says, pointing, "that this should be an eight instead of a nine. You can't have two nine o'clocks."

"Leo," his father shouts from the back room. "Remember. No returns."

Leo gives the man a pained expression, noticing now that he wears a Zildjian cymbal T-shirt like the one he stole two months ago from The Drum Shoppe. "You play?" he asks, nodding toward his shirt.

"Yeah." The man nods and taps a quick beat on the counter. "Yeah, I do play." Then he leans toward Leo and whispers, "Look, man, I don't care about the two nines. The truth is this was a wedding gift for a wedding that never ended up happening. So"—he shrugs and frowns—"it's depressing me."

"What happened?" Leo can't help asking.

"Apparently she had a change of heart."

Leo recalls for a quiet second the bride's crooked, helpless veil surrounded by those defiant spikes of hair, her pledge of love followed by a shrug. So, he thinks, even girls like her can leave you.

"Listen," Leo whispers, "just pick out a different clock real quick, and we'll call it even."

"Yeah, even." The man grimaces, then adds, "Okay. Thanks." He moves to the wall and quickly selects a very plain clock, blue and white with no designs.

When the man is gone, silence runs deep and aching through Leo's veins, despite the persistent shrill of voices on the radio, despite the methodic clearing of his father's throat. In half an hour his father will depart for lunch, and then, Leo thinks, he can play music. It doesn't matter what, just something smooth enough to slide beneath his skin and coat his bones, something loud enough to protect him from this dearth of sound.

HELEN RIDES to his house on her bike today after she gets off work. She arrives at six o'clock, and they go straight to Leo's room. Before he can tell her about the bride and groom, about his contaminated clock, she is kissing him, a long, deep catacomb of interlocking lips and teeth and tongues that causes Leo to get lost, to pull off clothes so quickly that he trips and falls into his drum set, cymbal crashing loudly on his back. Helen laughs, and he tries to join in her mirth, but his shoulder hurts from hitting metal and all he can manage is half a smile.

When they are on the bed, both undressed and ready, Leo says, "Let's not use a condom today."

"Are you crazy?" Helen pulls away.

"You just had your period. It should be safe."

"No way." She sits completely upright and scoots against the wall.

"You never let me feel just you," he complains. "I hate that there's a barrier between us."

She slides past him and hops off the bed, picking up her underwear and stepping into them. "You know how I feel about this, Leo. Quit bugging me about it."

"Okay, never mind. Forget I said anything. Come back to bed." He pats the space beside him.

She shakes her head and pulls on the rest of her clothes. He doesn't want her to leave while he lies here naked, so he rises from the bed and dresses quickly, feeling like a ghost of the deserted groom as he reaches his arms into his own black Zildjian cymbal T-shirt. "Want to go to Luv-it?" he asks.

She shrugs and walks to peer out of his blinds, sunlight slicing through the room with such intensity it makes him squint in pain.

"C'mon, Helen. I'm sorry."

"Okay," she says. "Let's go."

THEY WALK DOWN to the frozen custard stand and order chocolate cones. Soon she seems to have forgotten her anger. She allows Leo to sling his arm around her neck as they sit side by side on the bench, watching dying light move between the buildings of the Strip.

Still, he wants her to say something, anything to crack this shell of silence that has hardened over them. At last she does. Eating the final bite of her cone she says, "I read this poem today, and I can't stop thinking about the first line: 'And you wait, awaiting the one to make your small life grow.'"

She turns to him as if seeking a response, but he has no idea what to say, no way of knowing what will keep her gaze focused here, on him. "Sounds like an old REO Speedwagon song," he jokes.

She doesn't smile, only shakes her head and says, "Rilke."

"Oh." He nods, acting as if he's heard of this person, then finally murmurs, "I like that."

"Don't you think that's what we're all doing?" she asks. "Trying to find that person."

He shrugs. "I think I already have. It's you."

She smiles, and Leo thinks he's won, turned her toward him with a certain degree of permanence, but then she says, "How can it possibly be me? I don't know anything."

He leans across the bench and presses his mouth to her temple, blood beating fast and sure beneath him, then says into her ear, "Let's go across to Odyssey Records. I want to buy you a tape or something."

INSIDE THE STORE, the air is cool, and music—a band he's never heard before with dark, exotic chords and a moaning female singer—winds through the aisles. "Go find something," he tells her. "Whatever you like." She wanders off toward the new wave/alternative section and Leo begins his usual circuit. He moves through the heavy metal records, decides there is nothing new for him here, then takes a brief tour through jazz and blues before landing in classical. During his father's lunch today, Leo heard something on the radio called the *Moonlight Sonata*, and he decided right then that he must own this music, that he must be able to play it for Helen. It turns out to be a popular selection. There are ten tapes of this recording, and Leo takes one in his hand, then looks around the store before slipping the plastic case deep into the left pocket of his shorts. He'll pay for whatever Helen wants, but he can't afford them both, he reasons.

He's a little nervous as he makes his way toward her, the bright crown of her hair visible from every point in the store. He notices that the clerks all watch her, though Helen seems oblivious to their gazes, her head bent over some album, chin dipping slightly in rhythm with the music that plays everywhere, bathing him in color.

Leo comes up behind her and puts his arms around her waist, careful not to press too closely because she might detect the tape. "Did you find something?"

"Yeah, but you don't need to buy it."

"I want to."

"Why?"

He thinks of saying *because I want to be the one to make your small life grow*, but he can't. For one, her life does not seem small to him. It is almost overly gigantic. He knows that within this thin body she contains college in a different city, possibly a future far away from his. "I just want to buy you something. Is that a crime?"

She laughs. "Well, I want this new album by the Cure, but I know you're going to make fun of me."

"I guess it's better than the Violent Femmes," he tells her, then takes the record out of her hands and leads her to the counter.

HE PAYS FOR her present, and they are walking out the door when Leo feels a hand upon his arm. "Sir," a young, long-haired clerk says to him, "we need you to pay for that tape in your pocket."

Leo can feel sweat encase him, and he is certain his heartbeat is audible as he turns and answers, "What do you mean?"

The clerk sighs, reaches into the pocket himself, and holds up the Beethoven tape with a smug look on his face. Leo turns to Helen, who is watching him with a deep frown creased between her brows, and for a second all he can concentrate on is wanting to reach up his hand and smooth out her skin, but he quickly focuses on how to extricate himself from this crisis, telling the clerk, "I'm sorry. I completely forgot about that tape. I meant to pay for it." He pulls out his wallet and hands over his last ten-dollar bill. "Here," he tells him. "It was just a mistake, that's all."

The clerk snaps the ten-dollar bill out of Leo's hand, then passes back the tape, making no offer of change despite the fact that the tape is only $7.99. "You're banned for a month," the clerk tells him. "I don't want to see you in here until the end of August."

"But I come here all the time. It was just a mistake."

The clerk holds up his hand as if to silence argument, and Helen tugs at his arm. "Come on, Leo," she says quietly. "Let's get out of here."

OUTSIDE, THE SKY is beginning to grow dark and a wind has picked up, blowing Helen's hair across her face so that he can't read her expression. They walk diagonally across the parking lot to the stoplight, where they stand waiting for the green, not speaking, not touching. The silence is excruciating to Leo, who expected Helen to yell, to cry, walk to his house, jump on her bike, and pedal away from him as fast as possible. This is not the first time, after all, she has been made aware of his tendency to steal, and his current inability to predict her reactions strikes him as more disturbing than the old reactions themselves ever were.

They cross the street and begin the walk down Oakey toward his home. Cars pass them on the right, and one blue Mustang containing a trio of teenage boys emits a long wolfish, howl as it drives by. Helen doesn't even glance in the car's direction, but Leo shouts a loud "Fuck you!" and flips them the bird. The Mustang continues on, as if he has said nothing, as if he didn't even exist. Helen's face remains passive, even after his outburst, so Leo finally has to ask her, "Why don't you say something?"

She looks at him blankly. "What is there to say?"

"Look, I didn't steal that tape."

"I know you didn't. You got caught before you could."

"I meant to pay for it all along. I just forgot."

She nods and looks away again, back in the direction they are moving.

"What, you've never made a mistake before? You've never done anything wrong in your life, right?" He realizes he is shouting, and two children on a front lawn watch him with large eyes, but he can't manage to lower his voice. "Everything you do is right and good! Everything you ever do is absolutely perfect!"

She stops and turns back to him, long hair whipping out

around her face, as if this were the only body part able to release her agitation. "That's not true," she tells him quietly. "While you were in Denver, I slept with Miles."

For a second he cannot breathe, does not think he will ever be able to breathe again, and he sits down abruptly, Indian style, on the hot sidewalk, beside a strange house, then places his face in his hands and gasps for air. Helen crouches beside him, and he looks up at her, wanting to claw at her face, to ruin that young canvas of skin, bruise those yellow-green eyes, rip at her lips, and tear at her hair until there is nothing left of her for him to want. But he doesn't move. He knows that if he hurts her, it will be the end of everything.

"It didn't mean anything," she tells him.

And Leo is aware of how he used this line before on her, after he kissed that girl at music camp. Aware too of how false those words were when they fell out of his own mouth. That kiss meant many things, things he is unable to verbalize even to himself, but he remembers quite distinctly the soft feel of her hair beneath his hands, the chocolate taste of her mouth, and the sounds of a clarinet rising from the window of a cabin and distracting him. He would have slept with that girl too, if she had been willing, if there had been space and time available, but the fact is that he didn't.

"I hate you," he says so quietly it is almost to himself.

"What'd you say?" she asks him, though he is almost certain she has heard him, and he wonders if she is offering him some sort of second chance.

She stands, moves farther away, and he looks up at her,

momentarily thrown off balance by her extreme height when viewed from his current position. This last year he has come to accept that she will always be taller than he is. He stands beside her and takes her hand. "Helen," he tries out her name on the dark air. "Let's get married."

"What?" She takes a step away but lets him keep her hand. "That's not what you said a second ago."

"I know, but I mean it. I don't want to lose you."

"Leo, I'm only sixteen. I can't get married."

"I think that might be old enough in Vegas. And I'm eighteen. If it's not, we'll wait a year, just be engaged."

She pulls her hand away and drops her face into her palms. Her shoulders begin to shake, and the sight of her, softly crying on the open street, unwinds every particle of anger he owns so that pieces of his skin seem to disintegrate, to fall away onto the concrete beneath his feet and move him instantly toward her. Leo puts his arms around Helen and pulls her close, holding her face so near to his own he can feel her breath feather on his eyelids. A light comes on in the house beside them, and Leo feels as if he has turned this light on himself, as if anything is possible as long as Helen tells him yes.

"So," he asks her, "what do you think?"

She shrugs against him and raggedly sniffs. "I don't know."

"I need to know right now," he tells her, "or I'll die. I can't sleep another night until I know."

Helen pushes away from him. She has stopped crying, but still, she appears to be in pain. "Just give me some time to think about it," she tells him. "I can't decide right now."

He senses this is the best possible answer he will receive, so he nods firmly and says, "All right."

They walk the two blocks left to Leo's house in silence, holding hands and watching as streetlights burn on above them. The moon is nowhere to be found, and Leo thinks that there must be stars, but they are dimmed to nothing by the casinos' lights, less than a mile away. When they reach his house, she kisses him, then unlocks her ten-speed from the stubby palm tree on his lawn and flings a leg astride it, her new record tucked awkwardly beneath an armpit. She waves to Leo once, then wheels around and leaves him, standing on a brittle, darkened lawn in a city he knows he will most likely never escape.

The Egg

EDWARD'S WIFE WILL NO LONGER sleep with him. It has taken him a month to realize that this is indeed the case—their couplings are quite infrequent as it is—but last night, when she once again said no to his advances, then turned away and settled deep into her pillow, the sight of her cool shoulder in the slatted moonlight told him she would not be relenting anytime soon.

He sits in his office now, the Russian flag behind him lightly batting at his shoulder in the air conditioning's breeze. He is grading papers from his Russian film class, but Kathy keeps intruding on his concentration, and he realizes he's read this student's last paragraph at least three times. Perhaps this is the way it goes with married couples, he decides. Sex can be kept interesting for only so long, and they are homing in on their nineteenth wedding anniversary this September. Besides, whom is he kidding? Kathy never really relished sex to start with. Now, at long last, she is probably doing exactly what she wants by telling him to move away and go to sleep.

Edward sighs, then reads the final paragraph before him one more time. He red inks an "83%" across the top and stands to leave for class.

IN ROOM 202 he is greeted by the usual group of apathetic students. This is summer school, and while there is always the occasional A+ pupil, looking to get ahead for next year, most of his class is made up of the dregs. There are not even any great beauties on whom he might soothe his old, sun-battered eyes, and he remembers the secret notes he received last summer with a certain tingle of envy and regret. He should have found out who wrote those and acted when he had the chance.

He passes back the papers, then lectures for a while before turning off the lights and showing them the first half of a film. *Letter to Brezhnev* is what they watch today. Usually this is one of Edward's favorites, but this afternoon he simply sits in the dark back of his classroom ruminating on his marriage, oblivious to the characters on-screen.

He decides to buy something for Kathy after work, a necklace maybe or a book. Perhaps a nice bottle of wine for them to share tonight, though of course she'll drink only half a glass at most. There have been three sexless months thus far. Not so long a span of time, he reasons. Maybe he is making a big deal out of nothing.

When the bell rings and someone flicks on the lights, Edward blinks in the fluorescence like a newborn, his senses jarred out of all proportion. He remembers a staff meeting, years ago, when he brought up the scourge of fluorescent lighting to the dean. "What are you suggesting, Edward?" he asked, a wry smile pasted on his big pancake of a face. "Candlelight?" Everyone laughed, and Edward joined in too; the subject was immediately dropped and never taken up again.

He stops the film and removes the reel as his students flee, noisy and gleeful as a flock of geese. Edward feels disgusted with them. They do not deserve, he thinks, to learn about the deep pain and sorrow of the Russians or even of their joy. They do not deserve the knowledge he can give them.

When everyone has left, he notices that a lone girl awaits his presence at the desk in front, so he sets down the reel and moves toward her, between the maze of desks, trying to recall her name. Impossible, he decides, despite the fact they've been in classes for a month and he has only forty students total. Her face barely even looks familiar.

"Can I help you?" Edward asks when he reaches her.

"I was just, um, wondering, Dr. Larkin, why you gave me an eighty-three percent on this paper?"

She holds the paper up, and he takes it from her hand. It is the last one that he graded today, right before he came to class, but as he skims the first page, it seems to Edward that he's never read a word of it.

"Usually you put comments," she tells him. "But today it's blank."

"Right," he says, glancing at the girl. Her breasts are huge and sitting high out of her scoop-necked shirt, a pale brown mesa of flesh. Despite her otherwise thin body, she strikes Edward as gluttonous, and he tries to restrain a frown of distaste as she steps closer to look at the paper with him, her upper arm briefly meeting his elbow.

"Let me read it again," he tells her. "I should have written something."

"Great." She smiles, and he likes her overbite. One of her eyes is lazy, turned askew so he can't decide if she's looking directly at him or at the movie screen on her right. Maybe she is so overtly displaying her breasts to divert attention from this defect, a thought that causes Edward a momentary pang of sympathy.

"Thanks," she tells him, then turns to leave, but before she exits, she pivots toward him once again. "Dr. Larkin?"

"Yes?" He looks quickly at her paper for a name. Camilla! Lovely! "Yes, Camilla?"

"I just wanted you to know that I really really like this class."

"Well, thank you, Camilla," he says, genuinely pleased. "Thank you very much."

IN THE LATE AFTERNOON he drives over to the Strip in search of a gift for Kathy. He never shops inside the casinos, but he is picking Helen up in an hour and a half, and the idea of just one trip out into the world is too appealing to pass up. He chooses Caesars Palace as his destination, because of its longtime reputation for being a cut above the other hotels. However, once he is inside, the entire mission seems a bad idea. The casino's chilly air is choked with smoke, and tourists mill about in casual clothes that strike Edward as distinctly lacking in class. It's been awhile since he's seen such an array of fat midwestern legs, such an assortment of T-shirts advertising brands of shoes or food or just the company that made the shirt itself.

Turning down a corridor lined on either side by boutiques, Edward escapes the raucous ring of slot machines and finds air that is slightly easier to breathe. There is a men's suit shop to his right, followed by a cigar store, then a clothing store displaying a window of shiny, gold-braided warm-up suits that make him cringe. A bridal boutique is next, and Edward pauses here and peers inside, past the white-gowned mannequin in the window to the dresses, veils, and mirrors beyond.

He thinks of Kathy on their wedding day, exquisitely demure in a simple white dress that fell just below her knees, revealing well-shaped calves and her largish feet—size ten narrow—that Edward has always found charming, an anomaly to her thin five-foot six-inch frame. It was not a wedding dress per se—she insisted they keep all the details simple—but she looked so lovely with her long arms emerging brown and smooth from short, capped sleeves, he almost fell over.

A woman wearing an ornate, off-the-shoulder gown emerges from the dressing room in back. Her back is to him, and Edward watches as she climbs two steps to a pedestal where she stands before a bank of mirrors. Kathy should have had a dress like that, he thinks. She should have bathed herself in satin. He should have insisted that they create a day so drenched in otherworldly sumptuousness she would never be able to forget it, to turn away from him in bed as if he were merely an annoyance.

Edward steps closer to the glass and takes a better look inside just as the woman in the dress turns to face him. At the sight of her, he gasps and steps away again. The woman in the dress is his daughter Helen.

Quickly, before he can take a moment to think this situation through, he walks into the store and strides toward his daughter. She is facing away from him again, very still as she allows a middle-aged woman in a red wig to pin the bodice tighter. Edward comes up behind them and appears in the mirror over Helen's shoulder. At the sight of him, she frowns and turns around, yelping, "Ow," and rubbing at her hip where a pin must have pierced her skin.

The red-wigged woman straightens up and says, "I told you not to move, dear."

"Helen." Edward begins in a voice sterner than intended. "What is going on?"

"Nothing. I was just on break, and I got bored, so . . ." She shrugs.

The woman in the wig excuses herself and walks up to the store's front, almost out of earshot, but not quite, Edward decides. Close enough to hear if an argument ensues. The thought occurs to him that this woman might not realize he's the father, and he feels a sharp downward tug of disgust at the idea that to her he could be someone else. The groom? A jilted older lover?

He steps closer to his daughter and takes her arm. "Is there something you're not telling us? You're not about to elope with Leo or something absurd like that, are you?"

"Why would that be so absurd?" she wants to know.

"I shouldn't even have to answer that."

"I'm just playing around, Dad," she tells him. "That's all." She breaks free of his grasp and twirls in a circle, satin fabric flying out to hit his middle, then stops and faces him again. "What do you think?"

"I think you look like a child in her mother's dress, that's what I think," he says, though in truth he finds her beautiful, more a woman than he thinks she should be at her age. It's her carriage, he decides. The years he spent insisting that she stand up straight have definitely paid off. "Now, go get changed and come help me find a gift for your mother."

AFTER SHE HAS transformed into her old self, clothed in cutoffs and a T-shirt, they stroll together back into the shop-lined hallway. "Why are you buying Mom a gift?" Helen asks, and Edward thinks there is an underlying sneer in her tone, though he can't be sure.

"Because she's my wife, that's why. Sometimes one buys one's wife a gift just to say, 'I love you.' Has Leo ever bought you something for no reason? Maybe you should ask yourself that next time you start trying on wedding dresses."

"He bought me an album a couple of weeks ago."

Edward tries hard not to roll his eyes at this, a tic he's begun to pick up from his younger daughter, Jenny. "That's not exactly what I had in mind."

He pulls Helen into what appears to be a jewelry and dishware store, though there are also brightly colored scarves strewn here and there and a set of painted plaster elephants standing in the corner.

"Dad, I have to go," Helen tells him as he begins to look around. "I'm late."

"Oh, really?" He hoped she'd assist him in picking out a gift. "Can't you stay a few more minutes?"

She shakes her head.

"If you do, I promise I won't tell your mother about the wedding dress incident." He nods in the direction of the bridal shop. "I don't think she'd be very pleased with that scenario."

"I don't care what you tell her," Helen says, this time with a definite sneer. She turns to leave and on her way out of the shop calls back over her shoulder, "See you in an hour."

Edward watches her depart, then turns back to the bright, packed shelves, helpless before this vast array of baubles. The clerk provides no help, her plump elbows perched on the counter by the register, as she thumbs through a magazine. Edward thinks that maybe he should leave. He has no idea what to buy his wife, this woman he has lived with for so long. Lately she's begun to change her style too, so his judgment regarding what she'd like seems even more precarious. He is about to leave, about to return to the quiet heat of his car and turn on the air and NPR, but then across the store he sees it, sitting in a silver bowl: a perfect painted egg.

Up close, it is even more exquisite, and he sees that the egg is not painted at all, but intricately carved from a dark reddish amber substance that feels sort of like a piece of soap. The clerk informs him that it's made of cinnabar, and Edward buys it immediately, pleased that he's found something entirely new to give to Kathy, something from the earth he's never even heard of.

IN THE CAR, he retrieves his pocket dictionary from his briefcase and looks up cinnabar: "a heavy, reddish compound, HgS, that is the principal ore of mercury." The clerk wrapped the egg and provided Edward with a small card, which he opens now, and pens a note. "Katherine the Great [the sight of her nickname gives him a surge of hope], An egg made from the ore of mercury for my decidedly mercurial wife (whom I love dearly). With deep affection—Edward." He looks at his neat, even penmanship—like a typewriter, his daughters always tease him—and begins to rethink his use of the word *mercurial*. Sure, it works as a pun, but might she take offense? He doesn't consider her volatile, simply changeable. Then another thought occurs to him. Will she even know the meaning of the word? Will another argument ensue about Edward's tendency to show off his large vocabulary at the expense of other people's understanding him? Kathy once liked it when he used words unknown to her, but a month ago, when he referred to a colleague of his as an autodidact, she said: "Edward, we both know you're smarter than I am, but do you constantly have to remind me of the fact with the words you choose to use?"

He protested, of course, but she waved him away, then went into the bedroom and shut the door. Edward *did* know more words than his wife; he'd admit that much. He'd spent more time in school, and his grasp on history was far superior, but to call himself smarter didn't seem an accurate assessment. There was something intricate and dark woven into her fine bones, some mystery that made her shimmer, at times with such a brilliance Edward felt he'd never truly know her despite the many years spent in her presence. He, on the other hand, was transparent, wasn't he? His inner workings obvious to all who knew him.

He decides to keep the note as is—it's written in pen anyway—and tucks it beneath the ribbon of the gift box. He sits there for a minute, on the uppermost level of the Caesars Palace parking garage. Out his windshield sits the city. Its dusky mountains stretch down to cradle houses and hotels, churches and strip clubs, casinos and schools, tourists and workaday Las Vegans. It is not a place of peace or beauty. Edward knows this. It is a city both overripe and barren, both beige and fakely radiant. All the same, he loves it.

He backs out of the parking space and makes his way through the maze of the garage, imagining the moment tonight when Kathy will open the gift, the way she will flush the soft pinkish olive color that she does when flattered or surprised, and the way afterward in bed she will open toward him like a flower, like a book, as if an eggshell has cracked all around her and been shed. Edward smiles at these images, then goes to pick up Helen at the Dunes Hotel.

AT DINNER THAT NIGHT, he keeps seeing Helen in the wedding dress, though in reality she sits beside Kathy in a pale blue tank top, slurping up cold cucumber soup with a definite lack of grace. "Helen," he instructs her, "wipe the bottom of your spoon on the edge of the bowl like this"—he demonstrates—"before you eat it. You're dripping all over the table."

"Edward," Kathy interjects, "let her eat in peace."

"What, am I just supposed to stop fathering all of a sudden?" He smiles, trying to lighten the mood of the table, which, for some reason, is distinctly dour.

"Dad, I'm sixteen," she says. "What else can you possibly have to teach me at this point?"

Jenny, who sits beside him, laughs, then takes a bite of soup, carefully scraping the bottom of the spoon on the bowl's edge. Edward is so taken aback by Helen's statement—the audacity of it! The ignorance!—that he can't even muster a response. He looks across to Kathy for a show of support, a shared look of exasperation, a wry smile, something! But his wife sips at her wine with an air of detachment, looking across the table and over Jenny's head at nothing, at the blank wall behind her. "Is something the matter?" he asks Kathy now. She has begun to twirl her spoon in her soup, but Edward can see she is not actually eating it. Suddenly he feels surrounded by teenagers.

"Just tired out from this heat, I guess," she says. "Janice and I are going to take a walk after dinner. Maybe that will revive me."

"It was one hundred eighteen degrees today," Jenny informs them. "At least that's what our thermometer said."

"I don't think it got *that* hot," Helen says.

"Well." Edward really has nothing to add to this. "It'll pass soon," he says. It seems bizarre to him that they are discussing the weather. It is always hot in the summer. They all know this and therefore never discuss it. The women sitting around him seem to be transforming into strangers. Even his youngest, Jenny, who he notices for the first time is wearing eyeliner and maybe even a touch of blush. When did she begin putting makeup on that young, pristine face of hers? And Helen, *his Helen*, growing more caustic by the day and parading around in a wedding dress of all things in her free time!

He thinks about bringing up the wedding dress incident to Kathy later. It might serve to renew their intimacy, bond them together once again as worried parents, but she would probably fret over it for hours, and then any chance of sex would be erased for the evening.

"How's Leo doing?" Kathy asks Helen. "We haven't seen him around here in a while."

"Like you care," Helen retorts.

"Helen." Edward immediately reprimands her, wincing at the sight of Kathy's face, her momentary flare of pain. Even Jenny frowns across the table at her older sister.

"Sorry," Helen says, looking into her soup bowl. "He's fine," she adds, before asking to please be excused.

AFTER DINNER, Kathy leaves in her Honda, driving over to Janice's to take a walk. Leo picks up Helen in his Nova, supposedly to go see a movie. Jenny rides her bike over to a friend's, and Edward is left alone, in the quiet hush of his empty home. He pours himself another glass of wine, then goes into his study and shuts the door. The room is nicely cooled, from both the air conditioning and its lack of windows. There is only one small pane facing north, in the corner beside his bookshelf, so heat has not been allowed to invade the room from every angle throughout the day. He sits down at his desk and flips on the lamp before he retrieves Camilla's paper from his briefcase. Her class doesn't meet tomorrow, but he needs something to do, a task to remove his mind from the shifting currents of his wife and daughters, and he is already caught up on all his other grading. Before he begins to read, he takes out the small gift-wrapped box containing Kathy's egg and sets it beside him on the desk to serve as a reminder for what's to come, for the portion of the night he has been waiting for. It's only seven-thirty now, he calculates, so she should be home in an hour or so, and then he will draw her into the bedroom and surprise her.

Edward's mind wanders as he reads Camilla's paper, so he takes a long swallow of wine and forces himself to concentrate, pretending he is back in grad school, when he had to tune out neighbors through the thin wall of his and Kathy's first apartment, had to ignore the cries of Helen, who was being tended to by Kathy in the adjoining room. He wrote an entire dissertation under those noisy circumstances, for Pete's sake; he can grade one lousy paper in a quiet, empty house.

Another sip of wine, a deep breath, and the paper begins to take shape beneath him. He sees the grade should be far superior to its original 83 percent. The writing is lucid and insightful, and Camilla has chosen finely observed details from the film to illustrate her points. It is a short paper, just three pages long, but he reads slowly, absorbing each line deep into his mind, penning comments in the margins, and when he finishes reading it for a second time, he sees it is already nine. Impossible.

He rises, leaves his office, and walks to the front window, peering up and down the empty street before letting down the wooden blinds. The house has grown dark while he sat in his study, and he moves through the rooms, turning on lights, then retrieves the bottle of wine from the fridge and returns to his office, where he pours himself another glass and sits back down at his desk. For the first time the idea that Kathy is not with Janice occurs to him. She has been acting strangely lately. Are women entitled to midlife crises too? Has she met another man, a grade school teacher like herself, who has the days off to spend with her? The idea is absurd, he tells himself. For one, he can't imagine where she'd meet anyone of interest. He's seen the male teachers at her school. There are only two: an older man who wears an ascot and smokes a pipe, two affectations Kathy abhors, and a twenty-something boy with floppy hair and round, pimpled cheeks. Besides, his wife has never been particularly interested in sex, so what would be the point of seeking more outside the home?

He drinks half a glass of wine, then looks back down at Camilla's paper. It still needs a new grade and final comments, so he opens his red pen and thinks what to write. He is feeling generous, because of the wine, he supposes, or perhaps his loneliness, so he gives the girl a perfect grade of 100 percent. "It is not often," he writes between the grade and her title, "that a teacher is privileged enough to see a paper such as yours. This world can be desolate, and sometimes fine writing and the fine mind behind it are one's only inspiration, one's only hope that everything will once again be set back in its proper place. Order, my dear, precision and insight creating beauty on the page are potent necessities, indeed." Edward sits back in his chair and looks at what he's done. His writing, not as neat and small as it usually is, has overtaken the front page, gone sprawling, seeking space down the entire right-hand margin. And what on earth has he written? Where is his mind tonight? He tosses the paper back into his briefcase, deciding to deal with it later, then picks up his wine and the package and goes into the living room to wait for Kathy on the couch.

Jenny comes home first, fifteen minutes before her ten o'clock curfew. "Why are you sitting here not doing anything?" she wants to know when she finds Edward on the couch, without a book or music, the television blank and silent, a glass of wine clasped in his hand.

"Oh, I was just resting my old mind," he tells her with a laugh. "How was your evening?"

She shrugs. "Fun. Me and Angela—"

"Angela and I." He corrects her.

"*Angela and I* went for a bike ride, then got some ice cream. It's still hot out."

She retreats to her bedroom, and Edward hears the door shut, a soft, mocking suck of air on wood that seems to press down more acutely on his distress.

Fifteen minutes later, exactly on the brink of her curfew, Helen arrives, looking feverish and beautiful, Edward painfully observes. Her cheeks are flushed, and her mascara is smeared a bit beneath her eyes, giving her a smoky, older look. "How was the movie?" he asks her.

"Good," she tells him, and turns to go to her room as well.

"Which one did you see again?"

"Um." She turns back and bites her lower lip. "That new Tom Cruise thingy. I forget the name of it."

He nods, convinced suddenly that she's lying, that everyone in this house is lying to him, but he doesn't try to challenge her, just nods and says, "Good night."

HE HAS TO WAIT through another glass of wine, another hour on the couch, before his wife arrives, trying to come through the front door quietly, as if she hoped he were already asleep.

"Edward," she says brightly when she sees him. "I didn't think you'd still be up."

"How was your walk?" He is beginning to feel the wine, moving through his blood with leaden slowness. His arms are impossibly heavy, but he manages to lift one and pat the space beside him on the couch.

"Great," she tells him, moving to sit next to him.

"I have something for you," he says, lifting the gift.

Kathy takes the small box in her hands. "What's this for?"

"Just for you. No reason."

She opens it quickly, then peers into the box and smiles, though the smile does not seem genuine to Edward. Perhaps it is his slightly altered state. Does he see her differently through this haze of wine?

"Cinnabar," she says, touching it inside the box, and he is shocked by the ordinary way she says the word—cinnabar—as if it were an everyday item, a term she used all the time.

"You've heard of that?"

"Of course." She pulls the egg from its tissue paper and sits, frowning for a moment before she looks at him. "An egg?"

"There's a card too," he tells her, and she picks up the wrapping from the floor and retrieves the note. She reads it before she looks up and says, "Thank you so much." She leans to give him a kiss on his cheek, then stands and goes into the bathroom.

AFTER THEY BOTH have gotten ready for bed, Kathy and Edward lie side by side in darkness. He is waiting for her to turn to him, for the gift to embed itself into her heart, or at the least into her conscience, and propel her body onto his. After a long silence he worries she might be asleep, but then she says in a low, hushed voice, "Was that gift some sort of commentary on my approaching menopause?"

"What?" He props himself up on an elbow and looks down at her. "No, of course not. I just thought it was beautiful."

"It is." She nods and looks up into his face. "It's just, I don't know, an egg. It's kind of strange."

He searches for an explanation. "It's a symbol of perfection," he tells her, "of new life."

After a pause she says, "I guess I can see that."

He leans down to kiss her mouth and thinks he detects a foreign smell, something summery and rich like suntan lotion. "Kath, can we make love tonight?" he whispers. "I've missed you."

"I don't know." She turns her face to the side. Are those tears in her eyes, or shimmers from the windowpane above them? She lies there for a moment in silence, and Edward waits, hovering over her, hoping for a clearer answer. His arm grows tired, and he begins to feel foolish, so he flops back down onto his back with a sigh.

And then she is astride him, pulling up her long white nightgown and straddling his middle, leaning close so that her short hair brushes his cheeks, then, before he can even kiss her, sitting up straight so that her face is far away from his own. Despite this distance, he moves inside her with a deep feeling of relief, letting out his held breath and wanting to laugh out loud he is so glad to be joined to her, to be having sex with his wife again. But he manages to contain his laughter—it might offend Kathy, after all—and they rise and fall together in silence, his breathing growing louder and louder until finally he is released into the night.

Afterward she climbs off his body and turns away onto her side. Edward curves himself around her form, the satin of her nightgown an unwelcome object between them, but before he can ask if she'll please take it off, he is asleep.

By the time Edward awakes the next morning, Kathy has already gotten up and left to take Helen to work. The egg sits on her bedside table, as if it were some remnant of their coupling, and Edward experiences a pang at the idea that Kathy is indeed approaching menopause. The notion has not occurred to him before.

When he arrives at school, Camilla is waiting outside his office door, and her paper seems to burn inside his briefcase, emitting heat against his leg as he says hello and ushers her inside. Edward hopes she won't hang around too long because he needs to make a trip down to the teachers' lounge before his class and soothe his frazzled body with a cup of coffee, a glass of water, and three aspirin at least. The inside of his mouth, his stomach, the expanse of his chest are parched and dry as a desert, and he regrets again the amount of wine he imbibed last night.

"I just came by to see if you'd reread my paper," Camilla says.

Yes I read your paper, he wants to tell her, *but no, you can't have it back*. Instead, he sets his briefcase on his desk and unlatches it—what else can he do?—and there her paper lies for both of them to see, the wild-inked front page looking like something scrawled on by a madman.

Camilla seems to notice only the perfect grade. "Thank you," she says when he hands it to her, that young face unfolding into the widest smile Edward's ever seen. And then, without warning, her arms are around his neck, her body breaking onto his with such force he feels momentarily ill from the jolt. Then he notices the feel of her compared with Kathy, the generous expansion of her large breasts spreading out over his suit coat compared to his wife's ascetic curves. "Thank you," she says again into his neck as Edward stands there, arms at his sides, trying to figure out what he's required to do in the face of all this warmth, this spectacle of gratitude.

He places his hands on her waist, thinking he could pull her even closer, that she wouldn't mind, but instead, he moves her gently but efficiently away. "You did the work," he tells her. "There's nothing to thank me for."

One of her eyes is looking directly into his while the other flutters toward the Russian flag across his window. Is she gazing at him? He can't be sure.

"You don't give out many perfect grades, Dr. Larkin. I know all about your standards. I'm just really, really flattered."

"Well," he says, snapping shut his briefcase, then moving around behind his desk and sitting in his chair, "you're a very good writer."

"You think so?" she asks, perching on his desk, one eye continuing to watch him. Now he's certain that she's staring.

"Yes," he tells her, searching for the words that will expel her from his office. "Very good."

She doesn't move but continues to sit there, half of her ass flattened on the smooth mahogany between them. The idea occurs to Edward, takes shape suddenly and clearly in his mind, that this girl wants more from him than just a grade. Her embrace had been a beat too long for chasteness, and now the way she's sitting, here in silence, giving him what he supposes is a sultry look, though with that lazy eye it's difficult to say.

Edward is aware that at least one of his colleagues sleeps with the occasional student, and he tries to imagine locking the office door and undressing this girl right now. That part wouldn't be so bad—though he really needs a cup of coffee—but then he too would have to shed his clothes, and all he can conjure after this part of the scenario is her laughter. She can't be any older than nineteen. How could she not laugh at the sight of flab around his middle, at his sparsely red-haired chest, at the freckles running all across his back and shoulders from years of punishment beneath this desert sun?

Besides, she is a child. Edward is not necessarily against the idea of a sexual liaison outside his marriage, but he doesn't want a mere body to lie beneath him; he wants a fully structured mind, a human being who has known at least some small corner of the world well, someone who understands both the torture and the bliss of having children, a woman who has felt the months of dullness that can settle into bones until they feel brittle to the touch. He wants someone who knows all this, not another teenager to add to the list of people he deals with on a daily basis.

"Camilla," he says now, firmly, professorial, "I really need to get some work done before my class."

"Oh." She quickly stands. "Sure, Dr. Larkin. I guess I'll just see you tomorrow then?"

He nods a yes, and she leaves his office with a wave, a flutter of her hand, and a demure downward glance that strikes Edward as so elegant, so clean and poised for her sparse years that the image of it stays with him the entire morning.

AFTER THE DAY'S CLASSES he leaves to pick up Helen at the pool. Somehow, he manages to arrive half an hour early, and he debates waiting in the car and listening to the news or going into the courtyard in hopes that Helen may be able to leave now. He hasn't been on the pool deck since last summer, so he decides he might as well venture in, say hello to Helen's boss, and get a look at this Miles character, who kept his daughter out so late last month that she was grounded for a week.

The lounge chairs and both pools are swarming with people, and Edward shades his eyes to seek out Helen, whom he quickly spots, sprawled out in a lifeguard chair, legs open and spilling over the platform into empty air. Her demeanor is quite different from the neat way she perched there last summer, and Edward decides he'd better ask Kathy to talk to Helen about sitting in a ladylike position.

Miles must be the boy presiding over the other pool, and Edward instantly detests him. That outlandish spray of hair, the smug look of superiority as he scans the pool beneath him, as if he'd be doing you a favor if he deigned to save your life. Still, he goes to college and is doing quite well as a pre-med major, according to Helen, which is more than Edward can say for Leo and his beloved drum set. But Edward has an inexplicable fondness for Leo; perhaps it is his own blue-collar roots sprawling out beneath his feet—his father drove a truck; his mother checked playing cards for flaws—that helps him find solidarity with Helen's boyfriend. He can think of no other reason to feel a kinship with this boy.

Helen can't very well leave early if she is watching all those people in the pool, so Edward makes his way across the courtyard toward the red umbrella and the lectern where Helen keeps her things. Halfway across the deck he stops. Is that Kathy sitting beneath the red umbrella? On the other side of the lectern from Helen's boss? Edward puts a hand over his prescription sunglasses to cut the glare and sees that it is indeed his wife. Has he gotten the days confused? Was it Kathy's turn to retrieve Helen? He doesn't think so; it would be unlike him to forget. Then a hopeful frolic of a thought leaps up: Maybe she is here to meet him; maybe she wanted to surprise her husband. But the idea is absurd.

He'll be home in half an hour, and besides, she seems so ensconced in the scene it's easy to believe she's been here for a while, sipping from a glass of pale yellow liquid—lemonade?—and talking to Helen's boss. What is his name again? Gerald, Jerry. No something a bit more fancy and affected. Gerard. That's his name. Gerard.

When Edward reaches the umbrella and steps beneath its shade, Kathy looks up at him with obvious surprise.

"Did I get the day wrong?" he asks right away. "Was it your turn to pick up Helen?"

"Um." She falters and then smiles. "You know, I wasn't sure if it was my turn or not, so I thought I'd better just come over here and see."

Immediately he knows she's lying, but he still can't figure why. "But you're so early," he says.

"So are you," she says, then gestures toward Helen's boss. "You've met Gerard, haven't you?"

The man behind the lectern—shorter than Edward, he sees, but also broader, darker—stands and reaches out a hand.

Edward shakes it, then fights the urge to wipe his palm on his suit pants. "Yes, we've met. Once or twice, I think."

"Last summer," Gerard says, and nods firmly.

It bothers Edward greatly that he can't see this man's eyes. He has never trusted mirrored glasses. Just this year, when Jenny bought a pair, he made her take them back. Kathy defended them, he recalls now, and Edward can't help feeling that this makes his wife guilty, suddenly, of something.

"Would you like some lemonade?" Gerard says.

"Only if it's tart," Edward says automatically, then thinks that maybe he is being rude.

"Pardon?" Gerard says, raising his thick brows, and Edward notes that the word sounds foreign coming from his mouth. *Pardon* is not a word conducive to mirrored sunglasses and ball caps that read "The Dunes."

"If it's tart," Edward repeats more clearly. "I hate lemonade when it's overly sweet."

"Try mine," Kathy says.

Edward takes a sip from his wife's glass, then grimaces. "Much too sweet. But thank you anyway, Gerard." He isn't sure, but in the aftertaste Edward thinks he detects a hint of alcohol. Impossible. Kathy barely touches wine, let alone hard liquor. Still, there is something more relaxed about her as she sits here leaning back in that tall, spindly chair, black sunglasses hiding half her face. He has not seen her look so at home in quite a while.

While he is trying to figure out if he should sit down or not, Helen appears beneath the umbrella. "Dad," she says, ignoring her mother, as if she hasn't even noticed her! "I'm ready to go."

Kathy stands as Helen gathers her bag from inside Gerard's lectern. Edward says good-bye to Gerard, as does Kathy—Helen won't even look at the man—then the three of them make their way across the crowded deck and out into the parking lot.

"Well, isn't this funny?" Edward says, looking at his wife and daughter. "Both of us being here at once. Maybe we should all go out for a scoop of ice cream or something?"

"I'm not hungry," Helen says.

"Then maybe a cold drink?"

"I want to go home. Leo's waiting for me to come over."

Edward tries to exchange a look with Kathy, raising his brows and pursing his lips as if to ask, *what's with her?* But Kathy meets his gaze for only a second, not even long enough to receive and understand his look, before she glances toward the boiling rows of cars.

"Well, do you want to ride with me or your mother?" Edward asks Helen.

"You," she says, then begins walking toward his car.

Edward leans to kiss Kathy on the cheek. Again there is the foreign smell of suntan lotion in her skin. "I'll see you at home?"

"Sure," she answers, as insouciant as a teenager, then walks in the opposite direction, toward her Honda.

In the car with Helen, turning left onto the Strip, Edward ventures a question. "So, what do you think of Gerard? I noticed you two weren't very friendly."

"I hate his guts," Helen says in a voice so devoid of emotion it sears Edward, worries him more than the actual words. Despite the air conditioning blowing over him, Edward feels weakened by the heat. The sky burns above the car with a blue intensity, so pure and ferocious it seems alive. At a stoplight beside Caesars Palace, he chances a glance at his daughter. Her profile is still and pensive, damp hair clinging to her neck like tentacles. He decides he cannot let her hateful words rest between them, that he must speak, must step into the role of father before it is too late and he is just another stranger.

"What's the matter, Helen?" He begins. "Is something wrong lately?" When she is quiet, he adds, "Are you and Leo having trouble?"

She turns to him, and he is startled for a moment by how much she looks like Kathy. It's the same sadness, he decides, that he's seen so often in his wife. Nothing so obvious as a furrowed brow or downturned mouth, only a certain, haunted glow about the eyes, that greenish gold that always makes him think of pond water. "Sweetheart," he says, "what is it? What's the matter?"

"It's . . ." She falters, then tries a second time. "It's Mom and—" She breaks off again and turns back to the window.

"It's Mom and what?" he asks her, worry climbing up his spine with cold deliberation.

"Nothing," she says, shaking her head. "Mom and I just aren't getting along very well lately. I guess it's bugging me."

"Well, that much is obvious," he says, with a certain glimmer of relief. "It's normal, I suppose. It's hard for her, watching you grow up."

"*Right*," Helen says, so sarcastically that it makes him cringe.

But they are almost home, and he can't think of how to counter this, his daughter's anger or despair. Is it ordinary teenage angst? As he turns onto their street, then pulls into their driveway, he tries to dredge up an image of himself at age sixteen. He was happy, wasn't he? The everyday details of his life seemed extraordinary, resonant with possibilities. Or is this just the way he imagines those days now? Those heavy Ohio summers when he roamed the streets with friends, worked part-time as a bagger at the local grocery, and spent at least an hour every evening wishing he could kiss a girl.

Helen leaps out of the car the moment he cuts the engine off, and Edward watches his daughter cross their small brick porch and go inside. Kathy has not yet made it home, and he wonders what is taking her so long. He thinks again of Helen in that wedding dress and knows that his daughter has done a lot more with Leo than he cares to imagine, enough to lead her toward that long white gown. She hasn't spent any amount of time, it seems to Edward, wishing she could kiss someone. It strikes him that these days so many kids miss out on the yearning one should have to go through, the months and maybe even years of hoping for a look, a touch, and then, at last, a kiss. He remembers when a kiss was the most he dared hope for, and it makes him laugh out loud in the car now when he thinks of the past three months of his own life, how he waited so impatiently to have sex with his wife.

His first kiss was awkward, as most first kisses probably are, he muses. A girl by the name of Rebecca Fructman led him out of a high school dance and leaned herself against a wall beneath him, waiting. It all happened so suddenly he was uncertain what to do. Then he gathered his resources, breathed deeply, and moved into the kiss with every ounce of grace he owned—which wasn't much—and then it was over, too quickly, and they were back in the gymnasium as if it had been an ordinary evening, except that it hadn't. He was changed for good.

There is a tap on his car window, and he looks up, startled, to see Kathy. He laughs again that she has found him sitting here, mooning over his past, and gets out of the car. Behind her, the lawn stretches out like a speckled carpet of green and brown, the cry of cicadas burning in the air around them. He can have a kiss anytime he wants now, can't he? Though when he thinks to lean toward her, to open his mouth over his wife's right here in the driveway, he knows she will most likely keep her lips tight or turn her face to the side. It has actually been a long time since they've shared more than a dry, closed press of lips. Even last night in bed, he realizes now, they did not kiss.

"What are you doing out here, sweating to death?" she wants to know.

"I think something's upsetting Helen," he tells her. "I was just trying to figure it all out."

She nods and says, "I've noticed too. Probably just the usual teenage things. She'll grow out of it."

"The other day, when I was buying your egg, I caught her trying on a wedding dress." There, he's said it. He is surprised at the amount of relief he has already begun to feel, just having given half the burden to Kathy.

She frowns and adjusts her sunglasses. "What the fuck is she up to?"

Edward takes a step backward at her language. He's never heard her use a word stronger than *damn* or *hell*. "*Kathy*." He half reprimands her.

"Sorry," she says. "This just upsets me."

"I know." He puts an arm around her and leads her toward the door. "I shouldn't have told you. It's probably nothing."

Helen brushes past them on their way inside. She is leaving. "I'm going to Leo's," she calls to them, and then the front door shuts, and he and Kathy are alone, the absolute quiet of the house falling over them like a reprimand or a warning.

BY THE NEXT DAY Edward is still in an agitated state, thinking of Helen in that dress, of Kathy with that glass of lemonade beneath the red umbrella, of Gerard sitting across from her. But wait, should he really be worried about Gerard? It seems impossible that Kathy could in any way be drawn to him. He isn't particularly attractive, though he knows some women like that rugged bulldog look he has. Obviously the man hasn't gone to college if he's working at a pool, and Kathy values education. She's a teacher, for Pete's sake!

In his car, leaving the driveway for work, he decides to take a detour this morning. He is early, as he usually is, and doesn't want to risk running into Camilla before class today, especially now that she's read the crazy note he wrote on her paper. Besides, he can feel the temptation of her growing; a small crevice of his mind has begun to carve out a space in which to think of her— that graceful wave, that hapless lazy eye of hers, the way she perched on his desk yesterday like a grateful and adoring bird.

He doesn't have a destination in mind, as he weaves out of his neighborhood, but finds himself driving away from the university toward the older section of the city, past the Huntridge Theater, across Charleston, into the network of neighborhoods and run-down shops that surround Las Vegas High School. When he reaches the school, Edward peers at it from the safe quiet of his car and finds it empty and barren as a ghost town. Schools always look so forlorn to him during their summer months. Next year Helen will be a senior there, and as this knowledge rattles through him, he wonders if he's done a decent job as father. Who knew that it would be so hard? Jenny of course will only be a sophomore, and this idea relieves, a little bit, the pressure that has begun to build up in his chest. Is he about to cry? To weep for his older daughter's leaving? When had he begun to grow so sentimental?

He passes the school and makes his way toward Las Vegas Boulevard. He drives by a bank, an A&W Root Beer, a gas station, all the stores that make Las Vegas just an ordinary place. Then he comes upon a wedding chapel and is jarred back into the city in which he really lives. As he passes the small white structure with its paint-chipped steeple, its garish stained glass window, its sign advertising that "Axel Rose was married here," Edward wonders what effect this town will have, has had already, on his daughters' lives. *His* formative years were spent in Ohio, so he is able to see the notion of marrying in one of these spindly, gaudy structures as bizarre. But perhaps Helen thinks it normal. Perhaps the idea of pledging your life unto another's is as flimsy to his daughter as these dilapidated chapels are. He has always thought he could protect her from the lesser values of this town, but maybe he has been fooling himself all along.

The next building beside the chapel has a familiar name, Buying Time. That's Leo's father's store, he realizes, and pulls automatically into an empty space against the curb and steps outside. He enters through the glass door into a narrow, musty room clogged with strange-looking clocks and inundated by the gigantic sounds of a Bach sonata. Leo is behind the counter, and he appears to be the only person in the store.

The boy reaches behind him to a radio and turns down the

music, then gives Edward a nervous smile. "Mr. Larkin, what are you doing here?"

"Nice choice of music," Edward says, and steps up to the counter. "Bach?"

"Actually it's Handel."

"Oh, I sometimes get the two confused. Of course I don't think I've ever heard Handel played quite so loudly."

"My father's on break, and it's the only time I can play music." He shrugs. "Sometimes I get a little carried away."

"I didn't know you liked classical so much."

"I like everything," Leo says, then amends this a bit. "Except reggae. That stuff bores me to tears."

They both are quiet for a moment, as Edward looks more closely at his surroundings. The store is absolutely depressing, and he feels for Leo, having to spend his days here in this dim place, while Helen is surrounded by water and palm trees, up in her designated throne.

"What are your intentions for next year?" Edward asks, turning back to Leo.

"I'm going to the university, on a Pell grant. Didn't Helen tell you?"

The fact is that she hasn't, but Edward says, "Oh, of course. I'd forgotten. That's pretty exciting."

He shrugs. "Better than this hole."

Edward gives Leo a sympathetic grimace, then takes a breath and quickly asks, "Are you and Helen planning to marry?"

Leo appears frightened by the question. He runs a hand through his shaggy hair, then shoves both fists into the pockets of his jeans. "Um, I don't know. I'd like to marry your daughter. I'd like to have what you and Mrs. Larkin do. Eventually, that is. I know it takes time to build."

Edward nods, half pleased and half worried by this answer. He's glad that his own marriage appears intact and healthy, desirable to the outsider, even though *he* knows its deeper fault lines: the affair he had last year; the wide berth Kathy has begun to steer between them. Or maybe these cracks were always there? "It's good to wait," he tells Leo, and realizes how feeble this must sound.

"I'm afraid if I wait too long," Leo confesses, "that she'll get away from me. You don't meet someone like your daughter every day."

Edward smiles and nods. He felt the same way about Kathy, though he was twenty-five at the time, instead of eighteen. She seemed like an angel to him, sitting in that lavender dress behind her typewriter in the admissions office, an unknowable, capricious angel—maybe even a *mercurial* one—but an angel just the same. And now who was she? Someone he loved, but still didn't really know. Seeing her yesterday at the pool beside Gerard reasserted this information in his mind. "I understand," he tells Leo, then says, "I'd better get going or I won't make it to my class on time."

They say good-bye. Then Edward walks back out into the heat, onto the barren, cracked sidewalk, this wedding chapel beside him a reminder of everything he thought his marriage might turn out to be, but hadn't. It's peeling paint and small, sagging porch seem to mock him, to tell him: *This is what your marriage really is; don't keep fooling yourself just because you were wed in a perfect Episcopal church beside a glowing field of corn.*

He walks the short distance over to the chapel, across its driveway and lawn until he is standing by a window that is not stained glass but clear. It even appears to be freshly washed. He cups his hands around his eyes and looks inside at what he assumes is some sort of waiting room. There is a desk with a secretary behind it; she is speaking to a young couple dressed in jeans and white T-shirts. Even though it is almost noon on a weekday, two other couples wait in line behind them. Obviously, Edward realizes, people are still anxious to wed, despite all the signs that marriage is a delicate and precarious institution.

The next pair in line are quite young, maybe even Leo's age. They hold hands while she fidgets with her miniskirt; the boy stares straight ahead as if in serene contemplation, or filled with an impending sense of doom. Behind them are an older couple, in their forties. Maybe it's a second marriage, or maybe—and here Edward allows himself a more hopeful thought—they both merely waited until they found the right person, the one with whom they were certain they could spend their entire lives. The man has his arm draped loosely around the woman's shoulders, not possessive or overly protective, just a gentle reminder of his presence. The woman's arm is slung around his waist, her head, from time to time, dipping onto his shoulder. They are a little haggard in appearance. A pack of cigarettes peers out of the man's breast pocket. She has one long run in her nylons, though from Edward's position it's possible this is a trick of light. Still, they are able to emanate a certain degree of happiness, of expectation.

The man looks over at Edward, and their eyes meet through the glass. Edward raises his hand in greeting, and the man returns the wave, causing his soon-to-be bride to also glance toward the window. Not wanting to create a spectacle—some lonely man peering through the window of a wedding chapel—Edward steps away from the building and wanders back toward the sidewalk.

Standing beside his car, Edward gazes up the length of Las Vegas Boulevard. Far ahead are the silhouettes of all the casinos that make up the Strip. Closer he can see more wedding chapels, sprinkled here and there along the road like pieces of old confetti. All along this street, he muses, people are getting married. He is standing close enough to Buying Time that he can hear the strains of classical music spooling from beneath the door and through the building's single window. It is a melancholy sound, muted as it is by the concrete wall of the store, by the patter of traffic on the street before him. Still, it causes Edward to feel a swelling in his chest, a lifting all along his spine, of either hope or resignation. He can't be sure.

Molting

HAVING SEX WITH GERARD is unlike anything Kathy has ever experienced. It is an acutely physical event, yet it's not. She thinks of it as a conversation between body parts, a dialogue that moves beyond mere limbs and skin and becomes a deeper, wordless speaking. However, neither of them actually talks during the act itself.

With Edward, Kathy will sometimes ask him to get his elbow off her hair or not to lean on her so heavily, but with Gerard she loses words, loses language itself, and sometimes, while they move together on his twin bed, she watches the spackled off-white ceiling over his shoulder with a sense of floating, a feeling that she has shed herself completely.

After he is done, he whispers in her ear. "Do you need more?" he often asks her. "Are you happy?" She has no idea how to answer these quiet queries. Is she happy? Such a gigantic question simply to find out if she's had an orgasm. Usually she smiles and nods, not daring to send out a solid answer, but for some reason this always prompts further attention. He makes his way across and down her body until she is lifted even closer to the ceiling, nearer to a new Kathy, a self at once familiar and completely unknown.

Later, if they have time, he sleeps. Kathy watches as his face goes slack against the blue curve of his pillow. He doesn't snore, but his breathing is loud because of allergies, and the lines across his forehead and around his eyes deepen, now that his features are not in motion. In these sleeping moments, he is older, more foreign and unknown, and it is during these twenty-minute naps that Kathy feels the guilt of cheating.

While he sleeps, she leaves his bedroom and roams the rest of his small house in search of a new object that will tell her more about Gerard. The first time they made love, she didn't dare move after they were finished. When he awoke, she used his bathroom and was startled by the array of photos taped onto the walls. At first she was appalled by all the people gazing at her as she sat down on the toilet, especially since an overwhelming number of the gazers were young women. But then Gerard, upon seeing her look of distaste as she exited the bathroom, led her back inside and explained that one wall was designated for photos of his family and one for his life at work. A sensible explanation—even an endearing one, she mused—that demystified and made innocuous the sunburst pattern on one wall of smiling young lifeguards and the rows of people who closely resembled Gerard staring out, almost mournfully, across from them.

This first glimpse into his world, made her desire more, and on Kathy's second visit to his house, she discovered a note taped to the refrigerator that said: "Don't forget to pick up Christy." She didn't ask him about it, but on their third day of lovemaking he told her about his daughter, Christy, and the relief she felt upon hearing this inadvertent explanation told Kathy she was more deeply involved in this affair than she'd previously realized.

On subsequent afternoons she found a bag of marijuana in a kitchen drawer—at least she thought that's what it was—a gold wedding band inside his medicine cabinet—one edge dented as if it had been thrown against a concrete wall, or ground into the floor with an angry heel?—and a Visa receipt for a NordicTrack, which has yet to materialize. Today she starts in the living room. She is naked, but the blinds are drawn, and as she wanders through the room, the thick orange carpet feels gritty to her feet. An antique cherry buffet behind a pair of navy easy chairs beckons to her, and she runs her palm along its smooth, dust-free surface, surprised Gerard has such a nice piece of furniture in an otherwise cardboard-quality house. She opens one of its drawers and sees a stack of papers, bills and receipts that Kathy deems uninteresting after a quick perusal. Before opening another drawer, she stops to listen for any sound of Gerard's waking, but the house is quiet except for the air conditioner's steady pulse. The next drawer appears to be empty, but as she pushes it closed, an object rolls from the drawer's back into her line of vision and

Kathy catches her breath at the sight of it; it is another egg. This one is a faceted crystal, and she takes it in her hand and holds it up to the muted light, watching as colors move through its depths, then spray a rainbow on the wall.

"My ex gave it to me." She hears Gerard's voice on the edge of the room.

Kathy can feel herself blush. "I'm sorry, I was just . . . um, looking for a pen."

"Don't look so nervous." He crosses the room and puts an arm around her naked shoulders. He is wearing boxer shorts now, and flip-flops. "It's not some sort of sacred artifact or anything."

She laughs and is on the verge of telling him about the recent egg from Edward, then thinks better of it.

"I remember thinking it was such a strange gift at the time, especially to give a guy, you know. But it grew on me. It's really pretty, isn't it?" He takes the egg from her hand and rolls it through his dark brown fingers.

"Yes, it is," Kathy murmurs.

Gerard opens a third drawer and pulls out a pen, which he hands to her. "Here you go."

She looks at the blue ballpoint and wonders what she can possibly do with this instrument in her naked state, without a shred of paper anywhere nearby. "Thanks," she says, then drops her arm at her side, clutching the pen as if it is indeed necessary.

"I've got to get back to the pool," Gerard tells her. "Do you want to come along and hang out?"

"I'd better not."

"Suit yourself," he says, then returns the egg to its drawer, takes Kathy's hand, and leads her back into the bedroom.

She begins to dress, pulling on her underwear beside a giant poster of Hawaii, which shows a man and woman silhouetted against a dying sun. A full-length mirror hangs on the wall across from her, and Kathy catches a glimpse of herself trying to step into her underwear, that causes her to feel a mild tremor of shame. In this bent-up position her breasts sway, and the extra flesh around her middle and hips she's been slowly gathering since she passed the age of forty remind her that she is no longer young, that she has a husband and daughters, another life outside this bedroom that needs tending. It's her turn to pick up Helen at the Dunes this evening, and by the time they get home, Edward and Jenny will already be there, waiting for Kathy to make them a meal, then to sit with them around the teak table that they've shared for many, many years.

Gerard sits on the bed, where he takes off his boxers, then pulls on his black swim trunks. "I like that bra," he tells her, nodding toward the purple, push-up lace contraption she's just donned. "Is it new?"

"No." She lies, and shakes her head, quickly pulling on her long skirt and sleeveless top before stepping back into her sandals. She moves to the window beside the bed and slats the blinds. The sun is high and hot with summer, a fact she has forgotten in this room's faded cool.

He is behind her suddenly, his bare, thickly tufted chest pressed against her summer blouse, his arms around her waist. "It certainly looks new to me."

At his touch, the guilt she's been feeling since they coupled spills out of her and dissipates into the room. Her blood reaches, warm and dark, for the surface of her skin and she whispers, barely audible even to herself, "Why did your ex-wife give you an egg?"

He breathes against her neck, and she thinks he hasn't heard her or that he doesn't want to answer, to speak of this woman from his distant past. At last he says, quietly and maybe with just a hint of sadness, a wistful, remembering voice that Kathy's never heard him use, "She never said this, but I think she always wished we'd had more children." The room settles quietly around them. Then Gerard asks her, "Where's that pen?"

Somehow, it is still in her hand, and she unfurls her palm and offers it to him over her shoulder. He takes it, then pulls down the collar of her blouse in back, and Kathy feels him printing on her skin.

"What are you doing?" she wants to know.

"Don't worry, your blouse will cover it. Just writing you a little note."

She holds still, and when he finishes, he kisses the back of her neck, then repositions her blouse.

IN THE CAR, driving home, Kathy thinks about Edward. He has never written a note on her back, never noticed a new bra, never asked her for more children. Sometimes the problem seems to be that he doesn't care to know her. Certainly he knows the old Kathy—the Kathy she was when he met her, working as a secretary at the university—but he doesn't know this other person she's become since then, the one who is evolving daily.

As she plunges back into the traffic of Maryland Parkway, the idea occurs to her that she's never really taken the time to know Edward either. She has never been curious enough about him to go seeking further than the surface level. When he's told her things, she's listened. Of course she's listened. The details of his childhood in Ohio unfold like a familiar story in her mind. She knows that his favorite color is olive green, that he likes Vivaldi and Bach and pickled mushrooms with Brie. But these details don't seem to illuminate the true depths of Edward. That is why, she supposes, she's begun snooping around at Gerard's. Not that she is preparing to make him into a husband, not at all, but he provides a practice ground of sorts, a new terrain on which she can wander an alternate route, discover what might work better than the life she's led up until now.

Her house is empty when she arrives, and she sets down her purse, takes off her sandals, then wanders the rooms as if they are completely new to her. In the bathroom, she removes her blouse, takes a hand mirror out of the cupboard, and turns her back to the larger mirror, using the smaller one to decipher what's been penned across her back. Gerard's writing is childlike in its blockiness, its choppy show of emotion, and she leans closer to the mirror behind her, trying to decipher what he's written, not an easy task because the writing is small and caught, here and there, in a dip of skin. After a moment, however, the message becomes clear: "I THINK THAT I MIGHT LOVE YOU."

She stares at the words for several seconds, holding her breath, then puts away the hand mirror and retrieves a washcloth from the bathtub. Wetting the cloth in the sink, she feels conflicted.

The idea that their affair might mean more than simple sex both elevates it—lessening Kathy's guilt—and lends it a level of seriousness she had hoped to avoid.

She does not love Gerard. She knows this. She might be able to, she decides, wringing out the cloth and adding a squirt of liquid soap, but avoiding that emotion altogether strikes her as the wisest line of action.

In fact, she made a promise to herself that first Sunday in June when she accepted his offer of coffee. They went to a small café on Maryland Parkway, across from the university, and during their conversation Kathy began to realize that she would eventually sleep with this man. Okay, she told herself, sex is permitted. Just don't fall in love.

Gerard was so appealing that day in the dim café, slow jazz notes unfolding in the air around them, students chattering at nearby tables about classes and dates and the drudgery of summer school. The place was a bit dingy and affected, with giant posters of writers and musicians covering the eggplant-colored walls like goddesses and gods, but all this added to Gerard's allure. Sitting directly across from the college where Edward spent his days, in Edward's domain really (he'd most likely gotten coffee here once or twice), Kathy was able to appreciate the absolute contrast between this man and her husband. And she liked this contrast; she liked it a lot.

Kathy was so weary of Edward's neatly pressed suits and clean-shaven face. So tired of his grammatical corrections of their daughters (and sometimes even her!) at the dinner table. The sight of him reading in bed every night, his pale limbs clad in striped pajamas as he sat propped against the headboard, was beginning to depress her, and she couldn't explain exactly why except that she was tired of seeing him there in the identical position every night; she was exhausted by the sameness of it all.

In Gerard there was such newness. Such brown skin and stubbled cheeks. A red Adidas T-shirt paired with swim trunks and flip-flops. He was well spoken, but far from perfect in his use of language, and Kathy could never imagine him correcting anybody. Also, something about him, some shimmering sexuality in his smile, told her that Gerard would not view the bedroom as a place for reading books.

At one point in their conversation that day, he took her hand across the table and said, "You know, I have chocolate chip ice cream at my house. Doesn't that sound good?" His invitation was as simple as that, the touch of his hand sending a school of goose bumps swimming up her arm.

Avoiding love seemed easy that first day. She was so nervous, his mouth on hers so foreign and awkward she almost called the whole thing off and went home right then, while all their clothing was intact. But then she eased into the feel of him somehow, closed her eyes, and allowed his brown hands to remove her blouse, then her skirt, and eventually she was lulled into a certain dreamy peace, the dark, cool bedroom soothing her nerves until she actually began to enjoy herself. So this is possible, she remembers thinking: sex without the burden of worries it usually entails.

Of course later, as she drove home, the worry overcame her, the guilt of what she'd just done causing her to pull her Honda down a side street and stop for several minutes beneath the curbside shade of a palm tree. Edward has already done this to you, she told herself, but that knowledge didn't slow the rapid patter of her pulse. It struck her as a grade school argument, tit for tat, and she leaned her forehead against the steering wheel and positioned the air vents so that cool blew over her hot face.

Eventually she pulled back into the street and headed home. This will be separate from my family, she reasoned. Whatever happens with Gerard will not have any effect—she wouldn't let it—on her relationships with Edward or Jenny or Helen. This will just be mine.

But now, sitting on the closed toilet lid with this note glowing on her neck, she understands that this separation isn't truly possible. Her time with him is beginning to seep into the life she shares with her family. She can feel the emotion generated by her afternoons with Gerard flooding out from under his stucco walls, making its way across town, down the hot asphalt of Maryland Parkway, then through the neighborhood to her own front door. Despite all this, Kathy can't bring herself to wash off the note. She drops the washcloth back in the tub, retrieves her blouse from the towel rack, and puts it back on. The action, or inaction of leaving the note where it is, feels reckless, and she continues roaming the house, encased now in an inexplicable haze of elation.

Helen's bedroom smells faintly of limes, and Kathy sits on her daughter's unmade twin bed and lets her eyes wander over the multicolored butterfly chair, the bookshelf and desk, the dresser with drawers half open, the strap of a black bra flopping out of one like a helpless insect limb. She hasn't been in this room in quite a while, and Helen would not approve of her sitting here now. Still, she stays where she is, pulling her legs up and crossing them beneath her skirt as she absorbs every detail that she can. On the white wicker nightstand beside the bed is a yellow notebook. Helen's birdlike print has marked the cover: "Private, please don't read." There is no lock, only her daughter's flimsy warning, and Kathy takes the book in her hand and gazes down at it. It must be a diary, she muses, and the idea that she could read it, with no one's being the wiser is extremely tempting. She sets it beside her on the purple sheets, then stands and looks down at it. What would be the harm?

With one fingernail, she flips it open to a page deep in the interior, then moves away before she can see what's inside and walks across the room. Through a bank of windows, set genteelly over a window seat Helen never uses, Kathy has a view of the mulberry tree and dying grass of their backyard. A hummingbird feeds at the red bottle of syrup they have hung on a tree limb for just that purpose, and Kathy watches the small, quickly beating body for a moment before she takes a breath and wanders back to the bed.

The two pages visible of the opened journal are blank, except for a single word, printed in blue ink and ended with a giant question mark. "MARRIAGE?" Quickly she shuts the book and sets it back on the nightstand. Marriage? Helen is only sixteen. Such a word does not belong in her vocabulary, and Kathy worries afresh about Edward's seeing Helen trying on a wedding dress.

Should she ask Helen what's going on? Should she risk infringing on her daughter's privacy? Kathy sits down again, this time in the canvas butterfly chair, and ponders how she can talk to her daughter about Leo. Lately Helen's been hostile, and Kathy can't tell if this is just her teenage self fully emerging or if she knows about Gerard. She should not have spent so many hours with him at the pool while Helen watched the water. But Helen knows they're friends. At least that's how Kathy has justified these forays to herself. And isn't that what friends do? Hang out and have a conversation?

She leans her head back with a sigh and ponders the ceiling. What on earth, she wonders, did she think she was doing, sitting there lusting after the pool manager in full view of everyone?

AT FIVE O'CLOCK Kathy drives to the Dunes to pick up Helen. She waits in the parking lot, watching the baked white walls of the hotel as pop music floats over her and artificial air tries to provide the illusion that maybe it is cool outside. The radio announcer dispels this myth by announcing the current temperature: 105 degrees.

It is fifteen minutes past five now, and Kathy begins to wonder where Helen is. Her own need to walk onto the pool deck, where she knows Gerard is sitting right this second beneath his red umbrella, has been building as she waits here. It's only been two and a half hours since she lay beside him in his cool green grotto of a bedroom, and still, this yearning to see him one more time today threatens to overtake her wiser notions of propriety. She fidgets with the radio dial, trying to find a decent song, but nothing sounds appealing, so she shuts it off and sits in silence, waiting. Other employees exit the building, stepping out into bright sun in their maroon polo shirts and white shorts or pants, donning sunglasses and lighting cigarettes on the short walks to their cars. A white limousine enters the lot and does a long, slow circle of its perimeter before parking at the curb by the casino door. Its dark, unreadable windows give Kathy the feeling she is being watched.

At twenty-five minutes after five Kathy decides she'd better go and see what Helen's up to. The pool deck is still teeming with people, who now swim at their own risk since both lifeguard chairs are empty. Even the space beneath Gerard's umbrella is vacant, but Kathy walks over there anyway, worry beginning to build beneath her collarbone and rise into her throat. She sits in his chair beside the lectern and scans the deck for someone familiar. A cocktail waitress approaches her, then retreats back into the maze of lounge chairs, as if signaling to Kathy that she does not belong. A girl in a black one-piece slinks through a crowd of people on the far edge of the pool, and Kathy stands and waves, certain it is Helen; but then the girl turns to face her, and it is so obviously not her daughter that Kathy can't understand how she'd made such a mistake.

She sits again and is almost ready to cry—in fact, a tear has slid out beneath her sunglasses—when she feels hands on her shoulders and hears Gerard's voice near her ear. "Twice in one day. How'd I get so lucky?"

She shrugs him away, worried someone has seen this brief symbol of their intimacy, then swivels toward him. "Where's Helen?"

"She left with Miles awhile ago. She told me it was okay with you, that you weren't picking her up today." He shrugs and shows her his pale palms, as if to say *it's not my fault*.

"*Okay* with me? Of course it's not okay with me, and I especially don't like the idea that she's off somewhere with Miles."

"He's a good kid. Don't worry."

"A good kid? Do you know that this boy is quite a bit older than my daughter and that he once kept her out half the night at Lake Mead doing who knows what?" She stands and runs a hand through her hair with an angry huff of air.

"Kathy," Gerard soothes. "settle down. She's probably already home waiting for you."

"How would you feel if Christy did such a thing? Left with some strange man?"

Gerard laughs, and she feels a blistering urge to slap him in the face or knee his groin, something painful and dramatic that would quell his laughter, erase his nonchalance. "First of all," he tells her, "Miles is hardly some strange man. He's worked here for years, and I trust him a great deal. Secondly, Christy is practically a woman, much like Helen, and can do as she pleases, as far as I'm concerned."

"A woman." Kathy rolls her eyes beneath her giant sunglasses. "She's still in high school, for Christ's sake." It is unclear even to her, whether she is referring to Helen or Christy, but the difference seems negligible since they are both indeed in high school.

"Have a seat," Gerard says, gesturing to the chair she just rose from. "I'll get us a drink." He raises his hand to beckon the waitress, but Kathy bats it down.

"Don't bother," she tells him. "I have to go find Helen."

They are both silent for a moment, watching each other, and Kathy wonders if the affair is about to end, if one argument is all it takes to nullify such a new and strange relationship. The boundaries are murky, and even as Kathy tells him, "I can't believe you let her leave like that," she knows it is the wrong thing to say.

"Kathy, it's not like I'm her father or something."

His response spirals her back into her skin, places her more firmly on this pool deck, encased in this 105-degree heat, standing before a man with a lazy surfer smile and shaded eyes whom she had sex with less than three hours ago. Gerard reaches for her hand, but she backs away and says, "I have to go."

On her way across the pool deck toward the exit door, Kathy can feel Gerard's gaze puncturing the back of her blouse and reaching skin—the skin he's written on—and she has to hold her breath and listen to her clicking sandals on the pavement in order not to turn around and run to him.

When Kathy arrives home an unfamiliar truck sits in the driveway and she is forced to park at the curb. The truck's interior is cluttered with Slurpee cups and tape cases, and a lone tube of hair gel sits pink and sizzling on the dashboard. Stepping into the cool of her house, Kathy hears Helen's laughter silvering the air around the kitchen, and she walks across the entry hall toward the sound with a mixture of relief and anger braiding through her bones.

Miles sits at the kitchen table. Helen hovers near him, leaning on the counter in just her bathing suit, sipping languidly from a can of Coke. The scene is innocent enough, except that to Kathy's eyes Helen seems half naked and Miles's gaze betrays his sexual interest in her daughter. At the sight of Kathy on the kitchen's threshold, Miles sits up straight, then goes one better and stands, reaching out a hand. "Hello, Mrs. Larkin," he says with a smile.

She takes his hand reluctantly and murmurs a soft hello. Helen is locked into her same insolent position against the counter, and Kathy turns to her now, unable to rein in a frown. "I was worried about you," she tells her.

"We got off early." She shrugs. "So I figured it was no big deal if Miles drove me home. I tried to call, but you obviously weren't here to answer."

There is a hint of accusation in her daughter's tone, though what she is being accused of is unclear. "I don't know what you're talking about," Kathy says. "I've been home since two o'clock." Kathy turns to Miles now. "Would you please excuse us? I need to talk to Helen about something."

"Oh, sure." He pushes in his chair in an effort to neaten the table, which strikes Kathy as decidedly polite. Perhaps she has misjudged this boy?

"Miles, you don't have to go," Helen tells him. "Just wait outside for me. We can still go to the lake."

"No"—Kathy gives Helen a firm and angry head shake—"you are absolutely not going to the lake."

"I'd better head home anyway," Miles says, backing toward the kitchen door. "I'll take a rain check, Hell. All right?"

Helen shrugs but makes no further attempt at protest; she remains silent, eyes downcast, until they hear the front door open and then close.

They face each other in the kitchen, both standing beside the counter. Helen takes a long, loud swallow of Coke, and Kathy fights the urge to bat the can out of her daughter's hand. "What's this all about?" Kathy asks her.

"What do you mean?"

"Well, for starters you've been extremely rude to me as of late. Today is merely one example. And what are you doing spending so much time with Miles? Isn't Leo still your end-all, be-all of creation?"

"I thought you didn't want me to be so serious with just one guy," Helen says.

She tries to recall saying this and does. Long ago, it seems now, on a winter afternoon they sat eating soup at this kitchen table and Kathy attempted to dispense wise, motherly advice. "Well, that's true. But I don't like not knowing where you are."

"I don't always know where *you* are."

"That's different, and you know it."

Silence settles over them again, and Kathy worries that Helen will leave before they've finished what's begun, that she'll be left with the remains of two unfinished arguments, smoldering like stoked ashes in the curved base of her stomach. Gerard's words seep again into her mind: *Kathy, it's not like I'm her father.* Is that what makes him so attractive? The fact that he is not linked to this life?

"Mom," Helen says at last, "I know what's going on."

"What do you mean?" Kathy asks, worry beginning to flutter through her rib cage. She looks down at her nails, spreading her hand out on the counter, then decides she'd better meet her daughter's gaze.

"I saw you." Helen's face begins to redden, the way it does right before she cries, but then she shakes her head, as if to clear it, and continues. "I saw you at Gerard's. I know what's going on."

Kathy cannot speak, does not know what to say. Reflexively she covers the back of her blouse where Gerard's note rests with the palm of her hand as her mind ranges over every time she's been with Gerard, seeking any moment when she may have carelessly stepped into view. There *was* a minute once, the second time she went over to his house. After having sex, she dressed, then wandered into the kitchen, and there was the transient idea that someone was nearby, at the windows maybe, but she was fully dressed and merely eating ice cream, and the windows were glazed with light, so she couldn't have gotten a clear view from where she stood even if she dared look. By the time Gerard wandered out, naked and warm from his nap, she was lulled back into a certain complacent happiness, an emotion that right now shimmers in the distance as something she will never feel again.

"Aren't you going to say anything?" Helen wants to know.

"I told you before," Kathy says quietly, "that he and I are friends."

"*Friends*," Helen repeats, with obvious disbelief, with such an air of disdain Kathy knows she must amend her statement, explain whatever Helen saw so that it transforms itself into a benign vision, not the blistered picture of her mother she now sees.

"It's not what you think," Kathy tells her daughter. "Besides," she adds now, lifting her posture so that she is almost as tall as

Helen, "it's not your concern. I'm the mother. I'm the one who's supposed to worry about *you,* not the other way around." She attempts a smile.

Helen frowns and looks down at the floor. "Whatever you say," she says quietly, then walks past Kathy out of the kitchen.

The sound of Helen's bedroom door clicking quietly closed worries Kathy more than a slam would. It gives their argument more solemnity and truth, less heat-of-the-moment irrationality. She pulls out the chair Miles rose from, only ten minutes ago now, and collapses into it, dropping her face into her hands as she prepares to cry, but her eyes remain aching and dry, pained by the overhead light and waning sun coming in through the windows over the sink. Her giant black sunglasses sit on the counter, and she rises and puts them on, then opens the fridge, pulls out vegetables and chicken, and begins preparing dinner in the newly muted light.

IN BED THAT NIGHT, Kathy is wakeful, listening to Edward's breathing in an attempt to decide whether or not he is asleep. She pictures Helen on the other side of the house, strewn languidly across her twin bed, sleeping the dreamless, peaceful sleep of someone who has released a burden, shed an accusation that must have been constructing itself inside her for a while now, at least a month, maybe more? Kathy has been sleeping with Gerard for five weeks, but before that there were signs, of course there were signs, that they cared for each other. And her daughter was there to witness everything: Kathy's visits to the pool; the way her voice tended to get girlish and high in his presence (why hadn't she been able to control that?); her frequent laughter as they spoke, laughter that must've carried easily across the water to her daughter, high up in that queenlike chair.

Helen was quiet at dinner, eating little, then asking to be excused before anyone else finished. Leo picked her up at eight, then returned her at ten, and Helen made no mention to anyone—not even Jenny—about what transpired in her time away from home. Kathy knows, as she lies here beneath the silent ceiling, that her daughter is having sex, and now Kathy cannot even counsel or accuse her with any sort of authority. What right does an adulterer have to judge another?

Beside her, Edward releases a small cough, and Kathy turns toward him, onto her side, grateful that he's still awake. "Edward?" she asks quietly.

"Mmm?"

"Helen's upset with me, and I can't sleep."

His eyelids tremble and then open before he turns onto his side to face her. "What is she upset about?"

Here's her chance, she thinks, to release herself into the darkness, to tell her husband everything she's been doing wrong this summer. But he waits for her answer with such a gentle serenity settled into his features, the remains of sleep, she supposes, that she can tell him nothing. Besides, what would be the point? To make herself feel better? To cause him pain? "I don't know why she's angry with me," Kathy says at last.

"I have an idea why," he says.

She holds her breath, waiting for the second accusation of the day.

"She probably doesn't like it when you spend time at the Dunes. It's her territory, you know? I have to admit, it was a bit strange seeing you there myself the other day."

A cooling feeling of relief closes over her. He doesn't know. "I'm not there very often," she explains. "Once in a while I get there early, but that's all."

"I know, but she's a teenager. Remember what it was like to be sixteen? I'm sure you didn't want your mother anywhere near you."

Kathy tries to picture her mother during her own sixteenth year but can only recall an image of her sitting on a car hood, smoking, a red scarf covering her hair, cat-eyed sunglasses glinting rhinestones. It is a picture disembodied from time, and it lulls her for a moment, into a separate, more familiar pain, one that runs through her every couple of months since her mother died two years ago.

Edward has closed his eyes again, and in the blue light shed by the electric clock over his shoulder, she watches as he makes his way back toward sleep. Outside, she can hear cicadas vibrating in the August air, and she feels a stirring through her limbs, a call for contact, so she leans across the sheets and kisses Edward on the shoulder, then moves closer and presses the length of her body, still sheathed in its nightgown, against her husband's naked frame. He opens his eyes and smiles, then pulls her nightgown up and over her head before he rolls on top of her. She worries for a moment that he'll see Gerard's note, still scrawled across her back, but he makes no attempt to alter their positions, and she tries to ease into the movement and forget about what's written on her skin.

They have no need for birth control. Edward had a vasectomy long ago, after Jenny was born, and Kathy has found out from her forays with Gerard that she actually likes the feel of the condom between them; the thin barrier protects the need she has to keep her body separate. The idea that nothing rests, at this moment, between herself and Edward, that his very skin is swallowed by her own, unnerves her, causes her to experience, once again, the raw, wide-open feeling that she always does when having sex with him. But she does nothing to stop his rhythm; she'll finish what she's begun. She owes him this at least. Kathy puts her hands on her husband's shoulders and looks up into his face. *I'm sorry*, she tries to tell him, with her eyes, with the movement of her hips. *I'm sorry.*

IN THE MORNING Kathy drives her daughter to work, a sullen silence resting between them. This silence, however, is hardly new, and Kathy can almost allow herself to believe that Helen doesn't really know about the affair. Outside their car, the sky has turned an unusual gray-blue, and clouds pile up on the mountains to their right. As Kathy turns the car onto the Strip, lightning stencils the sky before them, giving her an excuse to turn to Helen. "You probably won't have to work today," she says. "Looks like a storm is almost here."

Helen shrugs. "I don't have anything else to do."

"We could do something together. Go shopping. Eat lunch. I don't know, whatever you'd like."

Helen turns to her now, and Kathy can see, from the red

spidering through her eyes, that she didn't get much sleep last night either. "I'd prefer to go to work," is all she says.

"You know, I always thought it was a treat to spend the day with my mother."

"*Your* mother wasn't fooling around with *your* boss."

"*Helen*, you are not to talk to me that way, no matter what you think you know."

Her daughter looks out the window so that Kathy can no longer see her face, only a solitary shoulder covered by her waterfall of hair. She glances back to the road and stops at a red light, beside the fountains outside Caesars Palace. When she was a young woman, Evel Knievel tried to jump his motorcycle over these very fountains and failed. At the time she thought the feat daring and romantic, but now it strikes her as just incredibly foolish. What mechanism in her brain has so thoroughly managed to change her perception of the world?

"Well," Helen finally says, continuing to look out the window, "maybe I won't talk to you at all then."

"Honey"—Kathy tries a different tack—"please don't act this way. You know how much I love you."

"Then why don't you tell me the truth?"

Kathy ponders this a moment. Maybe she should tell her. Isn't that in keeping with the moral outlook she's tried to bestow upon her daughters? But when she imagines the actual words emerging from her mouth—*You're right, Gerard and I are having an affair*—the damage to the air around them, between them now in this claustrophobic car, strikes her as immense, unfixable, an overwhelming mistake from which their relationship would not recover. "I have already," Kathy says at last, then stares straight ahead at the approaching sign of the Dunes Hotel, as more lightning carves its reckless way across the sky.

AT NOON the phone rings, and Kathy picks it up at once, expecting to hear Helen's voice since it has been raining for an hour now. Instead, Gerard's dark, varied tones seep into her ear. "I closed the pool," he hums. "Are you free?"

She can't decide whether to be angry—he's never called her at home before—or grateful for any form of human contact. "Did Helen leave again with Miles?" Kathy asks.

"Yes. I'm glad she told you this time." He laughs, then adds, "Sorry about our little misunderstanding yesterday. I was hoping I could make it up to you today?"

"Um." She is standing in the kitchen and turns to look now out at the backyard, which is being beaten down by rain. The house collects itself around her as if it means to attach itself to her skin, drain away her will to breathe. "Okay. I'll be at your place in half an hour."

She imagines she can hear him smile, the almost dimple in his left cheek creasing in against the phone's receiver. "I can't wait," is all he says, and then there is a click.

"HELEN KNOWS about us," Kathy tells him on the doorstep. Rain slants against her back, and Gerard pulls her inside with a frown.

"You're getting wet," he tells her. "We'd better get those clothes off." He smiles and draws close to kiss her neck before leading her down the hallway to his bedroom.

"Didn't you hear me?" Kathy asks, stepping into his room and sitting on the edge of his bed.

He nods, then taps his mouth, something he does, she's noticed, when he's not sure what to say. "I thought she might."

"What? Why?"

"One day I thought maybe I saw her through the kitchen window, but it was so quick and the sun was glaring that I figured I'd made it up, so I didn't want to worry you. Besides, you've seen how she acts around me at work now. Of course she's never been exquisitely charming toward me or anything, so that doesn't mean much, does it?" He tries out a laugh; but Kathy can't even return a smile, and she watches as his face shifts into solemnity.

"I told her that it wasn't true," Kathy says quietly. "I told her we were only friends. So I think I'd better change things so that's the case."

"Kathy." He moves to sit beside her on the bed. "Kathy," he murmurs again, leaning to kiss her neck as he runs fingers down her spine, through her cotton blouse, then reaches beneath the waistband of her skirt, in pursuit of skin, which he finds quickly. His hand is warm against her chilled tailbone, and she automatically leans into him, wanting nothing more than to shed these awkward, rain-damp garments and slide beneath his sheets. Lust is so new to her she imagines it might represent some deeper feeling, one she can't yet qualify with words. Could she love him? Kathy wonders, as they begin to molt out of their clothes, like locusts, she thinks, watching the dark brown of his chest emerge from beneath a red T-shirt. She puts her paler hands against his skin and wonders whether or not she's ever even loved Edward. Surely, she has never wanted to unpeel and shed her skin for him, as she wants to for Gerard.

"Let's not use anything today," he whispers. "I just got tested, and I'm sure you're nothing less than pristine."

She laughs, thinking he sounds like a teenage boy, bartering for something he has no right to ask for. "I don't think so," she says.

"Oh, come on. When's your period? Aren't you close?"

Actually, she's supposed to start tomorrow, but he doesn't need to know this. In fact, she is a bit appalled he'd even ask. "That's none of your business," she tells him.

She suspects he will not push the issue, and he doesn't, smiling at her and raising his eyebrows as if to say, *Well, you can't blame me for trying*, before he turns to the dresser beside his bed and retrieves a condom.

They are slow today, their movements matching the languorous patter of rain against the window, the Hawaii poster over Gerard's shoulder aglow with the storm's strange light. The note on her back was erased in this morning's shower, but Kathy knows it is still there, between them, as they move together on his sheets, deepening the meaning of their shared rhythms, imbuing the afternoon with a purple-blue shadow of possibility, the glimpse of another life Kathy could choose to lead. When they are finished, the shadow has dissipated, and as she lies beside this man, watching his face go soft with sleep, she decides she had better leave and not return again if she wants the lie she's told her daughter to become truth. She dresses quietly beside the bed, anxious now to be back in her clothes, to become the self she knows. He doesn't stir as she lets herself out of the bedroom, then out of the house into the rain.

HELEN COMES HOME LATE, after they have eaten dinner, after the storm has ended and the strangely humid night has made it pleasant on the porch, a rarity in August. Kathy sits on the front step outside their house, waiting. She has lied to Edward and Jenny that she knows where Helen is, that she went out with Kathy's permission and will simply be home later. When she arrives, Kathy has no idea what she will say to her daughter; she knows only that she needs to speak to her, to clean up the debris that has piled up between them. As she sits here, her insides skitter between anger and worry, leaving her to wonder which emotion will win out when Helen finally arrives.

Miles's truck pulls up to the curb after nine o'clock, and Kathy watches as her daughter says good-bye—no kiss or touch passing between her and this boy—then steps out of the high cab and crosses the lawn. The porch light is off, so that when Helen reaches Kathy, she stops short, obviously surprised to find her sitting here in the dark.

"Hi," is all Kathy says.

"Hi," Helen returns, continuing to stand before her.

She is still such a child, Kathy sees now, with her long, awkward limbs and turned-in knees, so much hair drifting out around her face and narrow shoulders she is lost in it. This week her daughter seemed to take on larger dimensions, to become an adult in Kathy's mind, an equal capable of casting judgment, and she is relieved to find her not so changed, after all, from the person she has always known.

"Have a seat," Kathy says, and Helen sighs, then drops down beside her on the porch step.

"So, I suppose I'm in huge trouble," Helen says.

"No." Kathy shakes her head. Cicadas throb in the soft air around them; otherwise the street is still. The sky is clear now, and Kathy searches for Venus, usually visible from this angle, but tonight she fails to find it. In fact, the stars are faint, only pale scratchings of light through the elm trees on their lawn. "Where have you been?" she asks at last.

"Just driving around. Talking to Miles."

"Talking?"

"*Yes*." Anger shivers through her voice, then subsides. "Talking."

"About what?"

Helen is quiet. Kathy chances a glance at her profile and is shocked, for a second, by the sensation of looking at herself as a teenager. In profile, and in this dim light, their differences of feature and coloring are indistinguishable. A summer night, when she was just sixteen, floats to her through her daughter's profile, fully formed: Her father had been dead for over a year, and her mother was out on a first date, the first date she attempted since his death; Kathy sat waiting on the porch, trying to decide whether or not she hated her mother. When the car pulled up, and her mother stepped out into the street in her pink summer dress, her foot faltered on its heel and she fell to the asphalt. In that second any hatred Kathy harbored was erased. She ran to her, down the lawn out into the spray of streetlight before her mother's date was even out of the car, and helped her rise. Maybe she should do something dramatic like that now, she thinks with an inward smile, throw herself supine on the street, or climb a tree and fall, force the moment to its peak.

"We were talking," Helen says at last, "about the fact that Leo has asked me to marry him."

Kathy nods, then asks, "Do you want to marry him?"

"I don't think so, but I'm not sure." She shrugs. "Are you going to forbid me to see him now?"

Kathy detects a certain degree of hope in her daughter's voice and smiles. "That would make things easier, wouldn't it?"

"Maybe. Maybe not."

"No, I'm not going to forbid you to see him. I know you'll do what's best." Even as she says this, she's uncertain if it's true. Why wouldn't Helen run off in the middle of the night for love? Wouldn't she herself have done so? No, actually she wouldn't have. The idea of it frightens her even now.

"How do you know I'll do what's right?"

"I just trust you, that's all," she tells her. The words drift between them, and Kathy wishes she could call them back; they strike her, on the open air, as an indictment of her own half-truths. Before Helen can seize upon the idea of trust, reaccuse her of sleeping with Gerard, Kathy rises and brushes off her skirt. "Let's go inside," she says, and Helen stands and follows without another word.

THE NEXT DAY Kathy's period does not arrive. She tries to tell herself that this is not unusual, as she drives Helen to work, cleans the house, reads, makes dinner for her family, but she knows it is. Her body has always been punctual, and as she sits at the kitchen table that night, after everyone else is in bed, she wonders whether she is pregnant or if menopause has struck with sudden cruelty. Is she experiencing any of its other signs? There have been no night sweats, no headaches. What else is she to look for? She has no idea, and isn't she still too young for this to touch her?

She rises from the kitchen table, turns off the light, then pours herself a glass of chardonnay in the refrigerator's anemic glow before returning to her place at the table. Light from the sky still slides through the kitchen windows as she sips her wine, waiting for the alcohol to move into her limbs with soothing darkness.

When she goes to bed, Edward is asleep, so she carefully places herself beside him. The cinnabar egg he gave her several weeks ago, sits on her nightstand, and Kathy reaches for it, takes its small carved body into her hands, and holds it until she falls into a state that she can't call sleep, but merely a more subdued and dream-crowded state of wakefulness.

Two

THE NIGHT IS WARM AND SILENT as Helen steps out onto the back patio in her summer robe, the filled-up condom cupped lightly in her hand. As she makes her barefoot way across the grass to the garbage can beneath the clothesline, she decides it must be 2:00 A.M. at least, hours from dawn, though the light from the moon is more than enough to reveal her presence, if anyone—Jenny, her father, or her mother—were to rise and look out the back windows of the house.

The garbage can is full, ready to be picked up on Wednesday, and Helen doesn't want to drop the condom right on top, so she removes a few of the tied-up plastic bags, preparing to nestle her evidence in the dark space below. Leo wanted to know, reasonably so, why she couldn't just flush it down the toilet, but their house is old by Las Vegas standards, with unpredictable plumbing, and she has fears of a family member's waking to find it floating in the bowl like some sort of artificial jellyfish, waiting to indict her for the crime of secret sex.

When she bends to place the condom in the garbage, she is stopped by the sight of a thin cardboard box. Leaning back a little, so that her shadow doesn't darken the words across its face, she reads "EPA Home Pregnancy Test." Quickly she shoves the condom between two bags and retrieves the box, shaking out the contents into her palm for inspection. The plastic spoon-shaped monitor has definitely been used, but Helen doesn't know how to interpret the results, and the directions are nowhere to be found. Is the person who hid this pregnant or not?

Her first thought is that it's Jenny's, though she's only been seeing this new boy, Ryan, for two weeks. Then the idea that it might be her mother's rises inside her throat, choking her and causing Helen to drop the box back where she found it. She covers the test with the bags of trash, then clamps the lid back on the can and looks across the lawn at the dark windows of her parents' bedroom, at her sister's panes, and then to her own window, where she thinks she sees the outline of hair, the glow of a turning shoulder. Is Leo watching her? She waves, just in case, then makes her careful way back across the lawn, aware for the first time that the night is not quiet at all. Rather, it is crowded with the cries of cicadas, a noise she has grown so accustomed to it has ceased to register as a sound.

IN HER TWIN BED, Leo sleeps on his back, the soft hum of his breathing a comfort to Helen as she removes her robe and curves herself around him. She wants so much to simply close her eyes and join him in sleep; but his presence is a danger, and she knows she must get him dressed and back out the window before anyone wakes up.

"Leo." She says his name softly, into the smooth skin of his chest, but he is instantly awake.

"Sorry," he whispers. "I didn't mean to fall asleep."

"You have to go."

Surprisingly, he offers no objections, merely sits up, rubs his eyes, then hops off the bed to gather his clothes from the floor. He dresses without a word. There is a large window beside her bed, and Helen rises to her knees on the sheets and opens it for his escape. This is the first time he's been in her room at night, and she can feel a thin fearful sweat collect across her back and arms as she waits for him to go.

Leo crawls across the bed, then hangs one leg out the window before turning to her with an unexpected smile. This has been a gift for him, she sees. Not the sex, but the risk she has taken having him here. "Dream about me," he says, then kisses her and steps out into the night.

INSTEAD, she dreams about her mother, round and heavy with child as she paddles around the swimming pool at the Dunes Hotel, Gerard watching her from beneath his red umbrella with all the contentment of a future father.

In the car the next morning, Helen glances across the seat at her mother's middle, looking for any signs of widening. It's been two weeks now since Helen accused her of sleeping with Gerard, and there has been so little evidence since then to support her claim Helen's begun to think her mother has ended the affair. Or is it possible she has been wrong all along? The memory of her mother standing barefoot in Gerard's kitchen eating ice cream, Gerard's brown, naked form huddled at her mother's back, has begun to take on the haziness of a dream, and sometimes she has trouble convincing herself of what she really witnessed.

"What are you looking at?" Her mother wants to know as she turns the car onto the Strip.

"Nothing."

"Is there something on my shirt?" Her mother looks down at her stomach and brushes it off.

"No." She watches the casinos pass her window for a moment, the mountains carved out behind them like a promise of the real, something tangible and nature-made, unlike these flimsy, neon-studded structures all around them. "Have you ever thought of having another baby?" Helen asks.

"What? Don't you think your father and I are a little old for that?" Her mother laughs, but the laugh sounds forced to Helen, and a little nervous.

"Lots of women have children way into their forties now. Don't they?"

"I suppose so."

"So why not you and Dad?"

Her mother doesn't look at her, but Helen thinks she detects a tensing of her fingers on the steering wheel. "Well, first of all, you and your sister are more than enough to handle. Besides, I'm practically on the verge of menopause."

"What's that?"

"I forget sometimes," her mother says, shaking her head with a smile, "how young you are."

"Oh, menopause. I know what you're talking about." And she does. Suddenly the word swims up with familiarity in her mind. "Don't some women go crazy when that happens?"

Her mother laughs. "Then I must be in the midst of it already," she says, before turning on the radio and ending the discussion.

MILES IS OUT in the parking lot when they pull in, drinking from a plastic container of orange juice as he leans against the wall by the door. When Helen emerges from the car, he raises the bottle in a small salute and gives her a smile that she can't quite interpret.

"What are you doing out here?" she wants to know when she reaches him.

"Waiting for you, little fiancée."

He has begun calling her that since she told him of Leo's proposal, and Helen is beginning to regret confiding in him since he has made the idea of her marriage to Leo into a joke. Inside the cool hallway that leads them to the pool, Miles pulls her elbow and brings her around to face him, then leans to kiss her on the mouth. Nothing physical has passed between them since the night, two months ago now, when she had sex with him at Lake

Mead, and she's not sure how she wants to respond to this kiss, so at first she does nothing, merely allows her mouth to sit quietly beneath his own. But in a second she is responding without thinking, enjoying, for a moment, the cool orange taste of him, before guilt seeps in and she pushes him away. "What's this all about?" she asks.

"What do you mean?" He smiles down at her.

A couple with a white sheepdog appears through the entrance to the pool and approaches them; the woman, shaking her head beneath a giant pair of white sunglasses, says, "Imagine, not allowing dogs around the pool. Did you *see* some of those *people*?" The man, bronzed and tall with no muscle definition anywhere on his Speedo-clad body, does not respond.

Helen and Miles are quiet until the couple has passed them and exited into the parking lot; then, at the same moment, they begin to laugh. This time, when Miles bends to kiss her, she decides not to worry about the meaning behind his attentions; in fact, she wants to try not to worry about anything at all.

Of course this is not something she is really capable of doing. In the chair she watches the pool, trying to ignore Gerard, who sits in his usual spot beneath the umbrella, writing a postcard. Miles sits in the other lifeguard chair, presiding over the larger pool, and Helen watches him for a moment, noting the way he has draped his body across the chair with the utmost confidence, slouching low in the seat with one leg thrown over an armrest. His posture seems to say: *This job is easy for me. Go ahead and drown. Saving you is a simple problem.* Helen tries to imagine Leo up in a lifeguard chair and decides that he would sit exactly the same way as Miles is right now, but the ruse of his confidence would be apparent. His unease would seep through somehow, maybe in a tapping foot or drumming fingers. The image makes her smile, and she recalls with a warm rush of blood the sight of his white body beneath her last night in bed, as she moved over him, listening with half of herself for the sound of footsteps in the sleeping house.

Ernie, the new girl (Helen still thinks of her this way despite the fact that she's worked here for almost three months now), is on vacation this week, a fact for which Helen is grateful, because ever since Miles broke up with Ernie, a month or so ago, she has looked at Helen with cold disdain, obviously blaming her for his departure. Helen has wanted to speak to her about it, to explain the situation, but she doesn't even understand it all herself, so has simply avoided saying anything. This strikes her now as cowardly, and as she leans back in her chair, the sun burns into her shoulders with such ferocity she interprets it as punishment for her unspoken sins.

A spray of water reaches her from below, wetting her bare feet with sudden cool, and Helen looks down to find a mother and her daughter, who is most likely eight or nine, floating together on a raft.

"Sarah, apologize for splashing the lifeguard," her mother says.

But before the little girl has raised her face, Helen calls down, "I don't mind being splashed. The water feels good."

"See," the girl tells her mother. "I knew she was hot."

They float past her, the mother waving once to Helen, then looking back down at her daughter. A line from a poem Helen read last night floats into her mind: "Your whole life you are two, with one taken away." In her butterfly chair the previous evening, she interpreted this as a line strictly meant for lovers and tried to conjure the feeling of deep and abiding attachment it suggested as she allowed Leo to sneak into her room. But now she decides that maybe the line is instead about birth, about leaving your mother's body for the world, but always retaining a part of her, whether you want to or not.

The poem was written by a man, Stanley Plumly, but still, he has a mother, Helen reasons. He must recognize the feeling as she does now, sitting beneath this accusing sun sensing her mother's movement through the day.

BECAUSE THEY ARE short one lifeguard this week, Gerard climbs the chair at noon to relieve her for a break. Helen tries to make the exchange without touching him, without even looking at his face, but this feat proves impossible. As they switch places on the stairway, Helen's arm hits his, and when she moves her gaze from her footing to the placement of her hands, she finds Gerard watching her, his mirrored glasses propped up on his head as he stares down from his position in the chair.

"Helen," he says with a smile, "why is it that you hate me?"

She almost falls down the rungs at his words but instead plants her bare feet firmly on the hot metal and stares back with concentrated calm. "I never said I hated you."

"I'm not an imbecile." He continues to smile. "I can read people now and then."

"I think you know why I might feel the way I do." There, she's done it, said something vague enough to allow her an escape hatch, while still managing to half accuse him. As he gazes down at her, she waits, expecting an immediate denial of anything and everything. Isn't that what grown-ups do, she thinks, deny what's obvious and true in order to protect her fragile teenage psyche? When he doesn't say a word, she continues down the ladder, but his voice stops her before she reaches the pool deck.

"Maybe I'm in love with her," he says quietly.

She looks back up at him, to find that his glasses are replaced, and she cannot read his face at all. "Well." She falters, heart in her throat, thinking that she must say something, anything, but what? "Well, that's no excuse." She finishes lamely, then hits the pool deck with both feet and makes her way to the lectern, where she retrieves her lunch, then continues across the deck and into the casino without once looking back.

At a table by a bank of tinted windows that look out on the pool, Helen unwraps a turkey sandwich and begins to eat. Her hand is shaking, she notices, as she raises the sandwich to her mouth, and goose bumps have scattered across every section of bare skin. Behind her, slot machines ring against the air and Helen closes her eyes and tries to imagine that the sound is instead a flock of geese, that the pool outside this window is a pond, and that she doesn't live in this city, but in a completely different place, a town that's green and lush and living, not this half-dead, dried-up desert with all its simulated lust and glamour.

She opens her eyes and looks outside, unsure why she feels so strongly, as of late, that she no longer wants to live here. One more school year, then one more summer and she'll go to college, someplace far away. But this does not seem soon enough today. A man approaches her table now and leans to ask her, "May I join you?"

He is old, even older than her father or Gerard, and he's wearing a blue, pinstriped suit. Helen guesses he works somewhere in the casino, maybe at the front desk, and she feels offended that yet another man is proving his inadequacy, his lack of judgment. "Are you that lonely?" she says, with a voice snottier than she'd intended. In truth, she merely wants to know his reason. Why would he be interested in a teenage girl?

"Pardon me?" He straightens up and frowns.

"Why would you want to sit with me?"

He nods to the other tables, and Helen follows his gaze. All of the tables are full, and he is holding a tray of cooling food from the snack bar. She blushes, then turns back to him. "Of course. Sit down. I was just about to leave anyway."

He smacks his tray on the empty space of table across from her, then sits and begins to eat chili from a plastic bowl without looking up. She has offended him and tries to decide if she should offer an apology, but no words rise that seem to fit the situation, so she merely continues to sit, sipping from her water bottle and looking out the window.

She can see Gerard stretching in his chair, raising both arms above his head, then turning from side to side before he drops his hands and shakes out his shoulders. *Maybe I'm in love with her.* The idea had not occurred to Helen, who assumed he was incapable of such a pure emotion. Or maybe, she thinks now, her mistake is in assuming that there is any pure emotion. Aren't they all mixed in together? Love and jealousy and lust and anger. Is it possible to feel something singular and true?

She turns back to the man at her table, watching him a moment before she asks, "Have you ever had an affair?"

He looks up, startled. His brown eyes are clear with crepey, shadowed skin beneath that gives his face a fragile quality. "I'm not married," he tells her, then smirks a little and says, "How about you?"

"I'm not married either."

"Ah, but you don't have to be married to betray someone now, do you?" He sips from a mug of coffee, then sits back in his chair and crosses his arms over his chest with an air of satisfaction. "I can tell from your face that you have. You don't have to say a word."

She thinks instantly of her night with Miles at the lake, of his mouth this morning in the hallway. How is she any better than her mother? "You're right," she tells the man. "I'm no better than an adulteress. Adulterer? Whatever word I should use. I'm that."

"Oh"—he leans forward with a smile—"don't be so hard on yourself. You're just a teenager. Everyone needs time to learn."

"No." She shakes her head. "That's no excuse."

He laughs now, loud and exuberant, and she feels a sudden urge to clamp her hand across his mouth and tell him to shut up. His laughter mocks her, mocks her youth and inexperience, her lack of kindness toward Leo and Ernie, toward Gerard and her mother and even Miles; it mocks the poor choices that she's made this summer, allowing her body to detach itself from her heart and mind, her conscience, and wander aimlessly through these hot, brittle days as if it were a stranger. Helen frowns and looks away, then rises from her chair.

"I'm sorry," the man says, looking up at her. "It's just that you're so serious. You should learn to lighten up. The world's not as important as you make it out to be."

You're wrong, she thinks, *you've just forgotten*. Helen wants to tell him this, but says nothing, merely shrugs, offers half a smile, then turns and walks away, tossing her lunch bag into a trash can before she emerges back into the heat.

When Helen opens the door of the lectern to return her beach bag to its slot, the postcard she saw Gerard writing that morning flutters out, and she crouches down to retrieve it, then decides that Gerard can't see her from this position, so she quickly inspects it. The card's picture is a snapshot of the Dunes Hotel, its teardrop sign blinking plaintively at twilight above a canvas of lighted, moving cars. It is addressed to someone named Kyle in San Diego and starts out with an innocuous "Hey, old friend, what's going on?" But the next line stops her breath. "I've met a fantastic lady. The only catch is that she's married. I'm trying to convince her to join me for a weekend out there at the beach. If I do, we'll stop by for a cocktail. Give my best to Annie." Helen shoves the card back onto the top shelf where Gerard keeps his things, then stands, shaky-legged, and sinks into his chair.

"Hey, Helen." She hears Miles shout to her across the water. "Any chance I might get a break today?" She looks up and raises her index finger, to indicate that she needs another minute; then she stands and strips down to her swimsuit, walks across the short space of deck to Miles's pool, and dives into the deep end.

LEO PICKS HER UP from work today. He is waiting for her in his Nova, tapping out a drumbeat on the steering wheel with more zest and energy than she's seen him display in quite a while. She slips into the front seat beside him and rolls down her window before leaning across and giving him a kiss. He opens his mouth over hers with such tenderness today, pushing hair off her forehead then releasing her with a subtle press behind her ears. Helen is reminded of something she learned once from a pregnant cousin, that there's a place behind babies' ears that when touched on both sides compels them to open their mouths in readiness to feed. "I missed you today," he tells her.

"You're in a good mood," she says, then smiles at him and leans against his shoulder, suddenly imbued with a sense of gratitude that he is here, that the two of them are going somewhere now, his house or perhaps on a drive, to be alone.

"I got my books today for school. And my music for orchestra. And you know what else? UNLV has this study abroad thing that I can apply to. I could go and play drums in Mexico or Germany for a semester. I had no idea they had so many cool things going on. I'd love to get out of this town for a while." He glances at her after easing into the traffic of the Strip and adds, "Maybe you could come too. I think the programs are mostly in the summer."

"That sounds perfect," she tells him. "Too bad it's so far away."

"Well, not really. Just a school year, I guess."

"That sounds like a long time right now," she says, looking out her window at the parade of giant palm trees and hot sidewalks, the sun reflecting so intensely off the mirrored windows of hotel-casinos she imagines they are poisonous, alive with radioactive waste from the nearby Nevada Test Site.

They ride the remaining distance to his house in silence, listening to the radio. He has it turned to the university station, which plays classical at this hour, and she leans back in her seat and lets the violins climb up along her arms and torso, then filter through the warm skin of her throat, where the music buzzes lightly, lulling her toward sleep. It has been awhile, she realizes now, since she's slept through an entire night.

At his house they retreat to the dark cool of his bedroom, the drum set presiding over half of it like some sort of prehistoric insect, its silver limbs glinting despite the closed blinds of his window. Helen moves to run her hand along the wind chimes, then undresses and sits down on the bed, letting her eyes roam over the album covers hung all along one wall as she listens to the ringing of the chimes echo through the room. "You know, I really like your room," she tells him.

"This dump?" He kicks off his underwear, then sits beside her, naked, on the bed.

"Yeah. It's just so filled up with you. There's nothing extraneous about it. Nothing that doesn't belong. You know?"

"I can't wait to move into the dorms," he says with a shrug, then turns to her and leans to kiss her collarbone.

"Do you mind if we just sleep today?" she asks him. "I'd just like to lie on your chest and take a nap. I'm really, really tired."

He pulls away and frowns, and she waits for him to protest; instead, he simply nods and says, "Yeah, that sounds nice."

THAT NIGHT, at dinner, her mother announces that she's going to San Diego for the weekend to visit an old college friend. Helen stares at her, then looks across the table at her father, who continues to eat his lamb chop and crumbled feta cheese without emotion.

"Aren't you going, Dad?" Helen wants to know.

He looks up from his plate. "No. I have finals to grade this weekend."

"Can Jenny and I come along?" Helen asks.

"I don't want to go," Jenny says.

"Then . . . just me?" She offers this alternative with hesitation. Does she even want to spend five hours alone in a car with her mother?

"Maybe next time. Alice and I have a lot of catching up to do. I haven't seen her in years. We have plans to celebrate our mutual ascent into menopause."

Her father looks up again at this and takes a long swallow of wine before he asks, "So it's official then?"

"Looks that way," her mother says, and shrugs. "I suppose I'm an old woman now."

"Stop it, Kath." Her father laughs, reaches across the table, and puts his hand on top of hers.

It strikes Helen that this is the first time she's seen them touch each other in a long time. Why has she never noticed before how seldom they show affection?

"It's true, Edward. I'm past my prime." Her mother is smiling as she says this, but Helen thinks she detects a definite note of sadness in her tone, her posture, the way she swirls her wine around inside her glass now before she takes a sip.

"I think it'd be great not to have a period," Jenny says. "How is this a bad thing?"

Her parents laugh at this, but Helen can find nothing funny in the conversation, and she asks to be excused.

SHE CANNOT SLEEP. Light from the moon spirals through her white, eyelet curtains; the mulberry tree scratches at her window as the wind beats out a steady rhythm. It is past midnight, nearing one o'clock, and the house is dark and quiet with sleep.

Her mother will leave in three days for a weekend in San Diego with Gerard. Helen can already envision the scattered pictures of this trip. Gerard will wait for her mother to pick him up on Friday afternoon, a duffel bag beside him on the front stoop, his ball cap pulled firmly down against the aging sun. They will stop along the way, in Barstow maybe, for some food, eating together in the car—something her father never allows—as they make their way across the desert. Their days will be spent at the beach, their evenings in dusky restaurants with sand scattered on the floor like stardust. They will kiss with long intensity on bluffs above the ocean. They will visit strangers and have cocktails. They will sleep in the same bed.

Helen turns over in her own bed now, her stomach roiling with worry. She has told no one about her mother's affair, not even her sister or Leo, and she wonders how much longer she will be able to keep the information close to her, what word or look will create the inevitable crack, through which the information will seep out and do harm. She thought that it was over. Or maybe she simply hoped that her words, her accusations, meant something to her mother. The idea that she is indeed going to San Diego alone to see her friend Alice moves through Helen's consciousness with a certain degree of hope. But then she sees the postcard again and knows the coincidence is simply too great.

Tossing off the sheet, Helen rises from her bed and dresses, removing a white sundress from her closet and stepping into it, then lacing on a pair of silver sandals that she's had for months and not yet worn. In the bathroom she splashes her face and applies a little makeup, brushes her hair, runs deodorant under her armpits, then walks as quietly as she can to the phone in the kitchen, which is at the opposite end of the house from her parents' room.

Leo has a phone in his bedroom, and he picks up on the very first ring. "What's wrong?" he asks before she can say anything other than "Hi, it's me." And Helen thinks that these are the exact words her mother would use to answer a late-night call.

"Nothing's wrong." She reassures him. "I was just thinking." She pauses and looks around at the dark kitchen counters, the half-full water glass glowing by the sink. Can she really say what she has called to tell him?

"What is it?" he asks, casual now, his voice so close against her ear she imagines he is with her.

"I decided that I want to get married. Yes, yes, I'll marry you."

He is quiet for a few seconds, and then she hears an outpouring of held breath vibrate through the lines. "Really?"

"Yes. Pick me up as soon as you can."

"Wait. You mean . . . tonight?"

She nods, then realizes he can't see her. "I don't want to wait another second. We can go to that all-night chapel by your dad's store, then drive to California or something for a honeymoon." She closes her eyes and waits for an answer, noticing for the first time how rapidly her heart is beating, how much moisture has collected on her throat and chest.

"Okay," he says. "I'll be there in twenty minutes."

Keeping the light off in her room, she packs a swimsuit and a change of clothes in her gym bag. Then she makes her bed and writes a note, which she sets on her pillow. It reads simply "I've eloped." She looks around her room once, wondering if she'll return at all or if this is it. Even the front porch may be off-limits once her mother discovers what she's done. Her diary and three books of poetry sit on her nightstand, so she grabs them and throws them in the bag, then opens her window and climbs out into the night to wait for Leo.

EVEN AT THIS LATE HOUR there is a small line at the wedding chapel. Leo is wearing his nicest clothes: black pants, a white oxford shirt, and a skinny gray and blue striped tie. His hair is neatly side parted and pressed close against his skull. Helen is not used to seeing him like this, and his appearance, the strangeness of him in the harsh fluorescence of the wedding chapel's waiting room, almost causes her to call it off. But she talks inwardly to calm herself. *He's still Leo*, she reassures her wary mind. *He's still the man you love*.

There are two couples ahead of them in line, both of them older than she and Leo, though not by much. No one else is wearing a dress or a tie. No one else is holding hands, though one woman has her palm shoved into the back pocket of her fiancée's jeans. Everyone looks tired.

"You look beautiful," Leo whispers to her now.

She smiles. "Are you nervous?"

"Not at all." He squeezes her hand, and she gives him a quick pulse back.

"We don't need a blood test, do we?"

"Not in Nevada."

She thinks of the note left on her pillow. Her mother will be the one to find it. She is the person who makes sure Helen is awake every day, and she suddenly feels a sliver of regret insert itself into her chest that she hadn't written more. But what else could she have said? What words could possibly make sense of what she's doing. *Your whole life you are two, with one taken away. The inadequate air and fire. The inadequate joy.* She can't remember any lines past that.

Leo pulls her forward. They have reached the receptionist. The second couple opens the doors to the chapel, slipping in to wait their turn, and Helen peers inside at the minister behind a podium, the first couple holding hands before him. A stained glass window of the Virgin Mary glows above him, lit at this late hour by some form of recessed lighting, Helen assumes, though she can't detect its source. The baby Jesus lies supine in the curve of his mother's arm, both of them blissfully unaware, Helen thinks, of what lies ahead for them.

The door closes, and Helen looks down at the receptionist, a young man with spiky hair who smells of cigarettes and taffy. Leo is filling out some paperwork, and the man looks up at Helen and winks. She gives him a wan smile, unsure what to make of the wink, and looks away toward the full-length picture window beside them, though all she can see is her own white-dressed reflection gazing back at her. It would be nicer, she thinks now, if she were wearing the wedding dress her father caught her trying on at Caesars Palace. Even this dim reflection lets her know that her white linen sheath is wrinkled, and she can tell that she forgot to comb the back of her hair. She wishes, suddenly, that her sister were here, her father, even her mother. Never in her wedding day imaginings had she pictured herself alone. Alone, of course, except for Leo.

"How old are you?" the receptionist asks Leo.

"Eighteen."

"And you?"

"Eighteen."

"IDs, please," he says, holding out his hand.

Leo pulls out his wallet and hands his license to the man, who inspects it closely, then says, "Thanks."

"I forgot mine," Helen tells him.

He shakes his head slowly and shrugs at her, offering his open palms. "I have to see it."

"Oh, just a second." She pretends to remember where she's put it and leaves the chapel to run outside to the Nova, parked at the curb. Maybe sixteen is okay, she thinks, retrieving the card from her wallet, then relocking the car, wind slapping at her bare legs and arms, sending hair into her eyes and mouth. There is nothing else she can do but show the clerk her license and hope the law is on her side. Or maybe that wink meant something. Maybe he will let her by just because he likes her.

Inside, Leo waits by the desk, tapping a rhythm on his leg. She hands the clerk her card, and he frowns, then laughs. "I see you dropped two years on your run to the car."

"I ran really fast," she tells him with a smile, realizing this makes no sense but hoping it sounds cutely flirtatious enough to get her way.

The clerk laughs again, and she joins him, feeling Leo's body tense beside her.

"Sorry, but you need parental permission if you're sixteen."

"Well"—she thinks quickly—"can we get married now and bring you the permission later?"

He shakes his head and passes back her license. "Sorry, dear."

The word *dear* rattles through her, making clear that he is an adult and she is just a child. Up until that second she pictured him as an ally.

She blushes and looks down at her license, at her own face gazing up at her from the laminated surface. The picture is a bad one, her smile too exuberant, her eyes stupid with innocent joy. What was she so happy about that day?"

"Let's go, Helen." Leo takes her arm, and she allows him to pull her out of the chapel, back onto the sidewalk.

"So, what do you want to do?" he asks her. He is so outwardly calm she can't believe it's really Leo. She expected anger, despair, a few raging tears at least, but his face is placid and kind. He didn't really want to do this, she realizes. He's not ready either.

"I guess I should go home," she says.

He nods with simple grace, then opens her door and helps her inside the car.

AT HER CURB, she gives him a light kiss, then extricates herself and her gym bag from the car, waving once as she presses his door closed as quietly as possible. Her house is still dark, and she lets herself into the backyard, then climbs back through her window, which she left open just a crack, as if foreseeing how the night would really end. Inside, she shuts and locks her window, then removes her white dress and hangs it in the closet, kicks off her sandals, and dons a cotton nightgown, then sits on her still-made bed.

Her note is visible, even in this dim light. A painful, naked message left to harm her mother, she thinks now. Though this was not its only purpose. She meant to leave with Leo, to change the way she has been living, to move from a life of careless indecision into one of love and honesty. Love and honesty. The words mean something to her, though not exactly what they used to mean. The dust of this summer has settled onto them with a certain permanence.

She tears up the note and throws it into her wastebasket, then pulls back the covers of her bed and tucks herself inside, preparing, she hopes, to sleep a dark and dreamless sleep.

Book Three:

The
Last
Summer

• • • • • • • •

Heartbeats

EDWARD CHECKS HIS HEARTBEAT every morning as he lies in bed, two fingers pressed against the pulse in his neck as he holds his wristwatch in the air above him. Each morning it is exactly seventy-eight beats per minute. After he's showered and shaved, donned a crisp white shirt, blue tie, and suit, the beats have increased to eighty-nine, and by the time he kisses Kathy good-bye—on the lips if she'll allow it, but usually he's given just a suntanned cheek—his heartbeat has galloped up to ninety-five.

It's the heat, he reassures himself as he drives to work. It has gotten hot this summer earlier than usual. June has seen several days of 112 or more. It's the heat and a bit of worry too, he concludes, pulling into his designated faculty space at the university and stepping out into the dryly buzzing cloak of air. Helen—his first and secretly his favorite—leaves for college at the end of August. Also, he has begun to suspect seriously that Kathy is in love with someone else.

In love. What a quaint term. He chides himself, climbing the stairs to his office. Maybe she is merely having sex, minus any love at all. This idea horrifies him even more. The thought that Kathy, his stately iris of a wife, would give her body over to another only for the pleasures of the flesh—the pleasures of the flesh! Another old-world term—makes his heartbeat quicken once again.

A colleague is waiting outside his office door. Anne Collins, a professor of French history who specializes in the late Middle Ages. She leans against the wall in a pose his daughter Helen might employ, arms crossed over her chest, one leg propped up behind her. It is the stance, he muses, of a much-younger woman—something distinctly girlish and charming in that propped-up leg—and he recalls again the faculty party last year where he drank too much wine and talked to this woman on a back couch about intimate matters he can't now recall. It was her gestures, surely, that drew him to her, the way she was able to evoke youth in certain poses, because now, as he reaches her in the hallway, she lets down her leg, turning to face him, and stands still and unattractive, dressed once again in her true age, which he guesses is somewhere near his own forty-seven years.

"I was hoping you'd stop here before class," she tells him as Edward says hello and unlocks his door before ushering her inside. "I have a bit of a problem."

"How can I be of assistance?" He spreads out his hands in a gesture that he hopes evokes generosity because the false jauntiness of his voice strikes him as transparent. What he really wants to do is fetch his first cup of coffee from the faculty lounge and nurse it for an hour alone, gathering himself before the day's first class.

She sits down in the chair in front of his desk and crosses a leg, which she swings back and forth with agitation, transforming herself again into that younger, more appealing self. "You have teenagers at home, don't you?"

He laughs. "You make it sound like a collection." She fails to smile at this, so he adds in a more serious tone. "That's right. Two girls. Seventeen and fifteen."

"I think my daughter worked with one of yours last summer at the Dunes Hotel. Ernestine? Well, they call her Ernie."

This is not a name he remembers hearing, but he nods, wanting to be agreeable, and says, "That sounds familiar."

Without warning, Anne lowers her face into her hands, and Edward fears she's about to weep. He watches the clean line of her part, cleaving through graying, chin-length hair, and takes a deep breath. In the next second, she looks up and tells him, "My daughter's pregnant."

Edward sits down in the chair behind his desk and nods, uncertain what sort of response to offer. Why is she telling him something so intimate about her family? Did they grow closer than he realized at that party? Since that evening they have rarely spoken, and when they do, only simple pleasantries are passed between them. "I'm so sorry," he says at last.

"I was hoping." She pauses and breathes out. "I was hoping Helen might talk to her. Ernie doesn't have many girlfriends, and I always thought your daughter had such a good head on her shoulders."

"Talk to her about what?" The idea that this Ernie girl might contaminate his daughter fleets through him, and he fights the urge to feel his pulse.

"Oh, I don't know. Just to talk to another girl her age, a nice girl like Helen, might be helpful somehow. Of course she plans to, you know . . . not to keep it. Oh, God, I can't even say the word. You probably remember I'm Catholic."

"Right."

"But of course that's what she should do. She has a scholarship to UC Santa Barbara in the fall."

"It sounds like the best decision."

"So you'll ask Helen about it?"

He sees he can't possibly say no, so he nods firmly and tells her that he will.

The relief flushing through her features is so palpable it brings color to her cheeks, and Edward allows himself to put two fingers on the pulse at his throat and feel the hammering of blood beneath skin.

BEFORE DINNER that night, he tells Helen about Anne's request, expecting defiance. This is her last summer with Leo, and she has told the entire family more than once that she wants to spend every possible second by his side. Helen is pouring water for dinner when he tells her of Ernie's pregnancy, and she stops, the ceramic pitcher from the fridge gripped tightly in her hand, and utters a soft "Wow." She fills the remaining glasses, then puts the pitcher back in the fridge before turning to ask, "Who's the father?"

"We didn't get into that."

"It can't be . . . hmm." She rubs her chin. "It can't be Miles."

"Her mother didn't mention the boy."

"But I don't understand why she'd want to talk to me. We weren't exactly friends."

"Her mother thinks you've got a good head on your shoulders, that you'll reassure her or provide wise counsel. If you don't want to do it, you certainly don't have to."

"No." She nods slowly as if deciding. "No, I'll do it. Shit, I mean, sorry, jeez, I can't believe it."

"I know, it's very sad." He puts an arm around her shoulders, and she allows him to pull her in for a quick fatherly embrace, the even thump of her heart like a momentary bird upon his chest. Its pace is slower than his own, and once again he fights the urge to feel his pulse. "She'll meet you tomorrow for lunch."

AFTER DINNER that evening he and Kathy take a walk. It's been awhile since they've done this, strolled side by side through their neighborhood of fifteen years. Things have begun to decay a bit as of late, he sees. There are more dingy-looking cars parked in the driveways, even one black-eyed Camaro draped across a lawn, and someone has spray-painted "Ron loves Julie" on the trunk of a palm tree at block's end. "What's becoming of the neighborhood?" he asks, trying for the second time that day to strike a jaunty tone.

Kathy shrugs, a gesture she's picked up from Helen, and says, "Maybe we should move."

They turn the block and make their way down another street. The last pink flares of twilight are beginning to dissolve into darker sky. "That's a bit extreme. I was thinking I'd just paint brown over that declaration of love and be done with it."

"That's another option."

They walk for a spell without speaking, though Edward wants badly to talk, wants to unlock this silence and step inside the comfort of words, so he tells Kathy about Anne Collins and her pregnant daughter, about Anne's request and Helen's agreement to meet with Ernie.

"Thank God it isn't Helen," Kathy says.

"Yes, we've been very lucky."

She stops mid-sidewalk, beneath the new glow of a streetlight, and bends to tighten the strap of her sandal. When she rises, Edward looks down into her face, hoping for a sign that it would be all right to kiss her. Lately it feels to Edward as if he and Kathy aren't even married, but caught once again in the uncomfortable flux of dating. There is a closed quality to his wife's features now, and he fears rejection, so he decides against the kiss. For the first time he notices a new chain around her neck, a chunky silver link which disappears beneath her ruby blouse. "What's that necklace?" he asks, nodding toward her throat. "Is it new?"

"Oh." She shrugs again. "It's nothing."

"Let me see." He smiles, all the nerves along his arms and across his chest buzzing suddenly with apprehension.

She pulls the chain out, and he sees it is not jewelry at all but a stainless steel whistle that hangs down to her middle, gleaming in the streetlight with a fierceness that makes Edward catch his breath. Where has he seen this whistle before?

"It's Helen's," she says. "For the pool. I found it in my car and put it on. I guess I forgot to give it back."

A reasonable explanation, he decides, but still, the story sits uneasily in his mind as they continue down the block. Kathy takes his hand now as they walk, and her touch, the unexpected cool of her palm in his hot one, causes him to worry more. She is not a woman given to linking arms or holding hands. When she walks, she's told him on more than one occasion, she needs her space. Still, he continues to hold her hand in his, thinking maybe she is simply changing. Stranger things have happened. And he is beginning to rise toward a singular buoyancy, a lightness running through his every limb, when he sees graffiti on another palm tree, a message written in the same small, blocky letters as the last. However, this chain of words sends a coldness through him and makes him clutch his chest a little as he takes it in, hoping his wife hasn't seen the words on the tree across the street that say, "Julie just likes to fuck Ron."

In bed that night his eyes roam across the ceiling, seeking solace in the dark expanse above. Kathy sleeps on her side, turned away from him, the pattern of her breathing calm and seductive; the intimacy it suggests causes a sharp ache to cut across his chest. If he were to suffer a heart attack right this second, would she wake? Would he make a sound, cry out in pain, or merely hold his breath in silent agony, unable to gather enough air for even a hearty whimper? By morning he would be only a still body beneath the radiant, green-eyed gaze of his wife.

Kathy laughed at the graffiti on the tree, laughed out loud, then covered her mouth with impish glee and said, "It looks like Ron and Julie need to get their stories straight." And to think he wanted to shield her from the words, to protect her gentle sensibility. He turns onto his side, facing the raised curve of her back in the half dark. Light bends through the slatted blinds above their bed and illuminates the back of her neck, each small bone of her spine rising through skin like a series of linked islands. He touches these raised knobs lightly, willing her to wake and explain the whistle lying on the nightstand by their bed now, to explain all the small ways she has changed in the last year.

In some respects she has become more responsive to him, so he can't exactly complain. She is more likely to initiate lovemaking, though this is still a rare event. She walks more lightly, toes rolling forward, then a lift at the heel so her calf muscle reveals itself for one sensual second. She has begun to wear deeper colors, which Edward finds erotic. The ruby blouse tonight, a deep plum-colored skirt that hits her knees, satiny chocolate dress sandals. Her whites and beiges are being slowly phased out. And then there is her face. It has always been a secretive beacon, a private flower, but now every smile contains a triple meaning at least; every gaze is the equivalent of an entire conversation.

He turns away with a sigh, a loud sigh that he hopes will wake her, but this is another change in Kathy's demeanor: She has become a person who sleeps deeply. The digital clock glows a blue 2:00 A.M., and he closes his eyes, trying to summon sleep. He can feel the blood running through his veins, feel the pulsing at his temple, his wrists, down the backs of his bare knees. Is he going crazy?

No, this is normal, he tells himself. When a man is worried that his wife is having an affair, he can expect his blood to speed its pace, to make itself a felt presence. Edward breathes in deeply, then exhales, counting the seconds it takes to expel his breath, a method he learned once to calm himself. But after five deep breaths he knows this isn't going to work, knows that sleep will be as elusive as the answers he both wants and doesn't want.

THE NEXT DAY he picks Helen up at lunchtime to take her to the rendezvous with Ernie. Ernie didn't want to return to the site of her former workplace, so Edward has agreed to be the go-between of sorts, ferrying his daughter now from poolside to a sandwich shop across the street from UNLV. Anne is going to pick them up at one and return Helen to the Dunes.

His daughter is stoic in the car, hair combed back in neat, wet grooves that give her the look of a much older woman, someone sleek and quiet he cannot comprehend. By the time Anne picks her up, he thinks now, her hair will be dry and flaring out around her face in the soft waves he is used to. He notices that Helen's neck is bare and feels a surge of reassurance that the whistle on Kathy's nightstand does indeed belong to his daughter.

"Where's your whistle?" he asks, turning the car onto Maryland Parkway.

"I lent it to Miles. He forgot his."

Edward's pulse quickens. "Don't you have more than one?"

"Nope."

He turns left into the parking lot of the sandwich shop. A dark-haired girl sits at a booth in the window and raises a hand in greeting as they pull up. "Thanks for the ride," Helen says, making no move to leave the car. Is she nervous?

"You know, Helen, if you don't feel like talking to her about this, you really don't have to. The three of us can eat together, or I can drive her to her mother's office and you and I can grab a bite."

"No." She shakes her head. "I want to."

And then she is out of the car, thin brown legs unfolding toward asphalt, her chlorinated sunscreen scent exiting along with her. He waits and watches through the window as Helen enters the store, then moves to meet Ernie. The other girl stands, and Edward strains to see the shape of a new baby beneath her gray T-shirt; but her stomach is flat against the cloth, and he remembers that it takes several months before there is any evidence of life inside.

BACK IN HIS OFFICE he eats a hard-boiled egg from home, the shell scattered across his desk like white shrapnel. He drinks coffee from a thermos and contemplates his Russian flag, his view of the courtyard and people wandering through. A student from two summers ago, Carl, floats by, turning to wave as he passes Edward's window. Edward waves back, then turns away, recalling that this boy was once smitten with Helen. To his relief, nothing came of it. She has remained steadfastly attached to Leo, a fact he and Kathy have sometimes found troubling, but now this knowledge strikes him as a blessing. A daughter does not learn the art of being faithful from a faithless mother, does she? Surely he has imagined Kathy is seeing someone else.

He sweeps the bits of eggshell into his hand and tosses them into the trash can by his desk, then stands and brushes off his shirt. Class begins in ten minutes, so he gathers up his notes and checks his pulse once more—eighty-four—before stepping out into the hallway.

THAT EVENING, across the dinner table, he tries to pry information from Helen.

"So how was your lunch?" he asks her.

"Fine." She shrugs, and he sees this will be difficult.

They are eating brand-new dishes tonight. First there was something Spanish called ceviche, raw fish in oil and lemon juice which was strangely exhilarating—Jenny even asked for seconds—and now Kathy is spooning up bowls of paella, a dish he tried once on a trip with a college girlfriend to Madrid, but has not tasted since. The spicy rice in his mouth immediately brings to mind the girl he was with at twenty-two, her misting of freckles and uneven brows, the evening he told her he didn't love her and she cried in the bathroom of their hotel.

"Great meal," he tells Kathy as she returns to her chair across from him and takes a sip of wine.

"Thank you."

She is not wearing the whistle tonight, but her wrist is marred by a silver bracelet he has never liked. It is too thick and indelicate for her small wrist, and the hieroglyphic markings that supposedly spell her name strike him as obscenely blocky like graffiti.

"Are you on some sort of Spanish kick?" He smiles at her across the table, and she gives him a brief glimmer of a smile in return.

"Sort of, I guess."

He turns once again to Helen. "So the lunch was fine. What exactly does that mean?"

Again the shrug. "I don't know. It's sort of private, Dad."

"Oh, it is." He can't decide whether this answer seems reasonable or it infuriates him. He is hovering between accepting her reply and asking another question when the phone rings.

Jenny leaps to answer it, crossing the short span of carpet to the kitchen so quickly it reminds Edward she has a new boyfriend, someone he has yet to meet, called, of all the silly things, Brazil. The enormity of what he has to worry about causes his current bite of paella to clog thickly in his windpipe, and he swallows his entire glass of wine in four efficient gulps.

"Dad." Her voice is strung with disappointment. "It's for you. Somebody named Anne Collins."

He doesn't usually like to answer the phone during dinner, but his curiosity is too acute to pass this up, so he rises and takes the receiver from his daughter. "Good evening, Anne." He greets her, standing in the doorway of the kitchen and watching the three women in his family continue to eat their dinner. "How'd the lunch go? Any word?"

"Helen didn't tell you how it went?"

Her voice seeps into his ear like ice water, and Edward pulls the phone away a bit before offering a simple "No."

"Well, let *me* tell you, then, that having your daughter talk to mine was the worst idea I ever had. I don't know where she gets the nerve, but—"

"What's this about?" He intensifies his tone to let her know he is becoming angry too. He doesn't like the way she seems to be criticizing Helen, who has done her a favor, after all.

"Somehow Helen gave Ernie the crazy notion she should have the baby."

"She did?" He looks at Helen, who is alert now, watching him with wide eyes from her position at the table, fork poised midair above her meal. "That can't be true."

"It is. Believe me. Ernie now refuses to terminate the pregnancy."

"Well." He searches for something reassuring to tell her. "Well, maybe it's for the best, considering your religious beliefs. Perhaps adoption is a better choice anyway."

"No, you don't understand. She plans to keep it. To raise the child by herself. All because your daughter told her that if she sets her mind to it, she can."

"Hmm." He stalls. "Well, that's good advice in general, but I can see why you'd be upset."

"Upset does not do *justice* to my current state."

"Anne, listen." He lowers his voice, turning away from Helen's frightened gaze and stepping out of view into the kitchen. "I'm sorry. There must be some misunderstanding. I'll talk to Helen about it tonight." He promises to call her later, then says good-bye and returns to his seat at the table. His paella has gone cold, and when he takes a bite, he has to force himself not to frown in distaste.

"I suppose you know what that was about," he says to Helen. She nods, solemn, and looks down into her bowl.

"What's going on?" Kathy wants to know.

He explains the situation quickly. Jenny lets out a low whistle, then looks at Helen and says, "Nice move," with a sarcasm Edward hasn't heard from her before.

"Helen, what were you thinking?" he demands, but when she wrinkles her brow as if in pain and looks at him across the table, Edward instantly regrets his accusing tone.

"I don't know. You just said to talk to her. That's what I did."

"Surely this woman can't blame Helen for her daughter's personal choices," Kathy says.

"Well, apparently she's decided to, because before Ernie had lunch with Helen, she was going to get an abortion."

"She loves the father," Helen says, so quietly Edward thinks he's imagined it.

"Pardon me?"

"You heard her," Kathy interjects.

"What does loving the father have to do with anything?" he asks. "Especially since the father is a seventeen-year-old boy?"

"She can't kill something that's his," Helen tells him.

"I don't want to get into the whole 'when does life begin' debate," he tells her, "but I think *kill* is an awfully strong word for this situation."

"It's what she wanted all along," Helen says. "I didn't talk her into anything."

"Yeah." Jenny chimes in now. "What is she, some sort of brainwasher? C'mon, Dad. It's not Helen's fault."

He can see the entire table is against him now, and not without reason, so he settles back with his glass of wine and says, "Okay, okay, but I'm the one who has to explain all this to her enraged mother."

WHEN HE FINALLY gets into bed near midnight, sleep eludes him. Kathy is awake too—he can tell by her breathing—so he whispers, "That wasn't Helen's whistle."

"What?" she murmurs. The whistle is no longer on her nightstand, but Edward cannot stop thinking about it.

"Whose whistle were you wearing?"

She turns onto her side to face him and touches his chest with her open palm. "I found it in the car. I assumed it was Helen's." She moves her hand up and down as if to soothe him. "What's the matter?"

Here's his opportunity, he sees, the question that could enable him to crack open and expose his every worry. But he knows how unattractive jealousy can be, so instead he takes her wrist and pulls her arm over his shoulder, willing her to move her body next to his, which she does, pressing the length of herself against him and kissing his ear, then his neck, then his shoulder. What is he so worried about? He kisses her forehead with care, an act that feels fatherly, so he attempts to drum up more passion as he finds her mouth in the half dark, but the kiss is foreign to him; her lips have become strange and thin, and he imagines they are opening beneath his own tonight merely to appease him, to satiate his worry. So he pulls away and removes her arm from around his neck, gently so as not to accuse her with his withdrawal. He wants to ask her a question that will allow for the possibility of truth, one that will not force her to lie, as he suspects his question about the whistle just did. But he can think of nothing safe. Even a simple *How was your day?* seems unreachable behind a scrim of duplicity. He is quiet for a moment, then asks, finally, "Do you think this girl, Ernie, should keep her baby?"

"God, I don't know." She flops onto her back. "No, probably not. But I can understand why she wants to. I can't imagine ever giving up a child. Think of life without Jenny or Helen. It would be completely different, and terrible, don't you think?"

"We're going to experience life without Helen after this summer."

"Well, not exactly."

"It feels momentous. Her leaving for school. Maybe we should've counseled her to marry Leo and stay close to home."

Kathy laughs; then they lie for a while in silence, the darkness carved out around them by the familiar shapes of the bedroom. They have lived together in this house, slept side by side in this bedroom, since the second year of their marriage, and it occurs to Edward that there have always been unknowns between them, always a haze of language and body parts they cannot completely dissolve. There have, however, been small periods of time when the passage has been cleared, when something—a communal sigh against the night, the overlapping of her foot on his just before the arrival of sleep—has served to open the space between them with a quick, hard brilliance. Her laugh right now creates one of these openings, and Edward takes her hand beneath the sheets, willing the second to stretch itself out and encompass him, to seal him in the security he seeks.

"Is that what's been bothering you lately?" she asks him. "The fact that Helen's leaving us behind?"

"Yes." He half lies, then releases her hand and turns away from his wife, onto his side.

ANNE IS WAITING OUTSIDE his office when he arrives at work. He did not call her back last night, as promised, and as he walks down the hall toward her prim, stiff-armed figure he tries to conjure an excuse, to find the words that might, just possibly, appease her.

"I'm sorry I didn't call," he says immediately upon reaching her. "By the time I discussed everything with Helen it was after ten, and I thought it might be too late."

She follows him into his office and sits in the chair facing his desk. Edward removes his suit coat—it's so hot today he could hardly bear to dress himself—then sits behind his desk, facing her across the expanse of maple and orderly stacks of half-graded papers.

Anne sighs and pushes the hair off her forehead. "That's all right. I went to bed early and slept like a dead person."

"Good, good. That's probably just what you needed."

"Well," she says, and looks at him.

"Well." He offers her his open palms, waiting to follow her lead.

"It looks like I'm going to be a grandmother, instead of the proud mother of a college student."

"Can't you be both?"

"No. I think Ernie should wait to go to school now. I want her to stay home with me."

"You know"—he smiles softly—"that part doesn't sound all bad."

When she is quiet, he stands and says, "Let me run down the hall and get us some coffee. It should be fresh at this hour."

In the lounge he finds two clean coffee mugs, fills them, then returns to his office and offers one to Anne. She accepts it with a smile, and instead of returning to his spot behind the desk, Edward perches on its front edge, waiting for his drink to cool so he can take a sip. They are less than three feet apart from each other now, and he notices her perfume. He thinks it is the same one worn by his ex-girlfriend, the one of the Madrid trip, and he tries to unearth the name of it from memory. It is flowery and musky too, what he thinks is called a floriental scent. It has a funny name, he remembers, something he and this woman used to laugh about when she sprayed it behind her knees before leaving their hotel. Milk of Heaven, no, maybe Liquid Heaven? That wasn't it either. Nectar of Heaven. That was it. "By any chance are you wearing Nectar of Heaven?" he asks Anne now with a conspiratorial smile.

She laughs. "What on earth are you talking about?"

"Your perfume. Isn't that what it's called?"

"No." She laughs again. "What a name. Mine's only called Dark Lily."

"That's pretty good too."

She takes a swallow of coffee and crosses her legs, swinging one back and forth in her usual girlish manner. "I feel sort of embarrassed that you know all my secrets now. Please don't tell anyone else about Ernie."

"Of course not."

"So why don't you tell me a secret of yours in return?" She smiles up at him, and Edward notices for the first time that she has perfect teeth.

He thinks what he can tell her. That he suspects his wife is having an affair? That he had one of his own two years ago? That he almost wishes it were his daughter who was pregnant and staying home?

"Here's one," he says at last. "I've developed this bizarre ritual of checking my heart rate every chance I'm alone. And it never seems to be the same twice." He smirks at her, trying to situate a look on his face that will make this seem funny, like something a kooky professor would do in a movie.

But she doesn't respond the way he hoped. Instead, she frowns and says with genuine concern, "Oh, Edward. If your heartbeat's erratic, you should definitely go get it checked out. We're not teenagers anymore, you know."

AT FIVE O'CLOCK he drives to pick up Helen at the Dunes. Air conditioning beats against his face as news plays on the radio. The hotels of the Strip are fast approaching through his windshield, and beyond these are the mountains, hard and bright and seemingly as unreachable as the moon in the midst of these strip malls, casinos, and convenience stores, though in truth they are only an hour's drive away. It's been months since he's been up there, months since the air has provided him with an ounce of cool. He should take the family up to Mount Charleston this weekend for a picnic, though he can't imagine the girls will be up for it unless they're allowed to bring their boyfriends, and Edward doesn't know if he can stomach four plus hours with Leo and Brazil, especially if he has to watch them being fawned over by his daughters.

The Dunes' parking lot is crowded, but he manages to find a place right by the pool entrance. What would Helen call this again? Rock star parking. That's what she would say about such a prime spot. It occurs to him that more and more he's begun to call upon Helen's various expressions and use them as his own, at least internally. Is this what one does, he wonders, when there is an imminent leave-taking?

He's ten minutes early and decides to go into the courtyard and pick up Helen in person. Fear pricks his stomach as he enters the cool corridor leading to the pool, though he cannot logically determine its source. Once on the deck, in the explosion of sun and heat, he can feel his heart rate increase, and he loosens his tie as he walks toward the lectern and red umbrella. He discarded his suit coat in the car, so he rolls up his sleeves while he walks, searching for Helen. He finds her perched atop her white chair, fanning herself with a piece of paper, her white visor pulled low over her sunglasses. Gerard is sitting beneath the red umbrella, facing away from Edward as he looks out across the water of the larger pool, the one over which Miles is currently presiding, and Edward walks to join him in the shade. "Hello," he says when he reaches him.

Gerard turns, looks puzzled for a moment, then offers his hand. "Good to see you. Edward, isn't it?"

Edward accepts his hand and shakes, their damp palms commingling in an unpleasant way as the smell of suntan lotion and cologne drifts up toward Edward's nose. Beneath this is the slightly smoky smell of sweat, causing him to grimace and then attempt to hide this grimace with a smile. "How's pool management treating you?" Edward asks, thinking this does not sound like something he would say. Where has he suddenly acquired this faux-jovial tone? This insipid line of male questioning?

"Oh, fine." Gerard shrugs. "It's not rocket science. Or even Russian history, for that matter. That's what you teach out at the U, right?"

"Right," Edward says, wondering how Gerard knows this and wondering too whether he is being flattered or mocked.

"I bet that's pretty interesting."

"Oh, I suppose it has its moments."

"So does this job. Believe me." He gives Edward an indecipherable wink that makes his stomach buzz with distaste.

"I'm sure."

Helen appears suddenly at Edward's elbow. "Here I am," she says.

He turns to her and is struck by the whistle, swinging from its linked silver chain around her neck. It is an exact replica of the one Kathy was wearing. "Hello, sweetheart."

Miles joins them beneath the shade of the red umbrella, and Edward sees that he too wears a whistle. Gerard stands and removes his shirt, exposing his own whistle against the deep, furred brown of his chest. "Time for my swim," he says, nodding. "Everybody have a great night. Okay?"

Edward nods good-bye, dazed by this trio of identical chains and whistles, feeling light-headed and overwarm. The thought that Kathy had been wearing Gerard's whistle moves through him, but he quickly discards it, not wanting to allow the idea to even enter his mind. But back in the car, under the air conditioner's persistent hum, he knows that if Kathy is indeed seeing someone else, it might be Gerard. Last summer the notion struck him as impossible, but he is no longer certain of anything having to do with his wife.

"Dad, what's the matter?" Helen asks him as he pulls out into traffic.

Her concern merely strikes him as further evidence something is amiss. Does she know what's going on? "I'm just a little hot, that's all," he tells her, then adds, "What does Gerard do in the off-season? Do you know?"

"I think he works at a golf course or something dumb like that. I don't know. Who cares?"

Her tone is abrasive, and he recalls that last summer she claimed to hate this man's guts. "Is he married?"

She sighs heavily. "Divorced, I think. Can we please not talk about him?" She is quiet for a minute, then adds, "I just don't want to think about anything having to do with work when I'm not there. That's all."

He nods and continues driving, bile rising in his throat as he makes his way home. When they reach the house, he quickly runs inside and vomits in the kitchen sink, then splashes his face with water and cleans out the basin. He pours himself a glass of seltzer and stands at the counter, looking out onto the backyard, willing Kathy to come home, to find him here and ask him what the matter is, but the house is quiet—Helen did not even hear him—so he finishes his drink alone, then goes to lie down on his bed.

ON SATURDAY he awakes to find Kathy's side of the bed already vacant, so he quickly rises and wanders the house in search of her. Last night at dinner nothing at all seemed amiss. Kathy made one of his favorite dishes, goat cheese risotto, when she found out he was not feeling good (though the rich dinner had not exactly helped his stomach). Her outfit had been composed of her past palette of colors—a white sleeveless blouse and long beige skirt punctuated by black sandals—and she wore no jewelry except for an amber brooch he had given her years ago. After dinner they watched a *Masterpiece Theatre* rerun, then ate some raspberry sorbet with decaf coffee before going to bed. In the darkness, they discussed Jenny's new beau. He came by the house for the first time tonight to pick her up for a movie, and they both were surprised and pleased by his polite, courtly manner and charmed by his crazy mass of red hair and thin black tie.

Edward fell asleep almost believing he had imagined any affair, any changes in this dear, lovely woman beside him, but finding her gone in the morning—since she almost always slept in later than he did—whisked up, once again, his collection of worries.

He finds her in the backyard, sipping coffee and watching nothing as far as he can tell, merely gazing at the row of oleander bushes in tense contemplation. She is already dressed—in a new peacock blue sheath dress, to his dismay—and doesn't even hear his approach. "You're up early," he says when he reaches her, and she startles, spilling coffee on her hands and the grass before she turns to him with a frown.

"Shit," is all she says, licking the spilled coffee from her fingers.

"Sorry." He feels awkward in his seersucker robe, his hair uneven and greasy next to her showered, freshly made-up hair and face. "Why are you all fancied up?"

"I'm meeting Jan for lunch."

"It's nine o'clock."

She shrugs, and he is reminded of Helen. "I was up so just thought I'd get ready. Plus I have some errands to run beforehand."

"Errands?"

"I need to return a library book, then pick up some flowers for Jan. Her daughter-in-law just had a baby."

"Really?"

"I told you about that."

He nods, unable to remember any conversation about Jan's being a new grandmother, but he has to admit that his forgetting is not unusual. In fact, the description of her day is typical. She often runs errands and meets friends for lunch on a Saturday, so why does he feel so sick standing here? Why does he have to fight the urge to check his pulse, which appears to be racing as if he had just swum fifty laps. "Let's go inside," he says. "It's hot."

She nods, then follows him across the fragile yellowed grass that breaks beneath his feet like eggshells. *I'm walking on eggshells*, Edward thinks with a wry grimace, listening to the crush of his slippers. *How ridiculous I've become.*

THE DECISION to follow her comes to him gradually. They sit together over breakfast, each reading a section of the paper, the crunch of cereal the only sound between them. Helen comes in around nine-thirty, drinks a glass of orange juice, then grabs a banana and says she's biking over to Leo's for cinnamon rolls. Edward thinks to forbid her—almost to test if he still could, if the order would take—but he merely tells her to be careful, then returns to the paper. He is attempting to read the sports page, but none of the information is entering his consciousness; instead, he is imagining how he can follow his wife without being detected. She knows his car, of course, but she won't be expecting him to be behind her. As long as he keeps a reasonable distance, he thinks he can probably do it. And if she spots him, what will he say? He takes a swallow of coffee and ponders the question. He'll have to pick a destination on the same route and just claim he was going there, and how difficult could that be?

"Where are you meeting for lunch?" he asks Kathy now.

"Um . . ." She looks up at him. "That Middle Eastern place by the university."

"Great Greek Salads," he says.

"That's what I'll probably get."

BY THE TIME Kathy leaves, at ten-thirty, Jenny is still asleep, so he pens her a note—"I've gone out. Back soon. Dad"—and leaves it in the center of the kitchen table. He gets into his car quickly and pulls out onto their street, but already Kathy is nowhere to be found. Has he been foiled so soon? Then he decides to make his way toward the library, hoping to spot her on the way. Of course he knows if she decided to pick up the flowers first, he won't find her. The other possibility—that she is lying—sits darkly in the back of his throat, but he decides not to allow that thought to flourish just yet. The library is his best bet. It's closest to the house, a straight shot down Maryland Parkway to Charleston, and firmly embedded in the Charleston Plaza Mall, which offers him several excuses if she spots him.

He sees her blue Honda before he reaches the library, its bright top stopped at a light, so he remains several car lengths behind her, straining for the sight of her dark head, which he finds, nodding back and forth, most likely to music. Glancing at the other cars around him, he feels suddenly foolish. None of these other people is on a mission of deceit. He assuages his guilt by telling himself that they possess other foibles. The woman to his right is smoking. The man on his left appears clean and alert, but Edward is certain something sinister lurks in his dark corners. No one, he reminds himself, is perfect. And with that thought the light changes, and he is off, in subtle pursuit, keeping his distance as he watches Kathy make her way toward the library.

Relief sweeps through him when she does indeed turn into the back parking lot for the library. He parks far away from her and watches as she disembarks, a green book in hand. Has he seen enough? Shouldn't the sight of her, walking straight-backed and graceful to the door of the library, reassure him? But doubt still crowds against him as he sits waiting, watching a lone boy skateboarding in circles around a lamppost.

Moments later she emerges empty-handed and walks toward her car, holding her hair off the back of her neck. Edward ducks down a little, sweat assembling itself across his brow as he watches his wife, waiting for her to look his way. The parking lot is fairly empty, and despite his distance, he would be easy to spot. Her eyes are shielded by sunglasses, but her gaze does not wander from its destination, her car. She shuts herself inside and pulls out of the lot.

In the parking lot of the grocery store he is less nervous. Multitudes of cars protect him from view, and the array of people wandering in and out of the entrance clutters his sight line so thoroughly he worries he won't see Kathy emerge. But there she is, walking across the crowded asphalt with a bouquet of coral roses, and Edward can't help admiring the sight of her, the dazzling reddish orange of the flowers against her blue dress, her dark, glossy hair and matching black glasses, the neat, erect way she carries her head, as if it were a precious object to be held aloft. But the roses seem wrong somehow, the more he thinks about it. Are roses an appropriate flower for a friend? He doesn't know.

He follows her down Maryland Parkway. They are heading toward the Middle Eastern restaurant. *Please let Jan be there to meet her*, he half prays to someone. Certainly not God, he thinks, analyzing his wish more thoroughly, since he considers himself an atheist. If he had to describe the workings of the universe, he would spin out a giant web of causes and effects, of muted grays and blues punctuated by an occasional bright pink thread of joy, but there would be no overseer per se, only a horde of discordant consciousnesses, all vying for a place to call their own. There would be no absolute definitions of right and wrong either, only possibilities and disappointments, only instances that could've been handled better, or ignored altogether. If Gerard is at the restaurant, instead of Jan, what exactly will he do? Punch him in the nose? Belittle him with his superior grasp of language? Offer to buy the three of them lunch?

The street seems to sizzle before him in the heat as Kathy escapes through a yellow light and he is forced to wait through red. Far off to his right he watches the casinos, dull and rotting in the sun as a condemned city. To his left is the Boulevard Mall, a movie theater, a megabookstore that repels him. Ahead he can see Kathy's car again, as they approach the strip mall that contains the Middle Eastern restaurant. Edward steels himself for what he will see there, deciding not to decide what he will do until the moment announces itself.

He turns on the radio, hoping to calm himself, but a bombastic march expands inside the car's interior, setting his nerves even more raggedly on edge, so he hurriedly turns it off. The air conditioner is already on high, but he adjusts all the vents so they are blowing onto his skin. Only a block to go, and then he will know . . . what, the truth? Possibly. Or Jan might be there, and he will know nothing, except that Kathy has been telling the truth today. A honk sounds behind him, and he realizes how slowly he is going, so he presses his foot against the gas, keeping his eyes on Kathy's car ahead of him.

What will he do if Gerard is there? Edward asks himself again, spotting the restaurant up on his right. Kathy is almost to the parking lot's entrance now, and he takes a deep breath, then exhales slowly into the car. He can't imagine a life devoid of this woman, even if she is sometimes a complete stranger. The truth is that he loves her and wants her to be happy. Of course, if being happy means sleeping with another man, he can't abide that. The thought of her pale caramel-colored skin beneath the touch of another sends bile into his throat, and he hopes he won't throw up again.

He watches intently as her car reaches the turn-in, but then, to his astonishment, she passes the entrance and continues on, toward the university. The clock tells him it is noon, the usual hour for lunch, so he doesn't think she is early. Then what is she doing? He continues to trail her, past the yellowed lawns of campus, past the tight unhappy clusters of fast-food restaurants, record stores, and copy shops, through the lights of Flamingo Road, Tropicana, and beyond. Speeding up, he draws closer, almost willing her to detect him in the rearview mirror. She turns into a neighborhood, an unfamiliar one with low stucco houses and aging muscle cars, and he follows her down an almost empty street, thinking she will undoubtedly see him now, and not caring, wanting her to turn her head and notice his presence so that she won't go wherever it is she's going, so that he won't have to know for certain what his wife is doing here.

But she continues on, oblivious of his car only two blocks behind her now, and when she turns again, down a dead-end street, Edward stops his car in the center of the road, unable to continue. There are no other cars around, so he stays just where he is for a minute. The street she disappeared into is called Elysian Court, he can read the sign from here, and the name seems to strike him with a physical force. *Elysian*, Edward recites in his mind, *a place or condition of ideal happiness*. What a ludicrous name for such a decrepit place, he thinks, looking around more closely from his spot in the center of the street. The house beside him looks like all the others: a lumpy beige ranch-style structure with ragged miniblinds and a small block of concrete serving as a front stoop. The thought of Kathy inside one of these houses, doing anything at all, makes him incredibly agitated and sad.

He sits for another minute, then sees a car approaching in his rearview mirror, so he flips a U-turn in the middle of the road and goes back to Maryland Parkway, speeding now, his churning wheels in tempo with the beating of his heart, sweat enveloping him as he tries to breathe in, then out, then in again. He turns off the road once more, into a different neighborhood, and pulls his car to the side. A palm tree opens over him, providing a patchy, depressing shade, and a Labrador, apparently homeless, lazes on the sidewalk beside him.

Edward rests his forehead on the steering wheel, pain imploding inside his chest so fiercely he can't decide if he's about to sob or have a heart attack, or both. He's short of breath and overheated too. Aren't these all the signs of impending death? The image of himself dying here, mere blocks away from his wife and her lover, strikes him as so pitiful he has to laugh. He drinks from a water bottle on the passenger seat, takes two long, slow breaths, and then the pain begins to subside. Another breath and his heartbeat slows. The dog gets up from its space on the sidewalk and limps over to stick his black nose against Edward's window, his mournful eyes so sympathetic Edward laughs again— quietly—then waves at the dog, which barks once before returning to lie on the sidewalk.

Edward sighs deeply, then turns on the radio again. The music is more appealing now, a soft piano and oboe duet that serves to make his pain more poignant yet more manageable as well, part of the larger fabric of the world all around him. It is a pain, he realizes, that many men and women have shared before him, a pain he himself has inflicted on Kathy in the past, because surely she knew about his dalliance. The mere term, *dalliance*, makes him feel better, lifts the weight off this seedy neighborhood and the picture of Kathy entering one of these houses in her beautiful dress carrying her explosion of roses. He turns the radio up and pulls his car out into the street, then makes his way home with the help of the music.

Turquoise Faces

HELEN HAS NO IDEA WHY she talked Ernie into keeping the baby. If *she* were in Ernie's situation, her belly beginning to widen with Leo's child, Helen would not do the same. Shame clouds her eyes as she admits to herself that she would end the pregnancy as soon as possible. There is college to think about—she's already promised herself to a semiprestigious school in the Midwest—her age (seventeen), the erratic temperature of her love for Leo, so many factors that would make her decision simple. Still, she counseled Ernie to carry out her pregnancy to term, to raise the child on her own.

It will be a girl, Helen thinks, looking from her perch into the turquoise water of the pool. She's not sure how she knows this, but she does. Ernie's child will be a girl. And she can become an honorary aunt of sorts, can't she? She'll bring her fresh corn from the Midwest, write her silly poems when she's done studying, baby-sit when she's in town for Christmas. After all, she is somewhat responsible for this child's life.

It's four o'clock, and the pool is empty. Gerard is absent today, supposedly at the doctor, but Helen suspects he is with her mother. Their affair did not continue through the school year, she's almost sure of it, but when summer began, the little signs started to emerge once more. Now, in the early evenings, her mother sits on the deck sipping a gin and tonic, oblivious, it seems, of the intense heat as she gazes out across the yellowed lawn toward the oleander bushes. Also, there have been a rash of Spanish dinners, and although Helen doesn't believe Gerard is Spanish, she connects this change in menu to his influence.

Then of course there are the changes in Gerard. The Dunes ball cap has been discarded, and his hair sits sleekly against his skull like a proud helmet. He's turned in his mirrored glasses for a pair of black Ray-Bans, and he's taken to wearing a high-level sunscreen and sitting in the shade so that his coloring is much paler than Helen recalls from last summer, still slightly olive but not even approaching his usual walnut brown. All these physical changes are alterations of which her mother would approve, and when she sees them together, waiting for her beneath the red umbrella, Helen can't help noticing how much they look like a nicely turned-out couple on the cusp of middle age.

Miles is currently presiding over the other pool. His appearance has changed even more than Gerard's. Back from his third year at college, he now sports a Mohawk and silver hoop in his left ear, and when she teased him about it, he looked suddenly fierce, as if he might contain a secret violence hitherto undetected. He's also taken to wearing a set of headphones every second of the day, so that whenever she tries to talk to him, he just shrugs to indicate he cannot hear her and walks away, brittle, jarring sounds escaping from his ears and trailing him like a fitful dirge.

Still, she finds him attractive. Helen can't believe it, but she finds something in his new persona strangely alluring. Of course she seems to be attracted to everyone this summer—the boy who sells her sandwiches at lunch, the man with copper hair who runs the thatched-roof cocktail bar, the thin Mexican hotel guest who's lying right now on a chaise lounge at her feet. All of them are calling to her, telling her to leave Leo behind even before she leaves for college. But on the other hand, she is even more in love with Leo this summer than she's ever been, and the odd dichotomy going on inside her is beginning to drive her just a little crazy.

AFTER WORK, she drives herself to Ernie's house. At last Helen has been given a car to use (at least part of the time)—her mother's blue Honda Civic wagon with tinted windows—and she delights in driving it alone, turning up the air conditioner until her skin feels chilled as she makes her way through the hotels and then the neighborhoods to Ernie's. As usual at this hour Ernie is home alone, and she leads Helen through the well-lit entry hall and high-ceilinged dining room to her own bedroom, a dark, drawn-curtained affair that contains a yellow bean bag, an unmade queen-size bed, a stereo, and a small television that is always tuned to MTV. As Helen enters and sits down on the edge of the bed, the small screen shows two forlorn women with sprays of pink hair splayed out on a runway beneath the belly of a gigantic airplane. A rock song she doesn't recognize knocks around the corners of the room.

"You look different," Helen says as Ernie settles down beside her. It's not her stomach, which is still flat, but Helen can't quite place what it is.

Ernie flutters her eyes. "Colored contacts."

"Oh, right. Green. They look cool."

"I wanted them like yours, with that little yellow center, but they don't make anything with more than one color."

"Oh."

They sit for a while, watching the music videos blaze across the screen. Then they begin to talk. Ernie gets off the bed, turns down the sound of the television, and eases into the yellow bean bag. These have come to be their common positions for conversation. Helen cross-legged on the edge of the bed, Ernie beneath her, knees pulled tight against her chest. In a month or two, Helen thinks, Ernie will not be able to sit in that position.

"Gerard sent me a check," Ernie tells her. "He claims it's for back wages he owed me, but he didn't owe me any money as far as I can remember. Do you think he knows?"

"I didn't tell him."

"I suppose word gets around somehow."

"How much did he send?"

"Fifty bucks." She shrugs. "A nice gesture, I guess. Are you sure you didn't say anything? I won't be mad. It's not really a secret anymore."

"Of course I didn't say anything."

"Okay, don't be offended. I just thought maybe . . ." She shrugs again.

Helen knows she didn't say anything about Ernie to Gerard, but she is trying to remember if she mentioned the baby to Miles. Maybe she hinted at it once. She thinks she may have done that, a month ago before she and Ernie were really friends. The thought makes the insides of her stomach curl, so she stands to distract herself and yanks open a curtain. Ernie's swimming pool, vast and glittering in the early evening sun, set into their pool deck like a jewel, makes Helen smile. The idea that Gerard thought fifty dollars might help this girl seems sweetly naive, a word she never would've associated with Gerard.

ON THE DRIVE HOME, Helen listens to music, watching the sun begin to settle itself between the uneven prongs of the mountains. She hasn't seen Leo for two days and is beginning to miss him, but he is at summer orchestra practice again tonight, so she heads for home, taking a circuitous route through new neighborhoods until she loses herself down a cul-de-sac. She pulls the car over to the side of the road to reignite her sense of direction and figure out which way she needs to go. It's not difficult at all with the mountains as her landmarks. She should head toward the lone, finely etched form of Sunrise Mountain off to her right. She knows this. But there is a pleasant sensation to be found in just sitting here, she thinks, a certain allure to being lost, if only for a moment.

So she pretends not to notice the mountain and simply looks around. The surrounding houses are vast stucco structures, almost mansions really, with red tile roofs and long, winding drives. This is a newer section of Las Vegas, and she's never ventured here before. Not a single person is in sight. Too hot, Helen decides from the cosseted cool of her car. The sidewalks are a pristine pale gray and the lawns are somehow still emerald in the middle of July. Helen sighs, then rolls down her window, heat immediately brushing past her into the car. "My mother is fucking Gerard," she says to no one, to this silent oasis. The words have been clinging to the back of her throat all day, and she feels better having released them, so she tries once more, louder this time, realizing she sounds a bit crazy but not caring, hoping that maybe she is slipping slightly to the side of normal, losing the absolute sense that her mother is doing something wrong.

There is a flicker of color to her right, and Helen rolls up her window, hoping no one has heard her, as she turns toward the house beside her. A thin girl in shorts steps out onto the porch, and in the next second Helen realizes that the girl is her sister. Jenny waves to someone inside—Helen can't make out who the person in the shadowed doorway might be—then walks around to the side of the house and pulls her ten-speed away from the wall. She hops astride her bike and coasts down the sleek driveway, turns right at the bottom, then flies past Helen's car without a glance.

Helen is too surprised to call out to her. She moves to honk her horn, then thinks it might startle Jenny and cause her to fall; besides, there is something secretive in the slant of her body,

282 • *Heather Skyler*

curved protectively over the handlebars of her bike, and then she rounds the corner of the cul-de-sac and disappears from view.

Does she have a friend in this neighborhood? Helen can't recall, but she doesn't think so. And she knows Brazil lives on the other side of town. So what would Jenny be doing over here? She'll have to ask her, that's all. It's as simple as that. She'll ask her tonight.

FOR DINNER THAT EVENING there is another Spanish dish, something with fish and olives, which makes the back of Helen's throat tingle. Her father is quiet tonight—actually he has been more quiet in general as of late—and he sips red wine now with a thoughtful air about him, sinking into himself in such a way that his pale blue shirt seems a flimsy second skin, necessary to his survival. He knows, Helen thinks, watching him eat the fish and nod a mild approval to her mother's "Do you like it, Edward?" Of course he knows what's going on.

Her mother, on the other hand, looks as if she might float out of her seat and hover just above the table. Her skin is a rosy bronze, made more beautiful by the iris color of her blouse. Her hair has grown out, Helen notices, and brushes against her bare shoulders now with feathery sensuality. How is it that deceit is making her so beautiful?

Jenny is oblivious, Helen thinks, listening to her talk again about Brazil, her boyfriend of a year now. Helen has debated whether or not she should tell Jenny what's going on, but the need to shield her is what always wins out, and she has been on the verge of telling Leo many times but hasn't. Infidelity is not a subject she wishes to discuss with him, in any form. The specter of Miles might rise once again and disrupt their fragile peace.

When Jenny is finished talking about Brazil's latest project—a teenage brass band, which he leads—her father says with a gentleness that surprises Helen, "We haven't had the pleasure of Leo's company in a while."

"You used to think he was over here too much." Helen reminds him, then smiles to show she harbors no bitter feelings.

"Ah, yes, when you were in the first blush of love and couldn't get enough of each other. Now you're practically an old married couple."

"Except that she plans to break up with him this summer," Jenny says, then covers her mouth. "Was I not supposed to say that?"

Helen shrugs. "Just don't say it to Leo. And who knows? I might change my mind."

"Oh, Helen, I hope you don't," her mother says. "You really need to experience other people."

"I don't see why," her father says. "If you love a person, you love them. That's it."

"That's not what you used to think."

"How do you know what I used to think or not think?" He settles back in his chair, as if this were merely a philosophical discussion, but Helen can see her mother's mouth set itself in readiness for an argument, if need be.

Sweat begins to pearl up on Helen's brow as she says, "Hey, let's just drop it already. The entire family doesn't need to be involved in my love life." She laughs and hopes someone else at the table will latch on to her false mood, carry it to a truer level; but everyone seems to recognize the laugh for what it is, and the discussion moves on to inconsequential topics—her father's work, then the weather, then the movie Jenny saw last night—until Helen's stomach resettles and she can finish her dinner.

GERARD IS BACK at work the next day, balancing his checkbook at the lectern when Helen arrives. Miles is already in the pool, swimming his morning laps, and no hotel guests are in sight. Acknowledging Gerard's presence is inevitable today. She needs to put her bag away and sign in, both of which have to be done exactly where he is standing.

On the way to work this morning, her father asked her why she had taken this job at the Dunes for the third summer in a row when she didn't seem to enjoy it much anymore. The question jarred her. Why had she chosen to work here again when the mere sight of Gerard, scratching his neck now as he leans closer to his checkbook, squinting a little behind gold reading glasses—reading glasses! She hasn't seen those before—repels her?

"I do like it." She lied.

"It doesn't seem as if you do."

She thought about what to say, something innocuous that wouldn't dip toward her distaste for Gerard. She must avoid speaking about him at all around her father. "I'm just getting nervous about school, I guess. Excited too, don't get me wrong, but you know, it's stressful. Plus I'm going to miss Leo a lot. And you too." She added this last bit with a hopeful flourish, thinking it might halt his current line of questioning.

"I'm going to miss you too," he told her, turning his head briefly to face her. His blue eyes were soft and a bit watery behind his glasses, and Helen feared he was about to weep. "Very much." He looked back at the road. "Very, very much."

But why did she decide to return? she wonders, walking slowly now past the immaculate yellow chaise lounges. She does love this part of the job, arriving in the morning to these neat rows of chairs, the sun still soft—at least by desert standards—cloaking the courtyard in an orderly white glow. The palm trees are revived from their night of rest and darkness, and no hotel guests have yet arrived, so only her fellow employees are on deck, people she's gotten to know mildly well over her three summer stints: Jackie, the cocktail waitress, who sometimes gives Helen half a kiwi daiquiri after work if she has to wait for her ride; Rex, the manager of the pool's bar, who turns the other cheek when Helen drinks with Jackie; Horatio, the janitor, who sweeps this deck so clean every morning and talks to Helen about the old Las Vegas, the one of dressing up and stepping out that he misses.

Then there are the pools. The hourglass is her favorite, though the teardrop is beautiful too, and now, when only Miles is breaking the still water with his movement, she loves their cleanliness and color, the way white patterns from the sun open and close across their floors when the surface is broken. The way their turquoise faces match the shade of sky above. All this she loves. It is only Gerard who contaminates the landscape, and she didn't realize how much his presence is felt until she already decided to take the job. Besides, maybe she should be keeping an eye on him, for whatever reason. Perhaps she can somehow limit the damage he is inflicting on her family, merely by hanging around as a reminder that her mother has a daughter and is not just a single woman with no one else to worry about.

"WELL, GOOD MORNING, HELEN," he says when she reaches him.

"Morning," she mumbles, stepping into the red umbrella's shade and shoving her bag inside the lectern. She signs in on the time sheet, quickly glancing at the checkbook beside it. The balance reads "$76.01."

"The end of the month," he says when she looks up. "I always get low right before payday. I bet your father doesn't have that problem."

"I don't know." The idea has never occurred to her before. Her father works, of course, and is paid once or twice a month, she's not sure which, but the notion that their bank account might rise and lower drastically at different intervals is not something she's ever thought about.

"Trust me," Gerard tells her. "He doesn't have this problem. And I can bet you money he's never bounced a check in his working life."

Helen shrugs and says again, stupidly, "I don't know." She turns away and takes off her tank top and shorts, readying herself for the water.

"How's Ernie doing?" he asks her.

"Fine."

"Poor kid," he mutters.

She turns back to him. "How do you know about Ernie anyway?"

"Oh." She can see him hesitate, his lips tightening into a pinkish white line. "I don't remember. Word gets around, you know. Las Vegas isn't such a big town."

And then it is suddenly clear to Helen how he knows about Ernie's pregnancy: Her mother must have told him. The idea that her mother is not only sleeping with this man but confiding in him, telling him things about Helen's life, threatens to unhinge her, so she walks quickly to the empty pool and dives in.

AFTER WORK, Ernie picks her up. Her hair is different today, dyed a lighter shade of golden brown, so that it approaches Helen's color. And she is growing it out too, Helen notices for the first time. Her once-cropped dark locks now reach her shoulders with shorter pieces winging out around her chin.

"You dyed your hair," Helen says, getting into Ernie's car. She can think of nothing else to say.

"I know. My color was so boring. Just dark brown, no highlights or anything. I'm hoping I can grow it as long as yours by the end of summer."

"It was cute short," Helen says.

"Pu-leez." She rolls her eyes. "I looked like a boy."

"I don't think that's possible."

They are on their way to the Boulevard Mall to buy Ernie maternity clothes, despite the fact that you can't yet tell she's pregnant. But when they arrive and begin walking down the mall's cool corridors, Ernie shuns every section marked "Motherhood" and instead heads for the teenage boutiques. She ends up purchasing only a shirt, an exact replica of one Helen wears all the time, a sleeveless yellow T-shirt with an appliquéd surfboard floating across the chest.

"I hope you don't mind," Ernie says, already paying for it, looking up at her with those fake green eyes.

In fact, Helen does mind, and is beginning to become a bit disturbed by Ernie's transition. She supposes she should be flattered but instead feels uneasy. The thought of a pregnant girl looking just like her sends little pinpricks of worry all along her arms. "I should call Leo," Helen says, looking at her watch. Five forty-five. "I'm worried I might be late." She is expected at his house for dinner in fifteen minutes, and it is a rare night because his mother is cooking and has invited Helen to join them. Why did she agree to go shopping with Ernie? It's obvious to her now that she was trying to cram too many activities into her day, but it helps her not to think so much, keeps her from brooding in her room over some new poem that seems written specifically for her.

She steps away from Ernie and wonders this: Could the condition another person is in, a friend, be contagious? Not that Helen thinks she could actually catch a pregnancy, but the idea arises that you could adopt a personality, become a person who is not as vigilant as you are, a person who sometimes forgoes birth control, telling herself that at this point in her cycle, the chance of pregnancy is rare.

"Let's just leave now," Ernie says. "I can get you to Leo's on time. Don't worry."

Helen agrees, and as they speed down Maryland Parkway, dipping in between cars, then out again as necessary, Helen decides that being pregnant right now isn't the worst condition she can imagine. There would be a certain security in knowing exactly what she needed to do: eat well, exercise moderately, try to love Leo enough so she could accept him as a father. And who would even have time to think once the baby was born? Who would have time to worry about whether or not your mother was in love with your boss? Who would care at all?

LEO'S MOTHER has made cheeseburgers for dinner and a salad composed of cherry tomatoes and iceberg lettuce, a vegetable her own mother doesn't allow through the front door. But it tastes very good to Helen, its cool, sweet crispness breaking nicely beneath her teeth, and the cheeseburger is delicious as well, the bun soft and white and sprayed with sesame seeds.

"We're really going to miss you when you leave this fall," Leo's mother, Lily, tells her.

"I know," Helen says, taking a swallow of Pepsi. "Me too."

Leo nods over his plate but is being strangely silent tonight, so Helen tries to fill in the dinner with talk of her day at the pool. In truth, there isn't much to tell, so she embellishes a little bit, making up a story of a woman going into labor today on the pool deck, detailing the hurried arrival of her husband from the casino. She even creates a role for herself: calling them a cab and helping the woman focus on a bottle of Panama Jack suntan lotion and breathe while her husband gathered things from the room.

There *was* a pregnant woman at the pool today, but she lay

silent and aloof, a straw hat shielding her face so completely Helen couldn't even tell whether she was asleep or awake. Lily is interested in the story; but Leo is barely even listening, and by the time she's finished talking, she feels ashamed. What inspired such a lie? She's never done such a thing before.

"I went into labor with Leo on a Greyhound bus. I was coming down here from my sister's house in Oregon. You know, they wouldn't let me fly so late in the game, but it was still two weeks until my due date, and I thought it would be fine. They had to pull over at the state line, and an ex-nurse helped me in a hotel."

"I never heard that story," Helen says, shaking her head. "Wow."

"It didn't happen exactly like that, Mom," Leo intones.

"How do you know? You weren't even born yet. Well, almost not even."

"Dad told me you made it to a hospital in Barstow with plenty of time to spare."

"Your father doesn't know what he's talking about." Lily laughs, then pushes away her plate, leans back, and lights a cigarette.

"I believe you," Helen says, even though she's not sure whether she does or not. Is everyone at the table lying tonight?

WHEN SHE HAS SEX with Leo later that evening, the condom they are using breaks, a fact they are unaware of until he moves his body apart from hers and flops back on the bed beside her.

"Shit," he says when he reaches to remove it and sees what has happened. There is a wide, ragged hole ripped across the tip, and he and Helen both stare down at the flimsy, broken condom lying in his hand like a torn piece of kelp, or maybe a dead jellyfish, something that was once alive but is now obviously life*less*. Classical music plays on the stereo, and suddenly a rush of discordant violins descends on them like a swarm of bees. "Shit, shit, shit," he moans, covering his face with his free hand, then rises from the bed to stand beside Helen, who still lies supine, covering her breasts protectively now because she can feel the anger beginning to burn in him, building itself inside the center of his chest, then flaring out through his right arm as he hurls the condom against the wall. It sticks to an Iron Maiden album cover, then slips down and falls to the carpet behind his drum set.

"Leo." Helen sits up and pulls her legs against her chest. "Don't worry. It's not that big of a deal."

"How can you say that? Not that big of a deal!" He rubs his face with both hands, then asks, "When did you have your last period?"

"Um, two weeks ago maybe. I'm not sure."

"Great. This is just fucking great. Right when everything is going so well for me, I get you pregnant."

"Leo, come on. I doubt I'm pregnant. And besides, if I am, we'll just get married. How about that? I thought that's what you wanted anyway. You can come with me to school, or I don't even have to go to school. We can just travel around or something, see the world."

He sits beside her on the bed and looks at his knees. "Look, Helen, I know that's what we planned last summer and all, but I really think we're too young for marriage. Don't you? You used to think so."

She did used to think so. He is absolutely right. Then why does she feel a rash of pain begin to burn down her throat and across her naked abdomen? Why does it almost sound as if he were breaking up with her? "So maybe I changed my mind."

"Why, because of this Ernie person? Do you want to be just like her or something?"

His voice is scornful, and Helen shifts her body away from him, surprised. "No," is all she can manage to say.

There is a knock on the bedroom door, crisp and insistent, and Helen and Leo both look to each other, fear weaving instantly between them so that for a moment Helen feels connected to him once again, but then he stands and crosses the carpet to the door, causing the bond between them to unravel.

"Yes?" he says from behind the door, still naked, his skin singed a pale orange by the room's single lamp on the bedstand.

"Helen's father just called," Lily says through the door, her voice barely audible above the music. "He wants her to come home. It is pretty late, Honey. I didn't realize she was still here."

"Okay," Leo tells her. "I was just about to take her home."

Helen stands and begins to dress. For the first time she notices it is past eleven, and she promised to be home by ten. She supposes she will be yelled at when she arrives, possibly even grounded, but at the moment she doesn't care.

Leo dresses too. Then they walk, without speaking, through the house to the front door. Lily is nowhere in sight, and every room is dark, the scent of hamburger and cigarettes accosting Helen as they move past the kitchen, then outside into the tepid night.

Leo's Nova is warm and humid as an incubator, and Helen rolls down the window, allowing the night to wash in as they drive, cicadas crying to her from the sidewalks and burned yellow lawns. At her curb, Leo leans across the seat to kiss her, then says, "Sorry about earlier. I'm just worried, that's all."

"I know," she says, turning to look at her house. The living room lights are still on, and she sees a shadow move behind the curtains. "Me too."

INSIDE, SHE FINDS her mother reading on the love seat by the ficus tree. Helen closes the front door behind her as quietly as possible, mentally preparing for her reprimand and punishment. "Sorry I'm late," she tells her mother, walking across the carpet of the entry hall toward her quiet form. Lamplight drifts down across her mother's hair, illuminates her collarbone and the hollow of her throat. She is as lovely and untouchable as a painting in a museum, and Helen can hardly make herself believe she'd allow a man like Gerard to touch her.

At last she looks up at Helen, appearing, for a second, to be utterly lost, unaware of the house around her, oblivious to the fact that she has a teenage daughter who has passed her curfew. "Oh, hi," she says, then frowns. "How late are you?"

"Not very," Helen says, deciding this is not quite a lie, that time is relative, after all.

"Okay," she says with a shrug, then looks back down at her book, a dark blue hardback whose title is indecipherable in her mother's shadowy lap.

Helen continues to stand where she is, unable to move toward her room. Her mother looks up again and asks, "Did you have a good time?'

"Not really."

"Um, do you want to tell me about it?" She closes her book and pats the space of sofa beside her.

Helen considers the offer, internally reciting a description of her day: *First, I worked with the man you're fucking, then went shopping with a girl who is beginning to look like me. I lied my way through dinner for no particular reason, then had sex with Leo and the condom broke, so it's possible I'm pregnant.* "No." Helen shakes her head. "It was just boring, that's all."

On her way to the bathroom, Helen passes Jenny's room and remembers she hasn't yet asked her sister what she was doing in that rich neighborhood the other day, but her bedroom is dark now, so any questions will have to wait. She splashes her face with warm water, brushes her teeth, then lies down on her bed and falls immediately asleep.

AT WORK THE NEXT MORNING, Helen keeps touching her stomach; the smooth Lycra of her black suit stretches flatly reassuring beneath her hand. The chances of her being pregnant are slim, she tells herself. She checked her calendar this morning and saw that her period is due at the end of the week, so she isn't really in the middle of her cycle after all. She considered calling Leo to reassure him, but decided against it, for some reason wanting him to worry just a little longer. Besides, her period is fairly erratic, so there's still a chance.

The pool is crowded today, and Helen has to force herself to concentrate on the people beneath her feet, the people whose lives are her responsibility. A flock of gray-haired ladies tread water together in the deep end, chatting. A middle-aged man is attempting to swim laps along the edge directly beneath Helen, but he keeps having to stop in order to avoid two kids in floaties whose mothers don't seem to realize they're blocking him. Helen considers asking them to move out of his way, but she doesn't have the energy.

Glancing up, she scans the deck. Gerard is in his usual spot, sipping Diet Coke and reading a magazine. Miles is peering morosely down into his own crowded pool. The deck chairs are no longer in neat rows, but dragged out of alignment by people trying to achieve the perfect angle of sun, and a crowd has gathered around the thatched-roof bar. Helen watches beyond the bar as more people emerge from the casino's dark doors, stopping to adjust to the sun, shading their eyes against the bright, then walking out onto the pool deck.

Helen looks back down at the pool, reassures herself all is well, then looks up again. Another group emerges from the casino, and Helen thinks for a moment that she sees Jenny among them. That *is* Jenny—she's sure of it now—wearing a white sundress and tortoiseshell sunglasses. Helen waves, but her sister doesn't see her because she's reaching for something in her purse, so Helen looks back to the pool, waiting for Jenny to approach and feeling happy for the first time all day, surprised by the blossom of pleasure that settled in her chest at the sight of her sister. She was dreading eating lunch alone in the casino, and now she won't have to.

But when she looks back up, Jenny is nowhere in sight, and Helen wonders if she merely saw a girl who looked like her sister, though this explanation is feeble. Of course that was her sister; she would recognize Jenny if she'd only been given a view of her elbow. So maybe she has just gone to use the rest room first. Helen's lunch break isn't for another twenty minutes anyway. She waits, watching the pool and then the deck and then the pool again, but by the time noon arrives her sister is still nowhere in sight, so she waits for Gerard to relieve her, then retrieves her lunch from the lectern and goes inside to eat.

AFTER WORK, Helen crouches down to get her bag from beneath the lectern, then stands to find Gerard facing her. His sunglasses are pushed up onto his head, and he's biting his lip, as if trying to make a decision.

"Can I ask you a question, Helen?" His voice is hesitant, threaded with a barely perceptible quaver; but Helen hears it, and it stops her, scattering goose bumps along her forearms.

"I guess so."

"Do you feel as if . . . hmm"—he rubs an eyebrow—"how can I put this? Do you feel as if your parents have a good marriage?"

"I can't believe you're asking me that." She steps back a little but doesn't turn to leave.

"C'mon. You're an adult. I'm an adult. We both know that you know what's going on." He sighs and touches his sunglasses but leaves them on his head. "Your mother would kill me if she knew I were talking to you about this, but I don't know where else to turn. I just need to get my hands around this situation somehow, you know? Is she happy at home and I'm just a diversion . . . or am I something else entirely?"

Helen feels as if her blood had stopped flowing. A cold heaviness presses against her lungs, and she can't find the air to offer a response, though she has no idea what she would say even if she could indeed find the breath to speak.

"Uh-oh, you look pale. Here"—he pulls out the high chair—"sit down."

She obeys without thinking, then leans back and closes her eyes.

"I'm sorry, Helen. Jesus, I'm really sorry. Bad idea, asking you something like that. I didn't mean to be so insensitive, it's just . . . I'm a nervous wreck right now. I guess I forgot you might be a nervous wreck too."

She opens her eyes and begins to feel her blood move through her veins once more, speeding up in a rush so that now she is hot and flushed. "I'm not a nervous wreck," she tells him.

"Of course you are, sweetie. And it's perfectly understandable, considering."

She stands and tucks her hair behind her ears. "Fuck you," she says, then goes to move past him, but he blocks her way and clamps a hand on to each arm, not tightly, but with a gentle pressure that makes her even more angry. His touch seems caring and strong—*parental*—and she yanks her arms away and says, almost crying now, "Yes, they're extremely happy. My parents are so in love it's sickening. You should see them together; it's insane."

And then Miles is beside them, his Mohawk so outrageously spiked up with gel today Helen barely recognizes him. He removes his headphones, sets his Walkman on the lectern, and says, "Hey, what's the matter?"

She can feel tears sliding down her face, and she wipes at them with her hands. "Nothing," she tells him, then moves past Gerard and walks toward the exit, legs shaking with every step.

THE NEXT DAY, Tuesday, she calls in sick. "You don't look sick," her mother tells her, pressing a cool palm to her forehead. "What exactly is the matter?"

"My stomach hurts."

"Well, I have to go run some errands." Her mother steps away and puts her hands on her hips. "Will you be all right for a while? Do you want me to get you something?"

"Don't bother," Helen says, unable to keep the meanness from her voice. *Don't bother coming back at all*, she wants to say, but doesn't.

Once her mother is gone, Helen settles in at the kitchen table with a glass of orange juice and a book of poetry. She's still wearing her green cotton robe, and she hasn't showered since yesterday morning, so her hair smells strongly of chlorine and her skin contains a buttery mix of sunscreen and sleep. Her stomach does not hurt, but she can't imagine going back to the Dunes. In fact, she may decide to be sick for the rest of the summer.

After half an hour Jenny wanders in, already dressed in a black, scoop-necked T-shirt and lavender skirt, her hair wet and sleek from the shower. Her sister wasn't at dinner last night—in fact, everyone ate leftovers separately—and she came home very late from a date with Brazil, after Helen had already gone to bed.

"Hey"—Helen begins—"what were you doing at the Dunes yesterday?"

"I wasn't at the Dunes." She pours herself a glass of orange juice and stands drinking it at the fridge.

"Yes, you were. I saw you."

"You think I'm lying?" Jenny laughs, not making eye contact.

"I guess not. Oh, and I saw you the other day in this rich neighborhood too, sort of by UNLV. What was that all about?"

"I don't know where you mean."

"I can't remember the street. It was some fancy place with a red tile roof and huge yard, in a cul-de-sac. You were riding your bike."

"Hmm . . ." She shuts the fridge with her hip. "That doesn't ring a bell."

"Now I do think you're lying." Helen makes this accusation with a lightness of tone and a smile, belying the giant mass of black she feels spreading through her chest. "Do you think I don't know what you look like, or something?"

"Lots of people look like me."

"Fine." Helen stands up and tightens her robe. "Lie to me. Join the crowd. You'll fit right in with this family."

Jenny sets her empty glass on the counter and crosses her arms over her chest, looking small and meek and suddenly unhappy. "What do you mean? Who's lying?"

"Nobody. Forget about it."

"Tell me."

Helen shakes her head. "I can't."

HELEN FEIGNS ILLNESS for the rest of the week, though after her mother leaves the house, Ernie often drops by to pick her up and they go get ice cream or swim in her pool. Leo hasn't called since the night the condom broke, Jenny is being quiet and elusive, and Helen is avoiding both of her parents, so she is beginning to feel as if Ernie were her only friend. Helen had other girlfriends once, she thinks, lying on her back beside Ernie's pool, but with the advent of Leo many fell by the wayside, most of them just as consumed by their own new beaus as Helen was by Leo. There are still other girls she sees, on occasion, childhood friends she knows she can call at any time, but in a way she wants to free herself from as many people as she possibly can; she wants to leave behind a bare minimum of friends to miss when she goes to college at the end of August.

"I got another check from Gerard," Ernie says, surfacing in the pool beside her. She has her forearms up on the deck, her chin propped up by her laced hands. "And a note this time. Read it and tell me what you think. It's over there on the table."

Helen rises from her towel and walks across the deck to the glass-topped table, sheltered by a bottle-green umbrella. Sitting down, she picks up the card—a greeting card with "Get Well Soon" splayed in pink letters across a silver background—and reads the message Gerard has penned. "Dear Ernie, Of course you're not sick, but you're probably not feeling exactly like yourself right now! I know thirty dollars doesn't go very far these days, but please buy yourself something nice, or maybe something for the baby. You know, my daughter, Christy, wasn't planned either, but she is my moon and stars. Stop by to say hi sometime. Yours truly, Gerard R."

Helen sets down the card and remains where she is, in the shade. Why on earth is Gerard sending Ernie money? Especially, Helen wonders, when thirty dollars is almost half of what he had in his checking account the other day. It's not as if he had cash to spare.

The only explanations she can arrive at are sordid. He's really the father of Ernie's child. But she knows that's not true. Helen has met the father on several occasions now. His name is Kelly, and he's a senior at Ernie's school. A soft-spoken boy with the most striking eyes she's ever seen on a real person. Large and aqua blue and so intensely colored Helen imagines that he hypnotized Ernie into having unprotected sex and getting pregnant.

Helen's second idea: Gerard slept with Ernie's mother too and wants to keep Ernie quiet. But the actual sight of Ernie's mother makes this idea sound flimsy as well. She is graying and prim and spends all of her time either teaching her classes at UNLV or holed up at home in her office doing research for a book on Joan of Arc. In fact, she's in there right now. Helen could hear the keys of her computer clicking away as they walked by her closed door on the way outside to the pool.

Is it possible, Helen wonders, that Gerard is just trying to be nice? So far it is the only explanation that makes sense.

She stretches out her legs and looks around. Cicadas have left their shells all along the red brick wall that conceals Ernie's yard from the neighbors, a sign that the close of summer is drawing nearer, that soon she will be far away from this city and everyone in it; soon she will be sitting in a classroom in Ohio, with high, latticed windows and wood floors, strangers sitting at the desks all around her like an extra layer of comfort, a shield that will conceal the person she used to be. At school she can choose to become someone entirely new, someone who would know what to do in this situation.

Ernie is swimming laps again, and Helen watches the rhythmic lifting of her arms, thinking that soon this girl in the water will be a mother, and one day she may do something that harms her child; she might fall in love with a man who isn't her husband, or she might not even have a husband, and this will radiate a certain pain as well. Regardless, in six months Ernie will be linked to another person for the rest of her life; every single thing she chooses to do will affect this person, whether she wants it to or not.

On Friday, the fourth day of her sick leave from work, Miles stops by around noon. Helen is home alone, reading and eating a cheese sandwich on the couch, when she hears his knock. His Mohawk is not slicked up today, so that the loose hair of the top falls over the shaved sides and he looks almost the way he used to last summer.

"I was worried about you," he tells her.

"Really?" she asks, then adds, "Thanks," before ushering him inside with an outward sweep of her arm and closing the door behind him.

"So what's this mysterious illness that's keeping you away?" He smiles down at her, and she expects to feel the old flutter of attraction, but there is none. "Oh," she begins, trying to decide whether or not she wants to lie. The truth is, she is too tired to do it, too exhausted from skittering back and forth through the jungle of her interior life to make the effort. "I'm not sick," she tells him, then leads him to the kitchen, sits him down, and pours two glasses of sun tea.

"It's because of Gerard, isn't it?" Miles offers quietly.

"I don't know." She shrugs and takes a sip of her tea, attempting to hide her face with the glass because she thinks it must be revealing too much. It must be clearly written on her features that Gerard is indeed the cause of her absence.

"At least your mother's healthy, think of it that way," he says.

"What the hell is that supposed to mean?"

"I saw them together," he tells her, "at his house the other day."

"And she looked especially healthy?" Helen tosses this out as sarcastically as possible.

Miles sighs and rubs his forehead. "I just meant . . . um, I haven't told hardly anyone this yet, but my mother is really sick. Like, so sick she is probably going to die. She has breast cancer, and they didn't catch it in time."

Helen nods solemnly, but doesn't speak. They sit for a bit, just looking at each other. With both their secrets now revealed, Helen wonders if there are any words left to them. What else can they tell each other? "I'm sorry," she says finally. "That's so terrible." And she tries to tell herself that cancer *is* worse, so much worse, but still, a part of her, a small mean part she can't completely control, thinks it is better. There is dignity in dying, a clearing of space, whereas adultery offers only shame and clutter.

"I'm on my way to visit her now," he tells Helen. "I was out all night at the lake and haven't been home to see her yet." He takes a swallow of tea, then asks, "Do you want to come with me?"

The day stretches out before her, vast and complicated, so she shrugs and says, "Okay."

HIS TRUCK SMELLS of lake water and suntan oil, and she sees he still keeps his tube of pink hair gel on the dashboard. Slurpee cups gather around her sandaled feet so she pulls her legs up on the bench and crosses them. Miles pushes a tape into the player as they make their way down Maryland Parkway, and Helen expects it to be something raucous and punk to match his new style, but instead Neil Young drifts out, low-key and mournful, singing about being young with a wistful distance Helen hopes one day to achieve.

She has never been to Miles's house before and has no idea what to expect, though as they drive through town, she imagines it will be something like Leo's house, cramped and dark with the added burden of illness emanating from a back room, medicine bottles scattered across the kitchen counters and floor, a jug of orange juice growing warm on a plastic patio table in the corner of the living room. She can't imagine why she agreed to go.

"How's Leo?" Miles asks her after a while.

"Ignoring me, I think," she says, then adds, "He's really busy with a summer orchestra at UNLV."

"Too bad about Ernie."

"Yeah. But actually, she seems pretty happy."

He turns off Maryland Parkway into a neighborhood that looks familiar. The farther in they drive, the bigger and grander the houses become, until Helen realizes they are in the same neighborhood she got lost in last week. At last he turns left into a cul-de-sac and parks at the top of a high, arched driveway, and Helen is unable to move, unable to speak or breathe. This is the exact same house from which she saw her sister emerge.

"Come on," he says, hopping out, seeming all of a sudden to be jaunty and in charge.

She doesn't move, so he walks around to her side of the truck and leans his face in through the open window. "What's the holdup?" he asks her.

"Nothing," she says, trying to shake herself free of the image: Jenny walking out, saying good-bye to someone inside, then hopping astride her bike and coasting down this very driveway. Helen unbuckles her seat belt and gets out of the truck. Does she care, Helen wonders as she steps down out of the cab, if her sister is seeing Miles? Why should it bother her? It's simply the secrecy, she decides. The fact that her sister would lie to her just like everyone else.

The house actually smells good inside—a curious mix of lilies and chocolate—and the entry hall is cool and hushed, presided over by an ornate, silver-framed mirror. Helen can't help catching her reflection in it as they walk into the house, and she decides that she looks secretive and tired, her hair uncombed and her clothing—cutoffs and a tank top—inappropriate for meeting someone's sick mother.

When they emerge from the entry hall, the ceiling soars above them, connecting a series of fluidly linked rooms—dining, living, kitchen—which are all open and inviting and painted in cool greens. Miles leads her down a hallway off the living room to a bedroom at the back of the house, but before he opens the door, he turns and says, "I should warn you that she doesn't look so great, and sometimes she can be out of it, depending on the day."

Helen nods. "Okay."

A very thin woman presides over a hospital bed set next to a bay window. She is looking out on a swimming pool and rock garden, but when Miles closes the door behind them, the woman turns and smiles. Her head is covered by an orange scarf, and her face is decorated by round silver glasses and raspberry-colored lipstick. She's wearing a red, bell-sleeved top, and her legs are covered by a patchwork quilt. The overall impression is one of a sick Gypsy convalescing in a posh hotel. Here there is decidedly a smell of illness, though it's overlaid by the smell of citrus because, Helen sees now, there is a nurse peeling an orange in the room's opposite corner, a Hispanic woman who nods and smiles at them, giving Miles a special, good-to-see-you wink.

"Miles," the woman on the bed says, clasping her hands together, "I thought you'd forgotten all about me."

"I brought a friend." He leans in to kiss her cheek, then straightens up and tilts his head toward Helen.

"Jenny," his mother says, smiling up at her. "You look taller."

Miles immediately flushes a dark pink and shakes his head as if to silence her. "This is Helen."

"Well, they look just alike." She brings her hands together again, not quite in a clap, but almost.

"This is her sister," Miles explains.

"Very nice to meet you," Helen says, offering her hand. His

mother's palm is cool and dry, and Helen can feel the bones of every finger as they shake.

"Your sister is such a dear girl," she tells Helen. "You must worship her. Oh, and the way she goes on about your mother! I only hope Miles will sing such praise for me when I'm gone."

"Mom, don't talk like that," Miles says quietly.

"I only speak the truth."

Helen attempts a smile, but it feels false and silly, so she straightens her face and looks out the window. A young man in a red T-shirt is clipping the bushes behind the pool, and Helen watches him for a minute, the steady, chopping rhythm of his arms soothing her a bit. Miles and his mother talk for a little while, and Helen pretends to listen, nodding at what she hopes are appropriate moments, but it is difficult to stop thinking—about her sister, and her mother, and Leo and the broken condom and death; now there is death to think about too. The death of a friend's mother, a friend who is approximately Helen's age, must mean something. Maybe this is a warning, Helen thinks, looking at the sick woman's thin, graying face, a warning to love her mother no matter what because tomorrow she could be dead. Helen tries to feel a new appreciation for her own mother swelling up beneath her skin, the appreciation Jenny apparently feels, but there is nothing new as far as she can tell, just the same old love she has always possessed, covered now by a bruise, a love grown almost indistinguishable beneath the tender layers of purple and blue.

ON THE WAY HOME in Miles's truck, Helen waits for him to explain what is going on. She wants to accuse him of something, she's not sure what, but he looks as if he might cry, so she holds her words, gazing out the window at the cars moving along with them, at all of the people's cramped, unhappy faces as the early-evening traffic begins to thicken. Is this what we have to look forward to as adults, she wonders, sharing the common malaise of a traffic jam on the way home from a job that, in the grand scheme of things, means very little? And if so, no wonder. No wonder people cheat and lie and seek out sex and love in as many places as they possibly can. Is her sister in love with Miles? she wonders. Is that what is going on?

Finally she can no longer stand the silence, so she clears her throat, testing out the air, and says, "You don't need to hide anything going on between you and my sister. It's not like I'm pining for you or something." She smiles, trying to act as if she felt as light as her voice.

"What?" He glances her way, then shakes his head. "No, it's not like that. I hired her to read to my mother twice a week. I asked her not to tell you. I don't know why. It seems stupid now."

"Oh," Helen says, but she can't find the next words, the ones that will help them laugh about the misunderstanding. She experiences a certain amount of relief—at last there is a reason for something—but a mild panic, one she has been unable to completely shake as of late, still runs through her.

"So you thought me and Jenny were having a torrid affair, huh?" He smiles. "Don't you think she's a little young for me?"

"I don't know. I have no idea what to think about anything anymore."

They are passing the university now, and it seems a small oasis of trees and clean, simple buildings amid the strip malls and fast-food joints that surround it. Her father is probably in one of these buildings right now, she thinks, teaching his summer Russian film class. Students stroll across the lawns, between the off-white sixties-style buildings, appearing very much at ease, even beneath the heavy summer heat.

"Hey, isn't that Leo?" Miles asks, pointing at a boy sitting cross-legged beneath a mulberry tree.

"Yeah," Helen says, watching him as they approach. He is batting a pair of drumsticks against his bare leg, looking down at the rhythm he is practicing, and nodding his head a little bit, hair swaying back and forth across his face with the movement.

"Do you want me to drop you off?" Miles asks.

It's as if she were seeing Leo from a strange distance, a distance farther than this truck she's in, passing by on the street. He looks happy and engrossed and beautiful, and Helen feels a surge of love for him, as if she had been suddenly injected with a serum, one that moved quickly through her blood, calming her, holding her panic at bay. How can she leave this boy, she wonders now, and go to school somewhere far away and foreign, a school filled with ordinary college boys who will know nothing of her life in this city, who will know nothing of *her* really, because the her they need to know has been created by everything here, by the heat and the casinos, by the swimming pools and bright skies, by the lives of her parents and sister, and by Leo too? All this will be impossible to communicate to anyone else.

They are passing him now, and Miles asks again, "Should I stop?"

Helen sighs and shakes her head. "No. I don't want to disturb him." And she doesn't. He is perfect to her right now, sitting alone beneath that tree. If she stops they will have to talk about the other night, and why he hasn't called her, and why she hasn't called him for that matter. No, best to keep him right where he is for as long as possible.

When they get to Helen's house, her mother's car is in the driveway. Helen kisses Miles's cheek, tells him good-bye, then goes inside, unsure what she will say to her mother, but wanting to say something, wanting to climb out of the mire she feels sunk in, to free herself from this paralyzing panic that is making it increasingly difficult to act, to move through each day in any normal sort of way.

Helen finds her in the living room, watching Miles drive away through the front window from her seat on the couch.

"Hi," Helen says, sitting in the chair beside her.

Her mother turns toward her. "Hi," she answers softly.

They are quiet as Helen constructs different beginnings in her mind: *You have to stop seeing Gerard; you're hurting Dad by doing this; the truth is, you're hurting me—don't you see how much you're hurting me?* But nothing sounds exactly right, and while Helen continues trying to unwind and organize her words, her mother speaks.

"I guess Miles probably told you he ran into me the other day."

Helen nods.

"Look, Helen. I'm trying to figure this thing out, and I'm sorry I wasn't completely honest with you, but I didn't want you to worry. Besides, this is a private matter and not really any of your business. I don't mean that to sound mean or harsh, but it's the truth. Every aspect of my life does not concern you."

Her look is a little bit defiant, but also sad, Helen thinks, sad and worried and very tired. Shadowy violet crescents rest beneath her eyes, and for a second Helen fears she is ill, and she feels in that second how much worse this would be, to see her mother lying in a bed, covered by a quilt, trying to chat as if nothing at all were the matter.

"Say something, Helen. Please."

"I've been lying about something too," she says, trying to keep her voice clear and level.

"Don't tell me what it is," her mother says immediately. "I don't want to know."

"No, I think you should know. Let's have everything out in the open."

Her mother shakes her head firmly but is quiet. She looks down at her hands resting in her lap, then back up at Helen, almost pleading with her not to speak, it seems, with the look of worry on her face.

"I'm having sex with Leo. I have been for two years now. I lied about it before. Every time you asked me, I lied to your face." Helen sends this out between them, knowing it will wound her mother and waiting, waiting for some feeling of triumph or at least a mild release.

"Okay," her mother says. "Fair enough. I suppose it's not my business anyway. I never should've asked you such a thing."

"Of course you should have!" Helen cries out, rising to stand before her, tremors moving through every limb. "Of course you should've asked!" She sits down on the couch and begins to cry, with such ferocity she can hardly believe the sounds she is emitting are her own. Surely this is someone else, a stranger, making such a spectacle of herself. She waits for her mother's arms to find their way around her, to pull her close and soothe her so that she can shake them off and tell her to go away, that really she doesn't need her. But her mother simply sits there, unmoving, then gets up and walks away toward her bedroom. Helen hears her door click shut, so she lies down on the couch and looks out the latticed window at the sky, wishing she were someone else.

Drumbeats

THE IDEA BEGINS to make noise softly in his mind, with the subtlety of wind chimes, more like background music at this point. He sits on the lawn at UNLV, practicing a new pattern on his leg, and he hears it every few minutes or so when there's a pause in his drumming: *Break up with Helen.*

He hasn't called her for five days, a veritable record, and every day he doesn't speak to her, the thought grows louder so that now it is becoming more forceful than the wind chime message, closer to the hard tat of a snare drum: *Break up with Helen, break up with Helen.*

Why would he entertain such an idea? he wonders. He has not

fallen out of love with her; in fact, the picture of her that rises in his mind right now, as he rises from the lawn and walks back toward orchestra practice, clutches at his heart, sends a tremor from chest to throat and back. But five nights ago, when the condom broke, something shifted between them. He could feel it, strongly in that cramped, awful bedroom of his but less so in the car, where the wind, singing through the windows with a plaintiveness that brought him close to crying, cleared out the space around and between them so that their old patterns returned. So that his love returned, his yearning, his wish to keep Helen as close to him as possible.

But then a day passed without a call between them. Then another. And each day he recalled what had happened in his bedroom, the simultaneous dread and rage that had boiled up when he saw the broken condom, when he felt what it could mean for him, and these thoughts made him keep his silence.

She is going to leave him anyway. If he once imagined she might continue their relationship long distance while she was in college, he no longer harbors such hopes. No, despite her claim she wants to marry him, despite even their midnight visit to the chapel last summer, he knows the truth, and the truth is that she will leave and grow and change and meet another guy, then another, and another, until they all are piled up along her past like a cast of extras, not true actors in the movie of her life. And he will be among them. Sure, he will have a slightly more important role—the first boyfriend, the first love—but it will not be enough. With Helen, it will never be enough, and he is beginning to realize this; little pieces of doubt are rising to the surface on a daily basis now, and soon, enough will be accumulated to convince him. Then *he* will do the leaving.

Inside the band room, notes, discordant and raucous, float toward him. Flutes and clarinets, the high whine of violins, a tuba in the corner, trumpets and trombones. Everyone is tuning up, preparing to go through the score one or two more times today. Then there will be a break, then dinner at the student union, then practice again until eight; then he will make his way home, where he will convince himself once more it is too late to call Helen.

He takes his place behind the timpani and stretches out his wrists and hands before picking up the mallets. The room is almost full now, though the conductor, an acerbic, demanding woman with radiant red hair whom everyone in the orchestra, including the girls, has a bit of a crush on, has not yet returned from lunch. Leo tunes his drums, then looks around the room. He has made a few friends here, the other drummers and one trombonist who lived in his dorm last year; but there are plenty of pretty girls, and he has hardly talked to any of them yet.

One of the flutists looks familiar. He has been thinking this for several weeks now, but can't figure out where he knows her from. She is plump in a very nice way, with short, firm arms that hold up her flute with delicate ease. Her hair is very dark brown and all one length, swinging at mid-neck. Leo has found himself watching that white, exposed neck—no bones visible at all, unlike Helen's—as he counts through his rests during a piece of music. Her face is round and pleasant and bare of makeup except for dark red lipstick, which she wears without fail. She has chosen the prettiest part of herself to emphasize, Leo thinks now, watching her talk to the girl on her right. Her lips are not especially full; but she has an almost perfect bow at the top, and when she talks, as she is doing now, they are a flashing bit of color on her otherwise pale face.

The conductor, Ms. Sullivan, arrives holding a cup from 7-Eleven and drinking through its straw. "All right, people," she says loudly, exchanging her drink for her baton and stepping up to the lectern. "Let's run through the Copland piece again, and try not to sabotage it so much this time." There is laughter from the trumpet section. "Oh, yeah," she says, "it's really funny what bad musicians we are." She smiles in a very small way after this, not too encouraging, but just a little, then sets the beat with her baton, and they are off.

ON THEIR WALK across campus to dinner, Leo decides to talk to the familiar flutist and find out, if possible, who she is. It seems incredibly lucky to him that she is walking alone tonight, off to the side of the other flutists, and he increases his pace until he is beside her. "Hi," he says.

"Well"—she looks up at him with a smile—"I was wondering when you were going to get around to talking to me."

He still can't figure out where he knows her from, and now it appears that he's been rude, waiting until now to speak. "We were in that history survey class together, right?"

She shakes her head. "I haven't started school here yet. This fall will be my first semester. I took a year off to work."

"Great," he says, stalling for time. *Who is she? Who is she?* "You'll love it here."

"You don't know who I am, do you?"

"It's coming to me. Give me a minute."

"I guess I do look really different, so this isn't exactly a fair test. Here, I'll give you a hint." She pulls at a thin gold chain hidden under her red T-shirt, then lets the necklace fall against the cloth.

The pendant is a small piece of cursive writing, and Leo leans closer to read it, then pulls away with a jolt of surprise. "Traci?" he says. "From the Dunes? It can't be you."

"I stopped dyeing my hair and wearing all that makeup. And"—she shrugs and frowns—"I put on a little weight. After I quit smoking."

"You look great." He gives her a large smile to show he means what he says. They are walking down a path now toward the union, flanked on either side by pale green lawns and mulberry trees. Most of the musicians are ahead of them. An evening breeze filters through their hair, providing a moment of cool from the sun, which still sits halfway down the sky, presiding over the campus with its usual yellow intensity. For some reason, he is inordinately happy to have found out who she is, and on impulse he takes her hand and squeezes it as they walk, then drops it back safely at her side.

She laughs. "I thought you were avoiding me."

"Of course not," he says, thinking his voice sounds insincere, although that is not his intent. It occurs to him she may not be so pleased to see him. After all, he did lead her on, then told her about Helen, then saw her a few more times after that. They spent a couple of afternoons in his bedroom, kissing and listening to music, removing one or two articles of clothing until he felt so guilty he ended it a second time. But that was two summers ago, and to him it feels as if a million years have passed.

"Well, I'm glad we finally got to talk," she says with a smile. "I need to catch up with my friends." She points to a group of girls ahead. "I promised I'd eat with them."

"Okay." He nods, then watches as she runs a little bit ahead of him, thinking maybe now he is ready for a girlfriend like her, someone who is completely different from Helen.

AFTER THE EVENING'S final practice session, he drives home, wishing he were still living in the dorms, or better yet, that he had his own apartment. Every night when he winds up at his house—his mother's house is the way he thinks of it now—it seems he's taken a step backward, out of his new life and into his old.

During the school year he had a single dorm room, some random stroke of luck bestowed on him, because almost everyone else had a roommate. There was a twin bed by the single window, a desk with bookshelves set into the wall above it, a soft swivel chair, and a small refrigerator in the corner. Leo kept it neat and spare, with only a drum pad for practice. (Mostly he used the equipment in the band room.) Books from his classes were lined up tidily on the shelves, and his desk possessed a notebook, several pens in a cup, a CD Walkman (a gift from Helen), and a small plant he bought at a campus sale, though when Helen told him the name of it—dumb cane—he regretted the purchase. Still, he watered it once a week, then transported it to his bedroom at his mother's house, where it continued to flourish, and he looked at it now as a symbol of his return, a promise that he would soon have his own space again.

He put no pictures on the walls of his dorm room, no rugs on the floor, kept nothing in his refrigerator but a quart of milk, and one of his drummer friends, Evan, took to calling him Leo the Monk, a nickname that he pretended to think stupid but secretly liked, because his life always seemed so cluttered to him—full of records and drum equipment and condoms and clothes and sex—so *un*monastic, and the idea that he could change, could free himself of his past, made him feel clean and talented and happy.

Leo parks his Nova in the driveway, behind his mother's car, then enters through the side door, expecting to smell smoke and hear the television talking nonsense as he usually does. Instead, he hears two voices spilling animatedly from the living room: his mother's and Helen's. He stops in the dark kitchen, listening to them for a few seconds, not wanting to round the corner and see them both sitting there, waiting for him. "I don't think I've ever heard of that before," Helen exclaims, but Leo has missed what she's talking about and feels adrift here in the darkness, privy to only a small sliver of this girl's—*his girlfriend's*—life. It strikes him suddenly that this is the way he often feels in Helen's presence, as if he were hearing only half a conversation. She doles out only small portions of herself at a time, and it seems to Leo there are layers and layers he will never even be allowed to glimpse. It also occurs to him that this is part of her hold on him, what creates the intense yearning he feels even now, listening from the kitchen.

"Leo, is that you?" his mother calls, and he is forced to turn the corner, to walk into the dim light of the living room.

"Hi," he says. They sit at either end of the couch, bodies turned toward each other, though now their faces are turned to him. He moves automatically to sit by Helen on the couch, putting his hand on her bare leg and feeling its warmth beneath his palm, a reminder of the day's heat.

"I was just going to bed," his mother says, standing up. She is wearing her lavender terry-cloth robe over a summer nightgown, and when she bends to kiss Leo on the cheek, he smells her too-sweet, lilac talcum powder. "Good night," she tells them both, and then they are alone. Leo removes his hand from Helen's leg, realizing that it may not be welcome with the lack of phone calls between them.

"Sorry I haven't called," he tells her. Why does he always speak first?

She shrugs. "You're busy."

He is strangely disappointed by her lack of anger, so he adds, "Not that busy."

"I could've called you."

"True."

They sit for a minute, looking at each other, and Leo tries to decide if this is the right moment, if he should break up with her right now and be done with it, but then she takes his hand and smiles, and she looks so beautiful that leaving her seems foolish. He likes her best at night, when her hair is messed up and the day's makeup has dissipated, leaving the occasional sultry smudge of black beneath her eyes. Her skin is warm and brown from a day's worth of poolside sun and she smells of chlorine, a clean scent he always associates as her own, though he supposes everyone who swims must smell that way too.

"I got my period today," she whispers.

He breathes out deeply and leans his head against the back of the couch. "Thank God," he says, then laughs. "I guess I acted a little crazy the other night. I ruined that album cover, you know."

She laughs too. "Oh-oh. Your Iron Maiden collection will be incomplete."

"Doesn't matter. I took them all down last night. The walls are completely bare. It's much better."

"I'll have to buy you a Miró print or something to re-liven up the room."

Miró. What is she talking about? Even with a year of college behind him she is still somewhere up ahead. Instead of speaking anymore, he pulls her head against his chest and holds on to her. With her chlorine-scented hair beneath his cheek, her rib cage expanding with breath beneath his hand, Leo knows he will never be able to do the leaving.

THE NEXT DAY during lunch Leo makes a trip to the mall. Helen is turning eighteen at the end of summer, and Leo decided last night that he'd better start looking for a present right now, since he has no idea what to give her. If he takes a month to find the gift, he can't go wrong. It must be something unusual, he thinks, a gift that will reveal in a perfect and beautiful way all the complicated lines of love that run through him when he thinks of her.

On his way to the car from the band room, he sees Traci, eating a sandwich beneath a tree. He crosses over to say hello and on impulse asks if she'd like to come along. She agrees, then rises from the grass to follow him, and he feels buoyant crossing the parking lot, but when they get into his Nova, heat covers them, weighing Leo down and making him wonder why on earth he asked Traci to come with him. Best to tell her everything this time, he decides, rolling down his window as he pulls out of the lot, best to enlist her as a friend before he does something stupid and unkind.

"So," he says. "I should probably tell you up front this time that I still have a girlfriend."

"Okay." She looks out the window so that he can't read her expression, but her voice sounds bland and happy, unsurprised.

"She's going to college in Ohio at the end of summer, though."

"Cool," she says, then turns to him. "I have a boyfriend too. Well, he's not exactly a boyfriend yet, just someone I like, and I think the feeling might be mutual."

"Who is it?"

"One of the trumpet players." She smiles, and he notices again the way her front teeth lightly cross each other. He found that appealing in her before and recognizes that he still does. "I don't want to say who it is, in case nothing comes of it."

"Fair enough," Leo says. There are five trumpet players, and Leo can't quite fill his mind with their faces. Later he will inspect them more closely.

THE BOULEVARD MALL is not very crowded, and when they walk through the revolving front doors, a sheet of cool air wraps around them, putting Leo back into a good mood. Benign, watery music hovers above them, and Leo recognizes the tune, some rock song he once slow-danced to in junior high. Hearing it now, turned into a harmless instrumental number, serves to calm him, helps him believe he can handle this situation: being friends with Traci.

They stop by a glass-topped map of the mall in an effort to spend their hour and a half as wisely as possible. "So, you're a girl," Leo says, smiling. "What's the perfect gift for Helen's eighteenth birthday?"

"I don't know. Jewelry? Perfume?"

He shakes his head. "She doesn't wear either."

"What is she, some sort of nun?"

Traci winks at him, to show she is joking, he supposes, but the wink riles him up, makes him in the mood to flirt. He grabs her around the waist with one arm and pulls her close with a laugh. "Yes, she is, and it's a good thing she's leaving at the end of summer and I can find someone else, or I might die from lack of physical contact. Humans need contact for survival, you know. There was a study, with babies."

"I've never heard of that study," she says, dipping away from him.

They both laugh, then stare down at the map again, but Leo is not paying attention to the lists of stores. Instead, he is thinking of the way her waist felt beneath his hand, neat and firm despite her plump limbs. There is something almost tangible between them right now, Leo thinks. It strikes him as a color, a series of reddish orange, zigzagging lines connecting her body to his.

"I have an idea," she says, turning to face him. "How about a pet?"

He nods thoughtfully, "Yeah, maybe a dog. I think she's always wanted a dog. Of course they probably won't allow it in the dorm rooms where she's going."

"It could be smaller. Maybe a fish . . . or a lizard!"

"Very romantic," Leo says. "Here you go, Helen. Here's a lizard to show you how much you mean to me."

Traci laughs. "Well, let's go look at least."

He agrees, and they make their way over to the pet store, which is playing different music, or not even music, Leo realizes, but sounds—waves rolling in and out, the cries of seagulls. Small, forlorn-looking dogs peer out at them through cages, and Traci and Leo hurry past to the back of the store, where the smaller animals are kept. The fish are beautiful, swimming placidly behind glass, but he can't help feeling that giving Helen a fish would say something negative about the quality of his passion, since the expression *cold fish* is one he often hears the other drummers use to describe a girl who won't put out. Of course he can't explain this to Traci, so he takes her arm and pulls her away toward the birds.

Leo considers getting Helen a lovebird, but it strikes him as too obvious and almost needy, asking too plainly for her please to remember him when she goes away. The parrots are fun but abrasive, and then Leo sees exactly what he wants to give her, a canary. The bird is thin and yellow and in a cage of its own, singing so poetically Leo instantly knows this is the bird for Helen. A gift of music, Leo thinks. A reminder of him, but not obviously so.

He can't buy it now—Helen's birthday is still weeks away, and she'll see it in his room—so he tells Traci he's going to see if he can reserve the canary.

"I doubt that's possible," she tells him. "It's not like a shirt or something. You can't put it on hold."

"Sure you can," he says, then on impulse grabs her hand and pulls her with him toward the front of the store, past the lizards and mice, down a pet food aisle before he turns the corner, too quickly, and bumps into someone.

The woman he's hit turns around, frowning, then sees him and smiles. "Leo," she says. It is Helen's mother, Mrs. Larkin.

"Oh, hi," he says, dropping Traci's hand, but it is too late; Mrs. Larkin's eyes flickered to their linked hands immediately. "This is my friend Traci." He points to her. "She plays the flute in my orchestra. Traci, this is Helen's mother."

Traci holds out her hand politely, and the two women shake. "Very nice to meet you," Traci says in a way that sounds more mannered, more *cultured*, than Leo would've expected.

"Hey, Kath," they hear from across the store, and all three of them turn. "What do you think of this one?"

There is a man holding up a very small white poodle, and it is a man Leo knows he's seen before, but he can't immediately place where. Then it hits him: the man is Helen's boss, Gerard.

"I'll be there in a second," she calls, holding up one finger. "He wanted me to help him pick out a dog for his daughter," she explains with a shrug. She says good-bye, then walks across the linoleum to stand by Gerard, where Leo watches her say something as she frowns and shakes her head. Gerard hands the dog back to a boy in a blue smock; then they both turn and leave the store. They do not touch or walk close to each other, Leo doesn't even see them speak again as they disappear around the corner of the store; still, he senses something is going on between them. He recalls, suddenly, that Helen saw her mother at Gerard's party, two years ago. Leo has completely forgotten about that until now, and he wonders if they've been having an affair and whether or not Helen knows. And if she does know, why hasn't she confided the information to him?

"C'mon, let's go ask about the canary," Traci reminds him, then asks, "Are you all right?"

"Um." He looks down at her. "Yeah, that was just weird. What if Helen's mom is having an affair?"

Traci shrugs. "It wouldn't be the first time in the history of the planet."

"Yeah, but, I don't know, Helen's parents are just . . . I just thought they were above those types of things. Everything always seems so perfect at their house." He can hear how naive he sounds but is unable to stop. "I mean, I have to say I kind of secretly looked up to them as having an ideal marriage."

Traci gives him a sympathetic frown and pats his arm. "We'd better head back," she says, "or Ms. Sullivan will give us hell."

"Okay," he agrees, and they are already in the car and halfway back to campus before Leo remembers he forgot to ask about holding the canary.

WHEN HE GETS HOME that evening, a little after seven, the house is empty. He makes himself a ham sandwich and eats it standing at the kitchen counter, looking out the window at the yellow, sun-baked lawn, at the dying palm tree by the driveway, at his Nova, which is beginning to look used up; the blue paint is starting to peel around the wheels, and he hasn't washed it in weeks. He presumes his mother is out on a date, and the idea depresses him. Her new boyfriend—a dentist, this time, with overly white teeth and rounded shoulders that make him look older than he is—depresses Leo. It's as if this man, Ray Washburn, hoped his perfect bleached teeth would block out all his other inadequacies with their bright glare.

When he finishes his sandwich, he picks up the phone to call Helen, then, after hitting the first three numbers, realizes he can't do it and sets the phone back in its cradle on the kitchen wall. If he speaks to her, he will want to mention that he saw her mother today, and he doesn't think this is a good idea, so instead, he heads back outside and begins walking toward Odyssey Records.

The chant begins again as he walks, increasing its intensity and depth so that now Leo imagines it is a bass drum telling him: *Break up with Helen, break up with Helen.* Why is this idea still a presence in his mind, he wonders, when last night on the couch beside the actual Helen he knew he'd never even consider such a rash move? Is it simply self-preservation? he wonders. Merely his rational self warning his love-struck one to get out before she cuts him off and he'll have both pain *and* embarrassment to deal with? If he were the one to leave, at least he would maintain a measure of dignity.

He walks past the last of the houses onto the wide expanse of parking lot containing the minimart and Luv-it Frozen Custard, and seeing the familiar white ice-cream store—he still insists on calling it ice cream; what the hell is frozen custard?—he is bombarded by even more thoughts of Helen. They have sat together on that outside bench so many times, talking about music or people at school or their families, or poetry and love—how very much they love each other—or even fighting, over who knows what, usually his jealousy, he guesses, and her annoyance with it. Even the memories of those arguments make Leo smile as he passes the bench, where another couple sits right now, a middle-aged couple eating sundaes without speaking to each other but looking content all the same.

Don't be crazy, he tells himself, passing Luv-it and approaching the stoplight of Las Vegas Boulevard. You hate fighting with Helen, he tries to remind himself, dredging up all the past instances when jealousy—for Miles or just some guy who looked at her too long—ate away at his insides until he felt like nothing, like an absence. As he waits at the light, he turns again to look at the bench, which is empty now, and tries to picture himself there with Traci. The image is a pleasant one, her plump white legs neatly crossed as she eats a dip of strawberry on a sugar cone, her free hand placed on his knee, maybe absently practicing a difficult flute passage, though he's not certain that would be possible with just one hand. Would they fight too? he wonders. Would the same familiar fires burn through him, leaving him blackened out inside, sickened with ashes. He doesn't think so; for some reason he expects any jealousy for Traci would be much less intense, if only because he is unwilling to let it reach so deeply inside him anymore. He is almost twenty years old, after all, and in college now. Leo decides right there, waiting for the light, that he will never let jealousy wound him again with such ferocity.

Across the street the sign for Odyssey Records glows red through the evening light, which is still quite bright as the sun is just now beginning its descent behind the mountains. Leo is welcome there again; in fact, the clerk who busted him last summer for the tape in his pocket was fired during the school year. He wants to listen to a new Moroccan drummer he's heard about and buy a Thelonious Monk CD Evan played for him the other night, and maybe he'll buy something for Traci while he's at it, a tape to say thank you for helping him shop for Helen today. That's all it will be, just a gift to show his appreciation for her friendship.

ON THE WALK HOME, an hour later, he feels a yellow happiness rising within him, the same joy he always feels after buying new music. When he gets home, he'll make some microwave popcorn, pour himself a glass of orange crush—or maybe a glass of his mother's wine if she's not home yet—then go into his room, put on his Walkman headphones and listen, listen to the new Thelonious Monk CD over and over until he is sick of hearing it, then tomorrow he'll be ready to listen to it again. His Odyssey Records' bag also contains a tape for Traci, a jazz flutist whose name Leo can't recall right now, and he knows he'll be tempted to open it up and listen to it too but hopes he will be able to abstain and present the gift intact.

The sun has set, but the sky is still very light with its memory, and streaks of orange cross the deepening blue to his right like a school of goldfish. The houses on his left look better in the dimming evening air, and Leo can almost ignore the fact that their paint is chipping away or that their curtains are yellowed with cigarette smoke and age. Of course they are still obviously squat and dull-eyed, flanked by balding, cluttered lawns, but who cares really, Leo tells himself, because soon he will be gone, tucked once again into his spare dorm room, listening to whatever new CD he happens to have as if it were a religion.

He is so anxious to get inside and open his music that when he sees Helen from a block away, pulling into his driveway on her ten-speed, he is disappointed. He'll have to postpone his listening session and pretend he bought the flute tape for himself. Of course, as a consolation, they can have sex, and this thought buoys him up a bit, but still, he is disappointed.

However, as he draws closer to home and waves, he sees that the girl on the bike is not Helen at all, but her sister, Jenny, and Leo hurries his step, extremely curious what she would be doing here and a little worried too: Has she brought bad news?

"Jenny, what's up?" he says when he reaches her. Her face, beneath the brim of a lavender ball cap is set into a worried frown, so he adds, "Is something the matter?"

She shrugs in the exact manner Helen always does and says, "Not exactly. I was just riding around and thought maybe, since I was in the neighborhood, I'd come and talk to you."

"Okay, sure." He ushers her away from her bike over to the front stoop, where they both sit down on the warm concrete step, facing out toward the street.

"I'm worried about Helen," she tells him. "She's been acting weird."

"What do you mean?"

"Well, she hasn't gone to work for two weeks; she's pretending to be sick or something though my mom knows she isn't. She seems to have stopped brushing her hair at all and she hangs out with that Ernie girl all the time and it's weird because they're starting to look alike, except for their stomachs, of course. She's constantly rude to Mom, and Mom just takes it! She doesn't punish Helen or anything. It's very strange."

So Helen does know about her mother, Leo thinks. She must know. So why hasn't she mentioned anything to him? He also didn't know she'd been staying home from work for so long. Two days off were all she'd told him about, and she claimed they were due to a sick stomach. This information makes him desolate, as separate from Helen as he has ever been, and the drumbeat pumps through him for the second time that evening: *Break up with Helen.* "What do *you* think's going on?" he asks Jenny.

"I don't know. I'm worried she has some fatal disease or something and nobody's telling me."

He puts his arm around her shoulders, in an attempt to be brotherly, and says, "Oh, I don't think she has any disease, Jenny."

"Then what?"

She turns to face him, and Leo sees how much she is beginning to look like Helen, enough to make his heart clutch with love. "I think maybe she's trying to protect you from something. You know, be a good older sister, and all. She'll tell you when she's ready."

"Why don't you just tell me what it is, and I'll promise not to say anything?"

Leo considers this. How exactly would he phrase it? *I think your mother is sleeping with the pool manager at the Dunes Hotel.* But of course he can't do this. It would wound her deeply, alter every perception of her parents, of her family, that she has. As he realizes this, it occurs to Leo how Helen must be hurting, how this knowledge must be changing her, altering her entire landscape, that hilly, complex inside that is becoming more and more like foreign ground. "I don't have anything to tell," he says.

"Right," she says with a touch of sarcasm, then stands up. "You know, I'm not a little kid anymore. I can handle the truth."

"Maybe you can," Leo says, looking up at her with a smile, "but why do you want to if it's painful?"

"See, you do know something!"

"I was just speaking philosophically."

"The truth shall set you free," she says, then asks, "What's that from again?"

"The Bible."

"Oh." She looks down at her feet and kicks at the brittle grass, then says, "Well, I'm not so sure I believe in God, so I guess I shouldn't be quoting from the Bible."

It strikes Leo as incredibly sad that she doesn't believe in God, even though he's not so sure he does either. It seems an admission of lost faith, of a jadedness she is too young to possess. He hopes Helen doesn't tell her about their mother and make matters worse. Leo stands beside Jenny and pulls her into an embrace, patting her shoulder and kissing the top of her ball cap. "Don't worry so much," he says.

She holds on to him for a moment, pressing her face into his chest, then pulls away and gets on her bike. "Don't tell Helen I came by." Then she frowns and adds, "Actually, I don't care what you say. Don't tell her any lies."

He nods and waves good-bye, then watches as she pedals off down the sidewalk and out of sight around the corner.

HE LISTENS TO his new CD for a while but can't really focus on the music as he usually does, and he accidentally burned the popcorn he made so that the entire house is corrupted by the smell. His mother's wine tastes bitter to him, but he drinks it anyway and feels a small headache creeping up his neck when he is finished.

He attempts sleep around midnight—his mother is not yet home—but can only lie there wide-eyed, staring at the bumpy stuccoed ceiling and thinking about the divide between himself and Helen, a divide she appears to be intent on widening. By 1:00 A.M. he is even more wide awake, so he rises and dresses in the dark, then walks through the house and out the front door.

The thought of walking occurs to him, but he is drawn to his Nova's promise of the radio, and once inside he feels almost content against the cracking vinyl seat, his hands resting lightly on the warm steering wheel as he pulls out onto the street, listening to a late-night classical guitar program he likes but rarely stays up late enough to catch. There are still a few cars on the road; but for the most part the night is quiet, and he takes the back way, through sleeping neighborhoods, around the curved edge of Circle Park, until he is in a nicer area, one with more trees and tidy lawns, each house a different pastel color like a line of ice-cream cones or Popsicles.

Helen's house is sky-blue, almost a gray, with white trim and a roof composed of peaks and valleys. The windows are dark, and Leo parks across the street, then shuts off the car and sits for a moment in the silence, though at this time of summer there is never absolute silence, since the cicadas continue to wail throughout the night.

He has sneaked into her bedroom before, so Leo does not need to create a plan. The chain-link fence on the far left side of the house is where he will make his entrance, so he crosses the yard, then steps carefully through the sagebrush and around the pomegranate tree before catching a toehold in the fence and leaping over into the backyard. Helen's bedroom window faces him now; it begins lower than his waist and rises above his head, shut tight to keep in the air conditioning and curtained to keep Helen from the view of people or cars passing by on the street, though in truth, the plants and pomegranate tree conceal this section of the backyard and house fairly well.

The moon is half full tonight and casts a chalky glow on this portion of the lawn. Several feet away he can see the neighbor's house, over the low wooden fence that divides the two properties. An older couple lives there with a large basset hound, and Leo worries, as he did the last time he completed this feat, that the dog will hear or smell him, come outside, and bark loudly, revealing Leo's unwelcome presence to Helen's parents.

He taps on the window with his knuckle, so softly he can't imagine Helen will hear him, even though her bed is directly beside the window; but in less than a second the curtain is pulled aside, and then the window is opened, and Helen steps outside, completely naked, into the night. There is not a shred of coolness to the air—in fact, Leo is sweating—but her nakedness makes him crazy with fear, and she must sense this because in the next second she reaches back in through the window and pulls out a silky yellow robe, then puts it on, tying it tightly at the waist.

Despite the fact Helen's just woken up, Leo can tell Jenny is right about one thing: Helen hasn't combed her hair in a while. It looks thicker than usual, arching out from her head in an intractable mass, and a single matted lock has escaped its confines and lies against her throat like the small paw of an animal. She pushes it back impatiently, then waits for him to speak.

"What's up with your hair?" is the first thing he can think to say, though once it's out he feels embarrassed; he did not come here to discuss trivial matters.

"I'm thinking of trying to do dreadlocks," she says.

This strikes him as a lie, and he hopes it will be the last one between them. "Helen." He steps closer and lowers his voice to a whisper. "Helen, why didn't you tell me about your mom and Gerard?"

She shrugs and looks away, out toward the street. "I don't know."

"I thought being in love meant telling each other everything." Once this is out of his mouth he longs to call it back; he has kept many things from Helen, hasn't he? No longer, he tells himself, from this moment on things will be different.

"How did you find out?" Her eyes flicker back to him.

"I saw them together. At the mall."

"Great!" She gives a whispered shout. "Now they're doing their shopping together too. What were they buying? A wedding dress? A bed? A set of china?"

He tightens his mouth to show her he won't even consider laughing at the situation. They are still not touching, and he wonders why this is. It strikes him as unnatural, so he moves a step closer and takes her hand, which is warm and smooth with long, thin fingers. Often her nails are dirty, a fact that strikes him as endearing since the rest of her is so clean and bright. He is going to miss this hand, he thinks now, pressing it more tightly; he will miss many things about her when she is gone. "You should have told me about it," he says, sounding more stern and reproachful than he'd meant to.

"Why? Why should I have told you? How is it in any way your business?" She withdraws her hand from his and steps back toward the window.

"Because I love you."

"Is that why you were driving around with some girl today? Because you love me so much?" He is shocked into silence, and she takes the blank space of air to add, "Ernie saw you."

"Helen, it's not . . ." he says, trying to devise an elaborate defense, but suddenly he changes his mind. "Nothing's going on with her," is all he says, though he knows even this is not quite the truth. "Look." He takes a deep breath and shifts his gaze to the ground; if he looks at her, he will not be able to do this. "I think maybe we should break up."

When he glances at Helen, she is crying, sitting awkwardly on the window ledge with her hands over her face. She is emitting no sound, but her shoulders shake; then a small sob escapes, propelling him toward her.

"Never mind," he says quickly, moving to sit beside her, putting his hand on her leg. "I didn't mean it. Never mind."

"You did mean it," she says, keeping her hands over her face. "You can't take it back."

"Yes, I can. I'm doing it right now. Forget I said anything."

"No." She lifts her face. "It's probably a good idea."

And with these words, he begins to cry, standing and turning to the wall, propping a forearm above his head, then leaning his face into the sky-blue wood and sobbing, as quietly as he possibly can, but sobbing all the same. Helen is behind him in moments, her arms around his waist, cheek pressed to the back of his head. It is a small warm pressure, as if a bird had landed there, and this makes him think of the canary he wants to give her, and he cries all the harder. He'll still buy it for her, he decides. He wants her to have that canary.

They hear a noise from within the house—a door shutting, perhaps, or a sleepy elbow hitting a wall—and both of them are instantly quiet. "You'd better go," Helen says, then unwraps herself and climbs back through the open window; in the next second she pokes out her head and tells him, "We can talk later. Tomorrow." Then she closes her window, and he is left alone on the grass.

He climbs back over the fence and begins to cross the front lawn, when he hears his name called from the direction of the porch. He turns and sees Helen's father sitting on the red-brick steps in his pajamas. Edward beckons to Leo with a wave of his arm, so Leo walks over to him, trying to devise an apology that might explain this situation, but he can think of none. He is too tired, too sad and tired to come up with anything that will save him.

"Did I wake you?" Leo asks politely when he is standing before Helen's father. The question sounds ludicrous once it is out.

Mr. Larkin shakes his head. "I was listening to this classical guitar program I like because I couldn't sleep, and then I thought I heard your car; it's pretty distinctive-sounding."

A polite way of saying his muffler needs work, Leo thinks, then sinks onto the step beside Helen's father, suddenly too exhausted to stand for another second. "I was listening to that guitar program on the way over," he says.

Mr. Larkin nods, and Leo turns toward him, trying to formulate his story. Helen's father looks tired and unguarded without his glasses on, though otherwise, he is neat and crisp in pale green, striped pajamas, his thinning blond hair parted on the side and groomed as if it were the middle of the day rather than very late at night. "I know I shouldn't be here," Leo says, "but I had to speak with your daughter."

"I understand." Edward nods. "Important matters of the heart and all."

Leo breathes out, noticing for the first time how tight all of his muscles feel, as if he were preparing to pounce, to spring into the night and seek out prey. "We just broke up," he tells her father. Once the words are out, he knows it is true, that if there is any talking to be done tomorrow, nothing will come of it.

Edward turns to Leo and creases his brow in concern. "No," he says. "No, you need to work it out, whatever it is."

For the first time Leo catches a whiff of wine and thinks that perhaps it is an explanation for all the emotion in Mr. Larkin's voice. "We can't," Leo says simply.

"Is there someone else?"

Leo shakes his head no, though an image of Traci—the soft dip in the back of her neck as she plays her flute—swims instantly into Leo's vision, and he realizes he is anxious to see her tomorrow, to give her the tape he bought today. "It's just," Leo says, wanting, for some reason, to be as honest as possible. "it's just that sometimes I feel as if I don't even know Helen. She has all these hidden parts to her, and it's interesting and even, I don't know, exciting, I guess you could say, but it's making me crazy. I want to know everything about her, and I never will, and I just can't take it anymore. Does that make any sense?"

Mr. Larkin nods. "It does, Leo; it does indeed, but one day you'll see it's not really possible to know *any* person completely. There are hidden parts to all of us. We do the best we can with what we're given, with what we can glean through conversation and lovemaking . . . and through separation too. Sometimes we learn a lot through separation, or bad times, if you will." He rubs his chin, then asks with a smile, "Do I sound like a dottery old professor?"

"No."

"But of course you and Helen are teenagers, and you're not married and she's going away and maybe it makes sense to break up, though it still makes me a little wistful." He pats Leo's leg, then stands up. " 'Do not go gentle,' " he says, "though I won't call the night good."

Leo rises too, confused by Mr. Larkin's good-bye and chalking it up to the wine and late hour. They shake hands on the porch; then Leo climbs back into his Nova and begins the drive home.

About halfway there, he realizes Mr. Larkin was quoting a line from a poem: "Do not go gentle into that good night." No other lines come to him as he makes his way through the neighborhood, but he knows that at some point Helen read it to him, maybe one day in his bedroom, sitting cross-legged on the floor by his drum set? He can almost conjure the image, and he realizes, as night air hums over him, that no matter how hollowed out he feels right now, no matter how much it seems as if Helen has only stolen from him, that he is taking away something too, that the store of words and images, the array of perceptions and knowledge and feelings that soar out of him when he thinks of her, will most likely remain somewhere inside him until he dies.

A Manageable Paradise

EDWARD OR GERARD. THIS IS THE CHOICE Kathy must make. Edward or Gerard. Two days ago, in the cool grotto of Gerard's bedroom, Kathy was given what she thinks is the first ultimatum of her adult life: "Leave Edward or I'm leaving you." Gerard was sitting in the depths of a green bean bag, wearing nothing but a pair of black satin boxer shorts and a silver chain around his neck (one Kathy herself had given him in the first green rising of their affair). They had not yet had sex but were merely in the beginning stages of an afternoon together—the slow, casual undressing, glasses of iced tea, conversation overlaid by music from the radio. And then the conversation took a turn, the removal of clothing halted, and Gerard said simply: "Please leave Edward; I don't want to share you any longer. It's just not possible for me to do it any longer."

The crucial part of the ultimatum was not actually stated, but the knowledge that he would end their affair stood resolutely between them in the small room. Later, as they lay side by side on his twin bed, she said, "I need a few days to decide what I want to do." He nodded, lips pressed tightly together, and told her quietly, "Okay."

The choice should be an easy one, she tells herself now, wandering around her kitchen in the moonlight. Edward is smarter, more secure financially, even better-looking, really, and of course there is the crucial reason why he should be her obvious choice: He is the father of their daughters. She pours herself water from the fridge, then drinks it standing at the sink and staring out into the dark backyard. She tries to imagine standing like this in Gerard's kitchen, with a glass of Gerard's in her hand as she looks onto his backyard. Even in moonlight the differences would be striking. Gerard has no real lawn to speak of, only a slab of concrete presided over by a clothesline and an old motorcycle he works on in the winter and early spring when it's cooler outside; Edward, on the other hand, has spent this cooler period carefully nurturing a small lane of tulips and snapdragons (though at this point in the summer they've already bloomed and died), a magical task in the desert.

Right now she can see the tall dark shapes of the oleander bushes, the mulberry tree with its red hummingbird feeder, the redwood deck off to her left with its glass-topped table and yellow chairs. All this is hers to share, and she loves it all. In fact, the thought of holding a jelly jar glass of tap water as she looks out at the carcass of a motorcycle depresses her to no end.

Of course there is much more to this issue than her place of residence, she reminds herself, and with her teaching salary plus Gerard's they could buy a new home; perhaps they'd even move away to another city. Helen's leaving for college anyway, and Jenny will soon follow. Still, Kathy is old enough to know that the way people have chosen to live, the things they have built into and around their lives, says something about their character. And these choices are not really about money. Gerard can afford to buy tulip bulbs and a set of pretty glasses from Pier 1 just as well as she and Edward can. He could plant a mulberry tree and dispose of his motorcycle. She's not asking for a mansion after all.

She finishes her water and walks through the dark house to her bedroom. It is 2:00 A.M., and Edward is asleep, but she gets into bed a bit noisily, shuffling the covers over herself several times and emitting a fake cough because she wants to wake him, wants to talk to him right now and see if something he says in ordinary, nighttime conversation might tell her what to do, might clarify whom she should choose; but he merely rolls away from her onto his side and begins to breathe more deeply. So she closes her eyes and attempts to make her way toward sleep.

GERARD IS WAITING for her at his house the next afternoon with a bundle of carnations and a new Lionel Richie CD. "I thought I'd better start trying to make my case," he says, then kisses her cheek. They've agreed to keep seeing each other while Kathy tries to figure things out, and Saturday has become their day together because Edward thinks she is taking a summer school literature class at the community college that lasts most of the afternoon. For some reason this particular lie pains her the most, pulls a shade over these hours spent with Gerard more than her other untruths do. The thought of Edward home with Helen and Jenny, imagining her studiously sitting in a classroom discussing classic novels wraps her entire body in sticky guilt. At the least she wishes she had chosen a different made-up subject, because now every Saturday when she gets home Edward wants to know what they discussed and how she likes the book she's reading. (She first pretended to be reading *Madame Bovary* because she'd already read that one but soon saw the immense folly of her choice and quickly had the class move on to *Moby-Dick*.)

Kathy sets her purse down on the couch, then takes the flowers and CD into her hands with a smile. The carnations are white with vibrant dyed blue edges, and she doesn't like them at all; but she smells them and says, "Thank you," then asks for a vase to keep them in, since she can't take them home anyway. Edward would never give her dyed flowers, she thinks, watching Gerard search through his cupboards for a vase. Edward already knows her favorite flowers are calla lilies. Of course he never buys them for her because he thinks flowers are a silly gift, and isn't it better to receive fake blue carnations than no flowers at all?

Gerard gives up his search for a vase and extracts a giant beer stein from the back of a cabinet, fills it with water, plops the carnations in, and sets them on the kitchen table. "*Voilà!*" he says, then moves to kiss her again, this time on the mouth. "I thought we might go to the lake today," he says. "A friend said I could borrow his boat."

"Oh, I forgot my suit." He asked her to bring one this weekend, but did not tell her why, and it completely slipped her mind.

"I think I might have an old one of Brenda's, if that wouldn't weird you out too much."

She gives him a frown and shakes her head no. Brenda is his ex-wife of five years, and Kathy is surprised he still has something as intimate as her swimsuit in his possession.

As if he'd read her mind Gerard says, "She hated swimming, and I'm bad at throwing things out."

But this answer only leaves Kathy with more questions. If Brenda hated swimming, why own a swimsuit in the first place? Did she leave swimming behind when she left Gerard? Had he forced her to swim because he managed a pool? She asks him none of these questions and instead says, "I can just go on the boat in this." She is wearing a reddish orange cotton skirt and a white, sleeveless top. "We don't have to jump in."

"Or we could go out really far and skinny-dip?" He dances closer and takes her into an embrace.

She sways back and forth in his arms, then joins him as he breaks into a quick salsa step, suddenly reminded why she might choose Gerard over Edward: He is more fun. "I'm in," she says, pressing closer to him. "Let's go."

THE BOAT SURPRISES KATHY with its new beauty. She expected a beat-up, faded fishing contraption, or something along those lines, so when Gerard pulls her down the dock, then onto a bright Sea Ray speedboat, she laughs with delight. "What friend lent you this?"

He shrugs, then begins preparing for their departure. "A guy I used to play pool with. He's owed me a favor for quite some time."

A green canvas awning is stretched high over the driver's and passenger seats, and this shade along with the wind of their motion provides some relief as they make their way out onto the lake, but the day is very hot and Kathy begins to worry whether or not they brought enough to drink. Gerard filled a sixteen-ounce plastic bottle with water and put that and a few root beers into a cooler, but it would be easy to become dehydrated beneath this sun. She has a sudden fear of being found dead beside Gerard on this boat deck, of the subsequent call to Edward and her daughters. Or they could crash or drown; she has opened herself up to all sorts of possible disasters by agreeing to go out on this friend's boat.

And who is this friend? She still doesn't know exactly what Gerard does for work during the school year. They practically stopped seeing each other from September to May, and the few times they did meet, they did not talk much about their working lives. She knows he works at a golf course but suspects he also hustles pool or does something a little bit shady, though she doesn't think he is involved in anything illegal or morally flawed. Hustling pool does not strike her as a big deal, though in this town, anything to do with gambling can make pulses run harder, and she begins to imagine this friend with the boat as some sort of Mafia don who joins Gerard in swindling pool players out of their money.

"So, why does this friend of yours owe you a favor?" she asks him.

"I saved his life. We were both drunk—him more so—and we went swimming at night, out here. It started to rain and it was really dark and I ended up having to pull him out." He turns his face away from the water ahead and looks at her through his sunglasses. "It changed my life. Seriously."

"I can imagine."

He looks back out toward the lake, which is racing toward them and beneath them, spraying up in a fine mist over the bow. "It made me realize I don't want to just screw around and let things happen to me. I want to live with purpose. I want to be with the people in my life who matter to me. That was when I went back to court to get partial custody of Christy. And that was right before I met you."

Kathy nods, then turns to watch the fast-approaching water, uncertain what to say. There are red cliffs in the distance and against the turquoise blue of the water they appear to be a manageable paradise, one cut down to earthly scale, which they can reach and enjoy before returning to their regular lives. "Let's go there," she says, pointing ahead.

"Where do you think we're going?" He smiles and increases their speed.

The lake is fairly empty today, though in the distance off to her right she can see the white shapes of several boats, lightly rising and falling with the water's movement. There is no one in the direction they are heading. She retrieves the water from the cooler, takes a long swallow, then passes the bottle to Gerard, and he does the same, before passing it back to her. They have become so easy with each other, she thinks now, taking another sip of water. At times like this, when they are connected by a quiet line of serenity and knowing, Kathy can imagine a life with Gerard. If she has ever had this with Edward, she can't remember. Now they are always bumping into each other, always asking too many questions of each other, always speaking more than they need to.

Does she love Gerard? That is the question she has been avoiding, the one she needs to dissect, though she knows even if the answer is a definite yes, it won't necessarily trump every other consideration. She glances over at him and sees he is humming, tapping the steering wheel with his thumbs. Dark hair swirls out around his head, freed from its sleek cap; the lines around his mouth are deeply drawn and bespeak his many loosely offered smiles. She recalls that at first he seemed a bit ridiculous to her— a weather-beaten playboy who preyed on young girls—but her view of him has changed over the past two summers. Now she detects a quiet core of kindness, an emotional breadth that sometimes startles her, and, above all this, a talent for enjoyment she wishes she could possess herself. He manages to savor what he has already; in him she feels none of the persistent questing that plagues her every day.

They are almost to the cliffs. Gerard slows the boat, and they approach with care; he steers them left into a small cove with a rocky beach, and Kathy suspects this is the area where her daughters always come to swim, though right now there is no one in sight. He cuts the motor and stands, then begins unbuttoning his shirt. "It's time to be bad," he says, and winks at her.

"As if we weren't being bad already."

"What do you mean?" he asks, then frowns and says, "Oh, that. I guess I just put everything so far out of my mind that I start to really believe you're *my* wife. Sometimes I even begin to think of Helen as my daughter. She's going through those difficult teen years; that's why she dislikes me so much."

Kathy laughs, but in truth, it jars her to hear him speak of Helen like this, to link himself to her daughter in any way more serious than employer to worker. She tries to shake away the irritation as he helps her remove her blouse and skirt, then folds them neatly and places them under the steering wheel, where they won't get wet.

She feels very exposed in only her bra and underwear beneath the bright umbrella of sun, but she can't get these items of clothing wet if she plans to make it home with some semblance of normality; besides, Gerard is already completely undressed and poised on the back of the boat to dive in, and he expects her to shed the rest of her outer skins and join him. Every time she is with Gerard, she thinks now, there seems to be some sort of test. Will she be able to put away the old Kathy, the one who is rivered through with fears and self-consciousness, with restrictions placed on what she can say or do or be? This entire affair is a test when viewed from that perspective. Sometimes she passes the test, passes into this other self, which feels lighter and looser-skinned and not entirely strange or new. She wants to enter this other self today as well, so she unhooks her bra, steps out of her underwear, and joins Gerard on the back deck, not looking down at her body, which would remind her to be embarrassed, but out at the glossy water of the lake.

They jump in unison, though they are not touching, and the water envelops her completely, immersing Kathy in a lukewarm cocoon of momentary silence. When she surfaces, Gerard is beside her, laughing with pure joy. "It's a little warm," he says, "but it still feels great compared to the boat."

She smiles her agreement, then swims out a bit, farther away from the boat, before flipping onto her back to float and closing her eyes against the sun. For the moment she is completely happy; her mind has at last traveled the distance it needs to in order to shed her guilt, far enough to step out of her worries about Helen and Jenny and Edward, and how she'll make herself look presentable after this swim, and what she'll make for dinner tonight and even what they'll talk about at the dinner table, because she is beginning to suspect that everybody in the family knows her secret.

She floats easily, listening to the little slaps of water against the boat and Gerard's breathing somewhere nearby. She shades her eyes and opens them, then turns her head to see Gerard floating about three feet away from her; if she wanted to, she could stretch out her arm and touch him, but it is enough right now just to be close, she decides, enough to float side by side in the same water. Is this love? she wonders. This feeling expanding through her right this second? Why does she have such a need to identify each feeling, as if they were all separate entities with no weaving in between? Why does each one need to be cataloged: This is love; this is merely taking pleasure in someone's presence; this is only strong affection. Why must what she feels be labeled and stored away in her brain to be considered later?

She flips over and paddles to Gerard, then kisses his stomach. He smiles but keeps his eyes closed. Treading water, she watches him and it occurs to her that she needs to label exactly what it is she feels for this man because she needs to make an important choice. And if this isn't love, how can she justify choosing him?

The sound of voices on the shore reaches her, and she turns toward the chatter then ducks underwater as quickly as possible, even though from this distance—several pool lengths away—it is probably impossible to tell she is naked. In her glance at the beach she saw a group of teenagers making their way onto the graveled sand, carrying a cooler and boom box. She can't remain underwater for very long—in fact, she is already running short of breath—so she opens her eyes to the green murky light and swims as close to the boat as she can. Surfacing near the back ladder, she turns to seek out Gerard, but he is nowhere to be found. He must be underwater, she tells herself, so she waits for him to break through the blue and swim toward her, but he is missing from view for what strikes her as too long, so she dives back under, opening her eyes again in an attempt to seek out his form. The water is cloudy and shadowed, and there is no sign of movement, only the distant sound of the people onshore jumping into the water, so she resurfaces and swims far enough past the back of the boat so she can look for him on the other side, but he is not there either.

She is beginning to grow frantic now with worry. Should she call for help? The teenagers, two girls and two boys, are close enough to hear her if she were to shout, though they seem oblivious to her presence, the two couples beginning to kiss and splash in the shallow water near the shore. If he has drowned, she thinks, scanning the water again for his bobbing head, what will she do? How will she find her way back with the boat? How will she explain her nakedness to these teenagers? Recognizing that her first thoughts are only worry for her own situation makes her sick with shame, so she begins to call his name, her voice breaking as she shouts three times, "Gerard! Gerard! Gerard!"

The teenagers look in her direction, and she is about to wave them over when she feels arms around her waist, then the small splash of a head coming up through the water behind her. She turns, and he is there, laughing, laughing at her, and she slaps his arms away, kicks at his legs, and begins to cry.

"Kath." He tries to pull her close, but she shimmies away, treading water and weeping. "Kath, I'm sorry. It was just a joke. I was behind the boat. Kath, don't cry."

"Take me home," she says, then swims over to the ladder and climbs back onto the boat, covering her breasts and abdomen as best she can once on deck, though she feels the eyes of the teenagers focused on her, burning holes into her fragile skin. She won't look over until she's dressed, she tells herself. This is the only way to get through it, to pretend she is completely alone.

In seconds, Gerard is up and dressing beside her. He did not bring towels, and her clothes pull on with difficulty, wet spots forming here and there where skin meets fabric. She won't look at Gerard or speak, and once she is back in her underwear, then her skirt and blouse and sandals, she removes a comb from her purse and sits in the passenger seat, running it through her hair and looking out at the cliffs. There are hoots of derision coming from the beach—at least that's what they sound like to Kathy—and she turns to Gerard, who is still fumbling with the buttons on his shirt, and says, "Get me out of here," with a controlled rage that makes Gerard give up on his buttons and start the boat immediately.

Once they are out on the open water he slows the boat and turns to her. "Kathy, I didn't mean to scare you. I didn't think I was hidden long enough to really scare you. I was trying to get out of the view of those kids, and then I just thought it would be funny to . . . I don't know. I don't know what I was thinking. I'm so sorry."

She nods, still unwilling to look at him but growing calmer now, out here in the middle of the lake with the wind skating in across the bow and cooling her, settling her nerves. For the first time in a long while she thinks about her father, the serene handsomeness of his face above the white clerical collar, the night she found out, when she was newly fifteen, that he'd been shot by one of his parishioners for no real reason at all, for the simple reason that the man who shot him was mentally unstable and angry about something. She has carried this death with her for so many years it sits almost gently within her now, an event from her past that rises above and over other memories but no longer threatens to choke her. But every time something happens that frightens her—the day Helen fell out of the mulberry tree and got a concussion, Edward's minor car accident, Jenny's long bout with pneumonia—her father's death is renewed within her so that she can barely breathe from the fear of what might happen, then what could've happened, and then the memory of what *did* happen rears up within her once again.

"Why are you making such a big deal out of this?" Gerard asks.

There has been a shift in his tone, and it seems he is now annoyed. She tries to figure out how to explain to him why she is so upset, but the idea of putting into words the terror she was feeling, treading water naked beside that strange boat, seems to require an explanation of her past she is unwilling to give, an explanation she doesn't think she could give even if she wanted to. The history is too long and complicated, weighted not only by her father's death but by her mother's as well, by her fears concerning Helen and Jenny and Edward, and the undercurrent of worry that accompanies the love she feels for anyone. So she attempts to smile, though it feels rigid and false, and tells him, "I guess I'm just a little tense, that's all."

"Well, loosen up for Christ's sake." He smiles back at her and pats her knee. "I'm a lifeguard, remember? It's not like I'm going to drown."

They speak very little on the drive back to his house, and once there she tries to neaten her hair and apply a bit of lipstick and mascara, so it doesn't look as if she's been swimming. Still, in the bathroom mirror she appears windblown and in a minor state of disarray; her hair could use some mousse to form it into its usual shape, and her nose and forehead are slightly sunburned. She looks like a person, Kathy thinks, who has been doing something she is not supposed to be doing.

At the door, Gerard kisses her mouth and presses the new CD into her hands. They did not even make love today, and Kathy realizes she is able to be more distant because of this. Her anger at his disappearance in the water is not all bundled up with the tender lust he is always able to draw from her body when given the time. "Try not to be too mad at me," he says, holding the door for her.

And she isn't mad anymore. Not really. She can see that perhaps she overreacted, that he was merely playing around and certainly didn't mean to cause her harm. So she kisses him again, then steps outside and waves good-bye.

WHEN SHE ARRIVES HOME, Edward, Helen, and Jenny are all inside, watching Wimbledon. "How was class?" Edward asks from his position on the couch. "You're talking about *Crime and Punishment* this week, right?"

Helen is in the armchair, and Jenny is sprawled belly down on the floor; they both look up at her, away from the television, waiting for her answer. Kathy cringes again at the book she has chosen for class, though every title she considers seems to contain a personal message, an insight into her secret life.

"It was stressful," she tells the three of them. "I'm not really enjoying it anymore."

Edward seems to sense she is speaking in code, because he smiles at this information, though, after smiling, he says, "That's too bad."

KATHY KNOWS she is doing something wrong. She is not a person who makes excuses for her follies or someone who believes the lines of morality are nebulous and questionable. She believes there is a God, though she does not believe he is always just; she knows there are definite rights and wrongs and that her affair with Gerard is definitely wrong. Sometimes she considers what she is doing—to her husband, her daughters, to Gerard, even to her solid set of values—and feels disgusted and ashamed, but underneath these feelings there is also an unmistakable elation, a shiver of triumph over her goody-goody beliefs that continues to fuel the affair. It is tiresome, she's decided, to always do what's good and right, tiresome to be the one who is never to blame. Her affair with Gerard has made Kathy better able to accept Edward's past betrayals, and she views her husband now with a certain quiet camaraderie, with a deeper empathy, one that fills in the holes of their old love, making it, in a way, more intact.

The affair has also given Kathy a more profound understanding of her daughters. So this is what it's like, she recalls thinking when she and Gerard first kissed—stupidly, in the parking lot of Luv-it; anyone could have seen them—so this is what it's like to experience your body more intensely than any messages sent down by your mind. The afternoon last week when Helen told her about having sex with Leo, Kathy wanted to say, "It's all right. I understand. I still think you're too young and you should be very, very careful not to ruin your life, but I think I understand." Instead, she fled the room, unable to say anything at all, too stunned by the despair that streamed out of Helen and filled the room, leaving Kathy breathless. What she is doing is hurting her daughter, she tells herself now, and still, it seems so difficult to stop, to return to the old Kathy, the person who never would have done something like this in the first place.

It is dark outside as Kathy sits on the deck, sipping her gin and tonic. Helen is out with Miles and Ernie. Jenny is out with Brazil. Edward is cleaning up the dishes in the kitchen, directly behind her, and even through the closed windows she can hear the occasional ring of silverware, the tap being turned on and then off. It is still hot outside, despite the fact it must be after nine o'clock, and she can feel the areas of her body that got too much sun today—nose, cheeks and shoulders—as if they were still being stung by the hot wind off the lake.

Edward comes outside with a glass of wine in his hand and sits down beside her at the table so that they both are looking out on the dark lawn. She can tell merely by the posture of his body that he knows, the way he holds himself slightly away from her so not even their forearms possess the chance of touching. Kathy has wondered why he doesn't say anything, why he hasn't questioned her or made any demands. At first she was hurt, telling herself he didn't even love her enough to bother, but she has come to see his silence as dignified, as a gentler, more mature love, a love that wants to allow her the room to make her own decision.

In the first years of their marriage he would have made a scene—put his fist through the closet door or thrown his briefcase across the living room—but no longer. They are older now, she tells herself, calmer, more aware of the space needed to allow a marriage to flower. Of course what they are doing right now is not exactly what she would call flowering; *wilting* seems a more appropriate term.

"I miss Leo," Edward says.

Kathy laughs a little, then says, "Me too."

"I hope Miles isn't his replacement."

"He's not."

They sit quietly again, and Kathy chances a look at Edward's profile. She notices for the first time that he is unshaven, and in the light filtering out from the kitchen windows it looks as if his chin and cheeks have been sprinkled with red-gold glitter. It is rare for Edward to forgo shaving, even on a Saturday, and this shimmer of new hair lets her know he is being affected by her actions more than she had previously thought.

"I was thinking, while I was washing up," Edward says, "about that time we took the girls camping at Zion. Remember?"

Kathy nods.

"When we were climbing and Helen fell and got that gash just above her collarbone, I remember thinking she had cut her throat somehow, that a rock had been sharp enough to kill her. All I saw was the blood, and from a distance it looked more serious than it was. I remember thinking as I ran over to her that I would give up anything if she would be okay. Anything. Even you." He glances over at her, then says, "I mean, I didn't want you to die in her place, but for that split second before I reached her and saw she was going to be okay, I was willing to give up our marriage. Absolutely willing with no hesitation whatsoever."

"That's understandable," Kathy says. She wants to touch his arm in a comforting way but decides against it.

"But I've always felt guilty about that. About having that thought. And now Helen's leaving, and I don't know what I'd do without you."

He says this last bit quietly, as if he were embarrassed, and Kathy looks away and takes a long swallow of her drink. She is supposed to reassure him right now; she knows this. Take his hand and promise that of course she'll be here, that they'll help each other through Helen's departure, but she doesn't move, doesn't turn to look at him, because if he sees her hesitation, she fears this fragile peace between them will erupt. So instead, she says, "We still have Jenny."

"Of course we do; I know. I'm getting to be a sentimental fool, I suppose, but I always remember our first years with Helen as some of our best, and it will be so odd not having her around."

"Those were great years," Kathy tells him, finally turning to look at him. Their eyes meet now, but it is not with the final release and understanding you find in movies; they do not share a moment of purely reignited love. No, this meeting of gazes is much more complicated, weighed down by history and age and the uncertainty that has always existed, at least for Kathy, within their marriage. Still, it is not unpleasant, this shared look. It does possess a certain energy of feeling, the acknowledgment of a common past that has contained moments of mutual joy.

Edward takes her hand beneath the table, and Kathy allows him to. They sit together like this—the air humming around them with heat and locusts—finishing their drinks and waiting for their daughters to return.

THE NEXT DAY is Sunday, but Helen has to work, so Kathy drives her over to the Dunes. She returned to her job the day after she and Leo broke up, and though Kathy can't quite figure out the connection—she expected Helen to feign illness for the rest of the summer—she thinks it is probably for the best. The idea of her daughter's spending all day around Gerard upsets her because she knows this recharges Helen's anger, constantly reminds her what a rotten mother she has. On the other hand, it keeps Helen's mind occupied, and more selfishly, it keeps her out of the house so Kathy doesn't feel the constant need to go outside and get away.

"Your father's pretty sad you're leaving so soon," Kathy tells her as they make their way down the Strip.

"And I'm sure you're really torn up about it as well."

"Helen, of course I'm going to miss you. What's going on . . . " she says, searching for the right set of words, "what's going on between me and Gerard does not in any way affect my feelings for you."

"But it affects *my* feelings for *you*."

"Well, that's a different story."

"Aren't you even a little bit worried about Dad? Haven't you noticed how weird he's being, always going through our old photo albums, making notes in the margins."

Actually, she hadn't noticed that but says, "Your father will be fine."

"He doesn't deserve this, you know. Lots of women would love to be with him, and he's stuck with you, treating him like shit. He doesn't deserve this."

Anger flares up in Kathy's chest as they stop at a red light. In the past she would have reprimanded Helen for swearing, and almost does so now, automatically, but instead takes a deep breath, cooling off her insides, and considers her response. She is tempted to tell Helen that her father is far from perfect, that he's had at least one affair himself and possibly more. She wants to explain that he started this really, that she had been faithful as the sun until last summer when she'd decided to say, "Why not?" for once, to discover what this sin was really all about.

In the distance she can see the sign for the Dunes. Soon they will be turning into the parking lot, Helen will be released from the close space of this car, and Kathy will be free; but right now, at this light, the distance seems immense, and Kathy feels more potently than she ever has the weight of having children. There is so much to protect them from, she thinks, looking at all the mangy, red-eyed men among the crowd of tourists streaming past them on the crosswalk, at the wild buildings all around her where people have been gambling and drinking all night and will continue. The thought that she also has to protect her daughter from herself, and from Edward too, from the things they have done wrong, exhausts her.

"You're right," Kathy says as the light turns green and they hurtle toward their destination. "Your father doesn't deserve this."

At home Kathy shuts herself in their bedroom and thumbs through one of the old photo albums. Edward *has* been writing in them. Beside a photo of all four of them at the beach in La Jolla he has penned, "Great day, despite the vicious sunburn." Next to a picture of her and Edward at their ten-year anniversary party are the scribbled words *Remember this*. Is he asking her to remember this party, which was held in a friend's backyard, lights looped over the trees like fireflies, or was he reminding himself to remember the evening? Perhaps he wanted to remind himself that there had been good times, to see the record of a night that might be able to erase or at least mitigate his wife's present digressions. On the next page of the album, beside a photo of Kathy's mother, he has written a simple, plaintive, "Why?" And this entry stops her breath, makes her shut the book in shame, and whisper a quick "I'm sorry," meant for Edward or her mother or both, she doesn't know.

And this is how she comes to decide—though the answer, really, has been sitting just in the back of her throat all along— that she will choose Edward. Or rather, she thinks of it as choosing her daughters, as choosing Helen and Jenny and Edward—*her family*—over a single man she doesn't think she even really loves, though she does care for him quite a bit, she must admit. She might see Gerard one more time, she thinks, as she shuts the photo album and replaces it on the shelf. Make love one more time beneath that poster of Hawaii, attempt to embed the newness he has given her deep within her skin so that she doesn't lose everything that's been gained, so that her old life doesn't feel quite like it used to.

She spends the rest of the day in solitude, reading the Sunday paper and cleaning the bathroom and bedroom, sharing brief hellos with Jenny and Edward when they pass in the hallway or meet in the kitchen, though her husband and daughter also seem in the mood for silent retreat. Her decision sits in her chest like a bird, quietly at first, its wings folded in, but by midday the wings have unfurled and begun to beat within her chest, so that by five o'clock, when it's time to go get Helen, there's a constant fluttering inside her she cannot quell.

Edward is supposed to pick up Helen today, but Kathy offers

to instead, explaining she wants to get out of the house for a while. She can see his hesitation as he hands over the car keys, and for the first time in all of this, she detects slivers of scorn and anger in his voice when he tells her, "Okay, if you want to go, go ahead."

His words sounded like a dismissal, and in the car, as she threads through her neighborhood, it occurs to Kathy for the first time that she doesn't have to choose either of these men, that she can simply say good-bye to both of them and live alone. She attempts to picture this as she drives and can conjure only one room painted a snowy white, adorned by a single bed, a desk and bookshelf, a chair, and a hanging plant, the one spot of bright in the entire room. She would need a small refrigerator, she supposes, and possibly a hot plate—something to make tea with in the winter—but that would be it. Her life would be stripped of all but the essential. She would teach her students, spend time with Jenny every other evening, then come home to grade papers, read, and go to sleep. Gerard and Edward both would become ghostlike in her mind, men she had once cared for but whose features and habits and gestures would fade into the white nothingness of her walls.

She turns onto the Strip, smiling to herself, then reaches for the radio knob and turns off the current barrage of unnecessary love songs. The mountains are bright this evening, radiant with late sun, the casinos outlined in the foreground like something from her past, a city of cupidity she hardly sees beneath the azure sky and lavender-white clouds, a city that looks dusky and small before the sweep of the Sheep mountain range. She turns off the air conditioning, rolls down her window, and lets in the heat and sounds of traffic, feeling an immediate whisper of sweat float across her chest and face, but it feels purifying and somehow essential, sensual, and healthy.

Closer to the Dunes her notions of a life of purity in a white room begin to dissipate as she thinks about seeing Gerard. What is it about this man that weakens her? He is silly and lazy, and even with his new sleek hairdo and lighter tan he looks like a person distinctly lacking in class. Still, he has an effect on her; she is drawn to him, inexplicably drawn, and right now, imagining his brown hands tracing the small school of stretch marks on her lower stomach with tender solemnity makes the bird in her chest beat its wings faster, so that she presses down on the gas pedal and speeds her way to see him. One more afternoon in his bedroom, she tells herself. That's all I want, and then I can return to Edward, or to no one, but I will not return to Gerard if I can have just one more afternoon.

A siren severs the air, and Kathy glances in her rearview mirror, then sees that the ambulance is ahead of her; it is turning onto the Strip from the side street that leads to the Dunes parking lot. Instantly all thoughts of Gerard and Edward fall away, and she is left with a single line of pure panic, the fear that something has happened to Helen. She is only three blocks away now, and she speeds up, cutting off a minitruck and scooting through a yellow light before she is able to turn down the side street then into the Dunes parking lot, where all is quiet. Still, the ambulance came from this direction, so she leaps out of the car, moves quickly through the cool passageway, then steps out onto the deck to walk quickly toward the lectern between the pools as her eyes scan the area for Helen.

Something is wrong here; she can see that. Both the pools are empty, and people stand in clusters, talking quietly. One woman holds a small boy close, his face pressed against her waist, arms circling her hips. No one stands beneath the red umbrella and the lectern looks bereft, white and insubstantial with a lone bottle of suntan lotion perched on top. She can't see Helen anywhere, or anyone familiar for that matter. Where is Gerard? Miles? Someone she recognizes? She begins to run until she is between the pools. "What happened?" she asks a woman wrapped in a giant beach towel.

"Some guy just died," she says, and shrugs, as if to say, *I don't know anything else, so don't ask me.*

Kathy is heartened, knowing that "some guy" can't mean Helen, and she takes a deep breath, shades her eyes with her hand, and searches the area for her daughter. She finds her across the larger pool, standing beneath a palm tree with Miles and a man in a white shirt and pants, a paramedic. Miles has his arm around Helen, and the medic is talking to her. Helen nods at whatever he is saying, looking stunned and on the cusp of tears, rubbing her eyebrows with two fingers the way she always does right before she cries. She is soaking wet, a blue towel wrapped around her shoulders, and she looks so young, so exposed and fragile-boned with her hair flattened darkly against her skull that Kathy jogs around the pool and over to her as quickly as she can.

When Kathy reaches the circle of three, Helen looks at her and drops her hand from her brow, then crosses the short space between them and moves into her arms, placing her face into the curve of Kathy's neck and shaking, with cold or crying, she can't quite tell, because Helen doesn't make a sound as Kathy moves her arms around Helen's back, holding her daughter as closely to her chest as she possibly can, feeling the wet of her swimsuit soak into her clothes and smelling the chlorine that emanates from her hair.

"What happened?" she asks Miles and the paramedic over Helen's head.

"It's Gerard," Miles says quietly. "He had a heart attack."

"Is he all right?"

"Your daughter pulled him out of the pool," the medic tells her. "She gave him CPR until we got here, but—" he shows her his palms—"we couldn't establish a heartbeat. He's on the way to Sunrise Hospital now. Your daughter did a great job, though." He looks uncomfortable and young, uncertain what exactly he should say. "We can give her a sedative if you want."

"Um." Kathy hesitates, wondering whether or not this is a good idea. "No," she answers, then adds, "She'll be okay."

"I was at lunch," Miles says. "I'm sorry."

"So he might still make it, right?" Kathy asks the medic. Heart attacks are tricky things, she knows. Many people are revived by machines even when CPR doesn't work. A defibrillator, she thinks it's called; that's the machine which might save him. "They're still working on him?"

"Well, yes, but . . . it doesn't look good. I'll make a call soon and let you know what's going on."

The medic walks away, toward the hotel, and Helen extracts

herself from Kathy's embrace, goes over to a chaise lounge, and sits down, covering her face with her hands. The towel falls away from her shoulders so that she looks even smaller, and Kathy tries to imagine this long, skinny-limbed girl, *her daughter*, pulling a grown man out of a swimming pool. Miles and Kathy both turn to go to Helen at the same time, but Kathy raises a hand to him and says, "Let me be alone with her."

She walks over and sits down beside Helen, then readjusts the towel around her daughter's shoulders. People are leaving the pool deck, or moving to stand in the long line forming at the thatched hut bar for drinks. The pools remain empty, though there doesn't seem to be any real reason for this now except decorum or possibly fear. Their placid water now contains the threat of death, even though the water itself probably had nothing to do with Gerard's heart attack. Helen is shivering despite the heat, so Kathy pulls her closer and kisses the wet top of her head. She no longer appears to be crying, but her hands remain over her face. We'll just sit here until she's ready to leave, Kathy tells herself. She won't do anything to jar her or rush her; then she'll take her home, make her hot tea, and put her to bed. She'll stay with her until she falls asleep, Kathy decides, as she used to do when Helen was small.

Suddenly the realization that Gerard could be dead weakens her, makes her stomach clutch up into a hard inner core of shock. The sky grows spotty and dark, and for a moment she thinks she's going to faint, so she closes her eyes and leans her head on top of Helen's, collecting herself around the hope that he might have survived, despite the medic's grim prediction. Time passes, though

Kathy has no idea how much time, and soon she spots the white figure of the young paramedic exiting the hotel doors and walking toward them.

When he reaches their chaise lounge, Helen raises her head to hear what he has to say. "I'm so sorry," he tells them. "Mr. Rasmussen was pronounced dead when they reached the hospital."

Helen nods, then begins to cry again, and Kathy wants, with every ounce of herself, to join her, to lie on this chaise lounge and sob. But she doesn't.

"Do you have any idea who I need to contact?" he asks Kathy. "No one else seems to know."

"He has a daughter," she tells him. "Christy Rasmussen. She lives with her mother, Brenda, but I'm not sure what last name she uses and I don't know the number. But I think Christy goes to Chaparral High School. I've never met her," she adds, thinking how ridiculous this is, how strange that in three summers she never got close enough to Gerard to warrant meeting his daughter. In the next second she recognizes what an absurd notion it is to think he should have introduced her—his mistress? His lover?—to his family.

The medic thanks her and leaves them alone. Miles wanders over next and tells Helen that he has to go watch the pool, but please to call him if she needs him.

"Thanks," Helen tells him, rubbing her eyes. "I will."

"Shouldn't you go home?" Kathy asks him. "You must be in shock too."

"Believe it or not," he tells her, "it's more cheerful to me here." He shrugs and waves, then walks across the deck to the larger pool, the hourglass, where he climbs the ladder and sits down in the lifeguard chair.

A sudden rush of hot wind moves over them, causing the palm trees to sway, and Helen looks up at the sky, then over at Kathy. Her eyes are swollen and shot through with red, the irises more vividly green in contrast. "I didn't want him to die," Helen says.

"I know you didn't."

"I hated him, but I tried my best to save him. I really did. I promise."

"Sweetheart." Kathy shakes her head and sweeps a strand of hair off Helen's cheek. "You did everything right. You did your best."

"You don't know that."

"Yes." She nods firmly. "I do."

Somehow they make their way to the lectern to retrieve Helen's bag, then out of the courtyard and into the car. By the time they reach their neighborhood, Helen is asleep, her head tilted down and hands clasped in her lap so that it looks as if she were praying. Kathy pulls into their driveway and shuts off the car, trying to be as quiet as possible. She cannot leave her here, and she doesn't want to wake her, so she remains in the driver's seat, looking through the large front window into the empty living room of their house.

Even though Helen is asleep, Kathy refuses to cry. She knows this is not just motherly strength of will on her part, but a sign she hasn't registered clearly in her mind that Gerard is dead. The sight of the ambulance revives itself inside her now, and she places Gerard inside it, lying on a gurney, looking, she would guess, as he did in sleep, his mouth soft and slightly open, his dark lashes lying long and pretty against his sun-worn cheeks, the pale crescent underneath his chin exposed. It doesn't quite seem true to her—the fact that she'll never see him again—and she thinks this is probably always the way with a sudden death. She remembers how after her father's murder she kept expecting him to come home, to walk through the front door and clunk his keys into the silver bowl on the table in the entry hall, to call out for her to come down and get her bike out of the driveway. So for a time, she tells herself, she will keep picturing Gerard beneath that red umbrella, gesturing for her to come over and talk to him; she supposes too that the promise of their Saturday afternoons will also remain for a month or two, even though she was about to end them on her own. She will continue to see him waiting for her on his front stoop, drinking a glass of iced tea and fanning himself with a magazine, then, when he sees her walking toward him, rising and smiling at her as if she had changed the entire shape of the day, as if she could grant him something beautiful that might alter every ugly thing around him, as if she held the power to shift his life onto a different, more pleasing plane.

The car is getting hot, so she rolls down her window, but this doesn't do much to remedy the situation. Soon she will have to wake Helen and take her inside to the cool of her bedroom. She considers turning the car and air conditioner back on, but thinks this will wake Helen up anyway, so she decides to just sit and wait. She watches her daughter, listening to her deep, even breaths and remembering with a sudden vivid jolt the weight and span of Helen as a sleeping baby, the way she sprawled out then, stretching against Kathy's chest and turning into her, kicking her fat legs out straight as if she were lounging on a beach. Now she is unmoving, curled over and into herself, and Kathy worries she has been irreparably changed, that her daughter has chosen to collapse away from the world rather than unfold toward it. Has she ruined Helen? Have her own bad choices made Helen a lesser person?

But her daughter attempted to save a man's life only a few hours ago. She was the one to drag Gerard from the pool. A damaged person could not have gathered so much fortitude; a cringing person could not have managed half as much as Helen had today.

The front door opens, and Edward steps onto the porch. It feels strange to see him—the pale skin of his legs exposed in his weekend shorts, his chin still unshaved, glasses slightly askew—and Kathy is apprehensive about telling Edward what just happened. He runs fingers through his hair, then places his hands on his hips and walks toward the car. Who is this man? she thinks, watching him approach. Why is she married to him? She can't recall a single thing they have in common, a single day that has blazed glorious in his presence. She doesn't even want to speak to him right now. But she will have to. She will have to tell him what just happened.

Kathy gets out of the car just as Edward reaches it, then shuts the door behind her as quietly as possible. "What's up?" Edward asks her, peeking in at Helen, who is still asleep, then straightening to face her.

His response will tell me what to do, Kathy thinks now,

preparing the words she is about to give to him. His response will tell her whether she should stay or go. She doesn't know what the correct response, the acceptable response should be, but she knows everything rests on it.

"Gerard just had a heart attack," she says. "Helen tried to save him—pulled him out of the pool and gave him CPR—but he died. Gerard's dead."

"My God, that's horrible." His eyes widen and he bends to peer in at Helen. "Is she okay?"

"I think so."

He straightens up so that they are once again facing each other and watches her in silence. She waits for him to say something more, thinking he may say nothing else to her, ever, that he may simply turn and walk back into the house, but then his brows draw together, and he steps toward her. "Kathy." He pulls her to him so that she is against his chest, her face above the hard line of his collarbone. "Kathy." Her name resonates through him, and she feels the vibrations against her throat. "I'm sorry."

She closes her eyes and leans into him, still not crying—she will do that later, alone—but feeling the tension in her limbs begin to rise out of her, like a song. It is hot being this close to Edward, and sweat is collecting where her forehead meets his throat; but she decides to stay right where she is for as long as he'll allow.

HELEN STAYED IN HER BED for three days after her failed attempt to save Gerard. Kathy ministered to her as best she could, bringing her trays of grilled cheese sandwiches and grapes, peanut butter and jelly with the crusts cut off, glasses of milk, and chocolate cupcakes sprinkled with candy confetti. She tried to make and offer up all the foods Helen loved as a child. Her daughter would eat a little, then push the tray aside and go back to sleep without a word.

Kathy wanted badly to crawl in bed beside her, to curl her body protectively around her daughter's in such a way that her own skin would absorb all the memories of this summer; then she would take them out of this room and dispose of them somewhere far away. But the closest she got was to sit on the edge of the bed and ask Helen how she was feeling. "Okay," was always the answer, and the notion that a true word might never pass between them again would surface quickly, then dip back into the black swirl of her worries.

In her own room, alone, Kathy finally cried. While Edward was at work, Jenny was at a friend's, and Helen was asleep, Kathy locked herself away and tried to get all her sadness for Gerard out in one sitting. There is no space provided, she realized as she lay facedown on the blue comforter of her and Edward's bed, to mourn a person who was a secret from your family, even if Gerard was no longer really a secret. Later she took Gerard's whistle and the Lionel Richie CD he had given her and buried them in the backyard. It struck her as a childish act as she dug a small hole with a trowel beneath the pink oleander tree and dropped the items into the dirt, but it seemed important to say good-bye with some sort of ritual, and she didn't know at the time that she'd be going to his funeral.

Helen asked her to go. On the third afternoon her daughter rose of her own accord, showered, dressed, and made herself a sandwich (an adult sandwich of turkey and havarti), then announced that she was going over to Ernie's house. On her way out the door, she turned to Kathy and said, "Gerard's funeral is Saturday. Will you come with me?"

"Okay," is all Kathy managed to say, too shocked by the request to say more.

THE FUNERAL, to Kathy's surprise, is packed with people. It is held at a large Catholic church on Maryland Parkway on an extremely hot day. Helen and Kathy stand in the back and fan themselves with their programs as a young priest spreads gentle words and generalities about Gerard and God over the audience.

After the priest, Gerard's daughter, Christy, speaks. She is small and dark with short spiky hair dyed olive green, and she reads from note cards. "My father loved animals." (Kathy thinks of his turtle.) "My father did not place great value on material possessions. My father loved the water, and he loved being with people." All this is delivered in a flat, metallic voice with downcast eyes, but to Kathy's surprise, when she glances over at Helen, her daughter is weeping. Kathy places an arm around her shoulders, but Helen shrugs it off and wipes at her eyes with the back of her hand.

When Kathy sees that the next speaker is Gerard's ex-wife, Brenda, she whispers to Helen that she needs some air, then slips away outside. The sun is still on its rise toward noon, and no shade is provided on the small concrete patio in front of the church. Kathy retrieves her sunglasses from her purse, puts them on, then sits down on a bench by the wall and watches the traffic. If Gerard were here right now, she wonders, what would we talk about? His daughter's hair, she decides. He would go on about how fun it is, and Kathy would pretend to agree. And after that? She cannot further the conversation. They would want to touch, despite the heat; that's all she knows. That couldn't have lasted much longer, she decides now. That strong desire to touch with so little talk to back it up. But maybe she is just telling herself this in order to feel better, and this strikes her as a selfish act when her daughter is inside the church crying. Just feel bad, she tells herself. You should feel bad.

Organ music seeps out from under the church's doors, and she can hear people rise and begin to sing, though their words are muffled by the stucco walls of the church and cars buzzing by on the busy street. A memory of her weekend trip to San Diego with Gerard rises up, and she closes her eyes, allowing herself to live inside it for a few moments, before her daughter steps outside and they share a silent car ride home.

The trip was behind them, and they were driving home through the desert. Gerard was at the wheel of her Honda, and they were nearing the Baker grade, an arduous hill in the middle of dry, speckled land that required most cars to turn off their air conditioners so their engines wouldn't overheat. But right then the air conditioning blew cool over her bare arms and legs, and the intense heat outside was just a theory, another reality from which she had momentarily escaped.

"So," Gerard said, turning down the music and putting a warm hand on her knee. "What was your favorite part of the trip? Christy and I always do this," he added. "Declare a favorite trip moment on the way home. It seals the vacation into memory better. At least that's my theory."

"Mmm," she said, looking out the window. Mountains rolled by in the distance, their sand a coppery pink in the waning sun. *This part*, she wanted to tell him, *going home.* But it was not only the going home, the anticipation of seeing Helen and Jenny and even Edward, of being back inside the walls of her own house, a house that she loved, that provided shelter and comfort; it was going home with this trip behind her, with Gerard and the nights they had spent together woven in, so that she would have all these things contained in one space at the same time. As long as the feelings of this trip held, she was both the old Kathy and new one at once. She would be able, for a few days at least, to hold this balance.

She always guessed that the worst part of an affair would be this duality, trying to live two lives at the same time and struggling to keep them absolutely separate. And it probably was the worst part if you were madly in love with the other other. But for her, this melding opened her up somehow to her husband and daughters, to the ordinary moments of her days, so that there was a constant gentle buzzing just beneath the surface of her skin that helped her appreciate more deeply what she had.

But she thought this answer would offend Gerard, that telling him her favorite part of the trip was the moment she actually left his physical presence behind, so she lied. "I guess I'd have to say our walk on the beach last night." She smiled at him across the bucket seat, then asked, "How about you?"

"I don't know. It was all so great. Maybe when we did it on the balcony," he said, winking. "But I do know what the worst moment will be—when you drop me off at my house in a few hours."

Kathy sighed and put her hand on his knee, trying to act as if she felt the same about their imminent arrival, but in truth his answer sent a small bolt of fear up her spine. He's going to want more one day, she realized, more than she would ever be willing to give.

THE DOORS OF THE CHURCH OPEN, and people begin to wander out, shielding their eyes against the sun and talking quietly. One old man walks by crying, and Kathy wonders who he is. Then a little boy runs out laughing, and Kathy hears a woman's voice calling from inside, "Justin! Stop right where you are."

Kathy stands and begins to search the crowd for Helen. She recognizes a few of the mourners: Miles walks by, clamping the headphones of his Walkman over his ears. Ernie trails behind him, holding the small, smooth mound of her stomach with two open palms. They don't see Kathy and she doesn't attempt to get their attention. She expects Helen to be close behind them; but many more people follow, and her daughter is not among them.

Gerard's daughter strides out, holding an older woman's hand, and Kathy backs up against the wall and watches as they move to stand at the patio's edge and say their good-byes to the guests. So this is Brenda. A short middle-aged woman in a flow-ing, flowered hippie-style dress and Birkenstocks. Her hair is long—dark brown threaded with gray—and hangs straight and thick to her waist. Beaded earrings dangle to her shoulders, and her face is stoic, faintly lined and devoid of makeup. She is not especially attractive and looks as if she wandered in from a dif-ferent decade; but there is a liveliness to her movements as she begins to speak with another middle-aged woman, who has just approached the mother-daughter pair, and her smile, when it arrives, is so unexpected that its momentary light almost causes Kathy to smile too. So, Kathy thinks, she is one of those people who are suddenly beautiful when they smile. Now she can pic-ture the two of them together: Brenda and Gerard. She sees them sitting in their swimsuits in spindly fold-out chairs on the shore of Lake Mead, fifteen years younger, drinking from cans of beer and laughing.

The daughter, however, is an anomaly. How did a hippie with a brilliant smile and an affable beach bum create this sour-faced daughter with spiked olive hair? Of course she may not always look so dour, Kathy reminds herself. Still, there is an air of seri-ousness to her that seems permanent, a sturdy kernel of anger behind her gaze. And now with Gerard gone, Kathy expects this kernel will expand, that she will grow up angry at many things, among them the fact that her father died when she was young. Later, of course, the anger will fade, and she will be left with even less, with an incomplete sense of how to navigate her way toward happiness.

And how will Brenda be affected? Kathy wonders. She has

never remarried, as far as Kathy knows. Perhaps she continued to pine for Gerard. The thought never occurred to her before today. His absence will be so much more painful for those two women, Kathy thinks, than it will ever be for me. The concentric circles waving out from his death must affect many people, she realizes, considering the size of his funeral.

SHE TURNS AGAIN to seek out Helen. The entire congregation appears to be on the church's tiny front patio now, groups streaming off to each side and walking to their cars, and still no sign of her daughter. Kathy waits a few minutes, then goes back inside the church. She finds the light dim after having sat for so long outside; voices from the patio burble through the closed doors, but other than that it is very quiet.

"Helen," Kathy calls out tentatively.

The young priest steps out from behind a curtain near the altar and calls, "Can I help you with something?"

"My daughter. I can't find her."

Kathy and the priest both begin walking toward each other down the aisle until they stand face-to-face in the center of the church. He is shorter than she is, with wispy blond hair that reminds her of a baby chick and a soft, open face that Kathy finds warm and appealing. "How old is she?" he wants to know.

"Oh, she's seventeen."

"Whew." He lets out a sigh. "We lost a little one for several hours last Sunday. This place is pretty vast. Maybe she went to use the rest room?" he says, pointing toward a hallway off to the right.

"You're probably right," she says, but makes no attempt to walk in that direction. Suddenly she is exhausted, so she says, "Excuse me, Father," and sits down in the closest pew.

He sits in the pew in front of her, turning his body to face her, and asks, "Are you all right?"

She takes a deep breath, then nods. "I guess it's the heat. And the funeral," she adds. "It's been a pretty emotional day."

"What was your relationship to the deceased? To Gerard?" He props his elbow on the back of the pew, then drops his chin onto his fist.

Kathy thinks about how to answer this. *He was my secret,* she tries out in her mind. *He was a man who caused me to hurt my daughter, to hurt my entire family very much, though it wasn't his fault. Only mine.* But of course she can't say this out loud, so she says, "He was a friend."

The priest nods thoughtfully. "I met him only once," he says. "When his daughter was baptized, quite recently actually. A late baptism. But he seemed to have the spark of life, as they say."

Kathy can't think who says this, it's a not a common phrase to her, but she thinks that it suits Gerard, that it suited him, and she smiles. "Yes, he did have that."

"Mom."

Kathy and the priest both turn in the direction of Helen's voice. She is standing in dark shadows near the hallway to the bathroom. "I'm ready to go," she says.

Kathy says good-bye to the priest, then walks to meet Helen by the front doors, where they step outside together.

Implosions, Quick and Slow

THEY ARE GOING TO IMPLODE the Dunes Hotel and Casino. Helen has known about the coming event for most of the summer, but it was only right after Gerard had his heart attack, two weeks ago now, that workers began carting away everything inside the hotel, so that as she sat in her chair watching the men walk by with furniture, with slot machines and blackjack tables—those worn green fans—she felt as if the hotel were shutting down because Gerard had died. The exodus of things was like a drawn-out funeral procession, and at the end of the week, when the pool finally closed down too, she was genuinely relieved to leave that courtyard for good.

She rode home with Miles that last day, and when he asked her what she thought about the Dunes' destruction, she emitted a short laugh that sounded painful to her own ears and said, "It seems pretty symbolic."

What this implosion was a symbol of, however, she couldn't actually say. She sits by Ernie's pool now, swinging her legs through the water as she thinks it all through. Miles is here too—the three of them have become close in these final weeks of summer—and Helen watches as he goofs off on the diving board, doing a handstand, then flopping over feet first into the pool. Ernie floats in the shallow end, the curve of her purple-sheathed stomach rising through the water like a tiny island.

Implosion. Helen looked up the word when she'd arrived home and was able to find the verb form, *implode*: to explode inward. Isn't this what she has been doing—imploding—since Gerard died? No, it began much earlier than that, she thinks, maybe the day she saw her mother eating ice cream in his kitchen. But the metaphor doesn't really work. She has been experiencing a slow inward crumbling for quite some time, and an implosion is quick and brutal, finished in seconds, not this minute chipping away over years until a man dies beneath your hands, causing the rest of your interior structure to completely collapse.

"Hey," Ernie says, abruptly standing up. "I just decided. I want you and Miles to be the godparents."

"Cool," Miles says, swimming over to Ernie and rubbing her stomach.

Helen thinks to protest—aren't godparents supposed to be a couple? And what if you're not sure you even believe in God; does that disqualify you?—but Ernie and Miles look so happy standing together in the waist-high water, both of them brown and radiant and smiling at her, that instead she says, "Sure, I'd be honored."

AT HOME her mother is making dinner, chopping yellow tomatoes for a pasta sauce. The Spanish dinners have disappeared, and Helen has found herself craving paella but has vowed never to eat that dish again. She wants to avoid the kitchen completely but is very thirsty, so she wanders in and pours herself a glass of sun tea from the fridge.

"Is it you or your sister who doesn't like tarragon?" her mother asks by way of a greeting.

"Me," Helen says, then adds, "But you can put it in. Maybe I've changed."

"No, it will work without it."

"Put it in. I've got to get used to eating whatever's set down in front of me. You know, for the dorms."

"There will be choices," she says, setting down her knife and turning to face her. "It's not a prison." Her mother has cut her hair again, into a shorter, more boyish style, and after all these years, she has suddenly stopped wearing eye makeup, so that she actually looks younger, more unfinished and wholesome. Perhaps, Helen thinks now, that is her intent, to help us forget she is not such an innocent. If this is the case, it appears to be working, at least on her father. Helen wouldn't say that a new romance has ignited between them, but they do seem to talk more, to touch a bit more. Last night in the kitchen they even broke into a thirty-second slow dance when an Eagles song came on the radio.

Helen watches as her mother opens the container of tarragon and sprinkles some on the tomatoes. "I think we should all go see the Dunes implode tomorrow night," she tells Helen, not looking up from her cooking.

"I don't know if I want to."

"It will be good for you. We're going."

It seems difficult to argue, difficult even to question her mother about how this weird event will somehow be good for her, so she just shrugs and says, "Okay, whatever."

AT NIGHT, she still dreams about it. The dreams, however, are in reverse, so that first Gerard is taken out of the ambulance, then her clasped hands are moving up and down on his chest, her mouth is fitting over his and blowing with as much force as she can gather, then she is pulling him into the water and swimming down to the bottom, where she lays him gently against the pool's curved concrete before pushing off alone for the surface. In the middle of the night, when she wakes up, this reverse order of events seems to mean something and she lies there for at least an hour trying to decipher the sequence, to glean some secret message that will help her make sense of everything, but by morning it simply strikes her as the surreal, unformed nature of dreams and nothing more.

No one has asked her to talk about it, to describe what trying to save another person's life was like, and she's not so sure she wants to, but she does think about it quite a bit. Strange details occur to her, and she almost feels guilty that she isn't pondering the larger issues, the gigantic idea of death itself. For instance, she is surprised that she was not disgusted by giving mouth-to-mouth resuscitation to Gerard. The thought of it now, putting her own mouth on top of his and breathing, makes her queasy, but at the time it had all been one fluid motion, fueled by panic and the intense desire to feel a breath of his in return, a small blossom of reassuring air, which never came.

She is also surprised by her strength. Pulling him off the pool's bottom was not that difficult—the water helped her all the way to the top—but dragging him out onto the deck had seemed impossible. She can't even recall how she managed to do it and just assumes she used the method learned in her lifeguarding classes. Then it was done, and she was beginning the next step, then the next without a thought of her own exhaustion. If he had lived, she might even have allowed herself some pride for this feat; but of course he hadn't, and she can only feel a distant shock when she conjures the image of herself doing the things she had done.

She remembers the way his chest felt. It was bare and hairy and a little chilled from pool water, and it did not give easily beneath her hands the way the practice dummy's had in class. His face was soft and closed off to her; she did not detect a presence the way she did, for instance, when she watched Leo sleeping. It was too still, and Helen thinks that even then she knew he was dead or going to die, but she kept trying. Of course she kept trying.

The longish hair of his eyebrows was wetly pulled down onto his eyelids when she swam with him up through the water, so that he looked sad and worried at once, and when the medics pulled her away from him, she was suddenly inundated by a memory: a day at the beginning of summer when he'd received a postcard from someone in Hawaii and begun to cry. She never found out why he'd been crying—it lasted for only a few seconds; then he rubbed his eyes and apologized—but she was struck by how natural this dip into sadness seemed when she always imagined Gerard as someone with a constant, half-witted grin on his face.

Has his death changed her? Of course it has, though how is not exactly clear. She feels older—years older than almost eighteen—and maybe even a little wiser, but also hollowed out and jangly; if someone were to knock into her, or handle her at all roughly, she imagines her limbs would splinter off from her body and fall to the ground. She almost wishes someone would ram into her and be done with it.

When her mother arrived at the pool that day, Helen had such an immediate desire to be close to her, such a need to curl up inside her chest as if she were not a whole person herself, but merely an extension of this woman. Somehow the idea that they had done this together—failed to revive Gerard—made Helen feel better, more protected, and for the first few seconds of contact when her mother had encircled her, enclosed her, all was forgiven, on both sides. She was sure of it.

But then Helen unlatched herself and went to sit on the chaise lounge, and all the pieces of the day fell back into place so that she was herself again, separate and alone and responsible, and the notion of forgiveness floated away from her until it was a tiny, unreachable speck against the sky.

HER MOTHER KNOCKS, then comes into Helen's room a little before nine. It is a Wednesday night, the night of the implosion. "Come on, it's time to go," she tells Helen. "Put your shoes on."

It is practically, Helen thinks, a command. "I've decided not to go," she says, closing the book in her lap and pulling her legs up into the folds of the butterfly chair.

"Well, you're not eighteen yet, so you have to obey me." Her mother smiles. "Tomorrow you can say no to anything."

"Tomorrow I could be dead."

"Helen." She frowns. "Please don't talk like that."

She shrugs and looks away. "Sorry."

"Come on, honey. Your father's even agreed to go." Her mother puts her hands on her hips, apparently waiting for Helen to do something, so she sets down her book, unfolds her legs, and rises from the chair.

"I'll be ready in two minutes," she tells her.

THE CROWD IS ENORMOUS, unspooling from the cordoned-off outer reaches of the Dunes parking lot all the way down the Strip. The next day Helen will read that two hundred thousand people attended the event, but as her family makes its slow, bumper-to-bumper way to a parking spot at the Desert Inn, Helen feels as if the entire country had crammed itself into this section of her city.

Outside the car on Las Vegas Boulevard, people whistle and shout and sing, drinking beer and liquor and Cokes and smoking cigars and cigarettes and possibly even pot, Helen thinks, as they pass a sweetly herbal-smelling cluster of college boys. Small children ride the shoulders of their fathers, and Helen spots the occasional baby strapped to a mother's front, but once the brilliantly raucous fireworks show begins—a precelebration to the implosion—Helen can hear the cries of young children and sees parents hustling their kids into nearby casinos.

It is warm outside, but no longer uncomfortably so, and the Strip is humming with light. The neon signs and casinos on both sides of the street seem like a giant parade of floats tonight, vibrant with glimmering festivity. The air smells of smoke, car exhaust, and a melding of sweats and perfumes, but beneath these odors is the scent of the desert. Helen breathes in deeply and appreciates the wild dryness of the air, the mingling of dust and creosote and sagebrush that she has grown up with, that she will miss when she goes away to school and leaves this city for good.

Her mother takes her father's hand and leads him into the crowd, so Helen grabs on to Jenny and does the same. They all four walk to a space more deeply ensconced in the crowd's center, until the view seems adequate; then they stop and watch the fireworks. Couples populate this section of the crowd, and Helen begins to miss Leo. She has seen him only once since the night several weeks ago when he broke up with her outside her bedroom window. Two days after that she biked over to his house to return a few of his clothes and a Miles Davis tape. Their parting seemed at once monumental and small. Here I am, she thought as they stood in his driveway, leaving the first person I ever loved, but it was as if she were watching the scene on a movie screen, and the person watching the movie was thinking, *They're just a pair of teenagers, and nothing's even happened to them yet. There will be other, bigger things to come. Really, this is small.*

But then two weeks later something big had happened— Gerard died—and that night in bed she wished so much for Leo to be there that she almost got up to call him in the middle of the night, but she made it through and the need passed and now here she was missing him again and it irritated her.

"What are you thinking about?" Jenny shouts to her above the noise of the crowd.

"How much I'm going to miss you when I go to school."

"You're lying," her sister says, but smiles and takes Helen's elbow, then pulls her close.

THE HOTEL IMPLODES at 10:10 P.M. A fake cannonball is launched from the Treasure Island Hotel in the direction of the Dunes, sparking a ring of brilliant fire at its base in an attempt to create even more drama out of an event that needs nothing extra. The sight of a building collapsing in on itself, releasing giant columns of charcoal smoke, is momentous enough. It is a sight that will imprint itself on the mind for years to come. Helen doesn't know why this is true. A building is not a person. It doesn't die in any true sense of the word. It is not beautiful in the same way a person is; it doesn't have sex or fall in love, stay married, or go off to college. It is an inanimate object, and one would think that to watch it disintegrate would mean nothing. But we attach meaning to objects, we leave parts of ourselves in certain places. We are affected when things are destroyed.

Helen was affected by the sight of the Dunes imploding more than she expected to be; as the smoke rose and the ground throbbed, she remembered her years working there; she thought of Miles and Ernie and Gerard—she thought a lot about Gerard—recalled the cool feel of the water, the turquoise color of the pools, the ring of palm trees, and the smell of chlorine and sunscreen. And through this remembering, she felt a melancholy drape across her shoulders, and then, when the dust began to drift down onto the new block of rubble, she felt it lift away from her, and she laughed and put an arm around her sister. Ahead of her, she watched as her parents stood together, then laughed too when it was over and embraced. Part of the laughing was the sheer ridiculousness of what they were all doing here: watching a building implode as if it were some sort of ceremony or show. And part of the laughing was relief.

Kathy felt it too, the sadness and then the lifting away of this sadness when the laughter came. She turned back to find her daughters and saw Helen watching her, so she chanced a smile. It was returned, with hesitation, she could sense that even in the midst of all this noise and smoke, but still, Helen had smiled at her.

AFTER THE IMPLOSION is over, Edward suggests they go get a late-night breakfast special together. The crowd is beginning to thin, migrating indoors to eat and gamble. Dense smoke still hovers above them, making it uncomfortable to breathe. Helen's eyes sting, and she has never felt so tired, but she agrees that breakfast is a good idea.

They choose a café in the Desert Inn where they are surrounded by people talking about the implosion, but her family doesn't speak of it at all as they receive eggs and coffee and pancakes. Instead, they discuss other, more mundane topics, as if the implosion were a touchy subject, one that is best put completely behind them.

Somehow, the idea to stay overnight at this hotel takes shape. Kathy suggests it as a celebration for Helen's birthday, which is tomorrow, and the more they discuss the possibilities—going to a show tonight, swimming in the pool tomorrow, ordering room service, and maybe even playing a little blackjack—the more the notion begins to appeal to everybody.

Edward and Jenny drive home to gather their swimsuits and a few other items, and Helen and Kathy remain in the café. They don't speak for a while, just sit watching people and drinking; Kathy has coffee, Helen, hot chocolate. The booth they are in is a deep red vinyl trimmed with gold, and the Formica table between them still holds their breakfast plates. Helen notices her mother didn't eat much of her hash browns or her eggs; everyone else's plate is practically clean. Is she suffering? Helen wonders. Does she badly miss Gerard?

As if hearing her thoughts, Kathy leans in and says, "I keep feeling like I should tell you something. I was going to leave Gerard anyway. I'd decided to stay with your father."

"It's none of my business," Helen says, looking down into her mug.

Her mother shrugs. "Maybe not, but for what it's worth, I just wanted you to know. Of course I'm sad that he died. Very sad. But not in the way you might be thinking I am. Does that make sense?"

Helen nods, then says, "I guess I just want to forget he ever existed."

"No." Her mother shakes her head. "No, that's not right. You should remember him. It's important."

"Okay," Helen says.

The waiter brings the bill, and her mother looks at it for a moment, then pulls her wallet out of her purse and lays a twenty and a ten on top of it before setting the bill at the table's end. The restaurant is emptying out now. Helen no longer hears anyone speaking about the implosion, though she can feel something different in the air tonight, an edgy excitement or even apprehension. Something new that has changed the interactions taking place here and outside and across the city. Perhaps the implosion is what has allowed her and her mother to discuss Gerard today, at last—nothing has been said about him since he died, even at the funeral—but the notion seems silly and ethereal, not a real explanation for anything.

"Guess what?" Helen says after they pay and step out into the casino. "I'm going to be Ernie's baby's godparent. How crazy is that?"

"I'm so proud of you," her mother says with a laugh, then puts her arm around Helen's shoulders; Helen decides not to pull away.

THEY ALL ENJOY the evening immensely. There are tickets available to a midnight show that involves dancing and comedy and a man doing tricks on a motorcycle in a giant latticed sphere. Then they all sleep in one bedroom. Helen shares a bed with Jenny, and it feels so good to be in a foreign room, in a different bed from her own, that she decides she will like college, that leaving is the best thing she could possibly do.

In the morning her father wakes her up with a glass of fresh orange juice. Room service has already been ordered, and she is served a blueberry muffin with a candle. They sing happy birthday, then eat, then Helen and Jenny take a midmorning swim before they all pack up their few items of clothing and check out of the hotel.

Outside, the city is ravaged but subdued. Las Vegas Boulevard is a mess of plastic cups and beer bottles from the previous evening. Helen even sees a baby's bottle among the debris. The Dunes hotel is now a vast expanse of rubble, cordoned off by yellow caution tape and already swarming with trucks clearing the site. Soon there will be no indication that the Dunes ever existed, and a new casino will be built in its place. The drive home is quiet, classical music coating them with a soothing shell of flutes and violins. Soon the chaos of the strip is behind them. When they pull into their driveway, Helen sees something strange on the porch, a light blue towel draped over an object that is a couple of feet tall and curved on top. A red bow sits on the towel. Jenny reaches it first and calls out to Helen, who is still extracting herself from the car, "It's for you."

There is a card beneath the bow that says, "Good luck in your new life. Love, Leo." Helen pulls the towel away to find a silver cage, and inside the cage is a canary, small and yellow and asleep, though once the towel is off it opens two black eyes and looks up at her.

Later in the day, her father inserts a hook into the ceiling by her window seat and hangs the cage up high. Helen sits on her bed and watches the bird, wondering if she should call Leo to thank him, then decides against it. When she is in Ohio, safely ensconced in her "new life," as he calls it, she will call him, or write him a letter. She doesn't think she will be allowed to take the canary with her—pets are not permitted in the dorm rooms—but even the idea of this bird waiting here for her makes her happy.

She has already begun to pack up portions of her room to take to school. There are no longer any posters on the wall, and only a few books remain on her shelves. Her desk is completely empty, as are many of her drawers. Her room is cleaner than usual because of this and no longer really feels like her room, but she doesn't mind. She likes the extra light and air, the extra space reminding her this portion of her life is almost over. In less than a week she will be gone.

She sits for a long while, watching the canary. It is the color of lemons, or honey, she decides, or maybe the color of sun-doused mountains. The bird watches her too, hopping back and forth on its wooden perch. At some point, she tells herself, she will have to name it, but she doesn't feel ready just yet. Helen continues to sit on her bed as the day winds down outside—her eighteenth birthday, she reminds herself—thinking how strange it is that she is just sitting here gazing at a canary. Then the bird hops toward her and begins to sing.

Penguin Readers' Group

---

www.penguin.co.uk/readers

Our exclusive area for readers group members and anyone who wants to start or join a group

Author of the Month Interviews with all your favourite authors and your chance to ask them questions

Group of the month Review a Penguin book in your group meetings and see your group's discussion up on our website

Themed books Get some inspiration for your reading from our monthly themes: first novels, unhappy families, translated fiction, war and many, many more

Penguin/Orange Reading Group prize Win a weekend trip to Edinburgh Book Festival for your group! This is an annual prize for the best reading group in the UK. See previous shortlisted entries and download an entry form on www.penguin.co.uk/readers

Cult Choice Every month, Toby Litt, one of *Granta*'s Best of Young British Novelists, chooses a favourite cult book

Events Check out which of your favourite Penguin authors is doing an event near you

A whole community of book lovers is just a click away

ESTHER FREUD

THE SEA HOUSE

When Lily rents a cottage in the seaside village of Steerborough to research the life of famous architect Klaus Lehmann, she's quickly entranced by the beautiful landscape and soon begins to question the hectic London world she inhabits with preoccupied lover Nick.

Uncovering the depth of Lehmann's passion, not just for his work but for his wife, Lily finds herself seduced into a new life by neighbour Grae, a man she barely knows. And she realises she must make a choice, between a past she thought she knew and a future much less certain …

'An intriguing, complex and deeply satisfying book about the bonds between lovers. I read it cover to cover in one sitting' Maggie O'Farrell

'Utterly gripping, evocative and seductive. A haunting and compelling read with lots of twists and turns' *Daily Express*

'Extraordinary, beautifully written. Resonates with history, but it's Freud's ability to evoke love – in all its confusing ramifications – that really makes this book unmissable' *Marie Claire*

GLENN PATTERSON

NUMBER 5

Number 5 is a three-bedroom terrace house in a suburban street. From the 1950s to the present day, successive occupants fill the house with their troubles and joys, simply trying to cope with all that life hurls their way, whilst outside the front door the city shivers and sweats with the passing seasons. As fashions and tastes change according to each generation moving into Number 5, so the social fault lines of the city shift. Yet the presence of those who have come before lingers on …

'Compelling, confident, funny… and abundant in all kinds of clever touches. Patterson's vigour and flair keep us reading avidly as he exercises his capacity to make the everyday engrossing' *Independent*

'Beautifully conceived and composed… articulates the poetry of the ordinary with understated humour and pathos' *Guardian*

'An exceptional writer, a magnificent achievement' *The Times*

REBBECCA RAY

A CERTAIN AGE

**'When I was fourteen I lost my
virginity to a twenty-seven-year-old man.
And on a school night too'**

Oliver's different. A grown-up. So what if he's old enough to drive or have a job? His hands feel no different from the boys' at school.

And it's just a phase I'm going through.

Just my hormones kicking in.

It happens when you reach a Certain Age.

I know because Dad told me.

A Certain Age is a startling, moving début novel about illicit love and the end of innocence. It's what your children never tell you, and what you're too scared to remember.

'Frank and endlessly touching' *Company*

'Ray captures the urgency of adolescence, the constant surprise, the imperfection of being human, the pleasure and the horror' A. M. Homes